PROUD GARMENTS

by the same author

I think we should go into the jungle
Girls High
Portrait of the Artist's Wife
All the Nice Girls
The House Guest

PROUD GARMENTS

Barbara Anderson

JONATHAN CAPE
LONDON

First published 1997

1 3 5 7 9 10 8 6 4 2

© Barbara Anderson 1996

Barbara Anderson has asserted her right
under the Copyright, Designs and Patents Act 1988
to be identified as the author of this work

First published in the United Kingdom in 1997 by Jonathan Cape,
Random House, 20 Vauxhall Bridge Road, London SW1V 2SA

Random House Australia (Pty) Limited
20 Alfred Street. Milsons Point, Sydney,
New South Wales 2061, Australia

Random House New Zealand Limited
18 Poland Road, Glenfield,
Auckland 10, New Zealand

Random House South Africa (Pty) Limited
Endulini, 5A Jubilee Road, Parktown 2193, South Africa

Random House UK Limited Reg. No. 954009

A CIP catalogue record for this book is available from the British Library

Papers used by Random House UK Limited are natural,
recyclable products made form wood grown in sustainable forests.
The manufacturing processes conform to the environmental
regulations of the country of origin.

ISBN 0-224-04319-6

Printed and bound in Great Britain
by Mackays of Chatham PLC

For Neil

Acknowledgements

This novel was written with the assistance of a grant
from Creative New Zealand.

My grateful thanks also to Marilyn Sainty, Lise Strathdee
and Dorothea Turner for all their help.

one

'There's a dead bird outside my bedroom window,' said Bianca. 'It's been there for some time.'

Rosa looked at her sister in silence. You wouldn't read about it. You simply would not read about it. 'Oh. Did you hear that, Henry?'

Henry Felton, morose and silent, was busy with doggerel. Hark hark, is that a sparrow carking / Or merely our Bianca farting. 'Yes,' he said, 'I did. And God already has.'

Bianca stirred in her tub chair. What did she have to do to achieve action in this house—kick? roar? scream? She spoke with emphasis.

'For quite some time,' she said. 'A sparrow.'

Henry continued his fight with the paper. One of those bits, those infuriating, unwanted, uncalled for *bits* fell at his feet. Vanity units were on special.

'Dead birds butter no parsnips,' he muttered.

'What's that supposed to mean?'

'I've no idea.' Henry rubbed his nose, a large, aquiline nose pinched about the bridge. A Roman nose, good for show, not for blow. 'There are many aphorisms I don't understand. *If the shoe fits wear it.* What's that supposed to mean?'

Bianca bent forward, gave a low husky laugh, a sound

forced from her by her brother-in-law's inability to tackle problems as they arose. To seize the day, the nettle, the hour. Unlike her late husband, Henry has no grip at all. Justin Lefarge had been trained to make decisions in a disciplined environment; to diagnose, to prescribe, to cure. His career as a psychologist in the Royal Army Medical Corps had been distinguished; change and decay had come as a surprise to him. His demise had been prolonged and Bianca had nursed him to the end. Letters from Hampshire to Meadowbank had been full of praise. *Dear Mrs Felton, I thought I should let you know how much we all admire your sister's courage and fortitude at this sad time . . .*

'It's quite simple, Henry, and anyway it's the cap, not the shoe. It merely means . . .' Bianca stopped; silent, appalled, her brain turned to mush. What did it mean? Which cap? Why wear it? She clenched the hands hidden among folds of navy and white, sat straighter and breathed again, blessed the saving grace of rational thought as it flowed once more. 'If I say you're being stupid and you are, you must accept my saying so. You must wear the cap that fits you, that's all. It's a metaphor. Shakespeare. The Maoris. *A mighty totara has fallen.* You should know that. You're the ones who live here.'

As indeed they did and did and do. Henry and me, and Bianca makes three. Rosalind avoided her husband's eye, rubbed her itchy thumb.

By the pricking of my thumbs something something this way comes.

But which crone is it? Witch one, two or three? Mother would have known. She was grateful for the works of William Shakespeare who, she told her two small daughters, had saved her sanity when Father died.

She had founded the Meadowbank branch of the Shakespeare Society and owned the concordance which is now Rosa's. She had organised play readings in her house around the corner, had quoted soliloquies and sonnets and heroic blood stirrers as they drove to Pukekohe to pick their own tomatoes and Bianca said she was sick of PYO and why did they have to. '*Stiffen the sinews, summon up the blood,*' cried Mother, as they swung in to park by the packing shed. 'Besides, they're cheaper.'

Mother had chosen their names from her hero's work with care. The tragedies had not been consulted. Desdemona, Cordelia, Ophelia, although euphonious words and fine women all, were impossible, irreparably damaged names.

Rosalind, however, did not suit. Its recipient's lack of height for one thing. The baby grew into a tiny scrap of a child with blue-black eyes and wispy dark hair. She became Rosa, or worse, Ros, neither of which suited her but what could you do.

Bianca remained Bianca. Now Bianca Lefarge, sitting in the small chair with the sun behind her, pretty as a picture beneath the pompom dahlias in a trough on the mantelpiece. The dahlias are the same crimson-cherry as the beaks of black swans, their ovoid petals resemble the feathers ruffled like the petticoats of cancan dancers but black as soot. They are mysterious, seductive animals, black swans, more so than the white.

Rosalind is also fond of the pottery trough. Bianca did not want anything from the house when Mother died, except, of course, the silver and something more personal, some more intimate remembrance. Her pearls would do. Bianca had her own things, she wrote, and besides, her taste had changed.

Rosalind looked at her sister. Bianca is well preserved, if you can stand the phrase, but not mummified. Fifty-five if a day and not a wrinkle in sight.

Laughter is bad for the face and not having children helps as well. They should put it on packets, like health warnings. Cereal perhaps, something seen every day so the effect is cumulative. *Families may endanger your face.* Rosa thought of her son Rufus and stopped quickly. Years ago a Christian on a bicycle had pressed Alexander Pope's words in tract form into her hands before pedalling on down the tree-lined street. *To err is human, to forgive, divine . . .*

Not that Rufus has erred exactly. In fact not at all. Rosa's thoughts skidded and returned to Mother.

Mother serene and cheerful in her navy straw and her dark silk speckled like the guinea fowl in the children's zoo. So many worries, so little money and always pleasant. Mother bending stiffly from the waist to enquire after her friends in Smith and Caugheys. Mother in the tearooms afterwards, her shopping done, her face wrinkled as a pleated skirt but still handsome. Mother in gloves and hat walking home from the Meadowbank bus stop one day to be bowled over by a taxi at the corner.

It was the greengrocer who had broken the news to Rosalind. Mr Desai had dropped the apple he was polishing and run to her, had taken the spade from her hands and led her inside. 'Sit down Mrs, oh sit down. Your lovely lady is dead.' She wept in his arms till Henry appeared, wept as though the Waitemata had ceased to flow and Meadowbank was no more and life had ended. Mother had gone.

She telephoned Bianca that evening. It was morning there. 'Did she ask for me?'

'No, no, dear, she was killed instantly.'

'*Instantly.*'

As though that made it worse.

Bianca resembles Mother except for her unlined face; even her seated shape is similar—the spreading hips, the shapely legs. Mother was soft to the touch, spongy almost above the waist. 'It has to go somewhere, Rosa,' she laughed, as the child poked the pallid tube above her girdle.

10

Below the waist she was firmer, constrained, subdued by latex even after Lionel died. He had been a good man, she told them, and a great tease and had liked her firm. Besides, she hated to flop about. Rosalind was seven when he died but her memories of her father are few: bony knees, a pipe, the pleasures of bonfires. Not much, in all conscience, and Bianca has no memories at all.

Like many larger women, Mother had elegant feet and ankles. They lightened her, she seemed to sail above them as does Bianca, who has the same walk, a slow, graceful surge forward. She does not scamper from task to task like her older sister. Bianca appears to stream along, to billow like the scarves she favours. (Bianca is a scarf person.) The carp kites which fly from Japanese houses in celebration of a son's birthday reminded Rosalind of them both.

The kites are a fine sight; anchored yet free, they lift the heart. Daughters do not have them. Rosalind, with Henry on a buying trip, had asked the interpreter what girls do have. There was something she cannot remember, dolls perhaps, but nothing airborne, nothing as triumphantly buoyant.

The three of them are quiet now, mellow as the afternoon sun warming Bianca's shoulders. Henry's feet continue to grind the carpet as he reads the book reviews.

Bianca sits thinking about her things. Her eyes move, her mind ticks. How can she fit them all into a room this size, even when Ros has got rid of all this stuff. Bianca's gaze checks spaces, areas, height (the longcase clock), rips down curtains and throws out sofas. Her shoulders move in a minuscule shudder at the worn florals, the flowers and the leaves and the songbirds singing on the ancient slip covers, the tired cushions and neo-colonial tat. Tat was a word much used by Barry at Arnold's Antiques in Fareham, Hants. Bianca tries it, her lips moving in silence. Tat.

And the dog trade. She saw Barry, his trim behind giving a little sideways shimmy as he edged past a badly cracked garden urn. 'Dog trade, Mrs L. Strictly dog trade.'

'Dog trade?'

'People who're putting on the dog. All hair oil and no socks.'

Oh, the joys of exclusion when you weren't, and where was Arnold's Antiques now and Barry who was such fun and knew the importance of contemporary armorials and that Mrs L had a wonderful eye and was not and never had been dog trade. Twelve thousand miles away and sadly missed, that was where. Sadly, sadly missed.

But Bianca's container is due to arrive in a few months. Her things are on their way.

'*Speed bonnie boat like a bird on the wing*,' she sings softly her head tilting from side to side. Bianca often sings softly.

'Don't *cross* on the solid white *line*,' she sang from the front passenger's seat when they picked her up from the airport. 'Full stop ahead.'

'Yellow,' snarled Henry. 'Double yellow. You're home now.' Bianca turned her face to the window, to bleached paddocks and wire fences and silly sheep huddling.

She was more robust when Ros drove, blocking her vision as she peered left, shouting, 'Now! I said now. Why didn't you go?'

'Because I can't see.'

'Of course you can't see. I can. You can scarcely see over the steering wheel. You need a cushion. That elf one would do, that extraordinary elf one on the sofa.'

Rosalind drew in to the side and stopped the car. Her normally brown face was pale, she was breathing fast. 'Bianca, it's time we had a team talk. That's what they call them. They go into a huddle on TV and have team talks.' Her hands sketched stadiums, snarling coaches and intrusive cameras.

'I have been driving a car for more than forty years and intend to continue doing so. And furthermore, Bianca,' said Rosalind, staring straight at her, her eyes sparking, positively sparking, 'we didn't ask you to come and live with us.'

Bianca burst into tears. 'What a terrible thing to say to your sister.'

'Yes, isn't it,' said Rosa and drove on to the asparagus farm where it was always fresh and half the price.

Rosa had come scuttling back to bed the night Bianca arrived. 'She goes to bed in gloves,' she told Henry, who was lying with his eyes closed. 'Gloves on top of hand cream. Little cotton ones.'

There was something about gloves and fat women and nobody loving but Henry was too tired. Too tired and too depressed. Rosa rolled towards him, her face suddenly serious. 'Henry. Don't die in the night.'

Henry's eyes had opened. 'All right,' he said, and closed them again.

Bianca was still singing to herself.

Speed bonnie boat, like a bird on the wing
'Onward,' the sailors cry!
Carry the lad that's born to be King
Over the sea to Skye.

'A Jacobite, a genuine, fully paid up Jacobite in Meadow-bank,' sniffed Henry.

Bianca looked at him warily. Her eyes, less blue than formerly but still sharp, met his. No, thought Henry, not sharp. Her gaze is knowing. He had met only one other woman in his life who had looked at him like that and she was dead. Dead and buried and laid to rest in Milan. Bianca should not look at him like that. She had no right. He stared out the window. Anywhere to avoid Bianca.

She made no comment on his asinine remark. She was no fool. He knew that.

Shadows and silence filled the room, deepened the crimson dahlias, bent the heads of host and hostess. Henry shifted slightly, tossed a cushion to the floor and worked himself deeper into cretonne.

Bianca broke the silence. Her voice was clear. She had a good ear and thirty years in Titchfield had left their mark.

'I'm sure you won't mind my mentioning it, Henry . . .' she said, leaning forward to stare into his eyes. Brown eyes are meant to be warm but nothing about Henry was predictable. 'But I've wondered so often. Well, you can imagine. And Justin as well. Was anything more ever discovered about Andrew's death?'

Henry's mouth dropped in disbelief. 'What do you mean, discovered? You know exactly what happened. He was drowned while fishing. Slipped and fell over the Huka Falls thirty-three years ago.'

'Rufus was two,' offered Rosalind.

Neither of them glanced at her.

'Yes, yes, of course,' said Bianca, flustered but firm. 'But nothing . . . Was nothing more ever heard about . . .' She faltered, tried again. 'About the reason for his taking his life.'

'Taking his life! You say that? You of all people.'

'It seems so odd.'

'In what way?'

'To be fishing there.'

There was a red blotch between his eyebrows. 'Are you mad? How could anyone fish at the Huka Falls? He slipped further upstream and was swept over. Death by misadventure, as you very well know.'

Bianca drew back. I have gone too far. Far too far because I dislike him. That awful mother, that ridiculous father, all of them. Why shouldn't I bring it up. The way I was treated, the cover-up. Everything. Justin had been appalled.

But that face, that beaked, stained face thrust at hers, those cold eyes. She could see the hairs in his nostrils, the hairs beside the hairs, the damp redness.

'I'm sorry, Henry. I didn't mean to imply . . .'

'What in heaven's name is there to imply?'

'Nothing, nothing. I'm sorry. I've said I'm sorry.'

Henry flopped back in his chair. 'And so am I.' He breathed deeply, felt his heart slow, find its own rhythm and quieten.

'My apologies, Bianca. But for God's sake let Andy rot in peace.' The newspaper sighed beneath his hands and lay quiet. 'Though I suppose he has by now.'

Sun filtered, motes of dust hung in slanting rays of unease and silence. 'Perhaps I should have said dead birds don't squeak,' he muttered.

The man was shifty and devious beyond belief. How Ros had ever been able to contemplate the thought of matrimony, let alone live forty years with a man like Henry Felton was beyond comprehension. He bore no resemblance to his younger brother. None. The textiles he imported were beautiful, Bianca would give him that, but what use were they with his wife sitting staring at her in crumpled cotton you could shoot peas through. Ros had no dress sense. Not an ounce.

Bianca had enjoyed her marriage and her life in England. She had drifted onto the local pond like a decoy, had displayed the right markings and been accepted by the indigenous flock. She had kept her own counsel on many things and it had been wonderfully, gloriously worth it, and now look at her. All money gone, all passion spent, expiring with boredom in this dump and men swearing at her.

'Incidentally,' she said, 'what about the dead bird?'

'Oh, for heaven's sake, Bianca,' said Rosa. 'Sparrows don't smell or blow up or anything. They just sort of wither. I'll give you a spade.'

Henry dragged himself to his feet and headed for the kitchen. 'What would you like to drink, Bianca?'

Bianca made a small regrouping movement. 'The one I had last night when the tonic ran out was so delicious, I think I'll have another. What was it, Henry?'

Henry's eyes closed briefly. 'Water,' he said, 'and gin.' He moved towards the kitchen, his fingers touching chairs, tables, a book, before reaching the top cupboard for the gin bottle. Rosa had once suggested changes to him. Why didn't Henry move the drink bottles into the cupboard beneath the book-case? There would be room for the glasses and all he would need to bring in would be a jug of water. He had declined. For God's sake, he said, don't make it any easier.

Rosa watched his back as he headed for the kitchen. His self-deprecating honesty was endearing and always had been. She knew there were things about him. Undoubtedly there were. His refusal to talk about Rufus's future, for example. 'Rufus will be all right,' was all he would say. 'Don't worry about Rufus.'

His blanket denial did not leave her any room to man-oeuvre, to discuss, to work things through and share.

Similarly with Bianca. It was all very well to say, 'Bianca must go', but where, and how, and anyway how could she. She has no money and she is my sister and Bianca now is Bianca then, when I was seven and she was two and I promised Mother I would mind her and did.

Henry stood with the open bottle in his hand, an old man with a dry mouth staring at a lemon tree. The lemons hung gleaming in the reflected light, their crisp leaves slicked with raindrops as bright as mercury and as separate. Any fool can grow a lemon tree in Auckland. It's simply a question of digging a big enough hole. People are mean about digging holes. Wide and deep, wide and deep, that is all that is required.

There are not many people you love. Not men. Not men like Andy, who had loved Bianca. She was now expressing doubts about the TV news presenter's beautifully white teeth. False, obviously false, too good to be true. Bianca could always tell, always, and furthermore she had never been able to trust anyone with false teeth. It was just something she had a thing about, and who did the woman think she was anyway.

'Must it *all* be sport,' she moaned, as men rolled to their feet clutching balls in triumph, and impossible putts were sunk and cups presented and held high for kissing.

Henry handed her gin.

'Thank you. I've never had it like this before, women don't in Hampshire.' She sipped, circumspect as a communicant. 'And why do they need two of them? The news is not a cabaret act.'

If I strangle her she won't know she's dead so what is the point. There is no point. There is no point at all.

Rosalind put her feet up. She was bored with opening and shutting her mouth between protagonists like a hungry fledgling. How could Bianca say that about Andy. And to Henry. My own sister, my sister who has descended on us. She saw Bianca, robed in blue and manhandled by angels, descending from clouds like a rewound Assumption. Why here? Why here? Because there is nowhere else.

'Bed,' said Henry. 'Come on, Rosa.'

Rosa looked into her husband's eyes and read his baffled heart. He was miserable and uneasy. He wanted solidarity, contact, he wanted to talk to his wife. 'Coming,' she said.

He climbed into bed, clutching striped pyjamas to his

midriff. The elastic had gone. 'And the husband was worse, *de mortuis* notwithstanding. But when she got on to Andy . . . No, Rosa . . . No.'

Rosa was drowsy, kicking the word notwithstanding around between doze and dream. Notwithstanding. Not forever.

> *Not forever by green pastures*
> *Do we ask our way to be*
> *But the sleep and rugged pathway*
> *May we tread rejoicingly.*

There is a man in Britain who climbs mountains on two aluminium alloy feet. It is the ankle joints he misses.

'What else can we do?' she murmured.

'She cannot just descend on us.'

'Don't be so daft. She has.'

'You'll have to tell her to go. I mean it, Rosa.'

'No.'

'Then I will.'

'She has no money.'

'That's dusty Justy's legacy, not mine.'

Rosa was wide awake now, her voice firm. 'She is my sister and she is penniless and she is welcome in this house till the day I die. Then you can toss her out the door. And you shouldn't have said that about rotting in peace. Things are bad enough already. Why didn't you just say rest. It was just gratuitous . . .' She stopped. Gratuitous what? Violence? Truth? 'It was cruel,' she muttered.

Henry leaned towards her in the dark to clutch her shoulders, misjudged and fell back. 'Look how she treats you. Me. The whole world. Why, woman, why?'

Ah, but how can I tell you, my lover, my friend. My sister is my responsibility and always has been. She is burnt into my software, as Rufus would say. Besides I promised.

Binky has lace on her panties and lace on her hankim. And so she had and was cherished as all children should be and are not. 'Where has Rosa gone? Poor Rosa will be missing me,' she wept, tears rolling down her nose when I went to play with Wendy down the road. So Binky came too and Wendy loved her as well and Mother rested with the blinds drawn.

'Is that your baby, dear?' Wendy's mother had asked as Bianca clutched a small round cushion to her chest.

'No,' said Bianca. 'It's my handbag.'

She refused to be a baby when Wendy and I needed one. There were no babies in our house, just Mother and me and Bianca. It was sufficient and there was much to do. Nothing happens automatically in houses, someone must clean up now and again and Mother preferred Shakespeare and Bianca the garden.

'You mustn't mind, Rosa, if no one . . .' Mother had warned before the dance. 'I mean there's always the cloakroom. Not of course that you'll . . . You look lovely, dear,' she said firmly. 'Lovely.'

When she arrived to pick me up, Henry and I were dancing with tears in our eyes. Our tears were those of laughter, but that is not so in the original song, which is a sad one. The singer's partner is not the one he loves and thus his eyes are wet. I always worried for his partner, but perhaps she didn't notice.

The look on Mother's face gladdened my heart further as Henry and I swept past. Surprise was followed by joy and joy outshone. I should have grabbed her—spun her around with us beneath the tethered balloons tugging like memories. See, I should have said. Don't worry, I should have laughed. It will be all right. I am a grown woman.

Tight buds were unfurling in the Parnell Rose Gardens, opening to butter yellow and fierce reds and pinks as Henry

19

and I walked beside them. I agreed they were beautiful, how could I not. They were and I did not care. I scarcely noticed them except the clashing colours. Roses are the only flowers whose colours can fight.

Make Henry Felton ask me to marry him, I insisted to a lurid pink. You were allowed to then, to hope and pray for love, to consider yourself lucky if asked. I do not know why I added the Felton. Perhaps I felt it was more formal.

'Rosa, will you marry me?'

'Yes,' I said instantly. 'Yes, please.'

Henry worked for his father. Mr Felton senior's textile importing business was well established and efficiently run. It was the rest of the world which worried the old man. His expression was often bewildered, even hurt. He felt that a more 'wholesome' (that was the word he used), a more wholesome life was slipping away.

Now I tell Henry. The world has not changed, I tell him. Old people always think things used to be better, it is one of the signs of aging. And now there is communication, there is TV, there are satellites. People cannot help but see if the switch is on. They see the bombs and the bodies and the misery. They do not need to have any imagination at all. It is not only you, Henry, my darling, my friend.

When he looks at me I see that his brown eyes are still beautiful despite the opaque band around the pupil which is called *arcus senilis*. I do not tell him this.

We lie side by side, tanned and wrinkled like two connubial old kippers.

I think of Bianca and of our son Rufus who is coming home soon and how wonderful and what will he do. Of Bianca's things which she says will be arriving soon and where will they go. Bianca says this will be no problem. I do not like this phrase. I am wary of it. Often I find that, contrary to what

20

the speaker says, there is a problem and, more often than not, it is mine. Bianca tells me I can get rid of my stuff and then there will be room. I tell her they are not stuff. I tell her they are my things but she does not agree. I will have it out with her tomorrow. Bianca, I will say.

Henry puts out a hand. 'Are you asleep?'

'No.'

'She'll have to go.'

'No.'

Henry takes me in his arms.

If I had a daughter I would tell her. Don't worry, I would say, it is just as good. It is just as good as ever. It is simply that it happens less often, I would say.

'*My love who could deliver,*' says Henry and sleeps.

There is no need to tell Rufus.

'Are you awake?' I ask later.

Even in the silent dark I know he is frowning. 'This is ridiculous. Hissing away in bedrooms at our age.'

'I've thought of a solution,' I say.

There is a muffled snort beside me.

'We must find somewhere else for Bianca to live.'

The light snaps on. We stare at each other in disarray; old, bewildered, not our daytime selves at all. Henry's hair is a fuzz of white light. He is an anguished saint, one of those attenuated Spanish ones. 'And who pays for it?'

'We could rent a nice little flat for her. A townhouse even.'

'Rosalind, have you the slightest idea how much a nice flat costs?'

I ignore the flick of distancing which comes with the use of my full name. 'Little, I said, a little flat.'

'However little.'

'I still think it would be worth discussing. I'll contact some letting agents tomorrow. Come to your office.'

'I will not pay for that . . .' He does not say it but the word hangs in the air, clings to the curtains, a spiky black snitch of a word.

He snaps off the light and we lie still.

His hand strokes my rump. 'Come anyway. Bianca,' Henry tells the dark, 'can attend to her correspondence.'

He rolls over.

'Did she really say that? About her correspondence?'

No answer.

two

Bianca pours liquid honey onto yoghurt as she has done every breakfast since she and Justin discovered Greece. The loops and swirls are precise. Like all her actions, small or large, Bianca's movements are meticulous, she likes to get things right. Seemliness, order, patterns of procedure are important to her.

She glances up as Rosalind runs back from the kitchen. 'Every time I see you you've grown smaller, you know that. There'll be nothing left soon. Remember that one at primary? *Rosie Maule is so small, a rat could eat her, cap and all.*'

'Yes,' says Rosalind spreading Vegemite, remembering the jeers and no one choosing her for goalie because she'd be useless being so minute, when she wasn't, not at all. Biting, chewing, blinking the moment to oblivion, she takes it out on toast.

And if I told her, *when* I tell her, that Bianca Lefarge is overly large she will be crushed, she will weep, will burst immediately into the hot, wounded tears of the misunderstood, the can't-take-a-jokes, the plain speakers.

'More toast?' says Rosalind and runs again.

'Not every woman can be a pocket Venus, Bianca,' says Henry.

23

He was handsome once, as Bianca knows, and is still impressive. His grey hair is thick and silky, the lines on his face are fine, not the deep ravines of lonely men on benches drinking out of flagons. He stands upright, giving a spurious appearance of confidence and attack.

Bianca reaches for her handkerchief. He is a fraud and I hate him. His double talk, his so-called wit, the accuracy of his jibes upset me. And now Ros, charging in and out being ridiculous in that poky little kitchen.

Bianca has a sharp tongue. She knows this and it worries her. Sometimes things she has said or done come back to haunt her. Mrs Spencer taking umbrage when she couldn't give her a lift in to Fareham because her basket might scratch the leather. Mrs Rowland and that wretched hamster. More serious things, horrible things such as Doctor Clothier's letter suggesting she find another medical adviser. Not even giving her a chance to explain, and why shouldn't she have a second opinion. I did not mean to offend, Doctor, it is just my way. I don't mean to be rude but things pop out and people have no sense of humour. They take things personally, Doctor, they cannot take a joke. There are some things would you believe, Doctor, which have stayed with me for over thirty years. Humphrey Watson leaving me stranded on the dance floor, striding off in the middle of the Excuse Me when I told him he looked like a Romney Southdown cross and he did. These are not big things, Doctor, I realise that. Nevertheless they stay with me, they return in the night.

Rosalind watched a tangerine-beaked blackbird rush an elegant thrush on the grass below. The thrush departed squawking. Good, good on you. Do it again.

She slammed the toaster lever down, remembered Saint Lawrence on his gridiron. *Turn me, devil, eat. And see if raw or toasted, I make the better meat.*

Such a help they are, her talismans. Rosalind smiles, the toast pops, life goes on. Last night's loving resurfaces and that is part of the problem. Rosalind knows she could live with Bianca more easily without Henry, although she has no intention of doing so. She knows Bianca, tries to understand her, can almost see her trying to be nice, then, wham—the boot is in, the game is over. Bianca is on form once more.

Bianca, her curls golden as those of the unborn Rufus, had sobbed in her arms over thirty-five years ago. 'People don't like me. Why Ros? Why don't some people like me?'

Rosa had had a long hot wait at the antenatal and the humidity hadn't helped.

'Men or women?'

'Women mostly.'

'Because you're beautiful,' said Rosalind, running the cold tap on the inside of her wrists as Mother had taught them because it was so cooling. She scowled at the red face at the bottom of the mirror. All mirrors were too high.

'Oh,' said Bianca. She paused. 'But I can't help that.'

Rosa was now slapping water on her face. 'No. It's tough, being a beautiful woman. Ask Elsa Maxwell. She organised parties for millionaires and all their dolly birds loved her. She was plain, plain as a pikestaff, plain as the east end of a camel going west. She'd got no class, see, she wasn't sexy, but she gave ace parties and she made you crack up laughing and why not love the funny old doll? She was no threat. It just depends,' said Rosa, rubbing her face on a lilac towel, 'whether you want to be a millionaire's doxy or organise his parties.'

Doxy. Doxy was typical of Ros. One of those words you know exists but no one in their right mind would use. A word used only by funny girls like Rosa. As were her hats. No one had worn hats then. No one young. No one but Ros. Where did she find them, those mad little black hats with turned-up brims which made her look smaller than ever; a squat

25

mushroom with a fringe of hair and dark eyes staring.

'Oh, Rosa, what would I do without you?' cried Bianca.

The toast flew upwards like sparks and trouble. Shakespeare.

Bianca and Henry were sitting in silence, an angry silence, which was rare in the house. Silences, as a rule, were amiable. There was not much chat, the permanent residents knew each other too well, their reactions were demonstrated by a nod, acknowledged by an eyebrow. There were few surprises. Rosa goes elsewhere for the unexpected.

Henry was still reading last night's paper with stern attention. When he and Rosalind are alone together he lays the paper flat on the table and reads it carefully as though it contained secrets which must be solved before he can leave the world unread until tomorrow.

Henry takes his news seriously, he is news-crammed. The more the world depresses him, the more careful attention he gives it, the more printed information he absorbs. He seldom reads books as he used to. He has forgotten how, though he does not realise this.

Rosa offers him toast. Old, worried and put upon by relatives, Henry is not the man he was. His skin is blotchy, his anger impotent and buried beneath the restraints of courtesy. If Henry were a Bedouin, he would give Bianca the sheep's eye.

'Bianca,' says Rosa, 'I have some business things to do in town. With Henry.'

She can hear herself saying it, her voice bright as a brass button rolling as she prattles on explaining the whereabouts of coffee, tea, kettles, the shaved ham in the fridge. 'You'll be all right on your own, won't you?'

'Of course,' says Bianca, her mind leaping to the glint of the retractable steel tape measure on the garage shelf, her outstretched hand disturbing cobwebs as she reaches. There

26

are kitchen steps there too. 'Don't worry about me. And I'll clean up this mess.' She waves a hand over the checked tablecloth, the Shasta daisies, the crumbs.

'Thank you,' says Rosalind.

It would have been different if the baby had not died, Bianca knew that. She would have had looks, that stillborn child, how could she not. She would have married a fine man unscarred by financial collapse. Bianca saw her daughter, blonde, blue-eyed, holding out pale arms to embrace: Of course you must come to us, Mother. We wouldn't hear of anything else, would we . . . There was a gap, rather a tall gap. Angus? Hugh? He didn't have to be Scottish. But he was insistent, pressing, he was . . .

Bianca swept toast crumbs with an angry hand. What on earth are you thinking of, woman? Justin had called her 'woman'. It had been a private joke. She saw him in uniform, unexpectedly home for lunch. 'Where's m'woman?' he called from the hall and she ran laughing.

If the baby had lived it would have been 'women'. 'Women,' she said loudly and burst into tears, bitter, stupid, angry, gulping tears of no use to anyone, least of all herself.

Sniffling, snorting with self-disgust, she pulled herself up and cleared the table. She shook the cloth out the window, watched the birds lined up on those hideous telephone wires as they swooped to peck. She washed the dishes with plenty of nice hot soapy water, put on Rosa's plastic apron with mad chefs dancing and headed for the garage. She had plenty of time.

'Hi,' called a voice from the hall, 'anyone home?'

Bianca swayed, teetered on the top of the paint-spattered steps, her heart thudding. She steadied an arm against a wall and scrambled down. The retractable measure, dropped in fright, lay at her feet, its end thrashing like a steel snake. The shame, the shock, the . . .

A man stood in the doorway, his shape backed by light. 'What are you doing?'

What was she doing? What could she possibly be doing except gaping in fright at the shadowed figure smiling at the door. 'I, that is . . .' Anger saved her. 'It's more a question of what you're doing in my sister's house. Get out at once.'

The smile widened, filled the face with laughing disbelief. 'Good God, Auntie Bianca.' Rufus dropped his pack with a thud and held out his arms.

Bianca sat down suddenly on the arm of one of the chairs. It gave under her weight, rocked slightly. She had no breath, no breath at all.

'Rufus,' she panted. 'Why didn't you write to me?'

He dropped to his heels before her, took her hand. 'You're so right. Why didn't I? Why the hell didn't I? When I think how good you've been to me. The presents. That coat, remember the coat? I've still got it, good as new.' His eyes flicked, smiled again. 'Yes. You know the first present I remember you giving me? At Uncle Andy's funeral. A Dinky truck. Well, I was too young to remember but Mum told me, and I reminded you of it in Titchfield, remember? The Dinky truck when Uncle Andy died?

'I've still got all my Dinkys, collector's items now but I'm hanging on to them, boxes and all. They must go up. They'll be like Steiff bears one day. There's a lot of money in toys if they're in good condition. People don't realise. Most of them are shot to hell, of course, that's why.'

Bianca slid from the arm of the chair into its depths with uncharacteristic clumsiness. How could the cherubic child of that time, of subsequent photographs on a stool with one leg

28

tucked beneath him and the other sticking out and curls as thick as Millais's *Bubbles*, have turned into this unusual-looking man. She had not seen him for years, since he had gone home from the UK the first time and Justin's long decline into dementia had begun. She looked at him carefully. In fact he had not changed, not even from the early photographs. He had merely expanded, stretched and enlarged in all directions. He still looked well fed, his curls still rioted.

Rosa had tried with the hair when he was young. Photographs throughout the years had demonstrated the close crop (I'd hide the skinhead if I were you, darling. Justin.), the semi-sheer, the mop. Nature had burst through them all. *All the boys look quaint at the moment*, wrote Rosa on the back of a pre-Raphaelite maiden astride his new bike, *and Henry says there are worse things than long hair.*

The hair now hung in curls the colour of pine shavings streaked with gold. His eyes were the unclouded blue of a sparrow's egg.

He was still smiling as he picked up the tape measure; a reserved smile, a what's-going-on-here smile. 'And what were you doing, Aunt?'

He had remembered her dislike of auntie. That was something.

'Justin died,' she said. 'Last year.'

'Oh my God.' He was beside her, hugging her, his muscles taut against her, enclosing her distress with strong-armed comfort. 'How terrible! And to think I didn't even know.'

'But why didn't you know?' she asked through tears. 'He had been ill for so long. Didn't your mother, didn't anyone . . . How could you not know?'

'Well, like I said, you lose touch. But with some people you have this conviction that when you meet up again it'll be just the same, and it's true. I hate not knowing about Justin, a fine man, a good guy, tragic . . . What a loss.'

Bianca shook her head. She was an honest woman. 'Not at the end. Not at the end at all, Rufus.'

Rufus, his arms still around her, kissed her.

He was now lying in the chair opposite her with his legs draped over one arm. 'You may call me Bianca if you like, Rufus.'

Rufus adjusted a cushion behind his head, considered. 'Bianca. It doesn't exactly trip off the tongue, does it? I'll call you Bee, if we've dropped the aunt thing.'

She opened her mouth to tell him that no he would not, that Bianca was a beautiful name, that . . . But he was so relaxed, his smile so friendly among the faded colours, the quiet streets of home. Leafy Meadowbank, Henry called it, but you never knew with Henry.

'So what's with the tape measure, Bee?'

She could tell him, she knew she could tell him. Rufus would understand. There was nothing shameful about taking measurements in a sister's house—nephew and aunt would laugh about it together, he would hold the end of the tape thing, no, he would be better up the steps. There was nothing furtive about the operation, nothing furtive about anything. *There is nothing*, she remembered, *either good or bad, but thinking makes it so.*

She laughed aloud, more cheerful than she had been since the day the Boeing had landed and every man, woman and dog at the Auckland airport had instructed her to have a nice day and her heart dragging like a lead balloon even before the plane doors had opened.

'I was doing some measurement—my things.'

The blue denim leg stopped swinging. 'Things?'

'Yes, I have a container of my things arriving any day. I was wondering where they would fit.'

Silence. Quite a long silence. Bianca's hand rose to her throat.

30

'Antiques?'

'If you call them that.'

'What do you call them?'

Bianca gave a little puff of mirth to show life was fun. Rufus did not respond.

'What about Mum's things?'

Bianca looked around the comfortable unco-ordinated muddle—the three-legged stools and sticks of furniture, the rags and patches were not things and never had been. That cushion, for example, that extraordinary cushion behind Rufus's head. It had red-capped elves on it, large canvas-work elves; someone had given them golden cricket bats, had stitched them and bound them and rested heads against them for a thousand years.

'Oh, Ros will be delighted,' she said.

Rufus was inspecting a dirty white shoe. His gaze was concentrated, his mind busy. He wouldn't bet on it.

'Tell me,' he said. 'Remind me about your things.'

Bianca did so. She told him of bun-footed coffers, of old rugs and rat-tailed spoons and . . .

Rufus was now upright, one foot touching the kitchen steps. 'So why were you up the wall when I came in?'

Bianca's blush took her by surprise. 'The longcase clock,' she murmured.

'Ah, the grandaddy. I like old clocks. I'll realign it, get it going for you.'

'Oh, I don't think . . .'

'I'm an expert. As long as it's genuine, of course. The old ones' mechanisms are a breeze.'

Bianca opened her mouth in protest and shut it. What on earth was he doing now. Rufus continued unbuckling the heavy bronze buckle of his belt and pulling it from its denim loops, his face stern as a puritan father's about to thrash his child for the sake of its soul.

31

He retucked his shirt, laughed his rueful laugh and smiled into her eyes. 'Something binding a bit.' He juggled, re-threaded, rebuckled. 'By the way, where are the olds? Dad's at the office, yeah. But where's Mum?'

'She had some business to do in town,' murmured Bianca, dragging her mind back from Titchfield when she and Justin were first married. Justin's brisk hands tugging at corduroys, his head ducking oak beams. The Tippetts had asked them in for a drink. 'The Titchfield Tippetts with the floy doy,' Justin had called them. And where were the Tippetts now? Gone. Gone. No floy doy, no floy doy ever again and who cared what in heaven's name it meant or ever had. It meant shared jokes and long twilights and Justin's legs like pillars against the light.

They had made their excuses to the Tippetts. Goodness knows what they had said.

And here was this ape, this retarded ape dropping his trousers a yard in front of her nose.

'For heaven's sake, Rufus, surely someone has told you not to take off your trousers in public.'

'Well, I'd have said more "dropped", wouldn't you? An old battleaxe in the VD clinic, well it was then, used to say that. "Drop y'tweeds," she'd yell. She'd be shot now, of course. Things were much rougher in those days.'

Bianca's head was spinning. No, that was ridiculous. Her head was not spinning. Her head was angry. Uncouth, unmannered, loutish, he had got worse, much worse. 'How on earth do you know?'

'I used to work there.'

'As?'

'Medical orderly.' He was sitting opposite her once more, his hands clasped, his eyes kinder than ever, his hair shining. 'You're quite right, Bee. That was a crass thing to do. Inexcusable. You get into bad habits living alone, don't you?'

'No.'

Rufus sighed, stared sadly into a corner of the room where sunlight was fading pale cushions paler. 'No,' he said, 'perhaps not.' He sat silent for some time then leapt up. 'Okay, Bee. Let's get the show on the road, get the measuring done. Where's your list?'

They worked happily, amicably. He was competent, supple, dropping onto his heels then rolling upright. He ran up and down the steps without looking, he jumped from the top and landed without a sound. He was nimble and measured quickly, he double-checked each figure. His grace, his agility, his competence reassured her. All she had to do was hold one end of the tape. He shot it along to her behind a sofa as they knelt at either end. She missed it and it shot back to him like an electric hare. They sat back on their haunches and laughed. It was fun.

'It'll be a tight squeeze, Bee,' he said finally, 'but you'll make it.' He rubbed a dirty shoe on the threadbare carpet. 'Lucky the carpet's so worn, the rugs won't canter all over the place. That'll be a help.' He walked around the room in silence, his hands in his pockets, his mouth pursed as he looked at the ceiling, ran a hand over the mantelpiece, walked into the hall. She heard a door open, close. He came back more thoughtful than ever, dropped to examine the deep skirting board and sprang up again.

'You could make money on this place, you know that? Rip out the furniture, lock stock and barrel, get shot of it. Stain the floors throughout, rush through with a lick of paint. People in their forties, the guys with money, they're into colonial villas, heritage, all that. Any fool can slap in an en suite, but where are you going to get joinery like this nowadays? Look at these doors, look at them. Kauri. Unobtainable. Class stuff. This place could be a showplace, an absolute showplace.'

'This place?'

'Genuine kauri villa. Ask yourself. Not many round here. Good locality, schools, shops, bus route. Tart up the garden. Cottagey—hollyhocks, roses, what are those little things that smell?'

'Pinks,' said Bianca faintly, one hand on the back of a chair.

Rufus snapped his fingers, ran a hand down an architrave. It was a small hand for a man, the fingers stubby and not entirely clean. A boy's hand. 'Pinks,' he said.

'You said, you said you could make money,' said Bianca staring into his eyes. They seemed to have lightened.

'So you could, no doubt about that.'

'But what about my things?'

The pause was infinitesimal, over before her mouth had closed.

'Hang on. I've got an idea. Sit down and I'll tell you.'

His idea was ridiculous, insane, not to be countenanced for a second.

'Bed and *Breakfast*. Why in the name of all that's merciful would I want to run a Bed and Breakfast?'

'Because you haven't any money.'

Bianca was shaking with rage, her face and neck mottled. They went blotchy with anger, shamed her more. 'How dare you say that!' Who had told him. Not Ros, surely not Ros. 'How do you know?' she whispered.

'Why else would you come home?'

'Home?'

'Back then. I've seen it before. People with no cash always come home. Or old age. You need a few rellies when you start packing up.'

Bianca laughed. How could she not laugh at this idiot, this child with nous, this astonishing nephew.

Rufus hugged her again. It was a long time since Bianca had been hugged with conviction.

'Now calm down, Bee, calm down,' he said. 'You've got it all wrong about Bed and Breakfasts. The B and B scene's changed completely. It's a fun thing now. There's a heritage input from people with fully restored colonials, decos, old barns out in the bush, squattocracy, the lot. I could rip through this place in a flash; four good-sized double bedrooms, triple, a couple of them. Put in a mini en suite. Then we put in your antiques. Can you imagine? Well, you can better than me, but I can remember a lot.'

He was now springing about the room on his toes like an excited child. 'Can't you just see them?'

Bianca could, very clearly. She could see her things; their limpid patina, the gleam of centuries bestowed upon them by the work of others, the rose and apricot rugs, the rosewood commode, the Meissen parrot. And people would see them, people would admire, ask her about them, get her to explain about stringing and inlay and things she knew about. Ros and Henry, she knew, would never even look at her things, much less appreciate them.

She could see Americans, courteous men in pastel jackets with sharp-eyed wives twittering, 'Isn't this darling, Arthur? See, it opens in back.'

Bianca sat straighter. 'What about Breakfasts?'

'Continental. No sweat. Put out a few cereals, fruit, toast and you're in business. You don't have to make a feature. Some do a full English but it's up to you.'

'I wouldn't want children.'

'*No pets. Unsuitable for children. No smoking.* Just put it in the brochure.'

They sat together side by side, their faces intent as children staking their claim for a hut in the lupins. They were united.

*

Rosalind was exhausted and ashamed. Emotion is draining, they say, but which one? Where does shame fit?

She sat silent beside Henry as he drove home through the Domain, her over-full bag clutched on her lap, her eyes wide as they searched the rough area of the gully to the left. It was verdant, that was the word, verdant and dappled and soothing to the eye, this place where a homeless vagrant had been murdered recently. A pleasant woman, apparently, known to local shopkeepers for her honesty. She had owned a house nearby originally and something had gone wrong and she had run out of money.

Rosalind's hands tightened as they swept through. It could never happen, not here in Parnell, and it had. It could happen to Bianca. But would not because Bianca had her sister Ros and her sister's kind husband Henry. Ros who had sneaked out of her house leaving her sister among toast crumbs so she could go to the city and plot against her.

Which had proved a fatiguing and unproductive exercise. Rosalind had sat all morning at Felton Fabric Importers in the small vacant office which was used only occasionally by a temp when the workload on Lorraine became unacceptable. Many things were unacceptable to Lorraine, from outmoded computers to all this fuss about land claims.

The back office had been occupied by Martin Brown, a war veteran Henry had insisted on employing despite increasing infirmities caused by mortar fire. Martin, as he told Rosa, had left half his innards at Cassino. 'Never seen hide nor hair of them since.' He had been declared fit in time to be captured at the Senio, and had learned what he called survival Italian, which had been useful in the firm. He had established contacts, had gone on some of the buying trips with Henry and been invaluable.

The survival joke was typical of the man. He picked up words and examined them as Rosalind did. She saw him through the years, his feet splayed wide and purposeful as a penguin's as he came to greet her, *'Ciao, bella.'* They became friends, unlikely well-tempered friends, and remained so long after the effects of Cassino had caught up with him and he had retired to a council rest home in Takapuna where he lies on his bed and smokes. Meals on Wheels are a lifesaver. He doesn't know what he'd do without his Special Bland Reduction Fruit, he tells Rosa as they crack the crossword together and find that the answer to *Jones takes the plunge* is *Inigo*, and are pleased.

Someone from the RSA visits him, and always on Anzac Day. People are kind, you wouldn't believe.

There is a desk in Martin Brown's ex office, a chair, a *Great Gardens of Italy* calendar and a telephone. The calendar is in Italian and continues to be sent every year by one of his former contacts. Henry offers them to their recipient each year but Martin says that although it is a kind thought he needs a calendar like a hole in the head, so Henry continues to hang the thing in the back office. Why, he does not know. Apart from anything else, it is in Italian. Easy enough to work out because *domenica* is in red but why bother.

Rosalind stares at the calendar for a long time. It occurs to her that they might be running out of Great Gardens of Italy but this does not appear to be so. The photo angles in the Villa d'Este seem infinite and may need to be if the series goes on much longer. She looks for gardens near Milan.

Rosalind works her way through Real Estate Agents from Access to Wyatt. Do you have a letting agency? she asks. No or Yes. In what area? Unfurnished? Yes. And the price per week? Oh dear.

The prices for flats, apartments, let alone townhouses or designer units with dip pools have gone, you could say, through the roof. Henry was right. It is impossible. Rosalind touches a red *domenica*. Nothing is impossible, but she is undoubtedly out of touch with rents.

Her last experience was nearly twenty years ago when Rufus had been studying law. He had not wanted to live at home; what student did in the days before the grants were slashed.

She had ignored the obscene graffiti on the wall of old houses in the deep-litter flats he had shared, had resisted the impulse to clean up, had walked past open doors and the crumpled bed of entwined male flatmates. We all take our pleasures differently, as Henry said, and she agreed. Nevertheless the first glimpse of two unshaven faces on the same pillow and the dirty coffee mugs alongside had startled her. Mind you, it had been early in the morning. She had been taking Rufus out to Pukekohe to see Granny Felton, who liked to get her visitors over early so she could get on.

Henry put his arms around her when she told him later, kissed the top of her hat.

'It's just culture shock. Forget it.'

'And the love bites. His neck's black and blue.'

'Any fool can bite a neck.'

True. Gone were the polo-necked jerseys, the bandages, the sticking plasters of their youth. Love bites were now proud trophies displayed like sabre cuts. As was pregnancy and so it should be, how else. But the vast profferings of pregnant bellies above bikini pants had confused her at first.

They walked slowly up the path to the house. Rosalind, her mind full of land agents, remembered that one of them had told her years ago that their home had street appeal. The man, his moustache eager, his hands juggling mythical sales, had assured her that this was of the greatest importance to would-be buyers. 'You want your house to sit up and beg,' he explained.

Which depressed her further. What street appeal their

house had once owned had been diminished by lack of attention to detail. The windowsills were flaking, the garden was in need of care and attention. Nature had encroached as it does in Auckland, control had not been maintained. The banana passionfruit had gone mad, tumbling over the white trumpets of the datura and heading for the pawpaws by the verandah. The curved path to the front door was overgrown, the buried treasures of its borders invisible.

She had become careless about the garden. And Henry had never been tempted to be otherwise.

He ambled along beside her, irritated both by her thinking for one moment that her hare-brained scheme could work and by the fact that she had not pulled it off. Had not produced the bijou flat from the hat for a song.

And some clown had parked a rusting Skoda too near the blind corner. And Bianca would be there and damn and blast and bloody hell.

She sat on the sofa, her pretty feet extended, laughing into his son's eyes.

Rosalind dropped her bag and ran. 'Rufus! Why didn't you let us know the day!' Arms around him, she was hugging, laughing, being swept off her feet.

Henry, his arms hanging, watched in silence. The words, the actions, but especially, oh especially the words of Rufus's home-comings had not varied in nearly twenty years. He put out his hand as he had done countless times, felt the same sensation of love plus the niggling guilt of dismay. He dropped the outstretched hand and embraced his son, banged his back like a veteran team-mate acknowledging a superb try from the new kid.

'Welcome home, boy, welcome home.'

There was a chortle from the sofa. No other word for it. Bianca had chortled. 'Boy,' she laughed. 'Some boy!'

Henry looked at her in silence.

'Wait till we tell you! Rufus and I have had the most marvellous idea.'

Rufus stirred. 'Now hang on, Bee, I'll . . . just . . .'

Rosalind, now scrabbling in her bag, its open jaws yawning in her hand, looked up quickly. 'Bee?'

three

They sat side by side clutching gin. Rosalind lifted hers and sipped, imbibing liquid like a small wary bird.

Henry drank deep. Bianca had declined his suggestion that discussion of the plan wait until after the meal, until tomorrow, until glaciers flamed over and Rufus grew up.

Rufus, after his first startled 'Hang on, Bee', had been equally keen to impart the good news.

Henry watched him. Nothing had changed. His son's bright-eyed enthusiasm, his sharing of joy, his frank delight at new schemes practical or impractical, from the totally ludicrous to the worth investigating, remained untarnished.

Did the man think, in his wildest dreams, that his parents would countenance such insanity? Would have their home gutted, be cuckooed out of their warm muddled nest for some get-rich-quick scheme which would not work, and which, even if, against all possible odds, it did work, would be of no benefit to either of them, in fact quite the reverse. It was farcical, it was burlesque; but Henry, like Rosa beside him, knew from past experience that Rufus must be heard out.

He needed, as he had often told them, time to explain, to extrapolate, to reveal the wonders of future profits to his hearers.

If they refused to listen life became impossible. Rufus sulked, nagged, withheld affection and went dog on them. He behaved, thought Henry, like a spoiled coquette. The fun, the happiness he engendered seeped from the house, the horseplay dissipated, the singing in the shower dissolved itself into a dew.

Until they would listen, would sit through what he called his presentations, which became increasingly complicated throughout the years, presentations which involved computer printouts, pie diagrams and spreadsheets demonstrating wealth waiting to be accrued, Rufus would not play.

When they had given him a fair hearing and kept their faces straight (a skill Henry had sometimes found impossible, with disastrous results), then and only then would Rufus reward their patience. They were allowed to say what they thought of the plan in which he was inviting them to invest money.

When Henry said no, gloom descended on the house like a damp tarpaulin, but gradually, sometimes within twenty-four hours, Rufus would accept the situation and reappear, would be available for loving, would make life good once more.

It seemed, sometimes even to Henry, that this was fair enough. Henry made the living, Rufus contributed much that made the living worthwhile. Henry enjoyed his job, was knowledgable about fine fabrics and their purchase and marketing. His firm continued to make money despite increasing competition. Not as much, certainly, as in his father's day but how could it? He loved his son. Why not indulge? Support. Learn to overlook his own apprehension.

The only thing we have to fear is fear itself, said Franklin D Roosevelt and Henry agreed. And apprehension is not fear, apprehension is a taste in the mouth, a dryness, a doubt. Nothing more. Why not relax? Enjoy.

Because he couldn't. Because he was involved. Because the blood of generations of hard-working upright men and women pumping through his heart forbade it. He would not admit his fears, not to his inmost soul, wherever that was. He would not admit the questions, let alone the answers. Questions which lay stretched like faceless dogs guarding the entrance to his conscious mind. Had Rufus a moral sense? Did he know right from wrong? Did he care whether he knew or not? Was he one of those people about whom Henry has read, people in whom there is some aberration in the genes, something lacking in the building blocks of conscience. 'I want, therefore I take.'

Yet what in the name of Heaven did he fear? There had been no brush with the law, no incidents, no slippery slopes. Nothing untoward had occurred and never would and he must not worry Rosalind with his vague misgivings.

He had not tried to interest Rufus in his business in the downtown Auckland warehouse. Rufus, he assumed, was not warehouse material. He was the antithesis of Martin Brown, he despised routine. Rufus wanted real money, serious money he told them. He would get a law degree and branch out.

He dropped his law studies after eighteen months. Useless crap. Need their heads read, the lot of them. Not one of them had a clue. Not an entrepreneurial skill in sight. The whole ethos sucked.

Henry, his hand lying on Rosa's as though anchoring it to the nest of singing birds beneath, remembered Rufus's infancy. There are words now for the infinite variety of childhood; phrases such as attention deficit disorder and over-achiever and special abilities. Where were the words in the '60s for business-minded toddlers. Words such as entrepreneurial, streetwise, financially astute. Then Rufus had seemed merely disarmingly different, enchantingly so. Which other three-year-old liked the Fat Controller better than Thomas the Tank Engine. Could not understand why another one (Edward, the blue?) was happy to be back on his own little branch line after tasting life on the fast track.

He saw his son's naked back view, the pink legs pumping, the cherub buttocks tight with excitement as he ran to stow Granny's half-crown in his little 'ootcase'. The little suitcase featured large. Every treasure was guarded and stowed away; unwrapped sweets, unread books and best, oh best of all, his monies, were all stored in a fibre lunch case left over from Rosa's schooldays. His pennies became cents when he was seven years old, a process which interested him enormously. Where had they gone, the big brown ones? Why were there all these little ones? How were the little ones the same as the big ones when they weren't?

His suitcase went everywhere with him. Like all obsession-ally loved items of childhood, it became a bore to his parents. Unlike some, it was never lost or mislaid.

Men or women of mild goodwill bent to ask Rufus what he was going to be when he grew up. He gazed up at them, his eyes rounder than ever. 'Rich,' he said. By the time he was ten he had decided to be a millionaire. He bred guinea pigs, kept accurate records of progeny and prices obtained. Perhaps out of habit he kept the records in the same battered brown case alongside those of his fish-breeding enterprises. Disaster struck the fish in the form of tail rot, but the guinea pigs sold well. He avoided pet shops. They were middlemen living on the profits of the workers.

He collected coins and stamps. He read deeply on his chosen subjects but the assets accrued too slowly. His schemes became more enterprising. He bought webbing belts from Army Surplus and kitted out his fourth form at considerable profit. The belts were declared non-uniform and banned, but by this time the money was banked and how could Rufus have known that old Benson would stuff things up. '*Caveat emptor*,' he told the puniest boy in the class and biked home from Grammar by different routes for a week or two. There is nothing cute about being dumb.

As far as his parents could see, he was happy at school; he passed exams, was friendly but not sociable. His schemes took up much of his time, he played a lone hand until the plan either succeeded, in which case why tell the bludgers, or failed, in which case why tell anyone. Rufus knew that greed was good long before the man wrote the book which told the world.

And yet it was not greed, thought Henry, enmeshed once more in the web of love and astonishment Rufus had engendered for the last twenty years before it dawned upon him that his son would not change. This blinding flash had enabled him to face facts. To tell Rosa in all honesty that Rufus would be all right. He did not mean, as he knew Rosa hoped, that Rufus would settle down, start paying income tax and breed babies with some shadowy devoted wife. Rosa had shown him a full-page advertisement recently from an English paper— one of those beautifully lit black and white ones of such perfection that you ignore the product advertised. Yoghurt? Designer underwear? A beautiful young man lay gleaming and naked on a beach, his eyes closed against the sun, a sleeping infant draped along his torso.

'Nice?' she murmured.

'Rosa,' said Henry, and was silent. What could he say, what could he possibly say. Rufus is Rufus. He will be all right. He is Rufus. He is different. He is ours.

He was fifteen when he came bursting into his father's warehouse one day on his way from school.

He was onto a marvellous option.

'Option?'

He, Rufus, had a contact. A guy named Tod . . .

'One d or two?'

'Aw shit, Dad, one I think. What does it matter?'

'One d means death in German.'

45

His son's shoulders slumped. Henry tried again.

'Tell me. Tell me about Tod.'

Tod was onto a good thing. Why no one had thought of it before Rufus could not imagine. What Tod was onto, was into looking at, was about to tender for, was the franchise for distributing cigarette vending machines for hire in your own home. 'And we service them. Keep them stocked up and that. How about that!'

Henry laughed. He laughed till he wept. He lifted his eyes from his mopping handkerchief to his son's white face, to acne and pain.

'Sorry,' he gasped. 'It's just . . . it's just, why would anyone want such a thing in their house?'

Legs apart, toes poised for flight, Rufus socked it to him. 'For convenience, of course. Saves going to the dairy, you thicko.'

'And don't call me thicko.' Henry spoke without rancour. People who don't understand dreams are thickos, always have been and always will be. Why did I laugh? Because I am his father, because I got it wrong.

'Sit down, tell me about it,' he said, dragging a hand across his face. A cigarette vending machine in the privacy of your own home. It could be a talking point, a conversation piece, this tin box regurgitating fags when primed could become a source of mild envy.

Ah, I see you have one of those new Instafags.

The proud but modest, Yes.

Then what?

Henry pointed to a chair. 'Sit down,' he said again. 'Tell me all about it.'

That one was easy. Tod left town. Other schemes followed. Would Dad lend him the cash to do up that old shack down the road? No, Dad would not.

Why wouldn't they let him work on an oil rig? Because you're sitting School Certificate and they won't take you.

'What about my cash flow?'

'Stuff,' said Henry carefully, 'your cash flow.'

Guy I know organises parties for his mates, his auntie's got a garage. Gets the liquor in bulk, anything, he can get it. Knows a bloke, back-pocket deal. Wants me to go in fifty-fifty. Going like a bomb. They want more. Lots more.

There's money in Grey Power, Dad, you know that? Well, some. I'd rent the buses at first. Plough the profits back in. The sharp guys are just waking up to the transport angle, old guys like being driven. Bus travel's a whole new scene now. Completely upmarket, none of those rough rides and kids tossing down your neck. Air-conditioned, huge windows, sheepskins, they lap it up. Gardens, little tootles, wineries, seafood restaurants, shopping trips, you name it, they're on.

Guy I know made a packet out of *Jesus Christ Superstar*.

Rufus left for his OE in '78. He had spent the time since dropping out of law organising a student co-operative of house painters. They were a cheerful crew; quick, efficient and cleaned up well. Their prices were reasonable, or seemed so to Henry. Rufus interviewed the prospective clients, mostly old ladies. 'We're not professionals,' he told them, 'but we're keen and quick. And what's more we come when we say we'll come and we stay on the job. None of this here today gone tomorrow stuff, Mrs Wilkes. I can promise that.'

Oh, the relief. No more waiting, no waiting in day by day for professionals who said, 'Monday it is, Mrs Wilkes', and where were they.

'You know how you can tell a professional, Mrs Wilkes?'

Mrs Wilkes looked into the clear eyes and passed the vanilla cremes. 'No.'

Rufus was on his feet, one hand holding a phantom brush

as he demonstrated on the window frame. 'A professional can paint one sweep down here, and there won't be a single dribble on the masking tape. If he uses it, that is, and he won't. He doesn't need it. That's the difference.'

'But . . .' said Mrs Wilkes.

'Exactly. So why mention it?' Rufus gave a shy laugh. 'It doesn't matter, but that's the difference. You know about the maharajah who commissioned the Taj Mahal, Mrs Wilkes?'

Mrs Wilkes, uncertain but anxious to help, had heard something, but she didn't know it had been, as it were, commissioned.

Rufus's hands clapped together. 'Same difference. For his wife it was, in memory of his dead wife. The architect that the maharajah chose, you know what his plan, his submission for the job was?'

Mrs Wilkes shook her head, though there was something in the back of her mind she would like to have shared with this friendly young man. Something to show that she knew and had always known a great many things. That it was just that nowadays some of them disappeared when required, to click into her mind when it was too late and her fellow conversationalist had gone home. You could scarcely ring and tell them.

'Circle!' she said suddenly. 'He drew a circle.'

'Right first time. Not many of the ladies get that. Like you say, the architect just drew a circle, a perfect freehand pencil circle and the maharajah knew he was dealing with a pro.'

'Yes,' said Mrs Wilkes. 'But I've always wondered how. And what was your telephone number again, Rufus?'

There had been a cloud, a mist of dissension when Rufus dissolved the co-operative.

Terry and Mike and Jake and Lloyd no longer piled into the house at Meadowbank as they had done all through the summer. Mind if I have a shower, Mrs Felton? I smell like a goat. No, no, Jake, please do. Nimble, there and back in a flash, Rosa distributed towels, beer, food and loved every minute. She felt, that summer, like a multiple mother, a warm-hearted, competent figure offering nourishment to many.

The team liked her in return, they spared her embarrassing questions. Mike bailed up Henry as he was putting the car away.

'Mind if I have a word, Mr Felton? It's about the co-operative. Things seem to be a bit slow coming through, the wind-up payments. Do you happen to know when Roof's coming back?'

Henry stared at his key ring, rubbed the bronze F and waited.

Mike wiped his palms on his jeans. 'Can you tell us where he is?'

'With his grandmother in Pukekohe, the last time I heard.'

Mike pulled an envelope and a stub of pencil from the back pocket of his jeans. 'And the name?'

'Felton.' Thicko.

The sunburned face lifted. 'It could've been the other one. And the number?'

'Don't bother. I'll get on to him right away.'

'No worries. I'll give him a ring.'

'I have said I will deal with it, Michael.'

Henry heard his son's footsteps, the distinctive prancing stride. 'Rufus,' he called. 'Come here.'

'Where?'

'My office.' Which was a joke. The back verandah had been glassed in, a double-sided patchwork curtain designed by Rosa in her free-form period divided the area in two. Henry's side was made from more manly remnants, in colours suitable for a masculine workspace; greys, blues, woolshed reds and rusty

49

browns hung beside a second-hand desk, old filing cabinets and two ten-dollar chairs. 'Why are they so cheap?' Henry had asked the man with the crew cut. 'Not good sellers this shape, I have to say. It's the legs.' The man laid a consoling hand on green leatherette. 'Very '50s, but a steal at this price.'

Rosa's end of the verandah was a riotous assembly of colour and mess. An ironing board sat beside an old-fashioned sewing machine crouched for instant action. Piles of treasured scraps, remnants and warehouse offcuts spilled from plastic bags or cartons on shelves alongside. A macramé plant holder containing a dead cactus hung from the ceiling beside an upside-down patchwork parrot. Something had gone wrong with the attachment to its wooden hoop and Rosa had never been a fixer; the fun was in the making. One day she would mend the thing so its proud yellow beak no longer drooped like an unused cutlass, one day she would finish her small hand-woven tapestry inspired by a 2000 BC Egyptian fish vase, one day she would replace the bobbles of her canvas-work cushion depicting bunches of square grapes. And what did it matter if she didn't. She had her own space which, she had read somewhere, was important and, what was more, so had Henry. And all because she had had the sense to run up a curtain.

The acid blues, sharp greens and stinging yellows of her side had startled Bianca. She put up a hand against the onslaught of colour, the jangle of bells. 'Ooh,' she said, *oranges and lemons.*'

'I'm so glad you like it,' smiled Rosa.

'What is it?' said Rufus.

'Have a seat.'

Rufus slid into the other chair, then sprang to his feet rubbing the thighs beneath short denim shorts. 'Shit, this stuff's hot. Talk about *Blazing Saddles*. Why did you buy this crap?'

'Because it's cheap.'

'Look, can't I get it across to you, Dad . . .'

'Rufus, I don't want to start . . .'

But he was off again. Henry had heard it a thousand times. The stupidity, the sheer insanity of buying crud. How essential it was to go for quality stuff. Top of the range. Mug if you don't.

'You've got to think, Dad, use your loaf. Look at this rubbish. You could be sitting on an ergonomically designed Italian number, upmarket fabric, ball-bearing wheels, shoot all over the place like a dentist . . .'

Henry looked at his son in silence. Perhaps he was in some way, in some indefinable way, in need of help. And yet who or what could possibly change the mindset of this young thruster with entrepreneurial ambitions, or would want to. He saw his paternal grandmother, a sad, withdrawn woman whom he had never liked, looking sourly at his father's new Buick, his father in a snap-brimmed hat anxious beside her. 'Champagne tastes and ginger-beer income,' she sniffed.

'Rufus, Mike had a word with me yesterday. He said the rest of the gang haven't had their final payout.'

'Oh, that's all under control, Dad. No problems. Bit of a glitch at the moment . . .'

'Why?'

A quick impatient flick of the hand. 'You know how these things go.'

'No, I don't. Mike said it was equal whacks. That was what you all agreed. Tell me more. Explain.'

Rufus didn't, not exactly. After much circumlocution he told Henry that he was entitled to a major share because who got the thing up and running? Who chatted up the old ladies? None of it, not one bloody lick of paint would have happened without Rufus's enterprise and initiative.

Henry sat searching the face in front of him, watched the

eyes veiled by pale lashes. How could he explain to his son about honour, integrity, the word is the bond. Laertes had at least *hearkened* to his father, had given him a hearing. Henry and Rufus, like Sidney Smith's protagonists, would be arguing from different premises. From premises separated by oceans of incomprehension and seas of dissent.

He saw Rufus in glory at the Sunday School break-up, singing with the passionate conviction he gave to everything, his arms moving across, up, down in three-dimensional demonstration of his knowledge that his Redeemer lived and loved him.

Wide, wide, as the ocean
Deep, deep, as the sea.
High, high, as the heavens above
Is the Lord's love for me.

That there would be stars in his crown.

'Equal shares,' said Henry.

'Oh, all right, all right.' Rufus was on his feet, his hand clutching patchwork. 'You don't understand a bloody thing, you know that?'

'I know,' said Henry. 'I know that.'

Correspondence from overseas had been limited but this was to be expected. Rufus had never been what he called a paper man but he had a good eye for a postcard. He sent Rosa barebreasted maidens gazing with *Wish you were here* on the back.

Henry smiled bleakly. 'I didn't know he was going to the Solomon Islands.'

'No,' said Rosa, still giggling. 'But he must have, mustn't he?'

'Presumably.'

Rufus sent shoes to Rosa. Elegant Thai silk shoes for Christmas, beautifully made Italian mules for her birthday. 'Why shoes?' asked Rosa, clutching a Bruno Magli to her bosom. 'They're lovely, but so expensive. And the postage. Besides, you know me.' She wriggled an aptly named Kumf for Henry's inspection.

Henry inspected the packing. 'Extraordinary-looking stamps,' he muttered.

Rufus rang collect from London. There was a killing to be made in rugs, especially Caucasians. And kilims, though that, of course, was a whole new ball game. They both went with the whole Habitat thing: clean lines, strong colours, nothing flowery. He'd been to see a guy in one of the big warehouses down at the docks. Acres of rugs, floor to ceiling, amazing. There are tricks to the trade. Not anything like chemical washing or phoney aging with scrubbing pumice or whatever, but they don't all have to be peed on by camels. The guy had contacts. They were going to join up, head off next month for Kirovabad. Small time at first but the future was looking good.

Henry sent the money. He heard no more. The postcards ceased, there were no more shoes, but Rufus rang occasionally.

Everything was 'good', that casual catch-all word which covers everything and tells nothing.

Even Bianca was good. You should see the stuff she's got. From top to bottom, from bottom to top. Good stuff. Very good. It's all Justin's, of course, but as far as she's concerned it's hers. Always banging on about her things, and besides the man's a real no-hoper. Not Bianca's fighting weight at all. He had refused to give Rufus his service greatcoat, even though he no longer wore the thing. Even the buttons would be worth a packet at his stall. Oh, hadn't he mentioned his stall. Down at the market.

'Which market?'

'The one near here.'

'Where's here?'

Bianca had bought him an overcoat which was kind but not the point of the deal. Bianca was very thick with a guy called Barry at the local antique shop. Nice guy, camp, very knowledgable. Good contact, very good. As was Aunt Bianca. All that stuff; a real eye-opener.

He followed Mrs Thatcher's career with interest, which surprised Henry, who had thought of him as apolitical. He called her Maggie without abhorrence. She reminded him in some ways, he said, of Aunt Bianca. Plenty of attack, straight shooter, knows where she's going, though Aunt Bianca won't go anywhere with that prick Justin. They're not unalike in looks, either, though of course Bianca's younger. He'd stayed a weekend with them recently. Terrible coffee and the smallest gin in the world. A gimlet, ever heard of a gimlet, Dad?

'No,' said Henry, smiling into the mouthpiece and shaking his head.

'Gin and neat Rose's lime juice. Neat. And God, the coffee. Do you reckon she puts salt in it?'

Henry was still nodding, nodding silently and lovingly through thousands of miles of ether to the fruit of his over-anxious loins. He laughed aloud.

'What is it?' yelled the voice.

'Quick, quick.' Rosa was at his elbow. 'It's my turn.'

Rufus had arrived home unannounced, unexpected and un-communicative. Henry tried to find out how he had managed to exist for six years overseas, and not only to exist, but to make money. The answers were inconclusive and dismissive. Rosa tried when Henry was absent as she knew Henry, although devoted, was not interested in how his only child had managed to cope. Rufus would be all right.

Henry took his son to lunch at one of those cool, unob-trusive, downtown restaurants with a good wine list and men

54

in suits. There was little laughter in their discussions. These were serious men.

As were Rufus and his father. Henry was not aware that his son owned a suit. Apart from his gilded hair, he melted into the background, was appreciative of the wine list and talked politics. He had come back, he said, as soon as he heard they'd got rid of Muldoon, floated the dollar and all that. Thank God for Labour. He had kept in touch. A guy he knew, New Zealander, had the financial guff sent over, has had for years. Now Lange and co. have taken over, the whole place'll open up, take off, the age of enterprise and initiative will begin and Rufus planned to be part of it. Buoyant economy, get-ahead attitudes, that's what we're looking at. New Zealand's the place to be in the '80s and Auckland's the place to be in New Zealand. No doubt about that.

His voice did not rise. His usual exuberance appeared dampened, he glanced over his shoulder occasionally. People don't believe me, he said. They think because I've been away for a few years I haven't a clue. Suits me. I've brought my money back and I'm ready to roll.

'How much money?'

'Enough.'

'What are you going to put it in?'

Rufus waved a hand.

'Have a word with Charlie Adamson,' said his father.

'That old dugout. He's still losing the Somme.'

'Wrong war. And for God's sake keep your head. The market's going mad. Keep clear of it.'

Rufus had made money, a lot of money. How else could he have lost so much so spectacularly on Monday, 19 October 1987?

Rosa rang Henry. He's just sitting here. He has been all day. People keep ringing him, every time it's worse. Oh,

Henry, I've never seen him like this before. He looks . . . I can't tell you what he looks like. It's all gone, everything. Every penny he had. Oh Henry, I told you. I told you I was worried.

Rufus departed overseas once more. His debts were not impossible. He had not been home long enough.

He came home several times during the next eight years. He was doing well. Business was thriving.

'What business?'

'Same racket as you, Dad, the rag trade. Kids' wear. Find a good design . . .'

'How do you mean find?'

'All right. Industrial espionage, if you must. The name of the game in the rag trade and always has been. Where've you been, Dad?

'Then off to the sweatshops of Asia, I presume?'

'Yeah. The main problem is continuity. Your contacts can fold on you. Whole workshops can disappear overnight.' But Rufus had got a reliable network set up at last. 'You have to watch them, of course. Talk about tough. Watch them like a laser. But you just have to take people as you find them. Everyone's different. Taiwan, ever been to Taiwan?'

'No.'

'My God, they put you through it there and not only as regards business. The entertainment, the stuff they produce for their honoured guests to eat. They're testing you, see; sheep's eyes have got nothing on it. I told you about live ducks' feet?'

'No.'

'And monkeys' brains? They bring them to the table live same as the ducks, slice the top of their skulls off and there's the raw brains sitting wiggling at you on the plate.'

Rosa left the room. She came back white-faced, beads of sweat on her upper lip and forehead.

'But you love animals,' she begged.

'I do. I always have, like you say. I nearly had a fight with a guy in the market. He had live snakes on poles, dozens of them writhing about. Just hack off a bit, hand it over, guy goes off munching. No way they'll allow photos, well, who would? So I told him I'd buy the lot and he went berserk. I had to run for it in the end.'

He looked sadly at his mother's censorious frown. 'What could I have done with them, I thought later? They weren't even whole, half of them.

'And the same in the restaurant. What did you expect me to do? What could I do. People are different. It was an honour, it was business.' Rufus leaned back on elves. 'I take people as I find them. You have to in business, don't you, Dad?'

Henry lifted his hand from his wife's. It rose as though release from pressure had buoyed it upwards. Rufus had not taken long to reveal the details of the newest plan. He and Bianca sat side by side, partners who understood and were grateful for the strengths of the other. Bianca's hand touched Rufus's arm occasionally. She liked plans and that was one thing about New Zealand, you can do the most extraordinary things and no one will care. Sometimes when she had been abroad with Justin, Rapallo say, or Portofino, Bianca had looked down dark streets, seen gaiety, young men smoking and angry, dark-eyed girls. 'Let's go down there.'

'For God's sake, Bianca, don't be so Mrs Wentworth Brewster.'

And she had laughed at his wit and they had walked back to the Hotel Miramar and the limpid beauty of the harbour below the balcony where they drank coffee. One drinks a lot of coffee abroad.

While in England, Bianca had missed her enjoyment of hard physical work. Idleness did not come easily to her and she disliked golf and bridge. What she was good at was the hacking, taming, slashing type of gardening which she had practised in her mother's garden in Auckland, where growth has to be tamed not cosseted, where sub-tropical lianes threaten to strangle, where old roses go mad and leap down gullies, where Schiaparelli pink passion flowers do not astound. Titchfield gardens do not need to be tamed. Even walks in Hampshire are tamed. Bianca could understand her friend Linda, who had married a farmer thirty miles in from Otorohanga, a man who later left her for another woman. She missed him, of course, she told Bianca, but more than that she missed the farm. Not the beauty so much as the life, the satisfaction, the visible rewards of physical effort; the yards emptied, the shearing ended and their work done. Linda retreated to Otorohanga and pined for a life of vigour.

And now, especially now, now as never before, Bianca needed a project, something to absorb her completely.

Happiness, she had read somewhere, *is a by-product of absorption.*

Bianca thought about it, let it sink in, saw herself in an overall (Ros would have one), her hair tied up in a bandanna (Ros again), stripping, scrubbing, achieving happiness as a by-product of absorption.

She smiled at Rufus, patted his arm.

'I will tell you right now, Rufus,' said Henry, 'neither your mother nor I would countenance this idiotic scheme for one moment. As you must surely have realised.'

Rufus said nothing.

Bianca stared at him in panic. Her things, her Pembroke table, her Davenport, her longcase clock, all were disappearing from their appointed places in the room around her. Her scheme, her new life was collapsing before her eyes. She looked at Rufus's inert form, begged his idle hands.

'But you said, Rufus, you said.'

Rufus rose to his feet and stretched, dropped his palms behind his neck and yawned. 'Just an idea, Bee, just an idea. After all,' he explained, 'it's not our house, is it? Yours or mine.'

four

'How would you feel,' asked Rosa, 'if I asked you to come with me to see Martin Brown?'

Rufus glanced briefly from the real estate pages. 'Trapped. Where's Webster Street?'

'Why?' said Bianca, licking her spoon.

'Saturdays, the weekends generally, are so boring for him. He'd love to see you.'

'There's a unit for sale there.'

Henry rose stiff-legged and pompous. 'I'd be glad if you'd bring the paper to my office, Rufus. When you've finished with it, of course.'

'I don't want a unit! I want a villa, Rufus, like you said. To do up.'

'Take the damn thing, Dad.'

Bianca intercepted the transfer, gave a practised flip and scan. 'Look. Here's another one in Webster Street. *Wanted. Home handyman and TLC to restore this little gem. Great investment in desirable area.* What's TLC?'

'Please may I have my paper?'

'Tender loving care. It means it's a dump.'

'But look at the picture.'

Rufus peered over his aunt's shoulder at a smudged grey

cottage almost submerged beneath wisteria. A straight path led to the door. There was a hollyhock.

'Give me my paper!'

Bianca's smile was tender. 'In a moment, Henry.'

My heart is lurching. I must keep calm. This woman could kill me. Bianca, you seem unable to understand. What can I do to make you understand? We do not propose to hand our house over to you. We do not propose to buy one for you. There is no cottage. No house. Nothing. Nix. 'Thank you,' he said and took the paper.

Bianca sat motionless, one hand brushing imaginary crumbs from the swell of her bosom. She had had an idea.

'Rufus, are you coming with me to see Martin or not?'

'I didn't like the look of the weatherboards.' Rufus glanced in surprise at the ruffled bantam beside him. 'Sure, Mum, we'll go in Gaby's Skoda.'

Henry turned at the doorway. 'Is that the heap on the blind corner?'

'Yeah. Unless there's two.'

'Who's Gaby?'

'Aw, come on, Mum, I've told you about Gaby.'

'Never.'

'Gaby,' said Bianca faintly.

'Gaby's my partner.'

'Business or sleeping?'

'Both. And I don't like your tone, Dad.'

'I apologise.'

'Like hell you do. I would have you know . . .' Rufus was striding about the room, springing from his toes. 'I would have you know that if it hadn't been for Gaby I wouldn't be here today. I'd be dead. You're talking about the woman who carried me, bloody well half carried me, down from Poon Hill.'

'Where?'

'Near Annapurna. I was dead, half dead with Delhi belly. My pack, her pack, the lot. I could hardly crawl. I won't have you patronising Gaby.'

'Nobody's patronising anyone,' cried Rosalind. 'It's just that we didn't know about Gaby, did we, Henry?'

Henry shook his head. 'Or Poon Hill.'

'We want to meet her, we must meet her, thank her, everything . . .' She held out her hands. 'Oh Rufus, how are we to know things if you don't tell us?'

'Gaby,' said Bianca.

'I did tell you.'

'Never, never. Did he, Henry?'

'No.'

More silence. Rufus stopped prancing. Bianca stood up and sat down.

'Where is she now?' said Rosa finally.

'Matamata. There's a family wedding.'

'Why didn't you go?'

Rufus opened his arms. 'Because I wanted to get back to you guys. And besides, Gaby wasn't sure the Skoda would make it. It's been with her ex de facto while she's been away. The guy's just let it fall to pieces.'

Rosalind stood very straight, her head high. 'Will it get to Takapuna?'

'Oh hell yes. No sweat.'

'Good,' said his mother. 'Good.'

'Well, that's just as well,' said Henry, 'because I need the Sentra.'

'Why?'

'It's time I went to see Granny.'

Did I invent that, did I dredge up my aged old mother. I could scarcely invent her at this stage, but did I summon her up as a bolt-hole, an oh-my-God-let's-get-out-of-here escape.

An escape to the small cottage and green paddocks amid

encroaching ten-acre blocks and murmurs of motorway extensions, to the peace of well-sheltered orchards and his geriatric, alternative-lifestyle mother. Mrs Felton had moved out to Pukekohe when his father died. She had refused to budge, which was a worry, but her independence had its advantages. What if she had been as dependent as Bianca, had regarded her next of kin as safety nets and money as something which other people gave her smiling. Granny F had insisted on choosing her own ice-floe to head out to sea. She was captain of her soul, she took no orders. She was a cause for concern and it was high time he went to see her. Besides, he liked the tough old boot, enjoyed her company. There's no law against it.

Bianca leaned forward. She seemed incapable of asking a question without physical commitment, without being engaged. 'May I come too, Henry?'

Henry gaped at her. Here, offering her unwanted company, was the woman who, half an hour ago, had attempted to engage his son in a hare-brained collusion over a dead cottage in need of tender loving care plus a great deal of work and considerable money. He wanted to grab her by her plump shoulders, to shake her till she rattled. *There is no money. You have none because your husband lost it. I will not give you mine which will later be Rosa's and eventually, God help us, our son's.*

'Why?' he said eventually. 'Why on earth do you want to see her?'

'I don't want to see your mother particularly,' said Bianca, her mind elsewhere, 'but I'd like a run in the country.'

She must keep track of that advertisement, get some time to herself to cut it out before they left for Pukekohe and it was thrown away. Then work out exactly what she wished to say to Henry. Make notes to remind. There probably would be no need to consult them, just knowing they were there would be enough. Julian had been a great believer in notes. They clear the mind, he said, and there was much at stake.

'And then I'll answer my English Christmas cards when we get back,' she said, brushing again. 'You realise surface mail from here arrives about November 6th?'

'No,' gasped Henry. 'No, I hadn't realised that. Had you, Rosa?'

Rosa nodded. Bianca had complained for years of the penny-pinching habits of antipodean well-wishers. But Henry, who had scarcely glanced at a Christmas card in his life, was stretching out to her, seeking connubial support. She put an arm around him, patted his shoulder. 'You do now,' she said.

Rosalind sat high-rumped to help as the Skoda toiled up the harbour bridge. Rufus was telling her how much he liked his aunt, always had. 'Sure, she's got her weird bits but living with Justin wouldn't help. I got him a new toilet suite once . . . they were gussying up the downstairs lavatory.'

'Why you?'

'I knew a guy, got him a good price. They've all got really gross names: Regal, Royale, Consort. He ended up saying, "Very well, Rufus, if you can't get the Sovereign, I'm quite prepared to make do with the Regent."' Rufus gave a loud laugh, startling a gull from the girder alongside. It disappeared, hurtling downwards to the flat blue sea below. There was not enough wind for the yachts. They hung motionless between sea and sky, dependent on forces of nature.

'And when do we meet Gaby?'

'Gaby? Oh, any day now.'

The wanting to ask how things are with your offspring when you're not told, how they are *faring*, is like having a pool of liquid somewhere inside. It is not pathological, this fluid, neither is it essential like the pulsing thump of blood which knows where it's going and gets on with it, or the ordered bump and slosh of digestive processes. The pool of longing lies still, a mirrorless lake somewhere above the midriff. It comes and goes. It can be drained by answers.

'Tell me about her.'

'Well, you'll meet soon.'

'Yes, but tell me about her.'

'God, the North Shore's taken off, hasn't it?'

'No, it hasn't. Not Lake Road. It's just the same as always, only worse.'

'Looks okay to me.'

'It always was okay. It's worse now because there's more traffic.'

'Have it your way.'

She could have hit him. She very nearly did hit him.

He stroked the Skoda's rump as they arrived at the Sunnydale Rest Home. Something was on his side if not his inquisitive old bat of a mother.

The smell of nicotine in the small room was overpowering. Martin Brown lay on the bed, his yellow face and arms backed by tartan. He looked as though he had been thrown there. *Unregarded age in corners thrown*, thought Rosa, and wished she hadn't.

His walking frame was to hand for assistance to the bathroom straight ahead. The lavatory lid was raised, its all-seeing blankness stared back at them.

To the right of the bathroom door a huge television was operating full bore. Oprah Winfrey was being instructed by a young woman in pink tights and lip gloss how to make her Easter decorations for next to nothing. Oprah seemed interested, the young woman frenetic, as she cut, pasted and cut again; ribbons, tinsel, sequins, shiny paper and plain were all essential. Plus, of course, Oprah's own personal creative identity which every one of you guys out there has as well once it kicks in, is, like, you know, tapped. Isn't that right, Oprah? Oprah, staring at the small, complicated, yellow and green construction in her hand, agreed. Merlita was so right.

'Turn it off,' shouted Martin. 'Good to see you. Good. Good. Sit down.'

Rosalind kissed his pleated cheek and handed over a carton of cigarettes.

'I'll undo it for you,' said Rufus.

Martin handed him a packet.

'Thanks a lot.'

'I tried being an other-people's-only smoker myself,' said Martin, coughing, wheezing, killing himself but what the hell, 'but I wasn't getting enough. Be worse now, my word. Pariah dog country for smokers out there. Thank you, Rosa, thank you. So you're home again then.' He looked at Rufus, searching for clues as he had always done. He liked the man as he had liked the small boy. Rufus had made him laugh, he told a good story and had done from the age of four. Not all kids like talking to adults. Rufus had been happy to yarn for hours.

Martin saw the small brown hand on the lid of Tess's tin box labelled *Odds & Ends*, the drawer slipping shut as Rufus turned. 'I was just putting it back, Mr Brown,' he explained. 'I came in to talk to Tess and she wasn't here, and I saw this fifty cents on her desk and I thought hang and I was just putting it back.'

He had been a lovely kid.

'You'll come for lunch on your birthday, won't you, Martin?' said Rosa.

Martin looked at his friend. She attracted what you could call contact. She wished the world well and was disturbed by its conflicting interests. The rain would please the farmers but wasn't it bad luck for the school fête. It's hard to make money outside in the rain.

66

'Make up your mind, Rosa,' he had told her twenty years ago.

And here she was still trying. Wanting him to come, half dead and coughing his head off, to meet the po-faced sister whom he remembered with distaste, and these things are reciprocal.

'What about your sister, Rosa?'

'Oh, Bianca would love to see you again. Besides, it's her birthday as well.'

Bianca. What a name. Martin's eyes met Rufus's, flicked away quickly.

'Well, it's day by day these days, Rosa,' he wheezed. 'Very kind indeed, but that's months away, we'll have to see.'

'Take a raincheck,' said Rufus slipping another Rothmans from his pack. He had his own matches.

Martin stroked his tartan rug. It was a pity the boy's here, but why fuss. He couldn't ask him to clear out while he talked to his mother.

There's a lot of bull talked about love. Cherish is better. Rosa is cherishable and has been from the first moment I met her.

'I think I've got it all wrong, Mr Brown,' she whispered to him at her first office party after matrimony. The firm had been larger and more profitable then, and Mr Felton senior, despite his fears for the world as he knew it, had liked a good shindig. Rosalind glanced around the hot fug of the Christmas party, the slink of oyster satin bottoms gliding by, the proffered cleavage or two, the gaiety of converse. 'Wearing a sunfrock. I mean, look at them.' She flipped a finger beneath her nose, declined a fish ball. 'What the hell. Tell me, what do you do here?'

*

'Rosa,' he said, 'when I fall off the perch I want you to have what's left.'

Rosa had helped Martin with his banking for years and knew the pitiable state of his bank balance. But still. 'No, no, Martin, I wouldn't dream of it. What about your charities—RSA, Salvation Army?'

'You're my charity, Rosa. All my holdings, equities, the lot, all salted away. You'll be so rich you can leave what you like to the other buggers—or better still, blow the lot. Fat cat Rosa.'

Rufus was on his feet, his face serious. 'I don't want to intrude on this conversation. I don't think I should. No, no. I'll wait outside,' he said and disappeared.

Rosa looked at the old man in dismay. 'What on earth did you say that for? Rufus . . .'

You cannot say to a half-dead compulsive smoker, even if he is your best friend and you trust him, you cannot say, My son is interested in money and he might not realise you are joking.

She gave up, touched his stained hand briefly and picked up the crossword. '*Soldier ants remark to a friend?*'

Martin finished his cough and lay exhausted. '*Passant,*' he gasped.

Bianca was biding her time. She was wary of Henry and there was no hurry. It would be better to broach the subject on the way home.

'I had the most extraordinary dream last night,' she said.

Henry turned onto the motorway in silence.

'Princess Margaret was worried about her committee work. She was wearing rather a nice little hat, like half a stove-pipe with a feather. One of those practically all stalk ones with a little black fluff at the end. I was surprised, really, she doesn't often wear a hat indoors, let alone black. She asked me how I managed. "Well ma'am," I said, "in my experience, it all comes from the top. If the chairman is enthusiastic then she engenders enthusiasm in the whole of her committee. Unless you have a hard-working, enthusiastic—" Watch that lorry!'

'Truck.'

'It could have killed us. But it was odd, wasn't it? I mean dreams are of course, but this one was so real. She was very grateful and a footman arrived with tea and . . .' Bianca sat silent for a moment. 'It was funny it was Princess Margaret though, wasn't it? I mean . . .'

The asphalt ribbons of the motorway streamed south-wards. A van labelled *Pandas of the Secret Dragon* passed too close. There was not much traffic.

He would understand, wouldn't he, if Bianca didn't come in to see Mrs Felton. Bianca was sure his mother would much prefer to see him alone. 'She probably scarcely remembers me.'

'Oh, yes, she does.'

Well even so, Bianca would be quite happy. She had brought the morning paper and the countryside is so pretty at this time of year. She might go for a little walk, though of course you can't walk here like you can in Hampshire. Lorries hurtling about all over the place.

She didn't walk. She checked her notes and reread the advertisement for the home handyman's dream and thought how she would make her point.

'And how was your mother?'

'Very well. She'd just killed a turkey for Easter. She gets very cross when they won't lie still.'

Typical. 'Did she mind my not coming in?'

'Not at all.'

Bianca glanced at him sharply. 'She never liked me.'

'No.'

'Does she still blame me for Andrew's death?'

69

'I didn't ask her.'

It is very peaceful near Pukekohe. Small green hills rise and fall, shelter belts grow tall, cows bellow but not often.

The time had come. 'Henry, I have something to tell you. I wonder if you would like to pull in to the verge and stop while I do so.'

Henry's idiotic eyebrows leapt high.

'For heaven's sake, woman, what can you say that would stop me driving?'

'Don't call me woman.'

'I didn't mean to insult you.'

There he was again. Joke or no joke. Insult or no insult. Hard to crack and tiresome with it. 'It's just . . . Justin called me that. It was an, an endearment, a compliment.'

Henry gave a snort of delight. 'I'm not surprised.'

Tears came easily to Bianca. Her emotions were near the surface, Justin had told her. It didn't in any way indicate weakness.

Nor did it this time, it gave her strength. 'I want to tell you why I broke my engagement with Andrew.'

'Why would that stop me driving?'

'Oh, do dry up about driving.'

'I loved Andrew very much. I know you don't believe me, none of you would except Rosa. It was because he was different, that was why, and of course his looking like that, and all he knew, and all he'd seen and all we would see together. Places I'd never heard of: Petra, Angkor Wat, Chichen Itza. I can remember them all, all the names and there were lots more. It was more than just his being an architect. He wanted to see the whole world, the wonders of it, to find out—and he wanted to show me. He seemed, I mean, to worship me—and don't look like that, I don't know how else to describe it.

'And all the other girls being besotted about him, I didn't

70

mind that either. Half the School of Architecture had crushes on him, boys and girls. That dark face, dramatic, always talking. None of us had ever seen anyone like him. All that, plus brains and brilliance. Remember?'

'Yes.'

'That was why I called him Andrew. Andy seemed—not large enough somehow. Not destined for the whole world. I know you hate it. I know you hate my talking about him at all but I'm going to. I'm going to go on and on and tell you everything, tell you why, and you can just keep driving like you said you wanted to and . . .'

He didn't look at her, he refused to look at her.

'Remember his clothes? Those beautiful shirts? Like Hamlet's, all wide sleeves and floppy collars. Andrew made his own patterns, everything. He made things for me and I wore them all, weird black things, all trailing. And shoes, you know he made himself a pair of shoes?'

'Yes.'

'Italian shoes he loved best of all. Women's shoes. He used to get his father to bring them back from Milan for me. Shoes like nothing in the world: four-inch heels, stilettos, stretch satins. And the colours: maple, tomato red, pistachio green, plum. They were works of art. Glorious things. I remember him picking up a pointy-toed one, you know how they were then, like a long black beak, and kissing it. Telling me what it would do for my legs. It is something to do with design, he said, the cutting. You land up slim as a model and six feet tall. They were magic, magic things. And Andrew, Andrew who loved me and wanted to marry me and be the best designer in the world, he knew all this. He knew it in Ponsonby in the '60s. You know what it was like then. You remember.'

'Yes.'

'He started borrowing the shoes, to show his design tutor, he said. Just one at a time. He kept them on the table by his

71

bed so he could see them first thing, he said. He had several on the grotty mantelpiece. Then.'

She was weeping now, silently, the tears flowing down her face.

'One came back all stained. It was a red and blue leather peep-toe, real Rita Hayworth thing. He said he'd spilt coffee and he was sorry and I knew he was. It was ruined. He would write to the makers in Milan. They always have thirty-sevens. It is the classic size, he told me, and I felt quite proud. I know it's silly but . . .

'I had seen him that day already, he was doing honours then, and he came in to say hello and how about . . . I said no, I had to go into town to get my hair cut but I gave him some coffee and said I'd get home as soon as I could and when I got to Antonio's my man had been sacked, sacked that very day for putting his fingers in the till and they hadn't even told me. I thought, Blow this, I'm not having any old cutter, and Andrew will be waiting and Mum isn't home and I couldn't get there quickly enough.

'I'll never forget it. Never.'

'What?'

She was still weeping.

'I'm telling you. I'm telling you exactly. I knew he'd be in my bedroom with the shoes and I went in quietly to surprise him and tell him I loved him, and that Mum wouldn't be home for hours.

'I saw the curtain first, blowing out the open window and then his back view and his bare legs and I laughed and said something like he was a bit previous, wasn't he, and he swung round with a shoe, my pretty shoe in his hand and, he was . . .'

No.

'He was making himself come in my shoe.'

*

72

Henry pulled onto the verge and switched off the engine. Three black heifers ambled across the paddock to stare, spit swinging from their glum mouths, their tails moving slowly from side to side. The pine branches of the plantation tilted and swayed.

'Why are you telling me this?'

'I think you should know.'

'I did know,' he lied, slamming into gear. 'And I can't imagine what you're making all the fuss about.'

The car leapt forward, stones from the berm struck paint-work, the heifers turned tail to lumber across the paddock and stare again.

Henry did not know but he had guessed. Or perhaps suspected is a better word. Where there is brilliance, astonishment at life, there is often difference. It doesn't have to mean sad men flashing, it doesn't have to provoke sniggers, though it often does. The nudge, wink and nudge again formerly reserved for unlicensed pregnancies and homosexuality, the sneers and the leers of good keen men and women now include those who take their sexual pleasures differently and at one remove; the fetishists, the dresser-uppers, the transvestites, the 'kinky'. All of whose behaviour is perfectly legal. There are magazines now for those his father would have corralled into his catch-all word 'unwholesome'. Henry knew about paraphilia, had read about it after Andy killed himself, if he had. He knew the names for various forms of compulsive sexual behaviour, the terms for specific fetishes—rubber, fur, leather, dozens of them. That involving worship of female shoes is called retifism. Not an easy word to remember, retifism. It is found in men of every sexual orientation, the book had told him, but Henry knew that already.

If Andy were alive now he would be prancing off to the Shoeman's Ball, subscribing to *Fetish Times* or *Super Spikes*, surfing the internet for sources of information. Henry gave a long sniff. Andy should not have died.

He saw him fondling a lace-up stiletto, his palm sliding from the heel, up and over and down the toe, his face intent, his hand slow. 'Do you think I've got one of those weirdo things about shoes?'

Henry put *The Tin Drum* face down beside his infant son's blue knitted bear. 'I hope not.'

The smile was dreamy. 'I don't mind if I have . . . To me beautiful shoes are the perfect art form, the ultimate combination of design, engineering, colour. Look at this toe,' he said, stroking purple leather. 'And the heel—tomato, the bloom of tomato. No other word. It's the leather. You can't get colour and the *bloom* of colour in any other material. The depth.

'And Bianca realises all this, you know. Have you ever looked at her ankles?'

'Of course.'

'Her feet are even better. Narrow, wonderful shape. Beautiful feet are important to me. Very important. People with dirty feet, filthy cracked toenails, I find that . . .' Andy stood up, picked the blue bear from the sofa, punched its middle and dropped it. 'I find that repellent. Worse than repellent. I find it . . . immoral.'

Henry reached for the pipe he had smoked then. He lit up, relit, puffed hard, gave himself time.

'Do you love Bianca?'

'You nuts or something?'

'Not just her feet?'

Andy flopped down. The bear gave a small muffled squeak. 'I saw a film when I was a kid. About eleven or twelve. *Madonna of the Seven Moons*, it was called. The girl had gone mad or something and cleared out and the hero kept moping about looking for her. At one stage he said, "If I had ten dreams, Maddalena Labardi would be in every one of them."

74

I remember thinking, Shit.' He closed his eyes, opened them. 'You don't think I should hit you?'

'No.'

'Or that I'm a raving perve?'

'Get off that bloody bear.' Henry knocked it into shape, twitched its ears. 'No,' he said.

'Good,' said Andy.

He left soon after. Henry identified the body a week later.

'If you had loved him, really loved him, you would have helped him. Not dumped him, left him floundering—left him to . . .'

Bianca was now dry-eyed.

'I was twenty. My world was him and it had fallen apart. I was shaking, shaking like a leaf. I took all the shoes and threw them at him one after the other, on and on. I was screaming, out of my mind, screaming and screaming and then I ran.

'I never saw him again. You should be grateful to me. Be quiet, I haven't finished. Grateful. All that time, before the funeral, after, I never told a soul. I never said how I had loved him. Why I had stopped. Nothing.

'And I knew, the moment I saw him there, I knew. I knew he didn't love me, had never loved me. It was the shoes, those beautiful shoes. It was them he loved. I was just a thing, a thing for the shoes. I took them to the dump next day and I flung them, every one, further and further as far as I could and they looked terrible, I mean it, ghastly, like painted traps, something from another world, a jungle; brilliant petalled things that snap shut on insects and eat them alive. Digest them. All those heels sticking up and the colours, acid green and lime and purple and pink. There were mules, stilettos, sandals lying in all that rotten mess and the seagulls whirling and that smell, that sour, burning dump smell and I went home and lay in the bath for an hour and I knew I'd never get clean again.

'It wasn't me who killed Andrew. It was the shoes.

'I thought I would never get over it and I wouldn't have if it hadn't been for Justin. Not only losing Andrew. It was how. Why. And people, what they said. Had we had a row? Had he left a note? Your mother thinking it was my fault, blaming me for his death even after the coroner's verdict. I felt dirty, dirty beyond words. And I did for years.'

'You told *Justin*?'

'Of course I did and he saved me. He was a psychologist, wasn't he? He knew about obsessions, explained how it's compulsive, how they can't change. Andrew would never have loved me, he was incapable of loving, of being intimate, of caring. I was just an object, a thing with feet to dress up, to wear shoes.'

'Why did you ask me the other night if anything more had been discovered about Andy's death when you know every last detail, the tragic blinding waste of his death . . .' He paused for his answer, received none. 'And why are you telling me all this now?

'Why?' he said again.

Her voice was calm, her face serene. 'I think you owe me something, Henry.'

He laughed from release of tension, from the sheer bloody absurdity of the woman, from despair. Andy, Andy whom he had loved, the younger brother who outshone him and always had and so what, had killed himself. The brother he had minded for years, had bought condoms for, had talked things through with night after night. Andy had died alone and desperate. Not from genuine love of the woman beside him, he agreed with her there. But from the realisation that his obsession was untameable, that he had loved the wrong things and the wrong woman, he had drowned himself, had killed the whole to destroy the part. It was a long time ago.

Henry looked at the bridge foundation beside the motorway, the hexagonal blocks fitting together in neat concrete patchwork. He could swerve, accelerate, crash. And Bianca would survive and he would be crippled for life.

'What did you have in mind, Bianca?'

'I think,' she said calmly, 'you should buy that cottage in the paper this morning as an investment for Rufus. It's time Rufus settled down, got a proper job. And he and I could do it up and I could live in it. If it will suit my things, of course. I've never been really happy with the Bed and Breakfast idea. I don't think Justin would have liked that at all.

'It would be in my name and when I die I would leave it to Rufus. I am very fond of Rufus. I had planned to leave him something before all this awful muddle about my money and having to come out here and everything.'

Henry did look at her this time. His sick heart was thumping as he turned to her.

'And if I don't?'

'I will tell your mother why Andrew took his life.'

This laugh was louder. A victory roll, a sucks to you, a yah yah yah.

'She wouldn't believe a word of it, let alone understand. And if she did she'd kill you.' He thought of the still-bloodied tomahawk in Pukekohe, the stained block by the implement shed and laughed again.

'And what about Rufus?'

Henry was humming, bowling along the motorway on a sunny Saturday morning singing to himself: *We're three happy chappies with snappy serapes, you'll find us beneath our sombreros.* Where on earth had that come from.

'What about Rufus?' he laughed.

'Ros showed me all those shoes he sent her.'

An articulated truck thundered by, followed by a fire

engine screaming for room, room and more room.

'Three pairs,' said Henry. 'Only three.'

Bianca shook her head. 'Poor Ros,' she murmured.

He got home. He got them both home. He drove back to Meadowbank like an old man in pain, slowly and carefully. He drove in to the garage and walked up the path. Bianca collected her notes and followed him, her skirt brushing against some ragged pelargoniums which should have been trimmed back and of course hadn't.

five

Henry had not told Rosa. The words did not sound well. Your sister tells me, Rosalind, that my brother was a sexual pervert. She is about to hand on this intelligence to my mother unless I buy her a house. I see no reason why my mother should be troubled in this way so I have agreed to her suggestion.

Nor did disinterested generosity. I have decided, Rosalind, that I will buy a house for your sister. Rufus can help her do it up. It should be an excellent investment and we will get shot of her.

He saw Rosa, barefoot in an elongated T-shirt with kittens from Girlswear which served as a nightshirt. Why? When you said you wouldn't. How can we afford it?

We can't.

Then how?

I'll take out a new mortgage on this house.

At your age?

Silence was the other alternative. Until the morning, silence was best.

'Why can't I take her tea and toast as well?' he had asked weeks, months, years ago before Bianca arrived.

Rosa, naked except for a plastic shower cap, had patted

his buttock. 'Getting a bit saggy. Sort of pleated at the edges. Because eating in bed is sordid. Didn't you know?'

So there they were, due solely to Bianca's views on moral torpor, sitting up like vultures; munching, drinking, passing, nodding and passing again. Henry cleared his throat.

Rosa, caught in mid-dash to the kitchen, paused. Bianca lifted her head. Rufus continued rolling his own. He had smoked his last tailormade.

'I haven't had a chance to discuss this with you, Rosa,' said Henry, 'but I've decided we should all have a look at the cottage Bianca saw advertised yesterday.'

The reaction was gratifying. Like Mr Bennet's virgin daughters at their father's admission that he had called on the new neighbour, Rufus and Bianca were loud in their praise. Bianca clapped her hands, Rufus seized his father's. Only Rosa looked puzzled. 'Why didn't you tell me, Henry?'

'I meant to, but it slipped my mind.'

Rosa watched the interesting jiggle of light on the ceiling and traced it to her cup of coffee. Why, she asked, would light reflect back from her coffee?

No one answered.

'I'll take a picnic,' she said.

Bianca's pleasure heightened. She had wondered when the ham and egg pie in the fridge was going to appear. She enjoyed picnics and all small treats arranged by others and Rosa was good at arranging them, so things worked out well and always had. Bianca hoped Webster Street was not too far away.

It was near at hand, though not, unfortunately, within walking distance. The sign drooped from its post at the entrance to a previously unknown cul de sac. Old cottages had been pulled down and replaced by townhouses, the majority of which crouched low as they guarded their concrete sweeps, their lock-up garages, their hydrangeas and their tiny lawns. Others

80

shot upwards, three storeys or more, all angles and unused balconies and pointed roofs.

'Postmodern crud,' said Rufus.

Henry, who was thinking of Andy's probable reaction, nodded.

'All the other old cottages have been gentrified,' continued Rufus. 'That's always a good sign.'

The land agent (call me Max) agreed.

'Why do they tart them up?' said Bianca. 'All that phoney ironwork.'

'That's not a problem with this one,' laughed Max. 'Mind you, you have to remember it's deceased estate.'

They saw what he meant, they saw immediately. Max was now talking rapidly. The beneficiaries of the estate would of course clean it out—all the junk would disappear. A lifetime of junk here, he said, kicking a mangle on the verandah as he shouldered his way beneath wisteria to unlock the front door. 'The mangle?' murmured Bianca. Yeah, the mangle would undoubtedly go. 'No,' said Bianca and Rufus simultaneously, 'We'll take it off their hands,' continued Rufus. 'Put it that way.'

The door swung open on to squalor and more finds. 'The butter maker also, if that'd be any help. Don't you agree, Bee?' Bianca nodded. 'If it's any help,' she agreed. 'In fact I'd go further. I would be prepared . . .'

She stopped. Rufus removed his foot from hers. They entered.

Bianca and Rufus moved around the house making small discreet mews of excitement at scrubbing boards, a copper, a wooden handle in the WC labelled *Pull*. Rosa and Henry stood close together, stupefied by the mess, the air of decay. The sense of human disintegration was overwhelming, palpable. There was plenty of evidence. Layers of newspapers lay on a table on which meals had been eaten and spilt. Someone had scrawled *Fuck off, Fraser* in large letters above the stained sink, empty beer bottles spilled from an unlocked shed.

It would be no problem at all for Rufus to get rid of that lot, he said, no problem at all.

The agent looked at him thoughtfully. 'That, of course, will have to be discussed with the vendors. Frankly, I was of the opinion that it should be cleaned out before we advertised. *Have your property looking its best at all times.* It's one of our best vendor tips. But of course you never know where you are with deceased estates.'

A floorboard creaked beneath his weight.

Rufus and Bianca were undeterred. Bianca began taking measurements with what Henry recognised with astonishment as his retractable tape from the garage, climbing nimble as a cat over discarded newspapers and last-gasp chairs to check and recheck and record the results in a small lined note-book.

Rufus was both professional and authoritative. Every aspect of the structural work was examined. He discovered bonuses; concrete piles, would you believe, and it was gibbed throughout except for the bedrooms. Otherwise not a scrap of scrim in sight. He was under the house for piles, up on the roof searching for leaks. Negative. He checked sash cords, knocked on walls. There was no insulation, he reported, but that was to be expected. Nothing wrong with the water pressure, the toilet was sound, the stove worked and the drains were as sweet as a nut.

Rosa wandered from room to room. It was a small house, two bedrooms, one recept, usual offices.

As Mother would have said, it sat out well to the sun. It would need to. Without sun the place would be insufferable. Rosa could see signs, glimmers of potential like those glimpsed in the faces of heroines in old movies before the hero takes off their glasses. The rooms were well proportioned, the ceilings high. Its bones were good, a help at any time but especially in decline.

She began to see Bianca and Rufus's point; enthusiasm, vision, is always infectious after the first shock.

She could see the three of them, Bianca, Rufus and herself, setting out each morning, hi-hoing their way off to their day's work. The clearing, the sorting and, above all, the discarding. Rosa enjoyed her visits to the tip, the dump, the landfill. She found them cathartic. Even the scrubbing, the refurbishing could be fun. Rufus would do the painting. Bianca would boss them rigid, Rosalind would bring the food. It would work out splendidly. She went to find Henry, who had disappeared. I have good vibes about this place, she would say.

But why had he changed his mind?

Henry was stumping about the tangled overgrowth of the ex garden, avoiding his wife. He had no wish to confide in her at the moment, or ever, but he would have to eventually. Reaction had set in. Why in God's name had he suggested this visit? He would have to consult Charlie Adamson about his finances. Everyone was so damn old. He needed, he thought with a stab of something like mirth, an entrepreneurial young man like Rufus. A spin doctor to transform a bad situation into good, to change his mindset. Which he could do himself, of course he could. Here he was, a man of plans, vision, an intelligent speculator, no, not speculator, a developer; a snapper-upper, a keen-eyed businessman.

He had assets, he had enough money, or could find it somehow. He saw his father, wealthier than he would ever be, his rampant moustache, his sad smile. 'I'm a terrible businessman, terrible.' A man with a talent for self-deception.

Henry turned to stride through knee-length grass. Positive, that was the thing to be. Positive. Rosa would not be impoverished, Bianca would be assisted and Rufus would be given a fresh start. And all because of his, Henry's, enterprise and initiative, his facing up to the situation, his turning bad news to good. He had put the right spin on Bianca's perfidy. He was doing something constructive. He would discuss things with his wife, he would explain everything. All would be well.

He tripped, tossed a dead bike wheel onto a mound nearby and trekked on to find the rest of the team.

Rufus was now on to rates, water rates, garbage collection, the proximity of schools. Max gave him his answers and told them other things. He told them the property was a patent to tranquillity. A handyman's special, like the ad said. Thirsty for a coat of paint inside and out, but think of the potential. He told them about location, location, location and to look at the lovely flow inside and out which was ideal for both formal or informal living. The place had one of the most conducive environments Max had seen in a long time.

'And what is the asking price?' asked Henry.

Max told him.

'Whaat!'

It was the location, Max explained. Location, location, location. He personally thought the vendors were perhaps a teeny bit unrealistic, still, early days, open to negotiation.

Henry opened his mouth.

'We'll let you know,' said Rufus quickly. 'Never hurts to make an offer, does it?'

'No.' Max laughed once more. 'Not if it's one we can pick up and run with.' And no, he didn't think the vendors would object to them having a picnic out the back.

Rosalind threw the bike wheel to one side and sat on the mound in her working shorts. Many of Rosa's belongings were categorised. She had walking shoes and sitting shoes, reading glasses and seeing glasses and an old pair for ironing.

She looked around at the collapsed tumble of the yellow

banksia rose plus clothesline. Buddleia had seeded itself. In summer, its lilac pendants would hum with bees. Rosa's eyes were bright beneath her pudding-basin haircut (Bianca), her change of heart evident. She took a large bite of ham and egg. 'Anything could happen here,' she said. 'Real *Secret Garden* stuff.'

'Oh, Ros,' said Bianca, 'you're so hopelessly romantic.'

Rosalind took another bite. 'Have you ever actually known anyone called Dickon?'

Silence.

'Even in books I've only known two. *The Secret Garden* and that Ngaio Marsh boiling-mud one. Such a good idea, the murderer changes the marker posts, remember? I always wondered whether she got it from *The Hound of the Baskervilles*, changing the markers, I mean. It's odd, isn't it, in the old ones, you don't mind how they die. Drowned in boiling mud! Imagine. And what was Dorothy Sayers' bell one?'

'*The Nine Tailors*,' yawned Henry.

'Yes. Imagine being belled to death.' She looked around, loving them all, glad of plans, projects, people.

Henry leaned uncomfortably against a small lacebark.

Bianca was right. Rosa was a romantic. She had committed herself like a fool, had given her heart to the world, had made herself vulnerable to its pain and delights. Her attempts to give warmth to life impressed him, her determination to maintain affection in the endless muddle of the day by day left him speechless. He was grateful to Rosalind.

Bianca and Rufus sat side by side on a tarpaulin, their backs against a dilapidated crib wall, waves of empathy flowing between them. Rufus rolled a cigarette and offered it. 'Give it a go, Bee. You won't know till you try.'

Bianca took it smiling. She was happier than she had been for months, although it was a tiny bit disappointing that her slice of ham and egg pie had had no yolk. She liked yolk.

'It depends on the price, of course,' said Henry.

They left the wilderness to silence and the drone of two insistent bumble bees and drove home. Nobody spoke, there was no need to. The visit had been satisfactory, extremely so for some, and there was much to think about.

Trim houses flashed by, well-mown lawns were remown, a small child fell off a bicycle with trainer wheels and was brave. Meadowbank was at leisure on this warm Sunday afternoon, although nobody was to be seen demonstrating either rest or recreation. There were no bodies lying or even sitting outdoors. Leisure for Meadowbankers happened when they went somewhere else. When they arrived at a place labelled *Leisure* and knew they were there. A place where there was no grass to be shaved or cars to be cleaned and the shopping was out of this world.

Rosalind waved to Mr Desai on the corner, who lifted a small bunch of chrysanthemums in reply. He was handing over to his son, he had told her recently. Fifty years and not even Christmas Day off and now the supermarkets. There was no room left for the small man.

Rosa glimpsed the legs between Bianca and Henry's back views. Their owner stood on the top step beside the largest pack in the world.

'Gaby,' roared Rufus.

Rosa's arms opened in greeting but the young woman had been enfolded, engulfed, her legs were now glued against Rufus's, her face hidden by his embracing arms. Gaby stood tiptoe in Australian snakeboots; yards of black leggings were topped by a flared mini surmounted by a width of heavy beige lace. Over her black T-shirt she wore a brocade waistcoat in faded crimson and ivory stripes with rosebuds like the ottoman

86

in Mother's bedroom. She slid a leg between Rufus's, raised her virtually shaved yellow-orange head to gasp for air and returned for more. She changed tack, was now sampling her man, making tentative little extensions of lips and tongue, coming at him from the side, above, below, like a male spider aware of the life-threatening aspects of courtship.

Rosa, Bianca and Henry stood staring; there seemed little point in doing anything else. This was a demonstration of affection.

Their reactions were different.

Rosa's hands were clasped in excitement, her mind already skidding through the contents of the deep freeze. Bianca's mouth was tight. This was not what she had in mind. Gaby's arrival was too sudden, too precipitate, *too like the lightning, which doth cease to be ere one can say it lightens.* And, what's more, Gaby would stay. And stay and stay. And she and Rufus had plans afoot, work to do together, like-minded comrades active in the cause. Damn. And blast.

Henry tugged his lip. Gaby was probably no worse than many of her predecessors in Rufus's affections, which had been wide-ranging and sometimes unusual and, furthermore, she had saved his son's life. But her timing was bad. Astonishingly bad, bad beyond bad peculiar. Bugger. Henry had planned to sit the team around the table and detail the conditions governing his suggestion. Special conditions would apply. Were Bianca and Rufus misguided enough to think otherwise? The question must be addressed without delay.

Gaby's bird-boned hand now lay in Henry's, her gaze from eyes the colour of peat tarns was unblinking, her hair yellow ochre stubble. She was astonishingly thin.

Rosa, wondering whether to welcome her with a kiss, decided against it. The narrow face seemed all red spectacle frames and angles and she was used to women who smiled.

'I hope you haven't been waiting long?'

'No sweat.'

And nor it was. If it had been, Gaby would have said so. Henry would bet money on that. Relax, Rosa, relax. We're dealing with nature here, untrammelled nature, forces of.

'I believe you saved Rufus's life,' he said loudly.

Gaby gave a wide grin, even the red frames brightened. 'Which time?'

'You remember, hon,' said Rufus quickly, 'getting me down from Poon Hill. Carrying the packs, all that?'

She shook her head, shared the joke with Henry. 'He colours the picture.'

Henry smiled back. He was not offended, anything but. He was pleased by this unexpected-looking young woman from Matamata where butterfat content is all, who had demonstrated within five minutes both passion for Rufus and acceptance of his endearing attributes. Henry had found a fellow researcher, a colleague. He felt like the animal behaviourist who put his eye to the keyhole and met that of the gorilla researching back. He had an ally in his field, a clear-sighted pragmatist, one who would be trusted not to massage the results.

'Yeah,' said Gaby now smiling proudly at Rufus, 'lies like a rug, don't you?'

Rufus demonstrated slicing his throat or hers.

Bianca smiled thinly.

Rosa was busy with the front door. 'Come in,' she said, 'come in.'

'Tell us about the wedding,' said Henry. 'Who was the bride?'

Gaby heaved her vast pack onto one shoulder. 'Gran. But he's a nice old guy. They did the hokey-cokey after they'd had a few beers.'

The hokey-cokey. Gran must be his vintage. The details of the dance were hazy. You put y'left foot in, y'put y'left foot out—then what? Perhaps Gran would teach him again one day. That would be nice.

And there was no reason why family discussions should not take place in front of Gaby, even if she had not saved his son's life in quite such dramatic circumstances as he had understood. Had coloured the picture.

Obviously Gaby, as a life-saving helpmeet and partner, had an interest in any family discussions.

'*Special conditions apply*,' said Henry, his eyes flicking around the table as he shuffled his notes.

Rosa was watching Gaby. Gaby, she decided, was her own person. 'Ashtray?' she murmured, lighting a cigarette. Bianca gave a small dry cough. Gaby offered her a cigarette, which was accepted. They shared the ashtray produced by Rosa. Bianca told Gaby that it was a present from herself to Rosa and she was glad to see it again. That it came from Andalusia. Gaby said, Was that right, and asked Henry why was it again they were here?

Gaby knew the essentials but she wanted details. Rufus had explained the situation to her after a quick connection in his bedroom, marred only by Rosa's arrival with sheets. Gaby had seized a towel and leapt to the knocked door. Why fuss. You're offered unwanted sheets by a small smiling grey-haired woman. You take sheets. You make up two beds, you sleep in one. You go with the flow, no problem.

She sat cross-legged on patchwork after Rufus's explanations and examined a verruca on the sole of her foot. 'Sounds okay.'

'And an old guy's going to leave a lot of money to Mum.'
'How much?'
Rufus didn't know. But still.
'Oh sure. Still.'

*

Gaby fixed her unblinking eyes on Henry's as he answered her query.

'Yeah, Roof told me that. But there's nothing to understand is there? I mean as regards "conditions". You buy the cottage after I've given it the okay.'

Bianca, caught on the back draught of shock and smoke, coughed. Rufus patted, Rosa ran. Water was provided. 'Why should you be consulted, Gabrielle?'

'Gaby. Because I'm his partner. He'd never dream of taking on anything without my okay, would you hon?'

Rufus nodded. 'Never have and never would.'

'Besides,' said Gaby, 'I'm a gun painter.'

Bianca was thinking. Another pair of hands would be useful, very useful. There was something Rufus had mentioned called sugar soap, which was required to bring up the old wood. She hadn't liked the sound of it. It could burn. You had to be careful, even with gloves. And all those high stud walls, who was going to get up there. Gaby. What a name.

'You might have told me of Gaby's talents, Rufus,' she murmured.

'You might have told us of Gaby.'

'Oh, give it a rest, Dad. I didn't know when she'd show up. We had a bit of an up and downer,' said Rufus, kneading the black-covered thigh beside him. 'Didn't we?'

'Yeah,' said Gaby vaguely. 'And the place will be in Roof's name?'

All hell let loose. Bianca and Rufus were shouting. Gaby the unknown sat silent, her head tipped to one side in attention.

Henry sat smiling in his chair with arms. He covered his mouth with his palm and winked at Rosalind. *Winked*. Rage and muddle and bad behaviour and all Henry could do was wink.

'Stop brawling,' she cried. They stopped, their faces quick

90

with surprise, Bianca's mottled, Rufus's a dull crimson. He took one of Gaby's cigarettes and offered it to Bianca. She took the peace offering without a glance and laid it in front of her unlit.

The scent of lemon blossom wafted through open windows; a fragrance flowing, stealing their senses all away, like it said in the carol. Rosa was about to remind them when Henry became operational.

'The first thing is the price,' said Henry. 'I will negotiate the price, I will consult Charlie Adamson, and take that look off your face, Rufus, get his advice as to the property's potential. If and when the price becomes more realistic, and I mean exactly that, I'll make an offer. The place is a wreck, it will take more than work, it will take money, and incidentally, Rufus, I'll want details of your and Gaby's competence and experience in this field.'

They were holding hands now, smiling those closed-lip smiles that indicate both intimacy and exclusion.

All the world loves a lover but not Henry. Or Bianca. Rosalind smiled at them, or as near to them as she could get. They were lovely. Quaint but lovely, and so young. Well, not Rufus perhaps. Thirty-five isn't as young as all that but Gaby looked like a punk eighteen-year-old. Not that she could be but her, how would you say, her wayward gaucheness made her seem even younger. She was vital yet impassive, as interesting as someone from another race or planet.

'Sure,' they said together, 'sure.'

'The next thing. The title will of course be in my name.' Henry lifted a hand. 'That is unappealable.' He felt faintly drunk. The freedom of power, the power of freedom, the desire of dominance, the dominance of desire. So many choices and all tasting good.

Gaby was not pleased. 'Unappealable?'

'Not open to appeal.'

91

Anger, and more than anger, and smouldering disgust from Bianca.

'Secondly, when the house can be lived in, the two of you,' Henry dipped his head to Gaby who stared back, 'three, will live there. Rent free for the moment but when it's liveable there will be a minimum rent to pay off the mortgage.'

Bianca snapped upright in her seat.

'Three, huh,' said Gaby.

'Sure,' cried Rufus. Very generous of you, Dad. Very generous indeed. I, we, that'd be great, wouldn't it, Gaby?'

Gaby was staring thoughtfully at Bianca, who stared back. Cold peat met blue ice, neither faltered. Bianca lifted her unlit cigarette, lit it with Rufus's lighter and smiled at the younger woman. It was in now, that blank, sexless look, but it wouldn't last. And Rufus was devoted to his Aunt Bee.

Gaby lifted one shoulder and dropped it. 'Hard to know,' she said.

Bianca smiled.

'One final thing, Rufus, which concerns you only.'

Rufus turned to him, happy with plans and enthusiasm. 'Yes, Dad?' The little suitcase days surfaced, Henry's elation dissolved.

Who's kidding whom, you clown. You're not helping your son from disinterested affection. You've been blackmailed into it by that woman, that woman preening herself across the table. Bianca's presence was beginning to make him feel physically sick.

Cowardice in fellow crew members, he had read in some Battle of Britain memoir, had not been treated with the contempt reserved for braggarts. Unlike bull artists, cowards were felt to have some unfortunate deficiency for which they could only be pitied, such as colour blindness or poor vision.

Not a helpful memory. Why had he allowed himself to

slip into Bianca's trap like a rat to its drain? Rufus's sexual preferences, he was sure, did not stray from irredeemable heterosexuality. Mrs Felton would laugh at Bianca's disclosures about Andy and reach for her tomahawk.

Henry looked at his wife. Her attention had strayed. She would be thinking about five down or four across or wondering whether the labelless carton in the deep freeze was plums or boeuf bourguignon and if so would it do five.

He heard Bianca's murmur on the motorway, saw the calm hands, the crocodile tears. 'Poor Rosa.'

My sweet Rose, my dear Rose, be merry.

And she would. Henry would see to that. He must.

He thinks I don't know, but I do. I don't know what is going on because he hasn't told me, which I find odd. But I do know that something is, and furthermore I don't like it. The atmosphere in this house is troubled, muddy, up the wop and out of kilter. There is an air of tension in both the formal and informal living areas, the flow is disturbed. I don't like it.

Why is Henry so troubled? Why is Bianca as smug as a cream-ingested marmalade cat? I can see why Rufus is happy, bless his heart, and I am sure Gaby will grow on me. I smile at Gaby. Again.

Gaby removed her over-sized red plastic spectacles, blew on them, rubbed them clear and replaced them. They were very large and glasses are small now. But Gaby, as Rosalind already knows, is her own person. She likes big ones. You get big ones. Yeah.

Rosalind's brief glimpse of the unshielded tawny eyes was startling. Gaby's eyes are weak, unfocused. She cannot see well. There is a chink in her armour. Goodness me and fancy that.

'As I was saying,' said Henry. 'This condition concerns you alone, Rufus.'

'Yes, Dad, you said.'

'I have decided to offer you a position in Felton Fabric Importers.'

Rufus ducked his head, stared from beneath his brows like shy Di from childcare days, when it was all good, when the romance had lifted the hearts of millions.

'Bit sudden, isn't it?' he said. 'You know me, Dad, I'm not much of a nine-to-five man. And besides, how would I get on to fixing up Webster Street? There's a ton of work to be done there. You said so yourself. It'll take months.'

'Webster Street,' said Henry, 'is not in the bag. Webster Street depends on my being able to make suitable financial arrangements. Do you,' he snapped, 'want your mother to be flung out of this house into the . . . into the street,' he said, resisting 'gutter' at the last moment, 'because it has been mortgaged for you and your friends?'

'What do you think I am?' Rufus hugged Rosalind, smiled at Gaby. 'We are.' He leaned forward to place his cards on the table. 'But how will you finance it otherwise?'

'I'll go and see Charlie Adamson.'

'Good thinking,' said Rufus.

'This is not a sudden decision. I've been thinking about it for some time. It is now or never, Rufus. A keen young thruster at forty is no longer young or a thruster. There's room for one more now Martin's gone. I had hoped to get by, it's a fine balance. And if I do give you a chance, take you on, train you, it's on this condition only: that the importing of textiles is your profession—other activities, if you insist on pursuing any, will be expendable as side salads. Is that quite clear?'

Gaby was all eyes. All eyes and bones and frames. She grabbed her lover's arm. 'Hey, Roof . . .'

Rufus ignored her. 'Well, Dad, my plans, our plans I should say, are a bit fluid at the moment.' He paused, thought, paused

94

again. 'But I'd like to find out how things operate. Very much. Very much indeed.'

'And one other thing. It will involve you coming on a buying trip with me to Milan. Quite soon. Milan's the nub of things for us. We've been there far longer than anyone else here, got the contacts . . .'

Rosalind was staring at him. Why on earth hadn't he told her? We should have discussed it, talked things through. What is he *doing*, this man?

'Thanks to Martin,' she snapped.

Henry glanced at her in surprise, flung her a crumb and returned to Rufus. 'To Martin, as you say, but not entirely. It's essential that you come with me to get a glimpse of the way things work, meet the people, shake the hand. These things are important in Italy.'

'As they are anywhere,' murmured Bianca, 'Justin used to say . . .'

With vicious stabs Gaby ground her cigarette butt onto glazed blue pomegranates. She had no wish to return to Milan, not at the moment. Rufus could get her boots. But to be left with this lot . . . She chewed her lip, thought hard. Milan? Meadowbank? Meadowbank? Milan?

'I'll stay and get cracking here,' she said.

Henry, hiding his amazement, agreed that would be a good idea. How had she thought, envisaged for a micro-second that she would do otherwise.

He turned with relief to Rufus.

Who was concentrating. Henry could hear his mind ticking. His hands were clasped tight in the same excited gesture which had greeted his first bottle of ink. He had walked up Queen Street to the car park, clutching his treasure in its little saw-edged paper bag, his face wearing the beatific smile of an acolyte with a chalice. That is one of the things about an only child, there is no confusion of childhood memories. There is only one fount. He smiled at his son.

'It will mean you starting on Monday week. Depending, of course, on what Charlie Adamson thinks. And if my offer is accepted.'

'And what is your offer?' asked Rufus.

Henry told them.

'You're joking.'

Bianca was not concerned. She knew the cottage would be purchased. There might be a bit of confusion until she had sorted out the title, but never mind. Never mind at all. Speed bonnie boat. All will be well and all manner of things will be well. Except . . . 'But you said, Henry, that Rufus would help do it up.'

'And so he will. In the weekends.'

'The *weekends*.'

'And statutory holidays. Also, there is an enormous amount of culling out required. You and Gaby can do that before the real work begins.'

Gaby and Bianca eyed each other. Gaby lit another cigarette, dragged deeply, exhaled smoke with the assistance of her protruding bottom lip.

'And me,' said Rosalind. 'I like taking stuff to the dump.'

Bianca's eyes caught Henry's. He looked away.

Charlie Adamson thought it was an excellent idea. A snip at that price but would they get it? They did. Rufus and Bianca were euphoric. They shared a love of both bargains and projects. They had vision. The cottage and the job offer had come at a good time. Rufus was aware of the need to consolidate his commercial expertise. As he told Gaby while they explored each other in his bedroom beneath the unseeing gaze of Auckland Grammar School classmates, a stint in a well-established business never did anyone's CV any harm. Especially when the firm belonged to his father.

He was glad he'd had the sense to inscribe the names on the back of the seventh-form photo. You never know your luck with school contacts.

Gaby remained thoughtful.

six

Rufus tried. 'But that's what business class is all about, Dad. You arrive rested, full of attack and ready to roll.'

They travelled as Henry had always travelled, strapped in knee-jerking economy, his shoulder propping the heads of strangers, his stomach belching in another's dreams. Occasionally father and son lifted a glass to each other as they discussed their plans, ran through their programmes. It was a productive flight. Henry enjoyed his son's company, marvelled at his instant rapport, his interest in each and every fellow traveller he was lucky enough to meet.

The American overlaying him on the other side confided that he had a weight problem. Rufus commiserated, his bright head nodding in sympathy. The man rubbed large pale hands on tightly encased thighs and moved on to jet lag. Did Rufus suffer from jet lag? No? Had he any idea how lucky he was to be spared? Jet lag had made serious inroads on the man's stability, had jeopardised his career expectations. The only thing was vitamins. Vitamins helped. He offered vitamins. Rufus took two rust-coloured tablets.

The man looked at him thoughtfully. 'Only thing, they make you randy as a goat, a goddamn hairy goat.'

Rufus's concern did not falter. He was a good listener.

Henry, who had been wondering why a hairy one, weren't they all, had forgotten that. You don't meet many good listeners, not people who take a genuine interest in another's problems rather than just sign off and wait for them to stop bleating.

Rufus had learned quickly in his four weeks at the firm, had been happy to start at the bottom, to understand every aspect; it was the only way to suss the whole thing out, in his opinion. He knew the names of the staff members in a day, which was not the achievement it would have been in his grandfather's time. He had been pleasant to Lorraine, had commiserated with her over her outdated software and been rewarded by smiles. He had liked the two men. Good guys. Didn't Dad think a few bonding sessions, the whole team nutting things out together would be a good thing? No, said Henry. The whole team comprised five people; Gary and Tim knew the job backwards, as did Lorraine.

But why had the staff shrunk like this? Rufus remembered when he was a kid. There had been double this number, the typists had given him sweets. Tessa.

Henry explained carefully. Things had changed in the textile business and would change further. Many textile manufacturers now have their own agents in Italy and have begun to have them here. Technology, global technology, entrepreneurial skills—all that is your field. Why I have offered you the job. The small man, said Henry, is struggling. Ask Mr Desai.

Then we change with them. Give people what they want. Cheaper range.

I sell quality merchandise.

They left it there for the moment. Henry reminded himself that he would not change, that the firm needed to, and that Rufus, as well as being quick on his feet and having his finger on the pulse, showed both aptitude and enthusiasm for the work. He was lucky to have him.

He wondered why he had not insisted on this career move for his son long ago, but knew the answer. Twenty years ago parental interference in one's children's choice of career had died, had crawled away to the Valley of the Bones to lie beside arranged marriages and pork pie hats and centre partings.

Your offspring's lives are their own, their choice must be untrammelled, they must lead their own lives. All sentiments with which Henry agreed wholeheartedly.

But nothing is simple. A neighbour had found his fourteen-year-old daughter climbing back into her bedroom from a school dance in the '60s. She confessed with shame that she hated it, all of it, all, had wanted to come home from the first minute but didn't want to admit failure. Oh Mum, oh Dad. Do I have to?

Or take born-again Christians. God will lead his children to the way, the lifestyles, the careers. But what if God doesn't. Lets his guidance slip, wants his children to be happy like any other loving parent. What if he withdraws into his all-embracing wisdom and lets them get on with it. Offers them freedom to make their own mistakes and go to hell in their individual handcarts. Decisions, decisions, decisions.

Henry was grateful for his second chance. Such thoughts, such self-engendered convolutions of the mind had, he felt sure, never occurred to his own father, that foolish, autocratic old man. Mr Felton had founded the firm, been successful and handed it on to Henry. That was what fathers did and elder sons accepted. There had been no discussion, no demur. Mr Felton would have been happy 'to make room for Andy', if it had been necessary, but was relieved when his younger son showed no interest. He was brilliant, Andy, undoubtedly brilliant, but was he perhaps too *sudden*, too, how could he put it, too mercurial for the day-to-day work of running a business; for the buying and the selling, the cut and thrust with textile manufacturers whose forebears' spinners and weavers had operated in Italy for five hundred years. In an uncharacteristic burst of metaphor Mr Felton had enlarged upon this to Henry. Andrew was excellent quality, first rate, but not made for hard wear; shimmering luminous stuff made for high days and holidays, not the plain slog of every day.

Henry, he told him, was also good quality, top grade. He would wear forever. An honest worsted, a bird's-eye perhaps. Henry need not fear. He too had style.

'Thank you,' said Henry.

It was impossible to tell how much the old man's attitude to life had to do with his younger son's death, but had he known the truth he would undoubtedly have been as appalled as Bianca. No cross-weave, no grey tones, had ever blurred the black and white patterns of his father's thinking. He was right, always and in every detail, and insisted on being recognised as being so.

'It was Wednesday not Thursday,' he shouted, apropos of something completely unmemorable—the day of the last bus strike, the loss of the cufflink, that extraordinary leader in the *Herald*.

'Thursday,' said Andy happily munching corned beef.

'I said Wednesday!'

'Yes, and I said Thursday.'

'Wednesday!'

'Okay,' said Andy cheerfully. 'Make it Wednesday.'

'But you don't believe me,' cried his father.

'No.'

'But I'm right.'

'Okay. You're right.'

'But . . .'

Andy forgave him. He reached across, patted the wrinkled skin of the hand beside him. 'You're not alone, Dad. Thousands of people would rather be right than happy.

Wednesday it is.'

Andy was quick and ruthless in his placement but knew when to stop.

Would he have killed himself if his father had been less terrified of difference and appalled by change?

Mr Felton had died soon after his favourite son, broken-hearted by his unnecessary death, which he hugged to his heart as one more piece of incontrovertible evidence that the world was going to the dogs. Brilliant young men had not slipped and drowned while fishing in his day.

His very stupidity was heartbreaking.

His wife had been glad to move out of Meadowbank when he died. She had kept her own counsel and continued to do so at Pukekohe. She was a strong woman, Mrs Felton.

It occurred to Henry that Rufus's career move, this promising surge of intelligent interest and enthusiasm for the world of fine fabrics, was directly attributable to Bianca's devious manipulations. He dismissed the thought, glanced with affection at his son chewing aphrodisiac vitamins beside him.

The man with the weight problem leaned across Rufus, his large pallid hand offering Henry succour from jet lag. Henry declined. He did not wish to feel amorous in Milan.

He sighed and fastened his seatbelt. He would ring Rosa tonight. Rosa, he would say, be happy, Rosa. Rufus is a fine young man but we have always known that, have we not. His eyes, for some unknown reason, filled with tears; not tears, just excess. Rosa had never been to Milan.

'I'd much rather take you when I retire,' he had explained. 'Then we can have fun together and I'll show you everything and you'll have one of those books labelled *My Trip* and we'll have thousands of photographs and bore people rigid.'

*

'Where are you going?' said Henry. 'The bus is this way.'

Rufus put his hand luggage down and shook his curls. '*Cherubino*,' giggled a young woman with *Imagination on Tour* plastered across her front. Where had it gone, Henry wondered, this instrument of creation which had left home.

Flushed, distracted by bosoms, irritated by the petty meannesses of age, Rufus had had enough.

'For God's sake, Dad, let's get a taxi. I'll pay.'

'Good,' said Henry and whose money was it anyway and yes, why not.

It was Sunday, he had forgotten that. *Domenica* would be in red on the calendars. In summer, families would be at leisure in the open spaces they passed. Spaces which then would look like flowering paddocks. Or meadows; paddocks don't flower. Italians seem able to accept the fact that grass grows and is green and does not have to be eaten or shaved to extinction; that daisies and buttercups may flower and children may roll and picnics may happen beside crumbling stone.

But not today. The spring air was cold. Softball was in progress but few spectators huddled beneath the gnarled stumps of the plane trees, one or two of which had begun to shoot. Perhaps resurrection, life itself, would make more sense in a land of deciduous trees.

In a drear-nighted December,
Too happy, happy tree,
Thy branches ne'er remember
Their green felicity.

Anthropomorphic rubbish and maudlin to boot.

Henry watched the dark cypresses swaying. In Meadowbank a neighbour amputated their heads with a chainsaw. He liked them neat.

Twice a year, autumn and spring, autumn and spring forever, he had travelled this straight road, had noted the window detail, the pediments, the small balconies which seemed designed for papal blessings, the ancient buildings which fade from terracotta to rose as the sun goes down.

He liked it here, love and the past returned each time he came, came with the first spring catkins against stone, the first stench of diesel, the white magnolia buds clinging to bare branches like small sleeping cockatoos. He liked old buildings and the fragrance of orange trees.

Hotel Garibaldi was a small old-fashioned hotel with a tiny hesitant lift, a place of dark wood and small lobbies on each floor furnished with a solitary chair and nothing more. All the rooms, or any Henry had met, were small. Every one had a large, dark wardrobe, an even larger window with a venetian blind and little else. At some stage during the last ten years formica-topped refrigerators had appeared in each room, and the full restaurant service had departed. Breakfast only was served in a room beside the magnolia tree. But the hotel was clean, there were business facilities available and it was situated in the heart of the fashion centre, the golden triangle of designer fashion; shops, boutiques and designer offices lay on every side. Location, location, location.

And the staff were pleasant. There is something endearing about a symbiotic relationship between hotelier and guest which is renewed twice a year for years with the same manly embrace beneath the vast ziggurat light-fitting in the low-ceilinged lobby. And Signor Battista spoke English.

And had known Carla. Had understood.

Henry introduced Rufus. Signor Battista was delighted.

'You are a lucky man,' he told Henry and pumped his hand once more. 'Congratulations.'

'Excuse me,' said Rufus, 'I'll just go and have another look at the lions.'

'Ah,' said Signor Battista, 'they all love the lions.'

*

104

I can't think why I did that. I'm thirty-five for Christ's sake, but I still want to have a good look. To see them immediately once we've got shot of the luggage and Dad'll be under-tipping some poor guy and I'd rather be out of it anyway.

It's raining now. And cold. The stone walls of the hotel are slick as silk. The two stone lions, or rather heads of lions, stand shoulder high on either side of the entrance door which swings and hisses as people come and go shaking umbrellas.

The lions stare back at me, their foreheads furrowed above retracted snarling jaws and stone fangs. Their manes are full, deeply carved and flattened at the back.

I can see why men like Heseltine are described as leonine. Tough, really. These are humanised lions, haughty old men lions, lions usurped but defiant. They remind me of Dad. Two Dads. The same hair, the same lift of the head so that, if you're not careful, you're looking up damp nostrils. The same hauteur.

Not that I've thought of Dad as up himself before. I have thought of Dad as a guy who is around. A cool old guy. I've seen him wear a cravat and still look human. A man with style.

You'd know if you have it and I've never given a stuff, who does. But the Italians on the plane, the guys in the hotel, you notice their clothes.

We've had rows about it in the past. Not rows, it's difficult to have a row with Dad. Discussions maybe.

You've got it all wrong, Dad, I'd say. Then him looking at me, pretending he's exhausted, surprised. Whatever. Stirring me up with courtesy. Keeping his cool.

In what way, Rufus?

You get your suits made . . .

I'm a fabric importer.

. . . by a bespoke tailor.

All tailors are bespoke. It means made to order.

At great expense.

Most works of art are expensive.

Why bother?

Because they look better. They feel better. If you had a well-cut suit, Rufus, your bum wouldn't stick out.

He's a specialist in the dirty crack, the sort that goes off in your head and you're meant to laugh.

I just can't see the point of paying for bespoke . . .

You don't have to spit. It's a perfectly normal word.

. . . suits, yet you keep driving an old heap and putting up with that crap in your office at home.

You're confusing money with style, with having an eye, with meaning to dress as you do. Gaby has it. Your Uncle Andy had it . . . It's something given. And it lasts.

'His didn't,' I remember saying.

I thought for a moment he was going to hit me. But as usual he just oiled out of it. 'No,' he said. 'It didn't.'

'When we buried Andy,' he said suddenly, 'I insisted he wore his pink leather tie and a yellow silk handkerchief in his pocket.'

I laughed. I couldn't help it. 'What did he look like?'

He looks at me, his eyes cold as marbles in frost. 'Different,' he says.

Henry sat beside his son stirring coffee. His jet lag seemed to be getting worse. No sleep last night, no sleep for a week last time when he arrived home. Age, he supposed, or lack of vitamins, but a bugger either way. He finished his coffee, thought of the randy fat man without sympathy. Did he have work to do, people to see, experts to meet on their own ground, snap decisions to make amid the bustle and roar of machinery. Not many manufacturers could afford the luxury of the offices in Milan they planned to visit today, discreet, well-hidden marble spaces within walking distance of the Garibaldi.

The designers' garments displayed in the small windows on the Via della Spiga were visible to all. Tourists crowded the narrow streets, staring at suede shirts with the sheen and colours of silk—coffee, ivory, coral. Two old women stood lost in awe before a window of brightly lit glass pillars. On the highest, enshrined, lit from below, above and all around, sat a single silver kid sandal with a five-inch heel. There was no price tag.

Skirts were still short but they could only hope for better things when they saw the new season's range at the factories. It was high time skirts came down. Ridiculous and bad for trade.

Henry stopped before an androgynous-looking white polystyrene model in the window. It wore a panama hat dipped low over vacant eyes above a bright pink jacket. A yellow silk handkerchief flopped from the breast pocket of the jacket.

He walked on in silence, his heart racing.

'Hey,' said Rufus.

'Yes,' he snapped. 'I saw it. Come on.'

Monte Napoleone was full of small, busy-fingered women calculating in yen. Never in their wildest dreams had they expected such prices. The skirt. How much was the skirt? Calculator buttons buzzed in astonishment. Giggling women demonstrated collapse on crowded pavements.

They liked the shoe shops best, as had Rufus and Gaby. They had looked last time, she had tried on dozens of boots. But they were on their beam ends, not a show of buying. She had shoplifted a long-handled shoehorn by mistake, she discovered later. He had told his father about it. Not the shoehorn, why bother, but the hours they'd spent while she'd tried things on. How much he'd enjoyed it, just watching. How he must get her a pair, two pairs, they'd be half the price here.

'I wouldn't bet on it,' said Henry. 'Some of these characters' wares are so expensive they're not even imported at home.'

'How do you know?'

'I've been coming here a long time.'

Since before you were born.

An image flicked into his mind. Rufus aged about fifteen, red-faced and breathless on his bed, clutching a towel. 'Why the hell didn't you knock?' Henry closed the door. 'Sorry, it didn't occur to me.'

He sat on the end of the bed and glanced around, then smiled at his son. 'Your hair'll drop out,' he said.

He would never tell Rufus about Andy. It was pointless and besides, he was the one who wanted Andy to rot in peace did he not.

Let him lie. Any young death is tragic. *Whom the gods love die young* is a lie perpetuated by ancients.

Perhaps it was his vitamin-deficient jet lag or the emotional shreds of loss that brushed against him at unexpected moments in this city which had temporarily made him forget his love for it. There were too many memories, too many glimpses to remind. Things sneaked up on him, even now. The droop of a dark female head, a play of light, an unexpected reflection.

These small shocks did not occur at home, these disconcertings which made him think death might not be such a bad idea. That there was a lot to be said for a sleep and a forgetting. For being tucked up in a nice padded bespoke box and laid to eternal rest. Or not. Same difference, as Rufus would say.

He tried self-discipline. Not his strong suit. Carla has been dead for six years. You lost her ten years before. Stop this maudlin wallowing.

He smiled to himself, distracted by a sugar-plum fairy outfit in an adjacent window.

A grey-haired vendeuse reaching into the window for a pair of pink frosted-almond shoes smiled into his eyes, lifted the shoes in greeting and backed out. How do Italian women know that they are not only beautiful and desirable but will remain so? If they play their cards right, if they pay attention to their appearance and, preferably, marry rich men.

But it is more than that. They must have learned the habit of sensual pride at an early age. Like a love for your native landscape, it must be as familiar as the air you breathe for conviction to take hold, let alone stay with you forever. Some people, would you believe, find the Desert Road boring.

'The major problems in this business,' said Henry in the cab on the way out to Cernusco, 'are time and money. How much can you spare of each? There's never enough time, three days maximum . . .'

'It used to be longer than that when I was a kid.'

'Longer?' Henry's smile hung in the air. 'Well, things were more relaxed in those days.'

'I remember clearly. Eight sleeps at the beginning then count down every night till, boom—there you were.'

'So I was. With presents.'

'Yeah.'

The present buying had bored Carla. Bored her rigid. She had trailed behind him, chosen impossibly expensive gifts for his wife and child and laughed at his parsimony when he replaced them on their shelves. He told her not to come, he told her she was being ridiculous. She agreed and stalked off weeping. The pattern was repeated every time.

Every emotionally loaded gift was received with pleasure in Meadowbank and sat around for years, disturbing his peace of mind. As it should, should it not? As it did; Italian fire engines, handguns, bears. Why had he *let* her come? Why had he not sneaked out, snatched, grabbed, hidden the evidence? Thought of a better way. Stop thinking, man, stop thinking.

'You're sure you can cope on your own at Prato tomorrow?' he said.

'Of course.'

'I could come, there are things here to tidy up but, as I say . . .'

'Dad, for Christ's sake . . .'

'The first problem then. Money. How much can you afford to spend? Now this sounds easy at this remove. We've got it all worked out for Prato, as we have for Como today. You've got all the details, how much viscose, how much lycra, how much money we can spare. But it's not so easy on the spot. You'll see today.' He paused. 'You realise they've been making fabrics at Prato for five hundred years.'

'You said.'

'*The Merchant of Prato.*'

'I know.'

'Have you read it yet?'

'Dad,' sighed Rufus, 'I'm not fussed about some old guy's business five hundred years ago.'

Suddenly, unexpectedly, he remembered the lions' heads. They looked tired. Arrogant but tired, hanging on in there against the odds. His father was going to have to be informed, dragged into the real world. 'The future of the fabric industry,' said Rufus, 'lies in man-made fibres.'

Henry glanced up in surprise, not so much at the words but at the pomposity of his tone. Rufus was making a statement, issuing an edict. His grandmother was to suck eggs and would be shown how. Amusement kept Henry calm. The pontiff's bull had gone off at half cock.

'They have their place, certainly,' he said, 'and in this, as in every other fabric, except possibly the fine woollens of France, Italy leads the world. It's just a fact of life. Their

110

designs, their textures, colours, fashion sense, the way the fabrics fall, their feel. I have never known an Italian manufacturer or designer without this feel, this literal and physical feel for quality, man-made or otherwise. Their viscose acetates, for example, are top of the range, and expensive.'

'Big money,' said Rufus.

'I thought you liked big money.' Henry was angry now. Bored by his beautiful switched-on son who was exactly what Felton Fabrics needed did it not.

He changed the subject. 'And remember, they're not so concerned about their image in Prato as they are up here. Tuscans are different. Don't go down tomorrow expecting to see the grandeur of the places we'll see today. These Como families have been the most famous silkmakers in the world since the eighteenth century. Made the best quality linens. They're not interested in man-made fabrics. These are proud men. Serious silk. Serious linen. Serious men.'

Rufus said nothing. Thank God he was going to Prato alone. He couldn't see the point of coming to Como at all. Prato had more reasonable linens, cheaper wools and an infinitely better man-made range. Okay, it had been producing fabrics, leading the world for five hundred years, but it was still funky, upfront, fun. Someone in Prato, he had heard, was into designer PVC. He had seen a woman in the street yesterday in a white PVC jumpsuit with a silver plastic handbag formal and unyielding as the Queen's. Drop dead glamour. Tomorrow today. Italian silks, in Rufus's opinion, were a dead duck.

China, Japan, the whole of Asia was where that market lay. He glanced at the old Europhile beside him with something like compassion. Henry had never quite got it together somehow. Had always been behind the eight ball. He couldn't wait to get Gaby into the firm. They would take off like a rocket, two rockets.

The back of her neck came to mind, the perfection of her sculptured ear, her narrow wrist. He closed his eyes. Gaby.

The reception area of Casa Monti was both grand and under-stated. Grey marble floors, green marble pillars, good lighting and one serene woman seated behind what looked like a slab of onyx. The only piece of technical equipment in sight was a reproduction antique brass telephone alongside a large round bowl containing two goldfish.

A mistake, thought Rufus. Over the top. Blown it. One or the other but not both.

The fronds of a huge palm tree almost brushed the woman's shining blue-black hair. She did not duck. She knew, perhaps, that tension is created by small gaps.

She smiled at them, glanced at Rufus and smiled again. He was becoming used to both the look and the smile. A smile and a look, he assumed, not unlike that which Gaby told him she received from her grandmother every time she went home to Matamata. A quick glancing sweep upwards. Friendly but enquiring, not quite sure. Pregnant or not? Slobbish or quaint? It was a look which made Rufus feel, not unsure of himself, no one can do that unless you let them, but an object of unwanted interest. He concentrated on the fish.

Which were behaving oddly. Very oddly indeed. One languid goldfish drifted, an ox-blood one flashed past at speed followed by another slow drifter through weed. Another flash, and an electric blue shot by. Rufus turned to the floor-to-ceiling windows on to the street in search of answers. Of course. The upside-down reflections of cars were reduced to fish size and encapsulated in the bowl. It seemed a pity the fish didn't know. He must tell Henry.

Henry was explaining that they had an appointment. The receptionist's smile agreed. How could they possibly have stumbled into this palace without one. She stroked the antique

112

telephone into action, spoke and nodded. Her gentle replacement of the receiver, her smile, indicated the smallest delay in the world.

'Signor Monti sends his apologies, gentlemen. He will be with you in seconds. He is with the button lady.'

In fact he was with them in minutes. Minutes in which Henry had time to explain that this was by no means and must not in any way be interpreted by Rufus as power games, delaying tactics or a put down. This was a compliment, an acknowledgement that Henry was of the *cognoscenti*. Henry would know the importance of the button lady, he would probably know her name (which he didn't), he would undoubtedly know the name of the firm she represented (which he discovered later he did). The best firm in Italy, the most esteemed makers of the best buttons in the world and God lurks in the detail, does he not. Signor Monti's designers were begging for answers. The final decision from the top could not wait a moment longer.

Signor Monti came through a heavy glass door. Tall, large, with a profile from a Roman coin, he came to greet his friend, to welcome his friend's son.

The welcome was genuine, completely genuine, and pretty to watch. Signor Monti and Henry embraced with enthusiasm, the sheer pleasure at meeting again engulfed the two old men.

The last time Rufus had seen anything approaching such warmth had been between two black men farewelling each other in Tottenham Court Road; their ritual leave-taking had been as stylised as the mating dance of some exotic bird. They shook hands and swung away, spun back on their heels to clasp each other's wrists, separated for a high five, gave one final prolonged and laughing shake of the hands and, with springing feet and heads held high, went on their way rejoicing.

'Come,' said Monti, 'come to my showroom.' The pride of the man made his jowls shine, his gestures widen. He had

113

something to be proud about; the age and history of the family company, its impeccable reputation, all pleased him. The grandeur of the building, the quality of the product spoke both for him and his deceased forebears. His pride, Henry knew, would not allow him to discuss his own son's views in front of Rufus. His son wanted change. Signor Monti knew the fabric industry was changing. There were newcomers even in Como. *Arrivistes* messing about in studios. Men and women described by his son with approbation as wacky. What is this wacky, he had asked Henry last time they met.

They had moved on to the changing dress habits of the wealthy young, their anything goes, their lack of respect for family traditions. Romeo did not want to go into the family business, could Signor Felton believe that. Signor Felton could and did. All that had surprised him had been Signor Monti's surprise.

He saw the old man looking sadly at Rufus. Rufus was at his best, attentive and serious and anxious to learn. It was a pity about his suit, but Rome, after all, was not built in a day. Henry was tempted to come clean, to relieve the old man's wistful envy with facts. My son, Signor Monti, wishes to diversify, which is his euphemism for lowering the quality of merchandise stocked by Felton Fabrics. I fear that, as far Rufus is concerned, for Como and, in particular, the top of the range fabrics manufactured by you, Mr Monti, it's Goodnight, nurse. Can you believe that, you good old man.

The showroom was an extension of the factory, a large space humming with noise and activity. The owner of the company was both its life blood and its soul. Employees dashed up to consult, waved bits of fabric in his face, were answered with voluble despatch; men and women stood back as they passed. Signor Monti's voice lifted, he called for *pezzo*, *pezze*, more, more, like a director shouting for light on an already well-lit stage. Workers moved to tug out rolls and more

114

rolls. Signor Monti touched, stroked, sighed with pleasure and begged Henry and Rufus to do the same.

He became more excited, his gestures more dramatic. He rubbed a brocade, stroked a silk velvet, held a patterned silk of green, bronze and apricot to his ear as though listening.

The decisions, the thinking on the feet began. The company had not entirely finished their sample collections, no one had yet, but the ones here were already available. For the rest— sample swatches, colour cards. Signor Monti would check with the studio in Via della Spiga before they left in case they had anything there other than these. 'You are at the Garibaldi?'

'Of course. Just around the corner,' said Henry. 'I remember your studio.'

'The fountain?'

'Yes, but more the spaces behind locked doors, the courtyards.'

Signor Monti smiled. 'You like Milan, my friend.' It came out as 'my fren'. More intense somehow, more comradely. He gave a quick tug at a bolt of black shiny material. 'New,' he said stroking. 'Completely new fabric, with viscose. Manufactured in Germany for us exclusive.'

Henry took the slippery stuff in his hands, let it flow. 'Nice. Very nice. Can you guarantee one hundred per cent stability?'

'Of course.'

'And the colour range?'

Signor Monti lifted a finger. A man placed the appropriate swatch in his hand. Henry flicked through. 'No yellow?'

'Our designers have dispensed with yellow this year.'

'And the colour stability?'

'A hundred per cent also.'

They moved on to prices. Delivery dates. These of course must also be guaranteed. Signor Monti hedged. To Rufus, who had been watching the man with interest from the moment they met, he seemed to deflate slightly. 'Of course, of course.

But sometimes. You know how it is. One colour may be cancelled, another very popular. Otherwise of course, a hundred per cent, completely one hundred per cent.'

Henry nodded his head in silence. The follow-up, he had warned Rufus, can go wrong in Italy. The Japanese are more reliable in this respect.

Rufus was impressed. Henry undoubtedly knew his stuff. The excitement, the drama, even God help us the challenge, was obviously good for him. Adrenalin was pumping, which was just as well. They had two more factories to visit before returning to Milan.

They lunched together in the factory restaurant. Signor Monti looked carefully through the menu and ordered something which was not on it. Omelette. No tomato.

He asked after Martin Brown.

'Bad,' said Henry. 'Very bad, unfortunately. Ah, *farinata di ceci.*'

'What's that?' asked Rufus.

'Chickpeas and watercress.'

Rufus had risotto. It was not bad. Not bad at all.

He caught the Intercity to Prato early next morning. He activated his ticket in its yellow box, the use of which had been sussed out by Gaby. She was the perfect travelling companion; enterprising, delighted by success and undeterred by failure, she could push the world over on a good day. And she was good-natured, extraordinarily good-natured, considering. Poon Hill, for example. Amazing.

Rufus leaned back, stared at the bright blue netting and polished wood of the luggage racks, and thought about her. In his private dreams and fantasies she was his girlfriend. His best friend who was a girl and proved it daily.

In public she was his partner.

He enjoyed first-class travel. Even the temporary illusion

of wealth which came with Eurail had pleased him, where journeys end in lovers fighting and heaving packs and quick exits are essential in the battle for cheap accommodation within walking distance. Gaby had designed a system. She shot out of the first-class carriage like a rocket as the train reached the station. He guarded the packs, shoved them out the window and they were away laughing. They saw fellow backpackers off time after time, but the illusion of privilege had gone.

But this was real first class. First class with a suit and a briefcase. First class with class.

The carriage was not full. Rufus watched an elderly man seated across the aisle. A man as complete and unruffled as a handsome game bird. Such a perfect example of the species that Rufus stared from behind the cover of his paper, his gaze intent as a watcher's from a hide. What did he mean by complete? He tried to work it out. Secure in his own skin for starters. Rufus knew instantly several things about the man; his range and habitat, for example. This man was solid, wealthy, professional, well established in his own area and breeding ground. Nothing fly-by-night or migratory about him.

This man was in control, his life ordered. He had risen from a good night's sleep beneath one of those white feather duvets which really do work in winter and in summer unlike the el cheapos of home.

Does he have a wife or mistress? Does he lie alone? It is irrelevant. He has performed his ablutions, has been brisk in bathroom and lavatory, not puddling about for hours like Dad. He has shaved with a blade razor and how could you know that. You couldn't, but the smooth bloom of his unlined cheek gave the impression of close attention. Rufus felt his own chin. The man was not an electric razor user, that was for sure.

Cologne? Aftershave? Too far away to tell. He wore a suit of Prince of Wales check with hand-stitched lapels. Italian or

English? Henry would know. Rufus was getting keener every day on this clothes business. He was beginning to understand Henry's pain when the backs of ill-cut jackets pleated about the ears of seated TV politicians as they smiled into the camera and declined responsibility for mistakes which were theirs alone. The mute button wiped their excuses, the back slits strained over their departing bums. Shoddy, muttered Henry. Shoddy.

Rufus stared harder.

The old guy opens his briefcase and takes out a black diary tipped with gold edges which he consults gravely. He has gravity, this man. I could learn from him. He consults his watch, gold but not kitsch. By squinting with my better eye I can see that the numerals are Arabic. There is no call for Arabic numerals, I am told. People are perfectly happy with Roman. Except for me and the old guy, and he has found them. He can find what he wants. He has authority and presence and he is rich. He is complete. He is all of a piece, has been for years and will continue to be.

I slip my watch into my top pocket and move over to sit opposite him. 'Excuse me, sir,' I say, 'but do you speak English?'

He looks at me, well shaved and not pleased.

The accent is very slight. 'Yes.'

'Would you be kind enough to tell me the time?'

His face moves slightly, not a smile but not exactly a rejection. 'About two minutes later than when you removed your own watch.'

I laugh. What would you do. It's a bit late for touché. The ball stays in the silent court.

'Why did you want to speak to me?' he asks eventually.

I should have thought this through. I have acted on impulse. Shit.

I smile, lean forward. 'I wondered what line of business you are in. Just curiosity, ha ha.'

'I am Swiss,' he says, as though that explained something other than clean camping grounds and well-made clocks.

'Ah,' I say.

'And you?'

'New Zealand.'

'How extraordinary,' he says. 'What is your name?'

'Rufus Felton.'

He looks at me, a look both solemn and embarrassing—as though it's my fault, as though he has asked me to say grace before meat.

'Felton,' he says and leans back on the smart little first-class antimacassar thing, as white and crisp and complete as he is. 'I knew a Felton from New Zealand. His first name was Henry.'

I am delighted and show it. 'He's my father.'

'Good God,' he says and stares at my face as though he had to memorise it, take a photo, something. His eyes shut for a second.

'And may I ask what your . . .' (Your what? Business? Line? This man is not a captain of industry. He has his own firm. He is complete.) '. . . business is,' I say. I hear myself spluttering and turn it to a cough.

'I, too, am in the fashion industry.' He produces a card, gives it to me without a smile. 'Marco Grisoni. Perhaps your father will remember me. However, it was a long time ago.'

His eyes stay closed for some time. At last they open and he looks at me as though I might know something important.

'How old are you?'

'Thirty-five.'

He looks odd. Very odd indeed. '*O dio*,' he says.

'Are you returning to Milan?'

'Why do you ask?'

119

'Well, ah . . . I'm sure Dad would like to see you again.'

I'm not sure at all. There are not many people Dad wants to see again. I want to see this man again. This man interests me. I envy him. He has something I would like to have. He is old and he is Swiss and he is obviously tired, but he has got it made and I want to find out how he did it. What's more, I'm going to.

But I don't.

'I think not. Now if you will excuse me, Signor Felton, I have work to do, as I'm sure you do.'

'Yes, of course.'

The test of a champion, I read somewhere, is how he reacts in defeat. Tyson, it was. He hasn't been knocked out yet so it's hard to judge the true calibre of the man.

I smile at Signor Grisoni, shake his scarcely extended hand and return to my seat and read up on Enrico Baronti, my main man in Prato. His father's family, I read, came from Lucca, sixty miles north of Prato. So what. I remember not to sulk. Gaby taught me. The trick is to recognise you're doing it then stop. She can't stand sulkers. There are quite a lot of people Gaby can't stand. I think about Gaby, the way she walks, runs, her thin, quick wrists and ankles. I move on, fantasise you could call it, see her legs round my neck, my hands busy. Gaby is a sexy lady with a mind like a steel trap. She is all for one and I'm the one. What a team.

Enrico Baronti is what matters now.

Henry sat beside a naked plane tree in the small damp square near the hotel.

A small boy and his mother walked past hand in hand. In the other arm the boy carried, with care, a newly pressed black cloak, a Batman mask hung round his neck. They reached an appointed rendezvous near the swings. Small boys proliferated, Batman slipped into his cape and mask, Mamma twitched the sateen folds, wiped a wet park bench and sat smiling as the chase began. Batman, pursued by the forces of evil, headed for the open country. His cloak spun in the wind, muddy water splashed at his heels. Mamma applauded. Batman won. No one else had a chance.

'Hi,' said Rufus, sitting beside his father. 'What on earth are you doing in this grotty place?'

'I like wet trees,' said Henry. He indicated a breathless and triumphant Batman waving his mask above prostrate combatants. 'I was thinking, would the drama of that seem as interesting at home? As endearing?'

Rufus examined the sole of his shoe. 'I don't know.'

'Tell me about Prato.'

Triumph, total triumph. Rufus told him in detail, opened his briefcase, ran through figures, showed lists, demonstrated swatches. He had indeed done well and Henry told him so.

'Signor Baronti sent his greetings, best wishes, whatever.'

'Thank you.'

A larger boy was attempting to disrobe a now weeping Batman. Mamma lowered her head and charged.

'Look,' said Henry.

'What? Oh yeah. And I met another man you used to know. An old guy called Grisoni.'

'There are lots of Grisonis.'

'Marco Grisoni. He said it was years ago. About thirty.'

'More than that.'

'So you do remember.'

'Vaguely.'

'Tell me about him.'

Henry's head was spinning. 'There's nothing to tell.'

He leaned forward, put his head between his knees and breathed deeply.

'You okay?' said Rufus.

His father opened his eyes to find Batman crouched flat-footed in the mud before him, his head skewed upwards to peer at Henry's face. Mamma now carried the cloak, but the mask remained. The dark curls hung heavy, the eyes behind the mask were concerned. He pushed it back onto his forehead, an infant welder taking a break.

'*Il signore sta male!*' he said.

Mamma, flustered and voluble, tried to drag him away. Batman gave one shriek of fury and stayed rooted. Henry coughed, Rufus beat his back. Mamma panicked, tucked her son under one arm like a loaf and ran, trailing black sateen in dead leaves and dog shit.

The sound receded, echoing. '*Sta male, sta male!*'

'You okay?' said Rufus again.

'Yes, just a touch of dizziness. I've had rather an unsatisfactory day.'

Rufus relocked his briefcase.

'Unsatisfactory?'

'Yes.'

seven

Henry bought spring flowers from a florist near the hotel. Those mobile stalls outside the cemetery gates, stacked with cones of bright paper enclosing roses or a few carnations, always depressed him further. He wanted lots. Carla had been a generous woman.

He had first met her at a fashion show in 1960, one of those extravaganzas involving skittery little gold chairs beside a catwalk where elegant women glide in clothes designed to demonstrate the cutting skills, the flair, the vision of the maestro. Women so sleek they could enhance any garment however bizarre. Women swinging this way, that, a hand on a hip, a smile, a smoulder, a look-me-over and buy my wares which are not mine to sell. I am a clothes horse. I know my role among the inflated egos, the hard-nosed businessmen and women of the Milan fashion world and it is okay by me, buster, I can afford to dip my head, to slip from wool and retie silk. I demonstrate the genius of others.

I am essential to the cause. I am available for hire. I am expensive.

A hand jogged his elbow, champagne spilled, the woman apologised in Italian. As always, the speed defeated him. He mopped, she mopped, he promised lack of concern, she called for reinforcements, gave a peremptory tap on the shoulder of the man beside her, demanded handkerchiefs. The man turned, lifted uncomprehending palms as she snatched the silk one from his pocket and continued, voluble in her distress, her apologies, her horror.

Henry recognised him. He and Marco Grisoni had met through the years. They had smiled, shaken hands and forgotten each other until the next time.

Grisoni was now attempting to introduce the mopper, a process hindered by her efforts to return the now sodden rag to his breast pocket. He backed instinctively, gave a small bark of disgust.

Her laughter died. She held the handkerchief between thumb and finger for a second, dropped it and looked at Henry for the first time. 'Italian Swiss, *Signore*, have no sense of the ridiculous.'

Grisoni's expression did not change. 'Carla, may I present Signor Felton, my sister-in-law, Signora Grisoni.'

Henry bowed his head, opened his mouth to speak, was interrupted.

'Am I still your sister-in-law now Roberto is dead?'

'Yes.' Grisoni turned to Henry, made a small gesture indicating something. Embarrassment? Apology? 'My brother died last year.'

'I'm sorry.'

'Yes, it was very sad.'

They moved away, The woman placed her stiletto heel on the abandoned handkerchief, gave a swift grind and turned to smile. '*Arrivederci, signore.*'

His hotel bedroom had been stifling that September. No air conditioning, no air to condition. He tried the window again. It was jammed tight as it had been yesterday and for generations. So why so did he try. Because people do.

He turned on the television and flopped onto the bed. Black and white images came from Rome, Italian voices filled the narrow room.

He should take off his shoes. Didn't. Christ, it was hot.

The commentators became more excited as men stripped off tracksuits and lined up to race. Henry snapped upright at the black singlet and shorts. He leaned forward, willed himself to understand the rapid-fire Italian. Final—eight hundred metres. He'd made it this far, then, that promising young man they'd been on about at home. An Olympic finalist. Good luck to him. He would need it. It would be blazing hot there, the temperature, the tension from thousands of screaming fans.

Henry pulled off his tie, leaned nearer to help his man who was hopelessly boxed in. On the last bend, when the two leaders, a black man and a white, moved into their final sprint, a gap opened on the inner lane and the New Zealander surged through. Past the black man, past the white, past the lot to storm on down the last thirty metres and lunge for the line.

Henry was on his feet shouting. What a race, what a triumph, what a race. He flopped back exhausted. Snell, that was the name. Snell.

He was still standing as the flags rose, flopped back onto the bed as the band played 'God Save the Queen' not 'God Defend New Zealand'. But still the flag was there, too like the Australians' but up there at the right moment, flying on top of the world.

He sat beaming back at the shy grin, nodded as the head bent to receive the gold, then lay back.

He woke to another all black kit in the five thousand metre finals, another win. By eight metres, eight bloody metres! The slight figure of Halberg collapsed on his back and lay motionless.

Two gold medals. Who could he *tell*. This is patriotism, this is national pride, outdated jingoism, glory. What a fool

Marx must have been to think it could be forgotten for his higher cause.

Breathes there a man, with soul so dead,
who never to himself hath said,
This is my own, my native land!

Certainly not. Not Henry. Not Snell, not Halberg.

Christ in concrete, what a place it was. He was now striding around the narrow space available, banging his knees on the bed end, grinning his head off. He wanted to rush into the Monte Napoleone, grab men by the tie, women by the waist. Three million people, and two gold medals within hours. Listen, you clowns. Listen.

Breathes there a man. Even a man who had never run in his adult life, except for a bus.

He would ring Andy. Sometimes you have to and damn the expense.

Then he would get outside and walk, walk for miles.

He sat watching the waitresses in the café. He had been coming here for years, since the day when his halting Italian had resulted in a glass of warm sweetened milk instead of *caffelatte*. A nasty surprise, corrected immediately with laughing good humour. The two waitresses, there had never been more than two, worked harder than any male equivalent he had known except the French, and seemed a good deal happier. Henry liked everything about the place: the ornate double curve of the mahogany bar, the steaming indoor warmth in March, the crowded pavement tables now. The three-tiered chrome fruit-stand of oranges crowned with triumphant bananas pleased him. The six-foot fan-shaped light fittings, made from green bakelite in the days when it was a man-made miracle, continued to impress. Lit from behind and shimmering with iridescent greens, they sailed resplendent above din and clamour and laughter and grief.

The coffee was excellent.

But it was the waitresses who drew him back. They changed, of course, over the years, but every replacement seemed as efficient and insouciant as her predecessor. They appeared to be imbued with the pleasure of serving others.

He was in danger of getting sentimental about Italy. Rosa would love it. He would bring Rosa and the baby as soon as possible. The waitresses would be ecstatic. He had watched them yesterday, cooing with excitement over an immensely plain bambino in a pushchair, a solemn child with an overly large head and constant dribble.

The senior waitress brought more coffee. Her clinging bib-topped black trousers reminded him of a male gymnast's. They brought images of parallel bars, suspended rings and strength upside down. He saw himself sitting with Rosa, round as a ball on the sofa beside him as they had listened to the Olympic gymnastics the night before he left.

'To think there's people like him and people like me and we're both people. Don't you find that amazing?'

'He's not pregnant.'

She patted his arm. 'True.'

The waitress wore no bra beneath her long-sleeved T-shirt. Her breasts moved as she placed his coffee. These were not the chaste busts of virgin girls, these rounded shapes had made welcome, had given pleasure and probably sustenance. They were beautiful. Henry stirred in his seat. The strong brown face smiled into his. This was not flirting, or not the tentative backings and advancings of his salad days. This was lust for life, sheer joie de vivre. He swallowed and shifted again.

'Beautiful, aren't they?' said the woman at the table beside his.

His mouth dropped.

She nodded at the iridescent greens, the changing light of the plastic art deco fans above them.

127

'They are what bring me back.' She smiled. 'Don't look so surprised. We have met before.'

'We have?'

'I behaved badly and was dressed for it. Rossini's show. Carla Grisoni.'

'Of course.' She certainly looked different. Her black hair was no longer smoothed about her head. It hung loose and thick and heavy around a face strong-featured as that of the bosomed waitress, but less welcoming. Gold rings of various shapes circled each finger of her left hand and two on the right. She touched her chest. 'Today I am dressed casually.'

Well, yes.

She wore creased white trousers, a magenta top, white shoes and pink flowered socks. Her complexion was dark, her maroon lipstick appeared to be outlined with brown.

He told her about his countrymen's triumphs.

She turned a hand palm upwards on the table. '*Bravissimi*,' she said.

He changed the subject. Did she live near here?

No, she was on her way to the Brera. She was interested in art. But in Italy art has a capital A. She was not interested in capitals. Her English was fluent and idiomatic, she was quick-witted and made him laugh. There was something vaguely subversive about her. Contradictory. Her ridiculous flowered socks and shapeless trousers did not match carefully shadowed eyes and crafted lips.

The shape of her thighs against the jersey was distinctly haunch-like, he noticed as they rose to leave. She was not overly thin.

She turned to him on the pavement and gave him her hand. '*Arrivederci, signore.*' She paused. 'On second thoughts, would you like to accompany me to the Brera? I want to check up on the Saint Sebastians.'

'In what way?'

'The number of arrows. I keep a list.'

Her mind operated in an unusual way. She was an unusual woman.

They walked quickly through hot crowded streets. The temperature, according to a street clock, was 30°C. She refused a taxi. 'I walk everywhere.'

'That's unusual, isn't it? For an Italian woman. In this heat?'

'I am French, French, French. I was foolish enough to marry young. A Swiss.' The words withered in the stale air. 'Italian Swiss. The worst sort.'

You have to say something. Henry tried compassion. 'And he died?'

'Last year. And his brother blames me. Your friend Marco Grisoni.'

'I knew he was suspect,' he said.

She turned to him and laughed loudly, a laugh so unexpected, so all encompassing that he laughed back. They stood united by mirth and friendliness, laughing at what? Censure? Smugness? Heartbreak? He felt an unexpected tightening, a kick of desire.

'Quick,' she said, 'let's get inside. At least it will be cooler inside. Their precious Art works.' She nodded at barricades and shutters and rubble nearby, at large signs saying *In restauro*. 'The whole of Italy is *in restauro*. It never stops.'

'You buy the tickets,' she said as they entered. 'You must improve your Italian.'

'Where are you come from, *Signore*?' asked the guard.

'New Zealand.'

A clutch of small boys being marshalled and shuffled into Art by a distracted nun stopped in their tracks. 'New Zeeland.' They demonstrated rucks, tackles, a mini scrum. Yelled wow, gee, hang, in Italian, and punched the air. 'All Blacks,' they shouted. Henry was tempted to tell them his good news. Snell,

129

he would demonstrate to their blank upturned faces, Halberg. Vroom, vroom. But the nun had regained control and they disappeared.

'Do you like children?' she asked.

'I hope so. My wife is pregnant.'

She sighed. 'One's own one can love. Just.'

A provoking woman, his mother would have called her. He didn't have to play. There would be no knowing glances, no smiling collusion.

'Good,' he said.

She gave a dismissive shrug. 'I apologise. I was being . . . What is the word in English?'

'Glib.'

'Glib?'

'A cheap crack. Facile.'

No use. Worse if anything. She turned away, her head drooped, her hair fell forward.

He took her arm. 'Come and tell me about the paintings.'

She was informative and unpatronising, knowledgable and fun. She led him gently, as presumably the nun would now be leading the rugby fans. She assumed nothing.

Yes, she had remembered correctly about Saint Sebastian's arrows. The saint gazed heavenwards above the five arrows in his beautifully modelled torso, his face pained but calm.

They moved on to a triptych. Saint Jerome's lion appeared in each panel like a large and hairy dog; hiding ineffectually behind a tree while monks fled in terror, looming from the shadows in the saint's candle-lit study, flattened with grief beside his master's laid-out corpse, he was faithfulness incarnate.

'I like the backgrounds best,' she said before a fifteenth-century Madonna and Child. 'They are the parts where the artist could let go, be free to explore, be true to his own vision, even if it's only blue castles and misty hills. To tell the truth. Do you know the work of Louise Bourgeois?'

'No.'

Her face was stern. 'A French sculptor. She lives in America now. Even photographs of her work are not easy to find. It is wonderful. Strong. As true, as honest, as pissing.'

Women in Meadowbank did not speak of pissing to strangers, male or female. They did not speak of pissing at all. They went to the bathroom and they shut the door. At picnics they sought a generous bush.

She was sending him signals he found hard to believe.

'What do you mean?'

'It wasn't Saint Sebastian's arrows.' She brushed them away. 'An excuse.'

He stared around the high well-lit walls, noted the exit on the right, gave himself time. The nun was now telling her team about the Piero della Francesca, explaining which figure was the donor and why he was in the picture. And, she asked their stiffening boredom, could anyone see an ostrich egg in the picture? Could anyone see *l'uovo*?

Sì! Sì! Any fool could see. The big fellow hanging above the head of the blessed Virgin.

'And what is the meaning, the significance of this egg, children?'

Total silence from all.

'I don't understand you,' said Henry finally.

Legs apart, arms at the ready, her smile crooked and accusing, she disagreed. 'Now you are lying.'

'No one is lying, we are just playing games. If you ask me to do a Saint Sebastian count with you and I agree we don't have to fuss about arrows or truth or you or me. You make things too difficult for yourself. Slow down. Relax.'

'You sound like Marco.'

'Why do you dislike him so much?'

'He pursues me like a dog and always has. He was glad when his brother died.'

Again that feeling of instability, that trembling shift. He thought of Rosa. Stopped. Felt himself ache for the woman beside him.

'He thought he could get me more easily. Have me like the bitch he thinks me.'

'Oh, for God's sake.' His palms flung apart. 'I don't want to hear all this. Why are you telling me?'

'Because you are a stranger.'

'I am married and my wife is pregnant.'

'The first?'

'Yes.'

She glanced at her fingernails. 'First,' she murmured.

'And will probably be the last. Rosa has problems.'

'Now you are telling me. "Rosa has problems." Sad. I am sad to hear it.' She put a hand up and turned his chin, stared into his eyes. 'What harm can a friendship with an unknown woman do to your Rosa ten thousand miles away, pregnant or not pregnant? Logically speaking, friendship with a woman is more understandable in a man when his wife is pregnant. Psychologically also.'

'And emotionally?' he snapped.

'Goodbye,' she said. She held out her hand for him to kiss. His lips met metal, brushed gold. 'Carla.'

She slipped her arm through his as they walked on. 'The exit is this way.'

The nun was now tackling perspective. The small boys sat cross-legged before Mantegna's *Dead Christ*. They had perked up a little and sat hunting for wounds. One was missing. 'Sister, sister, where is the one in the side?'

'It is hidden, Piero. I have explained to you. Why is the wound in the body of Christ hidden, class?'

132

Silence.

'Because of perspective. All is not seen. I have told you this before.'

The Milan Lions Club had restored a twelfth-century Madonna and Child near the entrance. Good on them. Good.

They became lovers that night.

All day in Prato he had felt alternately weak at the knees or walking on air, his longing tamped with tenderness or over-heated. Had he felt like this eight years ago with Rosa. Of course. Of course not. Of course.

Trees were visible above the balustrade of the roof garden opposite as he ran down the steps from the hotel. The sense always present in Milan of lives hidden from view, of seclusion behind locked doors and courtyards, seemed stronger than ever. Milan does not lie back and welcome. She has to be sought out. Entrée is required.

He pressed the button on the brass entry plate of the high stone wall. Carla's voice answered. The door opened into a cobbled courtyard. He walked past a statue of a boy holding a cornucopia trickling rusty water, turned left past unmown grass, lemon trees and large urns, into a walled garden. Rosa had a thing about secret gardens. She had kept her childhood copy of the book for the baby.

Carla ran to meet him laughing, skipping the rough patches, her hands stretched wide.

She had moved into the studio flat after Roberto died. She wanted to get away from all that *dolce vita* rubbish. She wanted to work and she wanted to live where she worked and she was delighted to be able to greet him where she worked and after they would go around the corner to the Girarrosto Restaurant which was not to be missed, and reasonable as well. When they were completely restored they could return for more love. 'Is that plan good?'

133

'Very good.'

Milan is made for love, she told him. For secrecy, intrigue, corruption and love. What more could he want. What more could he possibly want.

Very little at the time.

She licked his ear. 'Do you like chickpeas?'

'I don't know.'

'Chickpea fritters with watercress. *Farinata di ceci.* Very delicious. Very restorative. Lombardy's answer to the onion soup of France.'

He did not remember much about her studio. Just that it was astonishing, that he had never seen anything like it; swatches, patterns, design sketches, cards of buttons and metres of trim lay all around. There was a large coloured poster of Sophia Loren photographed against a red background, her face resting on a velvet sofa. Her mouth was fractionally open, her smile intimate and amused, her enormous eyes wide with welcome.

'Why on earth?' he asked.

'Because she is the most beautiful woman in the world and she knows it and she can still laugh. She can laugh at herself and at men also. Can love and laugh and break your heart. She is life. Life and love and death and despair.' Carla kissed her hand to the smile.

'Many Italians have photographs of the Pope. She is my Pope. I dropped the other one when I grew up. Shall I tell you?'

He nodded.

'There is a memorial in our town in France. One in every town, every village, always inscribed the same: *A ses morts glorieux.* Twenty-one dead in the last war and our town is small.' She demonstrated size with her fingers. 'But it was the *victimes civiles* that decided me. "Killed by the Gestapo —one; killed by the resistance—one; deported—four; *interné politique*—one; *défence passive*—one." All those killings, all those factions. God couldn't make up his mind. He saved no one.' She lifted an arm to her friend: 'Life is better.'

She was as extravagant as her studio, as lavish as the green fanned lights.

He was never entirely sure what she did, or rather which of her many activities was the most important to her. She had worked for five years as Rossini's assistant. She loved him dearly and he drove her insane. Never had she seen such nerves. She now worked closely with textile manufacturers and sometimes designed collections for them. She had been known to design printed scarves of great beauty. *Stampa personalizzata*. She was interested in detail. The right button could make or mar.

She taught him a great deal. 'A grey deal,' his father had said; why, Henry had never asked. Many things he had never asked and many things were unanswerable. Why, for example, could he tolerate the possibility of Carla's future unfaithfulness with comparative equanimity, when the same thought with regard to Rosa reduced him to gibbering panic.

It was not that he loved Carla less. He loved her passionately, loved her body and her large crooked smile and the way her back arched to meet him. Her unexpectedness, her body and her soul.

And he loved Rosa. His love who could deliver. His wife in bed and out.

It was all very odd. Ridiculous, even, he thought in his bleaker moments. Here he was behaving like some airborne version of the mariner in *Captain's Paradise* flying from the arms of his exotic mistress to the suburban felicity of his loving wife. And back.

*

He arrived home a month before Rufus was born. It was a difficult birth. Toxaemia. There would be no more babies.

And no letters from Milan, of course. That had been agreed on. He would return twice a year. He would be back regularly. To work; to work-related expenses and his work-related love.

Her variousness never faltered. She could slip from proud elegance to street-kid charm with only the lop-sided tug of her grin in common.

Her emotions appeared to work in similar fashion. She swung from hypo- to hyper-sensitive, from action to languor, from rage for the world to rage against it. Her pleasure in sex and his company appeared constant.

He could never understand why she asked so little of him. She made occasional snide remarks about Rosa and the child, but very few. 'Rufus! *Cristo*. No one can be called Rufus.'

'My son is.'

She had more luck with her contempt for anything pertaining to New Zealand. 'Don't ever talk about it. Not a word.'

He let it pass. Patriotism, like guilt, was suspended.

He came, they loved, he left. And he came again. Do not forget that. He came again and again and again.

He should have felt guilty about Rosa and wondered why he didn't. There seemed little point. Not a grey deal.

He and Carla fought occasionally throughout the years. Once or twice she had refused to meet him at first, but such occasions were rare. Mostly he remembered not rows but a kind of teasing banter; irrelevant opportunities pounced upon to belittle his background and education.

Cows, for example, at the café where she sat eating ricotta and jam. She was in elegant mode, her smooth black hair swept into a roll up the back of her head, her lipstick darker than ever. She put down her spoon with a small decisive click and nodded at the heavy gilt-framed oil on the wall above them.

Cows were ambling home to be milked. Or he assumed they were. Like the *Dead Christ*, all was not revealed, but the bonneted maiden had a switch in her hand. They must be going somewhere.

'That painting is *inglese*.'

'How do you know?'

'Sunbonnets. No Italian or French milkmaid would ever have worn such a thing. Never.'

'But look at the cows. Totally French. Huge, raw-boned, terrifying. These are not English cows. Nor New Zealand. Not the cows of Home.'

It was a game ritualised by use; a gentle stirring, a stoke-up. She lead with her chin.

'With a capital H presumably?'

'Of course.'

'Those are not French cows.'

'They're certainly not New Zealanders. Nothing rangy about ours. Neat and sleek. Brindled velvet. I'll send you a postcard.'

'Of *cows*.'

'It wouldn't all be cows. The cows would be incidental, browsing around the foothills of snow-capped mountains, ambling through scenic wonderlands.'

'And hot pools,' she snapped.

The thought appalled him, the agonised bellows, the pain. 'God forbid.'

'A terrible place. Even the cows lack direction.'

'It was you who consigned them to the hot pools.'

'Me! Never!'

Ridiculous. Idiotic. And memorable in every detail.

The worst times were always after they had met Marco Grisoni. These occasions; in the interval at La Scala, at fashion shows throughout the years and, one particularly disastrous time, on the train from Como, always followed the same

137

pattern. Icy greetings, flaunting ridiculous over-the-top behaviour from Carla, chill composure from Marco and inept bumbling goodwill from himself. No, not goodwill, never that, he disliked the man and always had, and if a fraction of Carla's stories about him were true, had every reason so to do; but something akin to it, something placatory, a social hypocrisy, an attempt to smooth.

It was his behaviour more than the chill calm of Grisoni himself which fired Carla to rage whenever they left the man's presence. Rage at Henry.

What had he done?

Nothing! That was the point. He had done nothing. He had crawled, he had compromised, he had *accommodated* the man.

Despair followed later. 'Even Giacomo, my own son, he turns my own son against me. Woos him. Lies to him. Money, money, money. He promises him the moon and lies about me. At his age, so young. Nine, ten. All lies.'

It was only at these times that she mentioned her son. He was at boarding school.

'Isn't that rare in Italy?'

'No.'

A letter addressed to the warehouse arrived on his desk in August 1980. It was a long letter, loving and elegiac and final. She was about to remarry. For security, she explained, and he believed her. And loneliness. Twenty years was a long time to be a mistress. Too long.

He agreed, he understood, he wept. He never saw her again.

Giacomo Grisoni's letter had arrived six years ago. His mother, Carla, had died. She had left instructions that Signor Felton was to be informed. Her death had been sudden and painless.

Her husband had been away when she was taken ill but fortunately Giacomo and his uncle Marco had been at her bedside when she died. Last rites had been administered.

Giacomo would be grateful if Signor Felton did not communicate further with him in any way, either now or in the future.

Henry left the office and walked, headed for the harbour bridge and turned back to search the envelope yet again. She must have sent him some letter, some words, a note. Something. The son had not sent it on. Henry would write for it immediately, demand it. No, he wouldn't. He would seek him out next autumn and tear him apart. He would get his rightful letter.

When he came to his senses again he realised she would not have written him one, even if she had had time. It would not have been right. Not true. She was a married woman.

Henry walked towards the Cimitero Monumentale with the bunch of flowers hanging head downwards in his hand. He did not come every time but was glad when he was able to, when it worked out, when he could think about Carla and nothing else, could stand in that cold crowded place and climb the ladder to leave the flowers in the vase attached to the front of her tomb. Could climb down again to get into the open air and wish for the thousandth time that she had been buried outdoors. That he could have stood by her graveside and thought. And what difference, what conceivable difference could it have made to those haphazard ramblings where she was buried.

It was better to visit the cemetery during the week. In the weekend, especially on Sundays, the chattering crowds, the queue for ladders and long-spouted watering cans, the general air of camaraderie, of people with a shared purpose going about their business, polite and helpful to each other as holidaymakers in the communal kitchen of a camping ground, reduced him to either despair or hysteria.

What could you remember up a ladder when there was a queue waiting? Would the flowers fit in the container? *My lover, my dead love.*

The sight of the Cimitero Monumentale itself always gave him pause. It was aptly named, the scale enormous as were the monuments. Five vast tombs adorned with grieving marble forms stood on the balustrades of balconies on three sides of a building adjoining a piazza large enough for a military rally, for a display of armoured might, an exhortation from Il Duce in his heyday. Death, Cimitero Monumentale believed, would have no dominion.

It began to rain as he arrived. Small gentle rain, coming, if he'd got it right, from the west.

Christ, if my love were in my arms
And I in my bed again.

Yes. Well. Thank God Rufus was in Prato.

He put out a hand to open the gate. It was locked.

He glanced around, noted the absence of flower stalls, the lack of people and finally, the large sign. *Chiuso.*

A small man in a cap moved forward from an attendant's booth inside the iron railings. He was sympathetic but cheerful. '*Chiuso,*' he explained, '*Chiuso a tutti.* Cleansing, cleansing.'

Grazie, grazie.

Prego.

Not at all. Shoulders slumped, Henry turned to the right. He knew where to go. He lifted the flowers and held them upright. It was not the man's fault. He should have checked. Everything requires cleansing.

Carla's remains were interred in the lower level of the right-hand wing of the building, in a storage system set in stone.

He found what he was looking for—a large fan-shaped

window, or rather crescent-shaped hole in the wall divided
by iron struts, which looked down the length of the wing.
Individual tombs lined the entire length of the area from top
to bottom. From the footpath he was at eye level with the
uppermost tombs and the row of large globe lights that ran
from one end of the space to the other. Long ladders, flowers
artificial and real, all were in position. It was well lit. He could
read the inscriptions of the tombs nearest, a Giacomo, a
baroness, a Lucia. He could see the photographs, a miniature
sculpture of a child. Carla, he knew, was further along. Her
inscription brief.

Carla Françoise Stephani 1933–1990.

Nothing more. No husband, no child. Nothing.

Henry stood watching. Cleansing was indeed in progress.
A motorised scrubber wielded by one man was making loud
slurping sounds on the wet marble. It was followed by a man
pushing a large mop attached to a huge red bucket on wheels.
Cheerful and safe as a child's toy, it trundled in front of him
as he sang loudly and tunefully. '*Your tiny hand,*' he roared,
'*is frozen.*'

Henry leaned his head against the wet railings. Rain fell.
He straightened, undid the complicated restraining ribbons
and wires around the flowers and pushed paper whites,
jonquils, daffodils and freesias through gaps in the struts. He
hoped the singer would pick up these offerings from on high,
would share them with the scrubbing operator, would delight
their wives or sweethearts. For you my beloved, *con espres-
sione.*

But perhaps they were in retreat, had finished this end.

Oh Christ—*Cristo.*

It had stopped raining. He walked back to the hotel, a long,
cold, mindless walk. He had reached the park near the hotel
and Batman and his dresser before he had another thought,
one he could have shared with Carla and no one else in the

141

world. The man with the bucket could have been a Nellie Lutcher fan, could have been singing with the same gusto and emotion the Italian version of *Hurry on down to my house, baby.*

'Hey, look,' said Rufus. 'There's Signor Grisoni. Who's the guy with him?'

Henry chewed a mussel and glanced. 'I've no idea.'

He chewed harder, looked again and saw that he had lied. That face, that simian charm, that male version of Carla must be a relative. Or, God help him, her child. Giacomo would be about ten years older than Rufus. It fitted. Henry's gut tightened. He felt weak, dizzy, not well.

Rufus's look was stern. 'What's the matter?'

Henry lied with more purpose. 'I don't like the look of him. Tell me more about Prato.'

'There's nothing more to tell. And why have we come to a French restaurant in Milan?'

'Someone recommended it.' Henry heard his own voice pitched too high. 'Rufus, there's something I feel I should tell you. Something about Uncle Andy.'

Rufus dragged his eyes away from Marco Grisoni and his bright-eyed friend; a dynamic character, voluble, obviously a good talker.

'What on earth? He's been dead forever.'

It was not crassness. Henry knew it was not. Nor disrespect. It would have been better left unsaid.

'Thirty years.'

'More. I was two. Bee gave me a Dinky.'

'Listen,' said his father and told him. He spoke fluently and well as he used Andy's death and probable despair as a diversionary activity. He took occasional sneak looks at Grisoni and his nephew. Grisoni senior had not seen them or, even better, he had seen them and chosen to ignore them while

Henry discussed the sexual predilections and likely suicide of his long dead brother with his inattentive son.

Rufus glanced at his newly delivered plate. 'I thought *fromage de tête* would be brains.'

'No, potted meat, brawn.'

'Bugger,' said Rufus mildly. He put out a hand to his father. 'Dad, do you mean to say you've been fussing about this for over thirty years? I don't mean his death, that's tragic, sure. But a) you'll never know whether or not it was deliberate, not for sure, and b) who would give a stuff about fetishism?'

'This was in 1962.'

'So?'

They never understand, the young. How can they. They weren't there.

'He and Bianca were going to be married. She screamed and roared and sent him packing.'

Rufus was silent for a moment. He considered the evidence. With the certainty of youth, the superiority of those who were not there and don't know, who saw-by-the-paper and know what they think, he considered the evidence and came down on the wrong side.

'Yeah, well. If she saw him at it. Bit of a shock, I suppose. Might put her off.' He paused. 'Still.'

'Still. As you say.'

'It doesn't seem enough to make him top himself.'

'For God's sake, man! It would have killed our father. He was . . .' What would you say, Henry, what would you say. Bigoted. Terrified of difference. Idiotic. 'He was very conservative.'

Rufus was watching the Grisonis, admiring a bit of napkin play; the uncle touching each corner of his mouth, the nephew mopping with enthusiasm. 'Ah,' he said.

Henry looked at him bleakly. So that's it then. The conversation is over.

'You've got brawn on your face,' he said.

Rufus mopped. 'Why tell me now?'

'I thought you might be grateful to know.'

'Oh shit, Dad. I mean about Andy.'

'Bianca knows,' said Henry.

'So?'

'And she also knows that you sent your mother several pairs of shoes.'

Rufus smiled that sweet smile which is rare in men but not unknown. The smile a patient and indulgent parent might give to a child who insists on doing up its own shoes when it can't and the whole thing is going to take hours. 'So what's the problem, Dad?'

Henry was getting angry. 'Your mother does not know about Andy being different. Bianca will tell her and she will worry that it is some hereditary defect.' Get it, thicko? Straight shooting from the old dugout. Get it?

'Memo,' burped Rufus. 'Never have *fromage de tête* again.' He leaned forward to explain, 'Dad, just because there's one, how shall I say, oddball in the family, doesn't mean there's going to be a genetic trickle-down. And who cares? Not me. Certainly not Gaby. She's got a very healthy libido.'

The lingo, the smugness, even the non sequitur infuriated Henry further. And why is it always 'healthy'. Any moment soon it will be 'serious'. A seriously healthy libido, after which there will be nowhere left for it to go other than to slide into a problem. My partner has a seriously healthy libido problem. Jesus wept.

Rufus, undeterred by his previous reception from Signor Grisoni, was on his feet. 'Come on, Dad. Let's go and say hi to Grisoni and his offsider.'

'No!'

'Why on earth not?' said Rufus over his shoulder.

Henry watched in panic. 'Hi' was not a greeting for this

over-priced French restaurant, and there were certainly no offsiders. People met by appointment and no one had made an appointment for him to meet the only child of his deceased mistress, a man who had told him in writing that he had no wish for further communication between them ever again.

He wiped his sweating hands on his trouser legs and followed his son.

Grisoni and his nephew stood and greeted them with composure. Grisoni invited them to join him for a brandy. Henry, who could see how much the man was enjoying the situation, thanked him and asked for a double. They were introduced to Giacomo, a man in his forties, charming, friendly and open. No, he was not part of the fashion world. He was a banker. Milan had more banks per capita than any other city in the world. Did Signor Felton know this?

'Yes,' said Henry.

Rufus, on the other hand, did not. This was fascinating. This was one of the most interesting things Rufus had heard for some time. He and Giacomo talked in English. They did more than that, they exchanged details of their working life, they compared notes, they yarned. Grisoni senior and Henry watched them in silence.

Marco Grisoni had not changed much throughout the years. Sleeker but not fatter, balder but not bald. Eventually he leaned forward, touched Giacomo's jacket. 'Signor Felton knew your mother, Giacomo.'

Calm as Lake Como in sunshine, Henry found his voice. 'A long time ago.'

'How long ago would it be now since you met?' said Grisoni smiling.

'Over thirty years,' said Henry.

Again that smile. 'Thirty-five I think.'

'That'd be right,' said Rufus. 'I remember Mum telling me you got back the month before I arrived.'

Grisoni junior stiffened. His shape, his whole personality tightened, focused—stared in disbelief. '*That* one?' he gasped.

What is going on here? Something is undoubtedly going on in this uptight place which was recommended by some airhead.

Grisoni senior is playing Dad like a trout in the Tongariro. Dad is hooked, beached at the feet of the scurrying waiters, the trays, the half-eaten fromage de fucking tête. He slumps in his chair, stares eyeball to eyeball at Grisoni senior.

Grisoni junior also appears to be in some sort of shock.

'Yes,' says his uncle. 'Thirty-five exactly.'

Dad stands. 'We must be going, Rufus.'

Giacomo Grisoni is on his feet. 'Surely not, your brandy half drunk? I must hear more. Memories of my mother, you understand, are so precious. Tell me more, please *Signore*.'

But it's the way he says it. I can feel it in the crotch. The guy has turned to ice. '*Epée ou pistolet?*' We had it in French.

Giacomo smiles at his uncle. Dad doesn't see this but I do. Marco drops one eyelid in a half-wink. Giacomo stares at him, still questioning, still not able to believe. He is mouthing something, some query.

Marco Grisoni gives the smallest possible nod.

Giacomo swings an astonished hand sideways and knocks over Dad's brandy. It sweeps outwards, a brown stain seeping to the edge of the stiff white cloth.

'No,' says Dad. 'I'm afraid we must go.'

Grisoni senior bows. 'Of course,' he says. 'We must detain you no longer.'

No one shakes hands.

So what's going on? Gaby would know.

'What was all that about, Dad?' I say in the cab.

'Grisoni's a thug and always has been.'

'I quite liked him.'

'Where did you meet him?'

'I told you. On the way to Prato. In the train.'

'Oh yes. The train.'

Dad closes his eyes. Blue, red, pink lights from the neon ads swing around, lie across our knees in stripes, day glo Dad's hair.

'You know,' I say, 'when we first arrived here I remember being surprised that taxis were called taxis. Nuts, eh?'

His eyes open. 'Yes,' he says. 'Not very bright.'

eight

The man at the tip told her he'd have to let her in free if she came many more times. Pleased by goodwill, Rosa grinned back. Better a job here than at the tip face; driving the bulldozer, the stench would stay with you, but here with the pines and the gulls whirling and a little row of salvaged items for sale—a pushchair, a suspect-looking heater, a cot—a man could be his own boss. Presumably he had a heater of his own in his hut; a kettle, sandwiches. And always the chance of a saleable find.

Rufus had had a student job at the domestic waste disposal unit in Otahuhu. The guys there, he said, had it made. The first one started his lunch-hour at ten and the last at three in the afternoon. They bolted their pie or whatever and spent the rest of the hour scanning the incinerated remains of the waste for treasure as it travelled past their eyes on its way to eventual resurrection as garden compost. If they found anything it was theirs. And the stuff they found! Diamond rings, bracelets, watches, money. It was understandable, but Rufus just hadn't thought about it before. A lot of the trove was useless, of course, false teeth, glass eyes, things of that nature. Still. It would add interest and the odds would be better than Lotto.

He didn't get a go. It was a perk for the permanents.

Rosa drove on and unloaded the trailer, her arms tugging, her eyes down for nails and sharp edges. The circling gulls landed, inspected briefly and wheeled high in disgust. This was non-biodegradable refuse, real dump stuff: ragged lengths of mouldy scrim, layers of dead wallpaper, pile after pile of newspapers. The sad and sorry mess of a life which had abandoned order, or been forced to admit defeat; had been unable to clean and maintain, or had got sick of it. Had run out of puff.

Despite her former enthusiasm for her role, Rosa knew how the previous owner had felt. The disposal of inorganic refuse is essential, yes indeed, but repetitive. She had hoped that her job in the triumvirate would be more exciting, would involve spells of action at the sharp end; of hacking, biffing, tearing apart like Bianca in borrowed overalls, or Gaby in a back-to-front baseball cap running up and down ladders shouting. Rosa's job was to load the trailer, drive to the tip, unload and return for more. She was beginning to realise that the catharsis of tip visits occurs only when you're getting shot of the fruits of your own labours, the mountain of your prunings, the waste of your years.

It was not the physical effort involved. She was strong as a Shetland pony, and would continue to be so as the years rolled by and the tall and languid wilted about her.

Her main source of job satisfaction was her minor skill in backing the trailer. It's not easy backing a trailer, quite an art, in fact. But after a few days she was bored; was tired of the dust and the red nose, the snorting discomfort and the head like a pumpkin. The muck and muddle of it all, the carting and the dumping.

'I think,' she said, as they sat eating her egg sandwiches in the derelict back garden, 'that we should take turns doing different jobs. I'd like to have a turn at stripping scrim.'

Bianca and Gaby chewed more slowly, stared at her solemn as two cows which had followed her across a paddock at Pukekohe last week, had stopped when she stopped, had moved on when she did; silent, attentive and puzzled. What was she up to now.

'Why?' said Bianca finally.

'I think it would be more fun. More . . . more meaningful.'

'You find the tip meaningful. You said so.' Gaby stretched, brushed away a passing bee from the buddleia. 'This stuff stinks.'

'I said it was cathartic.'

'Same difference.'

'Catharsis is emotional release, a purging. Not . . .'

'From the dump you get this?'

Again that feeling of unease, of unexpected slants and angles to words which seemed to characterise her conversations with Gaby. 'What I meant was . . .'

Bianca was not having this nonsense. 'Of course you can't do anything else, Ros. You're too short.'

'*We're the flowers in your dustbin*,' screamed a male voice next door.

'Sex Pistols. The guy's a nerd,' said Gaby and chewed again.

'And besides,' Bianca glanced at her, 'can you drive a trailer?'

'No,' said Gaby.

Bianca brushed her fingers, 'Well, there you are.'

Rosa stood up, stowed thermoses and let them have it. She was sorry to have to remind them but she had had enough. Henry and, by extension, herself were paying for this enterprise, totally, one hundred per cent and happy to do so for the common weal. Weal, she said again. If anyone was a partner in this enterprise, she was and in future she wished to be treated as one. If she wanted to strip wallpaper or hessian she would do so. And furthermore, someone else, she said, glancing around the still, enclosed space, the bees, the buddleia, the quiet, someone else could make the sandwiches tomorrow.

Having stood up and stowed, there seemed nowhere else to go. Sauntering was impossible. She scrambled across rubble to the rampant banksia rose.

Bianca and Gaby watched her rear. 'But who will drive the trailer, Ros?' said Bianca.

'*Flow-ers*,' yelled the voice.

Gaby said nothing. She couldn't stand people who sulked and when the hell was Roof coming home. This lot was getting to her. She looked at Rosa's behind upended over a pile of junk, her hands tearing at grass and weeds. Nuts.

She lit a cigarette, offered Bianca one. Bianca held up her own packet. Justin had not liked women smoking, let alone a wife. Gaby handed her lighter, was thanked.

The sun shone.

Rosa's mind was busy. She would stop and get her work gloves, any moment she would do that. It was ridiculous to be doing this bare-handed; there might be glass, twisted wire, anything beneath this choking weed, dangerous refuse awaiting transportation to an alternative site which had never been offered.

Who drives the trailer. *Who pays the piper.* And what on earth does that mean. Henry was quite right. They don't make sense, these old saws. None of them makes sense. Upended, flustered and breathing fast, she felt a surge of affection for Henry, who understood that all we know is that we don't know a thing. Not really. Just snatches. A glimpse, here and there.

She would stop this petulance, this rage, ignore this ridiculous sense of isolation and exclusion. Would stop snivelling into Wandering Jew and was that racist.

Perhaps Granny F had got it right. The thought depressed her. Mrs Felton had explained her real reason for going to

Pukekohe after her husband died. Had explained quietly and calmly to Rosa in her bedroom as they packed her 'personal belongings' before the packers arrived. 'I suppose they mean my knickers,' she said. 'Very wise. Old women's smalls would frighten the wits out of those heroes.'

She stood small, spry and neat as a pin. Her long white hair had been cut the year before when she broke her arm and could no longer cope with a bun. She was a walking oxymoron, a geriatric Peter Pan. Rosa opened her mouth to tell her and shut it. Even someone as ruthlessly clear-sighted as Mrs Felton might not be flattered.

Her bedroom was unlike any other Rosa had seen. Mrs Felton slept alone and had done since Henry was a child. Plain as a nun's cell, the room was whitewashed and minimalist fifty years before the style caught on. The furniture consisted of a narrow wooden bed, a kauri chest, a table and a chair. There were no pictures and only one black and white photograph in a leather frame on the table; a young man in uniform smiled, his cap on the slant, his pipe in his hand. Her brother Ian had been killed as a sub-lieutenant in the *Neptune*.

Rosa and Henry had tried to explain that it would be better for Mrs Felton to stay in town. They had not put it like that. You didn't tell Mrs Felton what would be better for her. She already knew. And they could scarcely have said it would be more fun. They had appealed to her pragmatism, had said it would make sense if they had found her a small flat or house nearby. They had not said, where they could keep an eye on her. They had more sense. You don't keep eyes on stoics. They might catch you at it.

So there would be no more popping in, no hot soup on the wing, no easy closeness with a woman Rosa admired. She would miss her.

Packing pink bloomers, she made one last try. 'Gran, why are you going all the way out there?'

'All the way? About thirty miles.' Mrs Felton finished folding a spencer, laid it with its fellows and sat down on her bed. Rosa remembered her faint surprise. Admittedly there was nowhere else to sit, but Mrs Felton did not sit on beds.

'I'll tell you the real reason, Rosa. Don't tell Henry. He wouldn't understand.' She paused. 'On second thoughts I think he might and that would be worse.' She picked up the fringe of the white cotton bed cover, ran it through her fingers. 'I have decided that I don't like people, people in general. I never have particularly, not the whole world. Some, yes, a few, but by and large I prefer my own company.' She gave what Henry called her honk. 'Don't look so worried. I was never gregarious. It must have been hard for Henry's father, a mismatch all round. But now I find I dislike too many, women in particular, so it seems sensible to go where I won't have to see them—other than family and by appointment. And I like the country, the life. Pukekohe will do very well.' She smiled Rufus's smile. 'Don't you find women trying?'

The playcentre young mothers, the good friends, the laughs. 'No, not at all.'

'Perhaps you're right. But there are too many rogue humming birds about for me. Flutterers. Women dripping syrup which turns to acid. Enchanting creatures, but the sting comes later.'

'You don't understand,' said Rosa, 'Bianca doesn't . . .' Mrs Felton brushed Bianca away.

'Devious women. Older women on the whole, but by no means always. Retailers of chit and chat who don't say what they think, don't mean what they say, don't ask what they want to know.' She paused. 'Though give them their due, it might be a difficult question. "Did your son kill himself? And if so why?" That's what lies behind their whispers, their turned heads, their intrusive smiles.'

There must be something to say, something not entirely

banal. Rosa couldn't find it. 'They don't mean to,' she bleated.

'Then why do they do it? I do not *require* such women.'

Her voice was calm. 'There was something wrong with Andy's death. Andy had more eagerness for life, more attack, than anyone I have ever known.' Her eyes flicked to the photograph. 'Anyone.'

'It was an accident!'

'I don't think so. There was something wrong.' Mrs Felton straightened her spine. 'I think I might keep bees at Pukekohe. I've always liked the idea of bees. The practice, of course, may be quite different. We shall see.'

Bianca and Gaby's rapport increased, became something more than a way of getting the work done. Gaby had decided that as long as she met up with a few of the guys she used to work with, got this lot out of her hair at night, she could hack it. You can get used to anything. Bianca soon learned that Gaby was what Mother used to call a lovely little worker, a term of approbation she had earned herself in her section-clearing days. They worked well together. Gaby seemed tireless as well as nimble. Her stretch was wide and high, her treatment broad brush; slash and burn, get back to the wood. 'Then we can tart it up, fling the paint around.'

Bianca took over the woodwork, got into the detail. Sugar soap no longer held fears. She was meticulous with the window frames. The wide kauri skirting boards came up well.

'Yeah,' said Gaby realigning her pot of stripper on the top rung of the ladder. 'Comes up a treat, like I said. But why do it now? Let's get shot of the stripping first.'

'No,' said Bianca.

Let her rip. Go with the flow. As long as she keeps at it. Bianca was earning her keep and once Roof got back she and he could steam ahead. After work, weekends, you wouldn't see them for dust. It'd be a pain having the old bat living with them but it should work out okay. A temporary nuisance but once they got the title all would be well. Gaby had every confidence.

As did Bianca. Blessed with equal strength of purpose, Bianca also had no qualms. The essential was to get the title.

They worked on, occasionally fencing around each other, learning how and when incipient battles should be avoided, which ones fought to a standstill and when to retrench. Their skills were complementary, they were united in work for the common cause of their two opposing ends.

Their dissimilar views of ultimate ownership enhanced their enthusiasm in the shared project. They were grateful to each other for their efforts; not overtly, but in their hearts each of them appreciated the other's disinterested acceptance of her role in the fitness of things.

They appreciated each other. They shared what each regarded as a unilateral interest. Admiration was not far away, though Gaby's was tempered by Bianca's implacable stubbornness and occasional loss of a word. She would go silent, you could see her mind groping before coming out with the wrong one. Telephone, say, for toaster; lamppost for lavender. Gran in Matamata did the same thing. Nuts really.

But Bianca was okay. They got on. 'Gee, you never miss a trick, Bee. Talk about observant. And sharp. I'd hate to be stuck in a stalled lift with you.'

Bianca sat back on her heels to stare up the ladder. 'Why? What were you planning to do in the lift?'

Gaby laughed, the ladder rocked slightly. 'There you go again. Sharp as a tack.'

Bianca's stubbornness could be fun to watch too. Especially her reaction to any suggestion of Rosa's. The more simple the proposal, the quicker Bianca's refusal to comply. Resistance was all. Rosa's incompetent parking this morning, for instance. 'Sorry, dear. I'm too near the bush. Don't get out,

155

I'll back.' In a flash Bianca flung herself out the door into the arms of an overgrown teucrium, found herself unable to open the door wider, pushed harder, burst through, only to be ensnared once more. Rosa got the hedge clippers.

Rosa at lunchtime, dispensing sandwiches and comfort. 'Here's a nice flat place, dear.' Bianca refusing, standing, willing another flat space to appear. She would choose her own flat places. She would be independent in thought and deed. She shared with Mrs Felton, whom Gaby had never met but knew from Bianca was a terrible old woman, terrible, a preference for her own decisions. It was just the scale which differed.

Bianca needed handling. She reminded Gaby of Dad in Matamata. Like Mum said, it was simple. Just a matter of personnel management and keeping the desired end in sight. *The politics of the harem*, she'd read somewhere. Well, go for it. Mug if you don't. All would be well.

The camaraderie which existed between Gaby and Bianca heightened. Rosa's demeaning sense of exclusion from this strange partnership increased.

The dump was her province and seemed likely to remain so. But Henry would soon be home, Henry and Rufus.

Yes.

And Henry and Bianca

Oh dear . . . Oh dear oh dear oh dear.

And how did you and Henry get yourselves into this mess in the first place.

Because of you. This was your idea. Remember.

Martin's condition was worsening by the day and Rosa was in need of rational discourse. 'I'm going to see Martin,' she explained at the back door. 'There's plenty of food in the fridge.'

'Forget it,' said Gaby. 'There's a shop round the corner from Webster Street.'

'Oh goody.' Bianca lifted a hand, added a cryptic 'heigh-ho' and returned to the *Herald*.

Meadowbank was bustling as Rosa drove through and Remuera more so; more trees, more shops, more people, more money. Remuera, it would be fair to say, was basking in autumnal sunshine. Long-legged young women were leaping in and out of large cars, their straight hair flying, their voices high as they herded well-padded young over crossings. One crashed on his behind as the lights changed; his calm expression remained, he was used to it. He was hauled to his feet by his mother. She gave the careful lady driver a smile, half rueful, half 'don't run over us, but I know you won't because old women care'. Old women are not irrelevant. They have their place and like to be useful.

Rosa snarled at the departing backs and swept onwards to the bridge.

A woolly-hatted woman at the next stop adjusted her shopping bag, leaned towards the decrepit old man on the bench beside her to chat as the torn clouds streamed above and the bus was late yet again. He nodded, sat a little sideways and crossed his legs. His mind was on something else.

Martin had given up on his TV. He might as well watch washing slapping about in a laundrette for all the pleasure he got from it. It still loomed, however. Large, vacant as an empty oven, it continued to make a statement of some sort; unused, unwanted, it hung on in there.

He had transferred his allegiance to the radio, was better informed and saved bits and pieces to tell Rosa. A young man had been granted the Delphic award for Pervasive Entrepreneurial and Promotional Ethos. He had been prepared to go that extra mile for Customer Focus.

And there was a good one yesterday. *Top-gallant delight.* Had she heard the phrase? No, he hadn't either. 'Top-gallant delight,' he murmured.

He had been told to give up smoking. Sunnydale couldn't take the responsibility any more. He was killing himself, they said. 'I know that, I told them, and it suits me fine. "But you must think of the other inhabitants," they said. I said why? I told them they needed more customer focus. They didn't like that. They came clean then. I'm a fire risk, they say. So it's very new, you see, this nicotine withdrawal, only a few days and I don't mind telling you it's hell. Let's have a whisky. The bottle's in the cupboard.'

Rosa sat relaxed and dreaming, wondering if she had an empty stomach and, if so, what a good idea. Something was undoubtedly hitting the spot.

A dog barked, one clear yap, then silence.

'How's the cough?'

'Fine.'

Liar. 'Do men have to learn how to spit?' she asked.

'I can't remember.'

'So forceful. Accurate. They must practise as boys.'

He shook his head. 'My friend—Signor Monti in Como always called us that.'

'Tell me about Italy.'

He coughed, and kept on coughing.

'What do you want to know?' he gasped eventually.

'Everything.'

He was breathless, wary, fighting for breath. She brought him water, helped him drink it, sat silent till he recovered.

'Henry's never talked about it. Hardly at all. You know how sometimes when you've done something and it's over you can't be bothered discussing it. Henry's always been like that. If it's over, it's gone. Done. Boring. Rufus is the same. It was like getting blood from a stone finding out, even at playcentre. What he'd been doing. Who his friends were. If you asked him—' her voice dropped, filled with gloom, '"I just played,

158

and played, and played." He's still the same. Don't ask. It's past, over. Like Henry.'

Martin could feel his heart racing. Rosa was not helping either his physical or mental condition. He would have to get on to Henry when he got home. It was a good time to be in Milan; he'd like to hear about it himself. The *lira* half what it had been in '91; about a thousand to the dollar instead of six hundred. Make the sums on the factory floor easier too. Just cut out the noughts.

Remember, Rosa knows nothing. Nothing. All you've got to do is keep off people. But why has she never talked about Milan? Presumably because Henry won't. She'll chat about Paris, the things she wants to see. The bridges, the boulevards she could see herself striding along. The Louvre was overpowering, Henry said. Henry said that snails taste of garlic and nothing else, that she would like the Pompidou, that some people thought it was looking a bit grotty already but that he didn't agree. That he had had little time, there or anywhere. They'd have all the time in the world when they went together.

Had she never wondered about the veto on Milan? Martin looked at her round face, her uncompromising haircut. No, she hadn't.

'And what about Rufus?' he asked. 'How did Rufus get on in Prato?'

She didn't know.

Martin saw Henry and himself returning from Prato in the mid-'70s. They were pleased with themselves, they had done well, extremely well. Henry was expansive, full of praise for Martin's expertise with the language, his quick-witted attack which had been invaluable. Enrico Baronti had been running for cover. They must celebrate, make sure Martin came on every trip.

Martin shook his head. 'No.'

'Whyever not?'

159

'It's an unnecessary expense now your Italian's adequate. I'd be more use at home.'

A dark-haired woman in black, chic as the early photographs of the Duchess of Windsor and as severe, rose from her chair in the foyer. 'Henry,' she said, 'I must speak with you.'

Martin moved quickly to the tiny lift. '*Piccolo, piccolo,*' gestured the large man beside him. '*Sì sì.*'

That woman and Henry are lovers. That claiming hand, that urgency, every movement of her body. Henry's start, the quick upfling of palms. Five words were enough.

'That woman yesterday . . .' said Henry at breakfast next morning.

Martin lifted his cup for more coffee, '*Grazie.*' His eyes watched the baggy waddle of the departing waiter. 'Don't bother,' he said.

'Was it so obvious?'

'Yes.'

'I'd be glad if you didn't . . . You won't, of course, but . . .'

'No.' Not for your sake. Don't think that for a minute. For Rosa. 'How long has it been going on?' he asked.

'I don't think there's any point in your knowing that.'

'No?' Martin stood up. 'Excuse me,' he said. 'Shit time.'

He had glimpsed Carla throughout the years, had met her occasionally. He did not warm to her. Their acquaintance did not prosper.

'Why do you suddenly want to know about Milan?' he asked.

'Because we'll be going soon. Once Rufus has settled in, when Henry feels completely confident about leaving him in charge we'll be off. We always planned to go as soon as Henry retires.'

He told her what little he knew. He told her about the

elegance and the slums, the grandeur and the kitsch, the pollution and the magnolia and the power of the church. The faith that moves mountains and the corruption in high places. You'll never know it, understand it. You can only love it or hate it.

'It's odd we haven't been before,' she said. 'Ridiculous really. It's easy to park one child. Granny would have been happy. They always got on well, used to make gingerbread men, can you believe. Toffee apples even.' She traced a red stripe on his tartan rug. 'But Henry went off the idea. He said it'd be more fun when he could show me everything, explore together.' She paused. 'You know something? I'd rather have explored by myself. The first time, I mean. I like not having to say things. In galleries when we go, I just want people to shut up. Henry even. I hate it when he talks.'

Martin moved irritably, was furious with her. 'Then why in heaven's name didn't you insist?'

She patted his arm, laughed. 'I can't imagine.' She gave a brisk movement of her shoulders. 'We'll go soon and that'll be great, so tell me more.'

'Let's have another whisky,' he said.

'It's eleven-thirty in the morning.'

'So? There's something else I want to talk about before I run out of puff.'

She came back with their glasses. A deep brown voice sang from the corridor.

Sing lula, lula, lula lula bye bye
Do you want the moon to play with.

Why not. Let us aim high. 'Is yours strong enough?'

'Just.'

'I'll bring a bottle next time.' She lifted her glass. 'Don't die in the night, Martin.'

'That's what I want to talk about.'

She put her glass on the bedside table among the clutter of

161

what remained of his life: *Best Bets*, crosswords, a *Listener*, tissues, pills and puffers.

'Don't look like that. Lift your glass a sec.' He scrabbled among the papers for a large envelope, waved it in the air.

'Here we are. I've been getting things teed up. I've asked a local padre to do his stuff, no date of course, but that's okay by him. I'll give you this now so you won't have anything to worry about later.' He paused. 'I thought cremation would make more sense. What do you reckon?'

Rosa lifted her game. 'Yes,' she said. 'I'm all for cremation.'

'Good. Good.'

He patted the envelope. 'It's all there, except one thing's a bit of a bind.

'Tell me.'

'The ashes.'

The heart can turn over. 'What do you want done with them?'

'At first I thought just dump them somewhere, but then I thought where? It might be a bit of a bind . . .'

'Don't be ridiculous.'

'They come in a wee box. Quite neat, apparently. I thought you could just tuck it away in the garage somewhere.' He took her hand, gave it back. 'I wouldn't expect you to put it on the duchesse or anything.'

'I haven't got a duchesse,' she wailed.

'The garage then.'

She gave a quick angry toss of her head. 'Right,' she said, smiling into his exhausted eyes. 'Good thinking, Carstairs.'

Rosa, her head backed by elves, sat on the sofa and thought of Martin. Bianca, as usual at this time, was tearing the television apart, tossing and goring the presenters, those idiotic little clouds in the weather map, the advertisements every five minutes. The whole thing made her sick.

162

Why watch it then? Bianca, the time Rosa had asked her, had replied with insight and a sniff at the garden beyond the window that there was little else to watch. Except the dead sparrow decomposing. Putrefaction, she noticed, had set in, it was rotting before her eyes.

'It is not putrefying.'

'Then what is it doing?'

'Disintegrating. Turning to compost.'

'Nonsense.'

Gaby disappeared each night in her ancient Skoda and returned at varying times, sometimes as they were sitting down to a chop. ('Don't *worry*, no *problem*.') Once in the dead of night she 'knocked something up in the kitchen', something involving pasta and garlic and cheap red wine. The remains were evident next day, the garlic melding with the overnight nicotine. Rosa explained that she was happy for her guests to cook what they liked when they liked, but please would Gaby use the extractor fan. Sure, said Gaby.

Rosa was not one of those people who refused to have smoking in her house. Not for Rosa the long-stemmed cardboard rose and the *No Smoking Please*, and what on earth was the connection? But would Gaby please empty the ashtrays. Sure, said Gaby.

The relationship, as Rosa had come to think of it, between Rufus and Gaby, seemed destined to continue. They had lived together for years and seemed at ease with each other. Toll calls to and fro from Italy had been frequent. Did Rosa like Gaby? Yes. And then again, no. Gaby's good qualities were obvious: loyalty to Rufus, courage in adversity, a lovely little worker and cool as two cucumbers. Yes.

And then again, no.

Bianca, having disposed of two frontpersons with one finger, was also thinking. It was good that her container had been delayed. If there had not been all that muddle and

163

mishandling at the other end it would have arrived long ago and storage in this place costs the earth. The boat had done well to delay. Better still if it became becalmed somewhere en route so the money required for storage on arrival would be negligible. Somewhere safe and possessed of a moderate climate. Excessive heat or humidity or insurrection among locals were undesirable, but so was paying money she could not afford and indeed did not have. She could only hope.

'When do they get back,' she said, 'Henry and Rufus?'

'They'll be in Paris now,' said Rosa. 'In about a week.'

'Good. It will be essential for Rufus to work full time on the house for a while,' explained Bianca.

Pillar-box red lipstick on old lips is a mistake and always has been. 'How on earth can he do that? His weekdays are entirely committed to the warehouse.'

'But what if my things arrive? Henry must be persuaded.'

Stubbornness is a gift as immutable as stupidity. Against which *the gods themselves contend in vain*. Henry had told her.

'Henry will not be persuaded.'

'My things might arrive.'

'Bianca . . .'

Bianca gave a small movement as though adjusting a fall of watered silk about her shoulders. 'We shall see.' Her glance sharpened. 'Why are you drinking whisky?'

Rosa's mouth moved. Was she developing a nervous tic? 'I thought I would like a change. Have you any objections?' She heard herself saying it. Petty, disagreeable, not nice at all.

Bianca ignored her lapse. 'And another thing. I hear that man, what's his name, that friend of yours . . .'

The word 'friend' hung in the air like smoke. It had an aura. It indicated a person who might conceivably be a friend to the misguided but not to those of taste and discernment such as the present speaker.

Auras are hard to fight. They do not come clean.

'Martin Brown,' snapped Rosa.

'Yes.' Bianca was not concerned at her loss of the wretched man's name. The trick is not to fuss, not to snap your fingers in the air mouthing away about things being on the tip of your tongue, how you almost had it, how it has gone again. The trick is to pretend you can't be bothered remembering, which was true in this case. A loathsome creature, Bianca had always thought so. 'One of your lame ducks,' she said.

Rosa's hand shook. 'What an appalling thing to say.'

'It's true, isn't it?'

'No, it is not. Martin is my friend and, even if he were not, no one in the world should be called that. Lame duck. The implication is that, that . . .' Rosa stopped. You cannot say to your sister that she is not only smug but has never known a twinge of lameness in her life when she sits before you, down on her uppers if not her beam ends.

Rosa drank whisky, blew her nose and drank again. 'Lame *duck*.'

'Reeks of nicotine too, the last time I met him. I hear he intends to leave you all his money.'

'Who told you!'

'Gabrielle.'

Exclusion from the playground gossip of others tends to make you puerile, the sense that things told in confidence may whirl around and acquire a life of their own is never pleasing. 'Why were you talking about me?'

'We weren't. You just came up. I can't think why you didn't tell me yourself.'

There was a gleam in Bianca's eye. Rosa saw her at Mother's dressing-table long ago, her small teeth closing on Granny's pearls with the quick instinctive bite of a sailor's moll on a proffered doubloon.

She was now licking scarlet lips. 'It's always so interesting,

I think, these deadbeats, recluses, whatever. There was a woman in New York, I saw last week. A bag lady, had all her meals at a soup kitchen or whatever they call them. Begged any remains and left two million dollars. You never know. You can't tell.'

'No.'

Bianca could wait no longer. 'Is it a lot?' she asked.

Rosa, miserable, distracted and enraged Rosa, lifted her head. 'Yes,' she said. 'It is.'

Martin died a few days later. Arrangements were put in train. The plan was implemented.

Bianca came to the funeral. She felt it was the least she could do for the wretched man.

Rosa told Henry of his death at the airport. He was distressed. They clung to each other. Henry wiped his eyes. He was surprised to find it necessary. He liked Martin and had always done so. Honourable, honest as the day, Martin would be missed, but not much by him. And what a life, the man would be glad to go.

A decent man but not memorable, except, of course, for loyalty. A good man he had worked with forever whose inner thoughts were unknown to him and vice versa. But not entirely. He wiped again.

'Great to see you,' said Rufus, trying to trundle the luggage and embrace Gaby at the same time. 'What's up with Dad?'

'The old guy's died,' she said, 'the guy with the cash.'

nine

It was great to see her again. Rufus couldn't keep his hands off her, let alone his eyes. He hadn't realised, not for a moment had he realised, what it would be like. Too long without loving, too fucking long. Never again, that was for sure. They wouldn't make that mistake again. Gaby must come next time. You bet she would. She couldn't wait. You're a natural, he told her, a born trader. She knew she was, she always had been, she came from a long, long line of wheeler-dealers and horse-traders. Milan, she said, passing the salad, would be a breeze and to hell with the dole suspension.

They laughed, they flaunted, their eyes stripteased. They might just as well have operated here and now, thought Henry sourly, have rolled onto the worn carpet and got on with it. Had they no modesty. Had they no reticence. No, they hadn't. Why didn't they just leave the table, donate their share of the welcome-home carrot cake to Bianca and withdraw to eat each other in private. Leave the rest of them in what he supposed you could call peace.

No, they wouldn't have any more, thanks. Rufus thought he would unpack. 'Coming Gaby?'

'*Honestly*,' said Bianca.

'Honestly what?' he snapped.

'You know.'

Rufus and Gaby lay side by side on the single bed. They talked briefly before love and more later. There was much to hear and tell, to discuss between partners.

Rufus moved a cramped arm. 'You know that weird thing I was telling you about Dad and the Grisoni guy?' She nodded. 'Well, wipe that. I'll start from the beginning. You should've seen him, seen his face. You know when they say "he went green". Fact, absolute fact, I'm here to tell you. I thought he was going to pass out. There we all were in this poncey place and the atmosphere was charged, electric. I mean it. I've never felt anything like it in my life. It was . . .'

'But what did he say, the guy?'

'He told his nephew that Dad had known his mother.'

'So what?'

'But Jesus, you should've seen them. Those guys had him licked, they had him on the ropes . . . It gave me the creeps almost.'

She is now sitting cross-legged by my head. I move my hand, she moves it back. Gaby is a one thing at a time girl. 'Tell me more,' she says.

So I tell her again about Grisoni in the train. I tell her about Grisoni junior. I tell her he's a good-looking guy in a funny sort of way. Dark, intense. I tell her he has a mobile face. I demonstrate. On and on I go, and she listens and she thinks and finally she says, 'I wasn't there. I didn't see any of it, the train, the restaurant, any of these nuances you're on about. *How* were they so real, so threatening? How did you know something was going on, what made it so fucking obvious?'

'Like I said. Dad. You know me, I never notice anything. Not things like, are people well or not. Not what colour they've gone. Normally you'd have to be lying there in a pool of blood, and even then you'd be lucky.'

She's still thinking. Thinking hard. Nutting it out. 'It's obviously one of two things,' she says, stretching; the side effect is her boobs look better than ever.

'Gaby,' I say.

'Mnn? Well, remember where we've got to after.'

'Sure, people can be half dead and I don't notice,' I say later, 'but I do know about power games. I've seen enough, made enough deals. I reckon I could watch a deal in a foreign language and I'd know which guy was winning and which was down the tube. And this time,' I say, kissing her navel, 'it was Dad.'

She moves away. Sits up. 'It's either sex or money,' she says. 'And I'll shoot for sex.'

'Naaah.'

She is serious. 'When Grisoni said Signor Felton "knew" your mother, was it like, you know, biblical?'

'Oh come on,' she says at my blank face, 'all that *and he did lie with the woman and he did know her* . . . I bet that's what Grisoni was hinting at. Sex.'

'I don't know.'

'I would've. Can't you even remember which was the most important bit?'

'Oh sure, but it was all . . .' I think hard, see their faces, the spilled brandy. 'The most important bit was where Giacomo said, "That one?"'

'"That Felton?"'

'Yeah.'

'I reckon,' says Gaby, 'that your father had an affair with Giacomo Grisoni's mother.'

I feel rather odd. Not only because the thought of Dad doing it at all is gross, but a mistress, if you see what I mean. How did he find this woman, how did he start, where did they go? And what about Mum? Mum loves him, loves him

169

more than she loves me. It doesn't worry me, never has, why should it. But an affair . . . Dad?'

Gaby has grabbed a used envelope and a biro from the floor and is doing sums. 'Are you thirty-five or thirty-six?'

'Thirty-five. That's what he asked. Marco Grisoni, in the train.'

She puts down the biro and nods her head slowly, rocks backward and forward on her neat little bum.

'Get it?' she says.

Henry peered over half-moon glasses at breasts sagging beneath pink knitted cotton. Faded pubic hair was visible below. 'That garment's indecent,' he said.

Rosa was unperturbed. 'No longer a pretty sight? Basically,' she said, climbing into bed, 'I'm a redhead. Or was.' She gave him a quick peck on the forehead and handed him a letter. 'Nice to have you home.'

He flapped the thing away. 'Why now? I'm dead with jet lag, Bianca's on top form,' his head tossed backwards, 'that lot's hot as monkeys. Why now, for God's sake?'

She pulled the duvet to her pale face. 'It's from Martin. He asked me to give it to you. Good night, dear,' she said reaching for the bedside light switch. She sighed, rolled over, remembered Mrs Felton scrubbing Jerusalem artichokes long ago. She had turned, given Rosa the sweet smile which had skipped a generation. 'Have I told you about the first night of our honeymoon?'

Mr and Mrs Felton had been married in Palmerston North. After the reception at the Grand Hotel they had caught the Limited to Auckland, had been shown into the tiny sleeping apartment with its stiff sheets and let-down handbasin. They had edged around each other, smiled, and undressed with decorum. Teeth had been cleaned. Mr Felton bent to kiss her in the bottom bunk. 'I won't bother you tonight, my dear,' he said and climbed the ladder to the top bunk. She lay silent, watching his striped pyjama trousers disappear.

In the morning there was only one *Dominion*. 'Didn't you order one for me?' she asked.

'Why would you want a newspaper?'

She knew then. Knew it was a disaster. It was terrible.

Henry gave a perfunctory pat of the duvet in the general direction of his wife's behind and opened the letter.

Dear Henry,

They tell me I have pneumonia. This is an odd letter to write. I'm not good at moral decisions, and putting things in writing is never a good idea. But does Rosa know about Milan? The way she looks, the things she asks about.

The writing became smaller, less precise.

I thought I ought to . . . God, I don't know. Come and I'll tell you.

Martin

Henry lay still, stretched his legs. They were aching as they sometimes did after flying. The bed was too small, they should have a bigger one. People have enormous beds now. You have a single and then you have a double and then you die as Martin had died, except his was single. A puriri branch was banging against the roof again. He should cut it off. He would get a man. Eventually. There was a window banging as well. He slid out of bed clutching the letter.

Rosa snapped on her light. 'Where are you going?'

'There's a window banging.'

'The last time it did that was in the *Wahine* storm. The window blew out, there was an awful mess. You were in Milan.' She tugged at the duvet. 'This thing walks,' she said and snuggled down again.

He walked past the now silent lovers and Bianca, who was snoring softly. The gentle nasal exhalations of the sound sleeper followed him down the narrow hall to the kitchen. Moonlight flooded in the wide windows, glinted blue and icy on stainless steel benches. His feet were cold. Rosa was awake—innocent and unsuspecting as a child, she might come padding out to help. He wouldn't turn on the light, couldn't, she would spot the letter immediately. He opened the back door, returned for matches and headed across the porch to the laundry door, removed the key, locked the door from the inside and switched on the light to coconut matting, the washing machine and deep, wide tubs. He held the letter by one corner, set light to it and watched it flame and blacken, then swirled the ashes down the plughole, careful and meticulous as a murderer with bloodstains, rerinsing and swilling till no trace remained.

Weak with relief, he leaned against the locked door. Nothing, ever, in his whole life had given him the security of that gimcrack lock and long-handled key. He stared around the space, sniffed the scent of washing powders, admired bottles, jars, free samples which had never been used. The bench was piled high with travellers' clothes and unironed washing.

Someone, Gaby presumably, had left a half-empty packet of cigarettes on the shelf beside a local builder's calendar labelled *Easy to See*. Above the inch-high numerals a large coloured photograph showed a small resolute child in a yellow safety helmet clutching a bricklayer's trowel and attempting to complete a half-finished wall. *A brickie's nightmare*, said the caption. Men would understand. Real men, do-it-yourselfers with expertise. Henry took a cigarette, lit up and dragged deep. It tasted of dry hay but the gesture seemed appropriate. If no one can see you can do what you like.

*

172

'Where on earth have you been?' said Rosa.

'Nowhere much.'

'Whose cigarette did you bludge?'

He was about to tell her about the packet in the laundry, how they must be Gaby's, how Bianca would never have been so careless, how . . .

'I don't know,' he said.

'That window's still banging.'

'Jet lag,' he mumbled and blundered out again to the hall. Jet lag, vitamins, nets closing.

She was waiting for him on his return. 'What did Martin's letter say?'

'I think he knew he was dying.'

She made an odd sound somewhere between a gasp and a sniff. 'Yes, but what did he say?'

'For God's sake, Rosa. The morning, I'll show you in the morning . . .'

No I won't. The letter no longer exists. 'I'll tell you about it in the morning,' he said. And where is the letter she would ask? Disappeared. Disappeared where? Down the plughole. Oh Christ.

The rounded curve of her back huffed at him. 'All right. All right.'

When Rufus was about twelve they had cleaned out the back shed, a process Rufus, his eye peeled for loot, had enjoyed. The local tip had been closed. They had driven around Meadowbank attempting to dump half a sack of solid cement. It had been, they told Rosa later, like attempting to dispose of a body. You wouldn't believe how difficult it is to get rid of something you don't want found.

'When are we going to Milan?' she murmured and slept.

Henry did not sleep.

Of all the idiotic things for a man to do. To ask a wife to hand a letter to her husband which dropped mysterious

173

unspecified hints about a place unknown to her. A place her husband went to alone and had done year after year after year.

The danger had not been in the delivery. Rosa, his love who could deliver, had done so without question.

But what was Henry meant to do with these words from the grave afterwards. Rosa, by her very nature, her affection for the man, would want to know his final message to his lifelong friend.

What was he meant to do with the bloody thing?

His irritation did not last. As he knew, he was blessed or cursed with the ability to see the other side. He had never known whether this was tolerance and thus a good thing, or detachment, which was more suspect. Even with Bianca he preferred to move away, to achieve absence or, failing that, evasion. You have to choose the weapons to suit your goddamn psyche.

And Martin, like so many well-meaning instigators of disaster, would have acted from the highest possible motives; loyalty to Henry and, as he had made clear, to Rosa. They had been good friends. She would grieve for the man.

Presumably, he thought, tossing and turning and tossing again, you remember the dead you have either hated or loved. He was a bad hater, but love had worked for Carla and Andy. The rest, by and large, just shuffled off, removed themselves, ceased to be present.

He had been shocked by Rosa's news at the airport; now all that remained was a vague sense of gratitude tinged with irritation for a man who had served him well in the past, if not now. 'Pneumonia, the old man's friend,' the doctor who attended Mr Felton had said. Something to look forward to.

Henry stirred, put his hand on Rosa's sleeping back. Tonight had not been a good start. He would do better in the morning. No, he wouldn't. The letter would loom. And Bianca. And Rufus. And Gaby.

Oh flaming hell. He flung off the duvet and stumbled down the hall to the lavatory.

There is no point in going for a piss in the middle of night unless it is essential, so why do it. There had been a song when Rufus was a child. A comic song about a dustman, a cockney voice drawling, *When y'get my age, it helps to pass the time.* He trickled, spurted, retrickled and trickled again.

He leaned against the wall, gave a despairing snigger. Now he could go back to bed and worry about Rufus and Gaby.

Gaby was a loose cannon, an unknown quotient, a cipher. Henry rubbed his aching shins. He must stop this jargon tossed off by Rufus. How splendid, how wise to be lying awake at dawn making meaningful resolutions about the purity of the language used in tearing what remained of his mind to pieces. Carla had called such sleepless nights *nuits blanches*. He tried again. Cannon was all right, but not loose. Gaby could go off, she could do a grey deal of damage but, like the guns for the defence of Singapore, she faced in one direction only. In Gaby's case, the direction which served her own interests and those of her partner. There would be no change of direction in Gaby's fire.

His mind churned back to Milan, to Rufus.

They had left Milan the day after the meeting with Grisoni. Rufus had made no enquiries, had not raised the topic either during their days in Paris or their journey home. He had, however, seemed preoccupied; not during business meetings, discussions or demonstrations, but during their free time together he had said little, he had not yarned with strangers. Rufus, Henry knew from past years, had something on his mind. Something other than the world at his fingertips—the air hostess at his elbow, his tiny packet of peanuts—was absorbing his thoughts.

Henry knew he should tackle the subject. He tried several

175

times. He tried at meal times. No, he didn't want his sesame seed roll. Certainly Rufus could have it, and by the way . . . He tried as the green line on the TV screen clocked up seven thousand flight miles and again at nine thousand. He gave up. There are some things beyond the range of words.

As zero five double zero showed on the bedside clock Henry faced facts. He was entirely dependent on Rufus and Gaby's goodwill or, rather, her reaction to his description of the Grisoni meeting. The thought did not cheer him. Nor the sounds of stirring in the room next door. They were talking again. They planned, he remembered, to go straight to the Webster Street house, get a full day's work in seeing it was Sunday. The calendar numerals would be red. People would be buying at the flower stalls of Cimitero Monumentale. Henry closed his eyes and slept.

'Fantastic,' said Rufus, springing about the bare rooms on the balls of his feet. 'Fantastic! You guys have done so much! Who did what?'

Bianca told him. She was happy to do so, she told him how she was an expert on sugar soap now, how it was a joy to watch beautiful wood come up and that she had really enjoyed stripping the scrim though it was an appallingly messy business. My overalls, you wouldn't believe, *and* my hair tied up. But it's wonderful when you see the result. She was quite sorry there were only two small bedrooms to strip, the rest of the house was already gibbed, as he would remember.

Rufus glanced at Gaby. She was at her best when ready for action. She wore black tights, a black long-sleeved T-shirt, and a paint-scarred baseball cap with a purple button. Great body. Tall and skinny, fantastic boobs. Fantastic everything— why didn't Bianca go away, drop dead, bugger off and leave them alone. And Mum would be here in a minute lugging lunch and looking for flat places. Gaby pulled on one of his old shirts spattered with undercoat and looked better than ever. Skinny women do in oversized shirts.

'Who did the high bits?'

Gaby dropped one side of her mouth, gave an exaggerated wink behind Bianca's back and tapped her chest.

'I've just lost a hard-boiled egg,' said Rosa in passing.

'And what did Mum do?'

'The dump,' said Gaby.

'She likes the dump,' said Bianca.

A doorbell rang. Bianca opened it to reveal a man and a woman standing side by side on the verandah. They resembled each other. Same height, same short dark hair, same friendly smiles above matching grey and blue tracksuits. Their express-ions, their obvious desire to be made welcome, to please, reminded Bianca of something. Of course, those two on the news, nodding and smiling and bobbing their haircuts at each other. Bianca closed the door slightly. 'No thank you,' she said, her voice firm.

'Did you think we were Bible-bangers?' laughed the man.

'Don't mind him,' said the woman fondly. She produced a business card, gave it to Bianca and smiled over her shoulder at Gaby.

'Phil and Bettina,' she said, 'Clarion Real Estate.'

They were partners, she explained, very keen, go ahead, pro-active but never intrusive, don't get her wrong. They had a special passion and expertise for old houses, especially those in good condition.

'We were just out for a run, lucky we'd just started,' she laughed, 'but actually we live just up the road and we couldn't resist whizzing in for a sec to say if you're ever in the slightest interested in materialising your assets on this highly desir-able—or it will be, won't it, Phil? It won't look like this much longer, that's for sure. I mean it was sad with the old lady, anyone could see that, but on the other hand an eyesore like this, well, it drags down the whole street. Sticks out like a sore thumb, doesn't it, Phil? There've been complaints, talk of getting the council on to it, it's been that bad, so really the whole thing's a mercy.'

Phil continued without pause. Yeah, he said. He and Bettina just thought they'd slip in and say hi. They didn't want to be pushy, hell no, but just remember—if you want to realise, capitalise, whatever, we're here. Johnny on the spot, so to speak. Know the locality like the back of our hands. Really taking off, this area, all the up-market gentrification going on, good schools, easy access to town.

Bianca was still at the door. 'Oh no, we're not interested in selling, thank you.' She handed the card back. Thank you,' she said again and moved to shut the door.

Gaby put out a long arm and held it wide. 'Why don't you guys come in and have a look around, see what we've been doing while this slob's,' she gave Rufus's buttock an amiable slap, 'been in Milan.'

'*Milan*,' squeaked Bettina.

Gaby pocketed the business card. *Clarion Real Estate— Action's our attraction. Phil Sharp. Bettina Rogers.* 'Come in,' she said, 'Have a good look round. Watch your feet.'

Progress on the house continued through the winter. Rufus, Gaby and Bianca reached the stage that, with luck, comes after chaos, upheaval and change. The stage when they could nod slowly at each other, their faces serious and tinged with something like surprise as they began to think that maybe they were getting there. Sometimes they said it. Bianca said it and was snapped at by Gaby for being premature. Rosa said it and was snapped at by Rufus. Henry told her a mother's place is in the wrong. He distanced himself as far as possible from Webster Street. He was paying for it and wanted nothing more to do with it. His main hope was that Rufus would be so engaged at the office and working himself blind at Webster Street that he would forget about Grisoni. Stranger things had happened.

As Bianca had told them several times, the days were drawing out. Not like Hampshire, of course, those long twilights, the croquet, the lazy summer evenings heavy with the scent of cherry pie. And the light, ah the light. The softness, the mellowness, the absence of glare.

The longer evenings in Meadowbank, however inadequate, were welcome to her. They meant Rufus and Gaby could work on while she came home with Rosa. Enough was enough. She looked forward to the long soak in the bath while Rosa organised the meal and she was, she explained to Henry's wooden stare, developing quite a taste for gin and water. What on earth would they say in Hampshire. No one drank spirits at home now. Well, hardly.

Rufus and Gaby came back at all hours. Sometimes Gaby did not come back at all. Rosa made no enquiries, offered to leave something to heat up and left it at that.

Rufus took her hand one such night, sat down on the ancient pouffe before her and smiled his smile. 'It's time we had a good talk, Mum,' he said. 'While I've got you alone.'

She smiled back, peaceful and friendly as she remembered them, herself and Rufus and Henry.

Rufus said how much he and Gaby appreciated what she and Henry were doing for them.

'Good,' said Rosa, 'I'm glad to hear it.'

'Yeah, well. But the thing is . . .' The thing was apparently what Gaby called Rosa's intensive care, ha ha. Her continuing never-ending concern for them both was getting to them. Gaby was not used to it, she'd been a free agent for years, they both had, what he meant was . . . Well, Gaby had said just the other day, she had asked, Why doesn't your mother get a life?

179

Rosa spoke calmly. 'If Gaby doesn't like it, she can leave. Gaby is free to depart any time she wants to. My life is here, in this house.'

Rufus's head jerked upwards. 'Then I'll go.'

Rosa met his eyes. The adrenalin of rage, outrage, frustration, was both liberating and absurd. 'Do that,' she snapped. 'Your father and I have managed quite happily without sight or sound of you for many years. Just as well in the circumstances.'

Rufus, after a quick glance at her flushed face, stared at his boots in silence. Finally he nodded. 'I see that, Mum, and you're a hundred per cent correct. This is your house, yours and Dad's. Not ours, no way. We fit in with you. Great, happy to do so, great to be here.'

He sighed, stroked a wandering vein on the back of her hand, released it, watched it slip back to its original lie. 'It's just . . . just if you'd just back off a bit, Mum. Gaby and I feel sort of, you know what I mean, threatened. Particularly Gaby. She's used to her own space, needs time out. She's into meditation and that helps but . . .'

This was too much.

'And what about Bianca?' Rosa cried. 'She seems to get on very well with Bianca.'

'Yeah,' said Rufus. 'But that's a different thing again and I'll tell you why. You know where you are with old Bee. She doesn't give a toss. Where does she sit? Easy—the best chair. Which bedroom does she claim? The one with the best outlook and most sun. Tough, Bee, that's the master one.' He paused, stroked the loose vein again, watched it move. 'You know where you are with people like Bee. Your trouble, Mum, is you try too hard. You know what you should do? Stop pussyfooting around, be more up front. Honest, don't give a stuff, state your aim and get on with on it. The three of us, me, Gaby, Bee, we all know where we're coming from. What we're

180

looking at. Where we're heading.'

'I see,' said Rosa. She lifted her head, took a long, hard look at this gentle smiling creature still holding her hand. She stood up, clutched briefly at the chair back. She had had a thought, a thought so disturbing it weakened her knees. You can be destroyed as well as saved by what you believe in. You can love too well. Shakespeare, she thought with rage. Shakespeare had it first. Mother, dreamily reading 'my favourite poet' while Rosa ran in with the tea. She was gulping now, gasping with rage. Damn the man. Sitting up there. Knowing it all. Damn the man and blast his genius. Oh God, dear God.

'I'm going to see Granny.'

Rufus, unaware of cross-currents, glanced at his watch. 'It's five-thirty. Be rush hour on the motorway.'

'Good!' said Rosa. '*Good.*'

He looked at her, opened his mouth and shut it again. He and Gaby could pick up a takeaway on the way home. It had gone off okay. Cool. Gaby would be pleased. He headed for the Skoda.

Wisdom lies in learning what to overlook. A useful thought. It fits in my normal system, my philosophy, I suppose you could call it. Forgive and forget. Unto seventy times? Nay, I say unto thee unto seventy times seven. But not today. Fat chance. That's a laugh, Jesus. And why am I so cross with Bianca? And what would Bianca want with forgiveness. Bianca has done nothing wrong. Bianca, as Rufus says, is operating in exactly the way she has operated from the moment she heaved herself upright and padded off to knock the world into a suitable shape for treatment.

So why am I driving too fast? Why am I speeding along the motorway in my husband's car which fortunately he did not drive to the office today, passing astonished vans and old men in Hondas? The motorway is alive with Hondas and I pass them all. I am tempted to make rude gestures but restrain myself. I pass another one and realise my eyes are wet which enrages me further.

I have never been envious of Bianca. Bianca the beautiful has always been cherished by me. Many people have been cherished by me. We all have our gifts do we not, Jesus, and mine is to be unselfish and drive people mad. 'Move *over*,' I roar at a truck labelled *Top Dog*. It blasts its horn. I blast mine. For a moment, one appalling, degrading moment, I think, They'll be sorry when I'm dead, and then I think, Will they? And the answer is not many of them. Henry. Henry will.

The reason I have never been envious of Bianca is simple. It is not from virtue.

Envy is the desire for something you would like to own and do not have. The desire for adulation and antiques has passed me by. That's all.

But jealousy—ah, jealousy is different; meaner, leaner and bitter to taste, jealousy centres on what you have and do not want to lose. Like sons. I am jealous of Bianca because my son admires her more than he does me. This is a shameful thought, corrosive, and piercing as a dart with poison. Jealousy is not a vague sullenness like envy. Anything but.

I am not jealous of Gaby. She has engaged my son's admiration and love. His passion for her is as it should be. Leavest thou thy father and thy mother and cleavest thou to whoever. Rufus had little enough familial affection before Gaby appeared and I want every ounce of what is still on offer, which is silly, for we all know, do we not, that love is limitless and self-engendering. It does not come in pots. It is a bottomless cup.

'Move over, you clown.' I shriek at a man on a yellow tractor at Granny's gate. He smiles, waves at me, I scowl at his red-pleated neck.

And why in the name of all that's merciful did I lie about

182

Martin leaving me money. What did I think I was doing. Rosa, little Rosa, Rosa honest as the day, lying gratuitously. That's the word—gratuitously—lying for free, for no reason, no sense, nothing. Lying as a child might lie, to counteract rejection, to be allowed to play too. Lying for love, and what do you mean by love? What do you know about love? Everything. Nothing. I am going to explode. Mad, quite mad. *Mad, bad and dangerous to know.* Caroline Lamb and Rosalind Felton. What a pair.

Mrs Felton senior waved from the sunporch. She was at leisure. She lay with her feet up on the ancient humpy couch reading *The New Zealand Poultry Farmer.* The previous owner of the cottage, an old man rake-thin and fading fast, had been asleep in the sun the day she had come to view the house. It had seemed to be a good omen; both porch and couch became desirable selling points. She made her offer that day and has never regretted it. You need sun.

She flicked the magazine in greeting. 'I was thinking about capons, lot of money in capons. Bit technical, of course, but . . .' She swung woollen-covered legs to the ground and sat up. 'Why are you here?'

That's a thought. Why am I here? Rosa picked an open book from the floor. *While female and infant capuchins socialise,* she read, *the males are somewhere else.* She sat down. 'No reason,' she said. 'Just one of those mad irrepressible impulses I have now and then.'

Mrs Felton smiled, slipped tiny feet into ancient shoes. 'Ah, one of those.' Her glance sharpened. 'All well at home?'

'Yes. I've just got a touch of the sours.' Rosa put the book on a table, repositioned it carefully, as though it were important, as important as the placement of a garden gnome with a fishing pole by a proud suburban pond. Rufus had loved gnomes.

183

'With which one?'

'Me.'

Mrs Felton adjusted her cardigan with a quick twitch. 'No point in that.'

'No,' said Rosa, her eyes still on wildlife. There are upstairs bush babies in the highest levels of the rain forest and downstairs bush babies far below. They never interbreed. They have fingernails. Howler monkeys make the largest noise in South America.

'I told the most ridiculous lie the other day,' she said.

'You haven't come thirty miles in the rush hour to tell me that.'

Rosa gave an unattractive damp snort. 'Oh, do stop going on about the rush hour.'

'I haven't started. Tell me the whopper.'

Rosa's face was strained, pulled tight about the mouth. 'I told Gabrielle that Martin Brown had left me a large sum of money.'

Mrs Felton restrained herself. Laughter is not the right medicine for the afflicted, however comic their wounds. 'Why on earth?'

'And she told Bianca. And Bianca asked me if it was true and I said yes.'

'Two whoppers.'

'Exactly. I said it because I knew it would infuriate her, make her jealous. I wanted her to be jealous. Of me, I wanted them both to be jealous of me. You know what I mean . . .'

'No.'

'That makes two of us.'

They sat in silence. A cattle beast lowed. 'Do you know why the sky's blue?' asked Rosa.

'No,' said Mrs Felton again.

'It's one of ten simple scientific facts everyone's meant to know. I saw it somewhere and I don't know. Not that one.'

How peaceful it is here. Grass oozing chlorophyll, cows chewing, clouds scudding. And no people, no people at all. I have backed the wrong horse as regards peace. Granny has been right all along. She has gone where people are not. You don't have to lie and fuss and grizzle. You can go someplace else. Take time out.

'May I stay the night?' she said.

'Certainly, if you like tripe and onions.'

Rosa grinned. 'Not much.'

'There's probably a chop somewhere. We'll feed the hens. And tomorrow you can go home and stop being so—what's that dreadful word they use now—caring.'

'I am caring.'

'Why?'

'Because I am.'

'Hopeless,' sniffed Mrs Felton.

'You're meant to love people.'

'Worse than hopeless.'

Rosa put her hand on Mrs Felton's knee, begging her to retract, to revoke heresy while the flames licked. 'No, Granny. You've got it all wrong.'

Mrs Felton's voice was stern. 'One minute you're telling lies so you can hate and be hated by your nearest and dearest, the next you're telling me I must love everyone. You're not making sense, Rosa.'

Rosa's face was anguished. 'If I'd made sense anywhere else I wouldn't have come,' she cried.

Mrs Felton stood, brushed her skirt with a quick, impatient hand and stared at her daughter-in-law. Goodness is completely natural to this woman. She is unaware that she is in any way unusual. The knowledge has not penetrated.

'Hens,' she said.

*

Mrs Felton's hens were in clover. Like Aztec sacrificial god kings, they were pampered, tempted with delights and cherished until the knife struck. They ranged far and wide, converging across green pastures at meal times like spokes to a hub.

Mrs Felton watched them, encouraged stragglers with a shake of the feed tin. 'Did I ever tell you about Andy?' she said securing the door after the final head count.

Rosa straightened from her inspection of a skittery white leghorn with blood on its head. It must be low in the pecking order. Or high.

'No,' she said.

Mrs Felton's voice was thoughtful. 'I found a magazine under his bed one morning beside a mummified apple core. Very unusual it was too. Fetishes, women's shoes mostly.' She placed a hand on the rough wooden door frame for a moment, her voice lifted. 'Goodnight, girls,' she called and banged the last chaff from the tin.

Rosa swallowed. There is no end to the surprises contained within this woman. Never has been and never will.

'Why are you telling me?' said Rosa.

'I don't know,' said Mrs Felton, staring across paddocks.

'Did you discuss it with Mr Felton?'

The pale eyes snapped. 'Why on earth would I do that?'

They walked in silence to the next gate. The breeze was soughing in the plantation, moving branches from side to side, lifting and lowering against a pale sky.

'What I do wish,' said Mrs Felton finally, 'is that I had the sense to talk to him about it. That is one of the things that worries me. Something like that, something as simple as a difference of that sort.' She turned to Rosa, her face fierce, her fingers gripping the rusting tin. 'That wouldn't have worried him, would it? Couldn't have affected him in some way? Made him desperate?'

'No,' said Rosa, her heart thumping and her voice firm. 'I couldn't have borne that. The waste.'

Parsley and mashed potato dripping butter and freshly picked spinach helped the tripe slip down, although that is one of its least attractive aspects. Give me bones, chew, texture. Slime and slide are not for me.

It is odd my being here at all. As a child I had gone next door and told old Mrs Buxton I had come to eat cake, which at least made sense. I am not sure that driving, through the rush hour, let us not forget, to eat tripe and sleep on a lumpy mattress in an arctic spare bedroom is rational behaviour at my age or indeed any.

Mrs F's revelation of Andy's predilection has not helped. I do not mean to be glib. I came to confide in Mrs F and she has confided back. Which I had not expected. I do not know what to make of either the revelation or the fact that Mrs F should tell it to me, as casually as if it had happened yesterday, as if she had just remembered this bit of chat. I must talk to Henry.

But a trouble shared is not a trouble spared or halved or whatever the received wisdom promises. Quite the reverse. It is a weakness revealed, by me in this case, to a woman without them. The kapok pillow in the spare room will not help either.

We are all on our Pat Malone. My friend Martin knew that and he told me. I should have told God or nobody. God. Hey, God.

And there is something else now. Another thought I do not like the look of. Why did Rufus send me so many pairs of shoes? Three is not many. Three is three. And he has already bought Gaby four pairs. She told me. Four, she said.

The hairs on the back of my neck rise.

'What are you going to do about your whopper?' says

Mrs F, pouring coffee. The telephone rings and I leap to answer it.

It is Henry. When am I coming home?

I am not, not tonight. I will come home in the morning.

'Why on earth?'

I need, I say, time out.

'Don't be idiotic!'

I nearly tell him he can't take a joke. I don't. I realise that Henry is angry. Very angry.

'I have to take the car in tomorrow,' he snaps.

'Oh. What for?'

Bad tempered, can't take a joke and puerile to boot. 'Servicing!' he yells in triumph.

'I'll take it in when I get back.'

More triumph. 'It's due in at 8.30 am.'

Calm, bitchkin, cool. 'Well, it won't be.'

Mrs Felton takes the receiver. 'Henry, do stop nagging,' she says. 'Rosa will be in tomorrow morning. Goodnight,' she says and replaces the receiver.

My calm melts. Mrs F has gone too far.

Henry stared at the receiver in astonishment. He replaced it, noticed how well it slipped into its mount. Yin and yang. *Home is the sailor, home from the sea.* He examined the fit. Someone had designed it, had made drawings, had worked, thought and dreamed this design. Had planned the ergonomic aspect, the aesthetics, the quality of the product. All this effort involving years of work by a team of experts to benefit the consumer, and he had never given it a thought until this moment.

It seemed wrong somehow.

ten

They sat by side by side backed by Geyser Grey walls, their legs extended on unsanded wood. Their hands dipped to fish, to chips, to chips again. There was a good guy around the corner.

Their silence, filled with chewing or otherwise, was contented.

'Finished?' said Rufus eventually.

Gaby nodded, reached for a cigarette. She lit it slowly, stared at the glow.

Rufus stood, jigged about, stretched and jigged again before collapsing. 'Numb bum.'

Gaby exhaled deeply. 'Tell me exactly what that guy in Milan said?'

'Oh Christ, not again.'

'It's important.'

Indolent, graceful as a cat, she changed position to lie beside him, to watch the smoke spiralling. She put her hand on his chest, waited till his covered it.

'You haven't a clue, have you?'

He yawned. 'What about?'

'How important it is.'

'For Mum?'

'For us, dumb fuck.'

He lay silent, closed his eyes. Two jobs per day was getting to him. She would explain eventually. He wouldn't have to ask.

Her voice was soft, soothing as the fingers removing his cigarette. 'You'll burn yourself,' she murmured.

His eyelids were glued together, his mind a blank. 'Nn.' He smelled the acrid stench, heard the small grinding movement of the butt on the old paint lid.

'Did you hear what I said?'

'Yes.'

There was a quick kick at his thigh. 'Don't go to sleep.'

He made a superhuman effort, dragged his mind back. 'Why for us?'

'Because,' she murmured, 'you know something your father would rather you didn't.'

Rufus's eyes snapped open. 'So?'

She is lying back on her elbows, her face amused, almost pitying. 'So,' she says back.

Something is shifting, floorboards, concrete piles, tectonic plates.

I clutch the ankle inside my old Auckland Grammar sock. 'What do you mean?'

'Oh shit, Rufus. Work it out.'

My hand tightens, she kicks it off.

Her voice sharpens. It happens with switched-on women, it's part of the deal and a pain in the butt. 'Why do I always have to think of everything?' she says.

'Okay. Tell me, smart arse.'

She rolls over on her stomach. 'This place is freezing in winter.' She sits up, brushes her front like Bee, but it bounces.

She is right. You can feel the draught through the floorboards. More than a draught, a bloody gale.

'Well, you can't have carpet.' I stroke the wood. 'It's rough now but it will come up, be a feature. Heart kauri, wood like this, it'd be sacrilege. Besides, there's Bee-baby's rugs.'

She hasn't heard a word. 'It will be freezing. Thirty below.'

I watch her like a hawk watches lambs' eyes. Gaby is thinking hard.

'We would be better off to sell it,' she says finally.

I explain as if she's slipped a cog. 'It's not ours to sell. And besides, the whole idea was for them to get shot of Bee.'

'Onto us.'

'Yeah,' I say. 'Onto us. Get it?'

She is getting mad too. 'I'm not going to live with that old bag.'

'I thought you got on okay.'

'Any old bag would be one too many. And stop treating me like I'm brain dead.'

'You act like it.' I put on a sweet sour voice like an old doll in a supermarket nagging the geriatric trundler beside her who's got parsley when she said persimmons. 'Sell the house, dear? How can we, dear, when it isn't ours to sell?'

'It could be,' says Gaby and uncurls herself. I could watch her stand, sit, bend, move forever.

The door bell rings.

'That'll be Phil and Bets,' she says.

Phil and Bets had just popped in for a minute. They weren't going to interrupt, no way. But they just couldn't resist a quick squiz to see how things were going. They couldn't believe how much had been achieved already. Not if you'd told them. They pranced around the house, demonstrating. Hey, Bets. Look at this. Hey, Phil, over here. Not an ounce of undercoat left, would you believe, and wow, look at those skirting boards. They knew, both of them had realised their potential immediately, or rather Phil had, the only time he'd had a glimpse inside. He'd been flogging chicken shit for the Lions, you

191

should have heard the old girl's language. Well, she had a point, Phil could see that, she was knee-deep in shit already like she said. But even then, just from a glimpse beneath the shambles and muck and newspapers for miles, Phil had seen the potential in those boards. Someone had done a wonderful job on them, that was for sure. He dropped on his haunches to stroke, looked up smiling. 'Great job. Who's the expert?'

Gaby's tongue slid from side to side behind her top lip.

'Bee, wasn't it, hon?' said Rufus.

'The English lady?'

'She's not English. She just talks like that.'

'My aunt,' said Rufus. 'She's going to live here.'

So Gaby and Rufus were doing it up for the old lady as well? Bets thought that was amazing. Imagine putting all this work in to a place you weren't going to own outright. Phil had to say straight out, he couldn't put that sort of commitment in to something he wasn't going to own, period. No, Bets didn't reckon she could either.

'It'll be ours eventually,' said Rufus. 'Come and see the gibbing in the back bedroom.'

They were proud of the gibbing. It had been a killer at the end, they'd been up most of the night, those gib boards can weigh a ton.

Bettina said Gaby must be Wonder Woman. Rufus patted Gaby's behind and told Bets she was so right.

'We haven't painted this one yet,' said Gaby. 'Come and see, before and after.'

They walked down the hall talking. Bettina's cellphone rang. She said she was busy right now but she would get back to the caller later. Not a problem.

They left soon afterwards. Bets promised she'd pop in again soon.

Gaby told her to do that.

'Nice guys,' said Rufus.

'Yeah.'

They stood at the door, watched them walk up the street. Bettina waved her cellphone.

A small girl in a pink satin-topped tutu and ballet shoes danced past clutching a balloon.

'Where do y'reckon she's going?'

'God knows,' said Gaby.

She took his arm. They stayed side by side at the open door. There was not much to see, asphalt, a picket fence, a bottlebrush in bloom. But they liked it here.

'What did you mean,' said Rufus carefully, 'when you said we could own this place?'

She took his arm, closed the door. 'Come and I'll tell you.'

'No,' said Rufus, 'no, I will not. What the hell do you think I am?' He was striding around the empty space, springing from the balls of his feet in outrage. Dust stirred beneath his feet, resettled, stirred again. He turned to face her, dropped onto his heels to squat face to face. 'Apart from anything else, it's illegal. Blackmail is, didn't you know?'

Her eyes widened. Beneath the cropped hair they were huge, misunderstood, famished. 'Who's talking about blackmail? I'm suggesting you talk things through. Find out what it's all about, see if you can help your Dad. The poor old guy's obviously fussed about something. He can't sleep. The toilet's going half the night. It can't still be jet lag after all these months. Talk things through. It's the least you can do.'

They were still eyeball to eyeball. 'Okay, so here we go. "Hi, Dad, what's fussing you . . ."'

'Right.'

'Then he says, "Nothing." Then what?'

Gaby dragged a hand through yellow stubble, wrapped her bent skull in both hands. 'God, you're hopeless.'

'We'll have the title eventually.'

She crossed her legs, lit a cigarette with a virulent pink Bic and blew. 'I wouldn't bet on it.'

His eyes stung with smoke. When he opened them she was standing staring out the naked sash windows to the darkening garden. He was on his feet beside her. 'Now listen . . .'

'Listen nothing. Talk about a dysfunctional family. What a shower, what a pack of screwballs! What am I *doing* here!'

'We're a team!' he yelled. 'The two of us.'

Sudden as rain in Auckland, she calmed down, nodded her head in silence, kept on nodding like a dipping duck. At last she raised her head, looked at him for a moment, then smiled into his eyes. 'Okay. So I'll talk to him if you're so shit scared.'

'Why?' he begged. 'What good will it do? We can't kick Bee out, title or no title.'

'Who said anything about kicking her out?'

Gaby stroked the pink lighter, turned it over, stroked again. 'You know something? I wouldn't trust your Auntie Bee with a flat tyre. She's as ruthless as your Dad's gutless. How'd she get him to buy it in the first place? I reckon she's got some sort of lean on the guy.'

She lit a cigarette, sighed through smoke. 'I'd hate to be in her power.'

'You smoke too much.'

She kissed him, her lips warm and smoky. 'Any other complaints?'

The rain began as they were tidying up, fat drops splashing from a dark sky. By the time they reached the Skoda it was torrential, lashed horizontal by the sudden storm.

'You'd better drive,' said Gaby. 'I can't see in this muck.'

The gutters were full, water was swirling across intersections, flash flooding down drives. The wind increased, broke branches, rattled and banged and roared through Meadowbank. The Skoda leaked.

194

Henry opened the door for them. 'A rough night,' he said.

'Yeah.' Rufus glanced around the dark sitting room. The only light fell from beneath a drunken pleated shade above Henry's chair. 'Where is everyone?'

Henry picked up the paper. 'Bianca is having an Early Night in capitals. Much good may it do her in this racket. And your mother, fortunately, had already decided to stay the night with Granny.'

'Why on earth?'

Gaby dropped her wet parka on the floor and sank onto the sofa.

Henry stared morosely at print. 'Carnage,' he said. 'Chechnya, Rwanda. When's it going to end?'

'I don't know.' Rufus flopped on the sofa beside Gaby. 'Is Granny sick then?'

'No. Your mother said she wanted Time Out. She's also in to capitals tonight.' He flapped pages, folded, soothed, laid them to rest beside his chair. 'The difference being, of course, that Bianca is always in capitals. Everything she says or does or eats or thinks requires them. They are hers, ergo, they cap. I hope to God Rosa's not catching it.'

'Time out? Mum?'

'That's what she said. To give her her due, she was sending it up. Rosa doesn't need cant. She just goes away and has a good sulk, like any other sensible human being. Or cat. Cats are great sulkers, but you can enjoy them.'

Rufus stared at him. Even a non-noticer will notice if the head is spotlit. The old man looked tired, his hair in need of a wash, the lines on his face deepened by shadows. He was banging on, talking crap, shuffling his feet back and forth on the non-existent pile of the carpet. Rufus could not remember Rosa ever having left him alone before, even for a night. It was mad, he had told her, crazy. Shit, he leaves you enough. And here was Henry, bereft, ill at ease already.

195

As was Rufus.

His father was still talking. 'Have you ever noticed Bianca's unusual emphases? She does it continually, some women do, saves thinking, I suppose. But Bianca's a ripper. She goes for the adverbs. She *thoroughly* enjoyed her lunch with Naomi Fitchett. Why are we told how thorough her enjoyment was? Unlike others' sweaty old enjoyment, Bianca's enjoyment was the dinkum oil—fully paid-up enjoyment while the rest of us slobs have to make do with . . .'

Rufus stopped listening, caught Gaby's eye while Henry rattled on. Her mouth moved, exaggerated, silent and pregnant with meaning. *Now. Tonight.*

Give us a break, he mouthed back. She didn't get it, but his face was enough. She yawned, put a long-fingered hand to her mouth. 'Pardon me,' she said, 'but I'm stuffed. Night.' She put a hand on Rufus's head in blessing and left.

He turned to watch, was rewarded by a wave and a damp smacking kiss in the air. He could see her bony arms clutched around her, her bounding strides along the passage, her unspoken trust.

Henry was lying in his chair with his eyes closed.

'Dad?'

The eyes opened, took a moment to focus. Rufus lit a cigarette, offered one and was refused. Had Rufus not noticed he was about the only person left in the place not puffing his head off?

'And Mum.'

'As you say.'

'Why hasn't she come home?'

'I told you. Time bloody out.'

'Oh, come on, Dad.' Rufus leaned back. 'The springs in this thing are shot.'

'Very possibly.' Henry heaved himself upright. 'Now if you'll excuse me, I think I'll go to bed.'

Rufus could feel his heart pumping. Adrenalin. Power. Shame.

'Does Mum know Mr Grisoni?'

Henry sat down. 'No.'

Rufus leaned forward to flick ash. Memo: Tell Gaby. Dad didn't ask which Grisoni.

'Why do you ask?'

'I just wondered.'

Henry stretched his legs, examined a polished shoe. 'How could she? She's never been to Italy.'

Rufus's jaw clamped tight. He nodded slowly. 'True,' he said. 'True.' There was a pause, quite a long pause before he looked up smiling, to ask the next idle question. 'What was Grisoni senior on about that night?'

No daggers in that smile. It was comradely, understanding. Henry's heart moved in response. Decent of the boy not to rush him, to give him time, to wait for the right moment to talk man to man.

He was tempted to confide in him. He had never confided in anyone, except Andy. You only need one.

There need be no details, just a sentence would do. I had an affair with his sister-in-law. For years. For years and years and years.

Rufus, perhaps, might understand. Isn't that what happens among comrades, between members of a fraternity. They do not need things spelt out. They know the rules. They tolerate, forgive, but most of all they understand.

But not sons.

The reason I cannot tell you I have betrayed (too strong a word, but then again not) your mother, Rufus, is because she is precious to me, essential. I have always loved her. In a different way from Carla, of course. In my fashion.

And, let us not forget, I never had these qualms of conscience, never felt the need to be absolved when the likelihood

197

of being found out was minimal. When Rosa was innocent and Martin loyal to the end, Henry was carefree. Too happy, happy Henry.

We are all going to pay for our train rides. The presence of the conductor merely confirms this intention.

He had lived a charmed life for thirty years. He would not lose it now, not what remained. He thought of himself snapping down the telephone at Rosa. He wanted her, needed her sitting beside him, her small hand in his.

Rufus's kind eyes were waiting for his.

Henry smiled back. 'It's a long story. How about a whisky?' He stared out the drenched window at the storm still flattening the garden. 'It's a good night for it. We must do something about that branch of the puriri.'

Rufus grinned. 'We?'

'All right. You.'

Henry walked slowly to the kitchen. He had the bones of his skeleton story hanging together, had had since Milan and the long flight home. He had taken them out to check occasionally, had shaken them briefly and put them back in their closet. Bare bones only, but available.

Henry squinted through amber. 'Happy days.'

Rufus raised his glass to the dark window. 'Nothing like a good storm when you're not out in it.'

Henry told his story. He explained that the mutual dislike between himself and Marco Grisoni went back many years.

'Like thirty-five years?'

'Longer,' said Henry.

Grisoni senior was ruthless, manipulative and had the business ethics of an alley cat. He was also abusive and a bully. The woman he mentioned, Henry had indeed known her . . .

'Carla Grisoni?'

'. . . Yes.' He had had occasion to rescue her, literally, once

198

many years ago, at a restaurant. Grisoni had been drunk, the other guests had left in disgust, Grisoni was storming, out of his mind, insisting she eat his zabaglione. She didn't want it, was in tears, begging for mercy, then Grisoni suddenly lurched off to the mens and he and Signora Grisoni had slipped away. The man had never forgiven him.

Henry gave Bianca's long, pained sigh. '"Terrible man. Terrible."'

Rufus took a pull on his whisky. 'Doesn't look the sort of guy to fuss about a pudding.'

'No.'

'Why did Giacomo say, "That one?"?'

'Obviously his uncle had told him of the incident. All those years ago. Extraordinary.'

Rufus lit a cigarette, watched the smoke. 'Festered, do you reckon? The insult?'

Henry looked up sharply. Rufus smiled back. 'So you didn't have an affair with the lady?' he said gently. 'Nothing of that nature.'

'Good God, no.'

'Mmm. Mum'll be interested. Be something new to tell her. She's always on to me about Italy. Who do we see, who do we meet in Milan? Human interest is meat and potatoes to Mum. It's a drag punting up stuff to keep her happy. Look, Mum, I say, give us a break. It's over. It's happened. I've forgotten.'

'No,' said Henry. 'There's no point in telling your mother.'

Rufus smiled, patted the bony knee beneath the tweed. He sang the weepie slowly.

'Hush, not a word to Mary,
She might not understand.'

Henry stared at him without emotion. He had none. It had disappeared, gone somewhere else. Left him dry as a burnt sack. Did he know what he was doing to him, this man, this buffoon in front of him.

Henry stood up, stumbled slightly, righted himself. 'Very well,' he said and headed for the door. He turned around, hesitated. Where was he going? There was nowhere to go. He turned, gripped the architrave.

'Rufus,' he said to this stranger. 'I think I should remind you that you are entirely dependent on my goodwill and your mother's. We own the house you and Gaby intend to live in.' He paused, a muscle twitched. 'With Bianca.'

'I know that, Dad. I've told you how grateful I am, we are . . .'

'We?' said Henry.

Rufus nodded. 'But the thing is, Dad. Come back and I'll tell you.' Rufus leaned forward, put his cards on the table. 'I don't trust Bianca. That's something you have to hoist in. That's my gut feeling. Nothing to do with Gaby. I like Bianca, don't get me wrong. We both do. But . . .'

Henry knew what he should say. He heard the words forming in his head. He should tell his son that he understood perfectly, that not another word was required, that he realised that Rufus knew the truth and if his father did not hand over the Webster Street title he would explain to his mother that her happy marriage of over thirty years had been a mockery.

He should tell his son to leave the house and not return. He should strip layers of charm from the man and tell him to fuck off. To publish and be damned. There are words to demolish treachery, words waiting for use.

Words he would not use.

A love affair of such length, which had begun while his wife was pregnant, cannot, however deviously, be presented as a casual fling to be expunged by time. Rosa would be the fall guy of a bad joke, her trust confounded, her innocence betrayed. Rosa, the proud loser, would leave him. She would love him, and leave him.

He came back and sat down, picked up his abandoned drink.

'Why do you not trust Bianca?'

'Now don't misunderstand me. Bianca and I get on well. She's been good to me. But she's a total egocentric, know what I mean?'

'Yes,' said Henry.

'I feel, and okay, yeah, Gaby does too, that when she gets all her gear around her she'll want to get shot of us, to expand. There's no room for all her stuff. It looks crowded already. Stuff like that needs space, room to be seen.'

'Rufus, I don't think you understand. Bianca cannot "get shot of you" because she doesn't own the title. And how could I be sure you wouldn't get rid of her?'

'For God's sake, Dad!'

Henry did not look at him. He took a gulp of whisky, held it in his mouth. The sensible thing to do would be to hate, but that had never been an option.

'I'll require confirmation, in writing, from you that you will make no attempt to get rid of Bianca.'

Rufus lifted his empty glass, peered through it. 'If you insist.'

'I do.'

'Okay.'

'And you'll . . . ?'

Henry heaved himself upright. 'Turn the light out when you come,' he said, 'and check the windows. It's getting worse.'

Gaby sat up in the dark. 'Okay?'

Rufus slumped onto the other bed, pulled off his Reeboks and stayed sitting. 'Yeah.' His hands hung low between his knees. 'Jesus wept,' he said and rolled over.

'Come over here.'

'No, I'm buggered.'

She tried again in the morning. Had he or had he not got

the title? What had Henry said? How was she to know what was going on if he wouldn't tell her what the fuck happened. She flung clothes on as though she hated them, strode around the room, waved her arms and snarled.

Rufus let her rip. It was unlike Gaby, cool, laid back Gaby. He continued dressing in silence: suit, tie, all the gears to keep him together, to stop him falling to pieces and hitting the fan.

Finally he rounded on her. He tugged his Italian silk tie donated by Signor Monti throttling tight and told her. He was virtually sure that Henry would give them the title to the house, that he had done as she had suggested and he would do no more. If she wanted details she could ask Henry. 'Ask him,' he yelled and stormed out the door to catch the bus.

He passed Bianca in the hall. She had had a terrible night. Terrible.

Henry also caught an early bus.

Rosa came home to watery sunshine and an empty house. She walked around smiling, plumped a cushion, plucked a dead daisy from a vase. This is what it would be like when they had all gone; old shoe comfort once more with her friend Henry.

No lies, no idiotic behaviour, no jealousy. Normal service would be resumed as soon as possible.

She would ring him. Hullo, love. It's me. Will you pick up the car? Great. See you later.

And today she would catch up on the *Guardian Weekly*s. She would read them as Henry read them. She would start at the beginning and go on to the end. She would no longer snatch and grab headlines, or life, on the run. She was no fool and would cease behaving like one. Time is the art of the Swiss and not only the Swiss. What you do with what you have is up to you.

*

202

Time passed, they used their days. What else could they do with them. Tensions ranged from Henry's, who was either virtually moribund or irascible, through Gaby's silence and Rufus's preoccupied frown to Bianca's blithe unawareness of anything unusual in the home. She stood and watched rain fall. There had been a lot of rain in Meadowbank, the dead sparrow had either sunk or been buried. She did not bother to inquire which. It had gone, which was an improvement, and soon she would be counting the days, soon her container would arrive. Soon she would be surrounded by her own things in what would shortly be her own house once she had had a word with Henry. She would wait until they had made the move. There was no point in rushing it. Things would fall in to place. Speed bonnie boat.

Rosa also was calm. Her brush with hysteria had passed. She had ceased going to Webster Street. Her dumping skills were no longer required. She would run up some new cushions. She had not yet confessed her lie but she planned to do so and would when the opportunity offered. She could not think how she had got herself in such a state.

Mrs Felton was definitely going into capons, she had been to see a man nearby and had Rosa got over the sours? Good. Good.

But Henry was a concern. He had always been a compara-tively silent man and, like his father, prone to sorrow at the state of the world. But he had been amusing, fun to meet and greet, an amiable man to have about the home and seldom bad-tempered. Rosa still felt pleased when she saw him loping up the street from the bus with his longer-legged version of Rufus's prance. Now things were different. His gloom was constant, his parsimony, or rather his concern for money, increased. It was like living with Scrooge McDuck.

At night in bed he was loving and tender. More so, if anything. And unhappy. She had tried to help.

'What's the matter?'

'Nothing.'

'Oh, come on, Henry.'

'We'll need new tyres soon.'

She felt like telling him not to mind, that she would kiss it better. 'Worse things have happened at sea,' she told him.

'The two back ones.'

And he was not sleeping. At night when not holding her close he behaved more like the Ghost Who Walks than a demented duck. It was not funny. It was not funny at all.

Rosa got into the garden and stayed there. Each day was filled with the resurrection of lost treasures and the restoration of mangled remains. The garden centres were in bloom: punnets of pansies for instant glow, groundcover and bright bedders by the mile.

They did the packing themselves and Rufus hired a van.

'*The great day dawned bright and sunny,*' said Rosa. 'Remember Bee? School essays. *What I did in the holidays.*'

Bianca inspected the last of the boiled egg she had requested. She was going to have a Big Day. 'No.' She peered closer and put down her spoon. 'This *egg,*' she said, 'has been *fertilised.*' She moved the plate away with a little shiver of rejection.

Henry laughed. 'Do you the world of good.'

Gaby agreed. A bit of what the rooster did would set Bee up a treat for her big day. She winked at Rufus. He avoided her eye, looked across the familiar room at the new cushions glowing in a corner. They showed up the rest, made them look more faded and beat up than ever.

He found himself on his feet. He just wanted to thank Mum and Dad for all they had done over the past months for them all. He couldn't thank them enough and he'd like to take the chance to say how very much . . .

Henry, his face tundra bleak, stood up and walked from the room.

'No, no, no,' cried Rosa. 'We were happy to, weren't we . . .' She stopped, confused by Henry's departure.

Bianca and Gaby gazed at the speaker. Bianca in surprise, Gaby with something like concern.

The timing of Bianca's boat was perfect. It sailed in to the container wharf a fortnight after the move and her container was transferred to Webster Street with dispatch. Bianca had to admit she was quite impressed.

She was excited as a child at Christmas, joyful and triumphant and determined to unpack each gift herself. No one must help. She stood in the centre of the still-empty sitting room and explained. Certainly Rufus could help with the furniture. She couldn't handle that. She gave a small throaty chuckle. 'But in the meantime—no thank you, Gabrielle, I'd rather do the china cartons myself. It will be lovely to see them all again.'

It was not. It was heartbreaking. Many things were broken. Many, many things. The toll mounted; shards of Derby lay beside broken Worcester, a Meissen parrot had lost its beak, a pug an ear, an early chocolate jug lay in fragments.

Bianca, who minutes before seemed about to hop on one leg from sheer wanton joy, was now beside herself with grief. She knelt beside the wreckage, her normally calm face twisted, her arms wrapped about her head as she rocked backwards and forwards, backwards and forwards, keening with the agony of loss.

Her things, her things, all her pretty things smashed to pieces, broken beyond redemption, lost and gone forever.

Rufus and Gaby stared at her in bewilderment. Rufus dropped on his knees beside her, attempted comfort. Mentioned insurance. Damages.

Bianca scrambled to her feet, tripped, stumbled, straightened herself and came at him, her fingers stiff, her face a mask of hate. 'Insurance!' she screamed. 'What use is *insurance*? They are *gone*. Gone, you fool. Gone.'

Rufus wiped spittle, backed instinctively. 'The container must have been dropped. You can sue.'

His lack of comprehension fuelled her despair. '*Sue*. What's the point of *sueing*.' She became incoherent, flung wrapping material about, wept for her treasures, her vanished trove. She seemed to have none of the blinding rage he would have expected against those responsible for the tragedy, no steely desire for revenge, for recompense to soothe her broken heart. This was true grief, naked and pure and incalculable.

'You can get some of them mended,' said Gaby.

Bianca stared at her in horror and collapsed. She fell in a heap on the bare boards and lay weeping. Gaby dropped on her knees beside her, took the grey head in her arms and stroked it. 'There, there, Bee,' she said. 'There, there.'

Rufus stood silent beside the wreckage, looking at his partner. Her eyes were damp with tears as she bent to comfort, to help the distraught old woman.

'Come on,' she said. 'I'll get you a hottie. Roof and me'll sort this out.' She helped the trembling woman to her feet, guided her to the door. 'Okay?' she said, 'okay?'

She came back to the sitting room, and sank cross-legged beside him. He had finished the unpacking of the damaged carton. It was a sorry sight. Totalled, virtually totalled.

'See what I mean?' she said.

'Poor old girl,' he muttered.

'That's not what I mean.'

Bianca's grief had disturbed him. He was no good at it. He frowned, focused his eyes on hers and waited.

'She's out of her tree,' said Gaby. 'Completely. One hundred per cent, like I said.'

He didn't remember her saying that and said so. Gaby lifted a hand, flicked the charge to the tiled fire surround. 'She's lost it. Completely lost it. Have you ever seen anything like that performance? She needs counselling, professional help. And quickly.'

'She was upset,' he muttered.

'You can say that again.'

They discussed Bianca at some length. Bianca was all right. Bianca was not, Bianca would need watching. Gaby had met hysterics before, some complete flakes, junkies, the lot, but never anything like this.

'Have we got any beer?' she said suddenly.

'A couple of cans. Why?'

'Let's go and see Phil and Bets.' She flung her arms about, demonstrated lack of air.

Bianca was asleep when they left.

'See?' said Gaby.

Rufus shook his head. He didn't see, he didn't see anything.

He had followed Henry after his abrupt departure during his words of thanks, had found him in the office staring vacantly out the window. He had tried to communicate with him, to get things on line. He stood at the door, hating the el cheapo desk, the sleazy chair. So much for fucking style.

'Dad?' he said.

Henry turned. 'I have changed the title to your name as you requested. If you say one word, and I mean just that, of this transaction, I'll change it again.' He smiled. 'To Bianca's name.'

The smile, that loaded smile reminded Rufus of Milan. He saw Marco Grisoni and his father. Saw brains which had turned to brawn.

He told Gaby about the title that night. She was delighted. He left out the smile. The smile had upset him, upset him a lot.

eleven

And then came the good weather, the early summer days with not a hint of humidity when al fresco hits the city and Aucklanders realise yet again they have it made. When the scraping of hulls and painting is finished, the rush to get the boats in the water over and the yachties' winter work done. Now comes the good part. They have earned it and will go for it, weekend after weekend the whole summer long, they promise each other in pubs all over town and glasses and stubbies are lifted and eyes acknowledge and wink back. This is the life. Work's a bitch but there'll be time over. All the time in the world. This is what life in Auckland's all about, they say. Too fucking right. Long summer days when North Shore commuters fall off the bus and down to the beach, in theory if not in fact, to be greeted by wives and lovers and small naked children scurrying to welcome. Gosh/shit, say the women as they slap sunscreen on wriggling brown bodies. Is it that time already?

In these days Bianca recovered her calm, or most of it. No one would ever know or understand her loss. She realised this immediately. Gaby, Rufus, even Rosa seemed to think she was fussed mainly for mercenary reasons. That she was some sort of snivelling miser who had met her comeuppance. They had no concept of her worship of the beauty of craftsmanship, her delight in the authority of each slashing brush stroke on an early blue and white bowl, in the depth, the warmth of old porcelain. How could they understand her sacred reverence for the skills of the unknown artists who had fashioned the fluted shapes, the fenestrations, the purity of line and colour she had owned and lost.

'You're the expert, darling,' Justin had said. 'They're your treasures.' And she was and they had been and were gone.

But Bianca was a strong woman, a woman of courage. She knew that, everyone in Titchfield had known it. No one, they said, no one but you, Bianca, could have nursed Justin for so long. And as lovingly. And she had. She had always treated the moribund husk of her husband with respect, had put his hand out to shake the hands of others, had covered for him, anticipated disasters and laughed off accidents when she could. But not at the end. No one could have at the end.

Bianca pulled herself together. Her loss was hers alone and she would deal with it. She unwrapped the shards Rufus had sorted and rewrapped them in clean white tissue paper from Whitcoulls. She had rejected the sheaths of rainbow colours proffered by Bronwyn. Bianca knew she was Bronwyn, the squitty little cash sale ticket said so. *Whitcoulls*, it said, *Sales person Bronwyn. Always something new.* Bronwyn, a funny little thing but pleasant, advised coloured tissue, but Bianca remained firm. She had been tempted for a moment to tell her why, which was foolish. This loss could be shared with no one. No one would understand. She stood feeling faintly sick, clutching her handbag with both hands in front of the smiling Bronwyn, backed by birthday cards and get well cards and sympathy and bereavement.

Bronwyn was as kind as she looked. 'Are you all right?'

'I . . . Yes, thank you. Yes.'

*

She rewrapped her broken treasures with the calm competence of a nurse laying out a corpse. The spirit had gone, only the broken shells remained. The remains of those beyond repair would be stowed with dignity. Her fingers lingered over special treasures, her eyes noted rare marks but remained dry. There would be no more nonsense, her treasures would be mourned in silence and should have been from the beginning. More were retrievable than she had hoped. She would mend them herself, take a course. The thought appealed, sank in, filled her sad heart. She would find a china-mending expert, apprentice herself, learn the trade secrets and set herself up. She would make money at home and work part time in an antique shop. She saw herself, polite but obviously knowledgable, moving forward to help, brushing aside a velvet curtain to assist, to explain, to share her knowledge. She would be well dressed but not intimidating. It would give her somewhere to wear her clothes. Now she was behind the velvet curtain with the owner, a figure faintly reminiscent of Barry and as amusing, but an older man, dignified and courtly as the experts on *The Antiques Road Show*. They sat side by side with two steaming cups of real coffee surrounded by the backstage clutter of their profession: the reference books, the lists of hallmarks, a Strawberry Gothic hall chair without a leg, an Irish cream jug in need of repair. Why had she not thought of it before? Vistas, whole new vistas could open up, would open up. All was not lost. Good things can and do rise from bad.

She divided the remains into two, those beyond redemption and those to be mended. The redeemable box she hid beneath the bed in her room, the lost treasures she stowed beneath the house when Gaby was out. She unlatched the little door in the foundations at the back, bent double and crept inside dragging the box of shards to lie with concrete piles, cobwebs and a few slaters trundling across baked earth. She sat in Rosa's overalls beside the cardboard carton for a few moments, breathing in the sour smell of concrete and dry clay. There was a spider spinning a web. You don't often see that, any more than you see a hen actually laying an egg. She watched it swing into space, fasten itself, scamper round to swing again. Fascinating, and remember Robert Bruce. Bianca climbed out, feeling at peace and strengthened. She would tackle the next box.

Which was better, infinitely better. Gaby returned to find her crooning the 'Eriskay Love Lilt' among lidded tankards and rat-tailed spoons.

'Hi.'

'Oh, hullo, Gaby.'

Gaby picked up a silver beer mug. 'Nice stuff.'

Bianca smiled at the odd-looking child. The clown-like hair was longer now, sticking out in clumps around the small pale face. 'I think I should tell you, dear,' she murmured, 'your roots are showing.'

Gaby clutched her head in mock horror. 'My Gaad!' She gave the urchin grin of a small boy, pulled out a packet of gum and proffered it. 'I'm trying to cut down.'

'No thank you.'

'I've been thinking. Would you like to borrow the Skoda tomorrow? Give yourself a break. Get out, go for a bit of a run. You've been working your butt off round here.' She looked around the room. 'Looking good though, isn't it?'

There is something hypnotic about chewing jaws. Bianca, touched and surprised, had a thought as she watched them. A thought so good, so strong and enterprising she almost whistled. 'That's very kind of you,' she said, 'I'd like that very much. I'm a very good driver, as you know.' She stood up. 'By the way, have you seen the Yellow Pages any-where?'

'Down the hall.'

211

Bianca skipped down the hall, laid the Yellow Pages on the newly wiped bench and turned to Antiques.

The Skoda's gears were interesting but not impossible. Bianca drove through the suburbs smiling. She had her map, her list, her plan. The whole of Auckland was sitting out well to the sun, waiting for her this clear sparkling morning. She could hear her voice. I'm not afraid of hard work, she would say. My nephew and his friend and I have just completely refurbished a derelict house.

Later, when they knew each other better, she would ask her employer, she or he but probably he, to see her things. She could hear his appreciative murmurs, his informed comments. She would own the house by this time and he would call in for a sherry on his way home and they would sit and talk, discuss their day together, the laughs they had had, their customers, the sales made or hoped for. Gin perhaps, when they knew each other well. And champagne to celebrate the partnership.

Her glow abated as the day wore on. Half the people who called themselves Antiques were Collectibles and many were Second-Hand Tat. Colonial were the worst, acres of rose-wreathed chamber pots, a scrubbing board, a flat iron, a mirrored umbrella stand with knobs. And teddy bears. Bears, black, white and khaki, dirty bears and clean, cross-eyed and squinting, everywhere there were bears. She gave one startled glance at an enema can and left.

It was getting hot. Bianca ate a dubious slice of quiche and felt worse. It was not till well after lunch that she came to a real shop, a small and beautiful shop owned by someone who knew what he was doing.

There was even a velvet curtain of the right colour, that faded, muted no-colour Barry had laughingly called Elephant's Breath. Seated behind a flat leather-topped desk in front of it, a plump pussycat of a man was attending to his affairs. He looked up, smiled politely. 'Can I help?'

Bianca sat opposite him on a ballon-backed mahogany dining chair and explained her business. All around her wood gleamed and colours were subtle. She caught her reflection in a pretty little French mirror. She was a collector, she explained, well, in a sense, not so much a collector as one who happened to have . . . she waved a hand, the man put down his Parker and nodded. But unfortunately some of her treasures had recently been broken and she wanted to learn how to repair them and could Mr . . . ?

'Holmes.'

'Thank you, Mr Holmes, could you help?'

Mr Holmes explained that there was a very good woman in Levin.

'*Levin*.'

'Yes. She charges the earth but they all do. Time consuming. Very, she has jars full of spare fingers, rosebuds. It's a life's work.'

'I can't go and live in Levin.'

Mr Holmes, with infinite courtesy, indicated this was not his problem.

Bianca changed tack. She had no hesitation, she was as direct and purposeful as ever. She wished Mr Holmes to know that when and, of course, if, he needed a part-time employee she would be happy to help. She looked around the small, beautifully furnished room, the perfect groupings, the curtain. 'Very happy,' she said.

Mr Holmes picked up his fountain pen once more. It was one of those gold-nibbed mottled ones; new, but pretending to be old. He gazed at it thoughtfully then put it down with a sad little smile.

'How long have you been back in New Zealand, Mrs . . . ?'

'Lefarge. Bianca Lefarge.'

His sorrow appeared to deepen slightly. 'Bianca Lefarge,' he murmured.

'I've been back, good heavens, over six months. More.'

He nodded. 'And may I ask how long you've been away?

Bianca gave a light little laugh of astonishment at her reply. 'Thirty years.'

'About five years longer than I.'

'Ah,' Bianca laughed again. 'I thought so. Your voice.'

Mr Holmes looked more miserable than ever. 'New Zealand, Mrs Lefarge, has changed. Is changing every day.'

'Oh I realise that. All this awful . . .'

'Let me explain. People like ourselves, expatriates who have returned to the land of our fathers are now as outdated, as irrelevant to our country as the returning members of the British Raj were to theirs. Those men and women who spent their working life longing for Home . . .'

'I didn't.'

'I did, but let that pass. I could not employ you, Mrs Lefarge, because I do not make enough money. I make very little money. The days when the emergent wealthy, the young or not so young bought old furniture in New Zealand have gone and very sensibly so. Our light does not suit the past, Mrs Lefarge. It is fierce and strong. Old things, particularly furniture, bleach, fade, fall apart, require cherishing and time and effort, none of which people here are prepared to give to things any longer. If, of course, they could afford them in the first place.'

Mr Holmes's pleasant voice flowed on. 'However beautiful, however treasured, our antiques, Mrs Lefarge, are old hat. Some things fit, of course. Pine, anything which can . . .'

'*Pine.*'

'Pine.' He smiled. 'Our possessions, like ourselves, Mrs Lefarge, are an endangered species.'

The man was mad. Barking mad. 'All my friends . . .' Bianca

paused, distracted, appalled. Friends? What friends? Naomi. Naomi who? Oh please God. 'My nephew,' she cried, 'my nephew loves my things.'

'Good,' said Mr Holmes limply, and continued. 'Besides, even if I could afford to, I would not employ you. One of the species is bad enough. Two would frighten the horses.' He smiled his gentle infuriating smile. 'You and I, Mrs Lefarge . . .'

'Oh, do stop calling me Mrs Lefarge.'

Mr Holmes gave a dry little chuckle. 'You and I are not considered user-friendly, Mrs Lefarge. We should take lessons from the user-obsequious . . . The ad men, the PRs, the media personalities.' He rose to his feet. Small, studious and still smiling he showed her to the door, paused at the polished brass doorstep to give her more bad news.

'You realise, one can no longer buy Gauloises in this country?' He shook his neat head. 'However, fortunately my sister sends me a couple of packets a week secreted in . . .' Again that chuckle. 'But we mustn't tell all our secrets, must we, Mrs Lefarge? I like it here, love it, and fortunately so does my partner.'

'So you do have partner?' snapped Bianca.

'Ah yes, I do have a partner. He worships the sun.'

'There is too much hellish sun,' cried Bianca.

'If you say so.' Mr Holmes held out a small pink hand. 'Goodbye, Mrs Lefarge,' he said. 'Goodbye.'

Bianca could scarcely bear to touch the thing. She drove away twitching with disgust. Deranged. Mad as a coot. Two coots. And what about her plans, her behind-the-curtain visions; so clear, so bright, her hands realigning minuscule china fingers, adjusting rosebuds, making as good as new, though not, of course, as regards commercial value. But her clients, these grateful people who became her friends, who sought her help, would want their things restored, not sold.

215

'There's a wonderful woman in Meadowbank.' She could see friendships developing between the like-minded, goodwill and shared interests flowing on through the years.

She would borrow Gaby's Skoda again. Tomorrow, why not. I'll go further afield. I haven't scratched the surface. They can't all be mad.

Rosa, better late than never, was getting somewhere with the garden. In the past week she had hacked, slashed, cut back and divided. Like all foolish virgin gardeners, she had rushed to the garden centre for instant help; for colour, long flowering periods, showy perennials and a few architectural greys for the back. Her knees hurt but her garden glowed with strong-eyed marigolds, gentle verbenas and bright, splashy begonias. Her natives were trimmed, her edges cut.

She had gone outside originally because she could not bear to remain indoors. She wanted the wind in her hair and got it, she wanted peace of mind. In this she was not so successful, though work and a strong hoe had helped, as Kipling had told her it would, but not enough.

Rosa, to her surprise, was not happy. Shakespeare, as usual, had beaten her to it, '*Nought's had,*' she muttered crossly, '*all's spent, where our desire is got without content.*'

She had longed for Bianca to leave them and she had done so. All was going swimmingly at Webster Street, the new house was beautiful, its occupants pleased with life and the rent was paying off the mortgage, well almost.

She and Henry had got Bianca out of their hair with dignity, had extracted her gently, no knots, no painful tangles, not a tug. They had acted generously. They were free.

And more miserable than they had been since Andy's death.

There was something wrong with Henry. Unease hung like a pall over their comings and goings, their companionable silences became less so.

Rosa, digging with her red-handled grubber, came to a decision. She would speak to Henry tonight. Before she could help him he must tell her what was wrong. If he was clinically depressed he must seek help. Enough was enough and more than.

She looked up smiling as Bianca strode up the path, heaved herself up from her gardening frame and greeted her warmly. She gazed around her lovely show of colour. 'Looks nice, doesn't it?'

'Parks and Reserves.' Bianca sighed deeply. 'Annuals,' she murmured. 'Dear old annuals.'

There seemed little more to be said.

They sat side by side in silence on a garden bench left over from one of Rufus's less successful cut-price enterprises. Videos had been another. There was still a box of the things awaiting transport to the new house. It sat, appropriately labelled, in the garage beside Martin's ashes.

Midges danced in the late afternoon air, jigging, dissolving and jigging again. 'Crepuscular,' murmured Rosa who had lost heart with words and crosswords since Martin died. The cryptics in the paper, yes, but not his half-finished books. They waited beneath her handkerchiefs in her chest of drawers—the closest thing to a duchesse she could find. It occurred to her, watching the endless quivering of life, the disturbed air above the garden tap, that she could have told Martin about Henry's decline. Not his mother, not his son and certainly not the woman sitting rump by rump beside her. She could have told Martin. After a whisky, perhaps, when the final clue had been pencilled in.

Martin, Henry is behaving very oddly. She saw the friendly eyes, the concern. Then what? Nothing, nothing ever again. She shut her eyes.

'What?' said Bianca.

Rosa jumped slightly. 'What?'

217

'Oh for goodness' sake, you said something.'

'Oh. Crepuscular. It means twilight, or rather . . .'

'I realise that.'

More silence. Bianca wondered whether to tell her sister about Mr Holmes and decided against it. Rosa had never been any good at nuances.

Bianca put out a hand, plucked a lemon verbena leaf. An idea clicked into her brain, appeared from nowhere in the moment between the crushing of the leaf and its fragrance.

'What are you going to do with all the money Martin Brown left you?' she asked.

I have been expecting this. This is when I tell her I lied and I apologise. When I tell her I knew she would understand. When I agree my behaviour was inexcusable, one of those mad impulses, like a child really. That Martin hadn't a bean. That it was a joke. That I knew she would see the funny side.

'I haven't got it yet,' I mutter.

'Yes, but when you do?'

Now! I brace myself. 'I'm glad you mentioned it, Bianca. I've been meaning to tell you for some time . . .'

But Bianca had stopped listening. She was up and running with her idea; instant, vivid and good. Blow pots of spare fingers and glue and Mr Holmes and all his works. His balderdash, his pink hands, his gall, none of them mattered. All were irrelevant, completely irrelevant. There were better ways of making money. She put a hand on Rosa's thigh.

'The best thing, dear,' she said, 'would be for you to buy another villa and I'll do it up.'

'Bianca, I must tell you . . .' Rosa stopped, leapt to her feet to embrace Henry as he mooched slowly up the path. 'Hullo, darling,' she cried.

He detached himself gently. 'What must you tell Bianca?'

'We were talking about what Rosa is going to do with all

the money Martin Brown has left her.'

Henry changed his briefcase to the other hand, put it on the ground and looked at it. 'Ah,' he said.

Typical, absolutely typical of the wretched man to arrive at the wrong moment. There was no point in pursuing the splendid thought now. And perhaps it would be better to wait a little, to get her thoughts down on paper, to strengthen her arguments.

And at least she would get a gin. Two gins. Gaby and Rufus scarcely drank spirits and gin had gone through the roof since she had last bought any here. The bow-tied Jason at Liquorland had also asked her where she'd been for the last thirty years.

And that Bettina child would probably still be sitting around at Webster Street. She and Gaby spent hours smoking and drinking coffee at the kitchen table. There was nothing wrong with the child and Bianca could always go and sit with her things, but . . .

Henry picked up his briefcase. 'Gin,' he said.

Rosa turned on the sprinkler as she left. The midges regrouped, foamed higher as the drops fell.

Bianca had two strong gins and left.

Rosa lifted the remains of her glass to the collapsed figure in the chair. 'To Scrooge McDuck,' she said.

He gave a brief snort. 'Thank you. Any particular reason for the duck?'

'That's what you look like, lying there. If you could see yourself. You've shrunk, gone all hopeless-looking, halved in size.' Rosa took a sip of gin, remembered that she had meant to be gentle and kind to this man in need of help. It still came out wrong. 'What on earth's the matter with you, sitting there miserable as a bandicoot?'

'It was a duck a moment ago.'

219

'Tell me.'

Henry stirred, smiled at her concerned pink face. 'Why did you tell Bianca Martin had left you a lot of money?'

'It seemed a good idea at the time.'

'*The Heart Has Its Reasons*?'

This was too close for comfort, too perceptive, too like the lightning etc. Rosa sat straight. 'We're not talking about why I lied.'

Then whose lies were they talking about. Not his, surely. Henry was drained bone dry, exhausted. She couldn't mean that, not Rosa, his generous, loving Rosa. He gave a brief cough and waited.

'We're talking about why you've gone into some sort of decline. We're talking about how we should be happy and peaceful like we were, not talking much, not enough probably, but knowing it was all right, that we were on the same wavelength. That you didn't cheat or lie and nor did I, well not much. That you are, at heart, a decent man, generous even. You huff and puff but look what you did to help Bianca. That was a generous thing to do, very generous, though I've never been able to understand why you didn't discuss it with me first. You've been a good father, though again you won't talk, won't discuss Rufus. Let alone Gaby. I don't like Gaby. Do you like Gaby?'

He moved his hands. 'I . . .'

'There you are, you see! You don't know. And if you did know you probably wouldn't tell. Where have you *gone* Henry?'

He opened his mouth to tell her he didn't know and shut it. She was upset, deeply upset, her face pinker than ever, her eyes bright with tears. All his hopeless bewildered love flowed to her. He flopped onto the unicorn footstool beside her and took her hand. 'Rosa, my dear.'

She snatched it away.

'I must talk to you, Henry. I used to talk to Martin but he's dead.' She was crying now, noisily, her face blotched with damp and pain. 'And what was in his letter to you? You said you'd lost it.' She gave a deep, shuddering gasp and turned to stare. 'I don't believe that, Henry. I've never believed that for a moment.'

He walked to the window, stared at nothing. 'So what can I do?'

'Tell me what was in it.' She waited, listened to silence. 'It was Italy, wasn't it?'

He turned. 'Yes.'

She seemed smaller than ever in the large chair. A wide-eyed bush creature; small, gallant and fierce.

'A woman?'

'Yes.'

She had never felt like this before. Weak as a kitten, strong as a lion, appalled, humiliated and seething with rage, Rosa demanded facts—'Tell me,' she said.

'Twenty years!'

'Longer.'

The length of time is the thing. The most unforgivable thing of all. A life sentence of deceit.

When I was pregnant this deception began. When the woman remarried and not before it was ended. By her. Those are the facts. And all this, all this he has told me in *my own home.* It is better to die in your own bed but not much, less than much, if you're murdered.

I am going mad. Have gone.

And so I am and so I do and all these feelings rage and I am outraged. And then I begin to laugh, and I laugh and laugh and laugh and tears roll down and splash on my hands and my front and still I laugh.

Henry, not unnaturally, is alarmed. He gets water, wonders what to do, holds me in his arms, hushes and begs me for help and sanity. 'Rosa, darling Rosa, don't. Rosa, please.'

I calm down. I lie in his arms on the sofa where we have landed up. We are close, locked together like parents at airports awaiting bad news.

I sit up, blow my nose. 'After all,' I say, 'I had Martin.'

Henry is staring at me in disbelief which turns to horror. Rank terror. Terror I can see, hear, smell. 'You were lovers?'

'Yes. But not forever.'

'When?'

'When do you think? When you were away. He begged me for years but I wouldn't.' I think of my friend Martin, so much older, so much wiser. 'He knew, I suppose. About the woman?'

'Yes.'

This is it then. This is life. This is men. This is the love that needs a fall guy and I am it. I look at this stranger, this wet hen, this man. I shake my head.

'What a fool,' I say. 'What a stupid idiotic fool I've been.'

'No. Rosa. Rosa. I love you.'

'Thank you,' I say.

They talked for hours, they tossed about on a sea of words; words for recrimination, rage, betrayal. They struggled for air, half-drowning on the surface, they submerged and rose spluttering in despair.

They begged for reason, for sense, for understanding. They did not mention forgiveness. They clung to the wreckage.

'Do you want me to sleep somewhere else?' said Henry eventually.

'Oh, for God's sake,' snapped Rosa. 'And turn off the sprinkler.'

222

twelve

The gardening talents in Webster Street also combined well. Bianca knew about the cottage-garden effect desired, Gaby did not. Bianca was strong and Gaby stronger and Rufus took the stuff to the dump. Bianca's plan, easy care with colour and plenty of self-seeders, was approved. The last thing Gaby and Rufus wanted was to have to fart around in the section every weekend, especially as Gaby was looking for a job. Weekends were for unwinding, for lying on the as yet unlaid grass, for absorbing energy for the trip to the supermarket then on to the wine bar.

Gaby continued to be generous with the Skoda, was quite insistent that Bianca should have it once a week. Bianca owed herself a break, hell yes, and Gaby could shoot off any time.

Bianca accepted with thanks and was meticulous about petrol. She did not bother to tell Gaby or Rufus of her change of interest, that she had abandoned her search for a niche behind the velvet curtain of the antique world. She no longer sought Antiques, Collectibles or Colonials. She sought old villas in need of care and attention. She bought a map entitled *Auckland, City of Sails*, with the harbour bridge on the front, and set off every Monday on a treasure hunt which was hers alone. She bought her own *Herald* on real estate day and studied it with care, marked the possibles with her yellow highlighter, packed her lunch and set off with heart aglow. She was positive. Like Rufus she had no time for negative wimps. You could keep them.

She went to a different area each week, called first on any likely real estate vendors but ignored the obviously useless two-man outfits squeezed between TABs and Cambodian takeaways.

Having obtained the essentials of location and likely price of any villas for sale, she rejected offers of further assistance. But you won't have a key, they cried. Bianca explained that that would not be necessary at this stage. As she told Ken and Douglas and Trish and Soph, she just wanted to get a feel for the place. Make what her late husband used to call a 'recce'. Time spent on reconnaissance, he used to say, is never wasted. She would be back.

She kept careful notes in a small 3B1 notebook labelled *Bianca. Do not lose.*

Her sense of direction was a help. She had always done the navigating while Justin drove. He couldn't have managed in town without her, he told her every time they sailed over the hog's back on their way home. And she would smile and slip her hand under his on the wheel and be happy.

She learned quickly that she was too late for Freemans Bay or Ponsonby or even, she feared, Grey Lynn. She wasted no time on repining. She knew what she wanted: a villa at a reasonable price which Rosa could buy with the man's money and Bianca could do up. Her assistants in this enterprise were uncertain at the moment—Rufus and Gaby would both be working—but these details could be worked out later.

In the meantime she must get on to Henry about the title of Webster Street. This, again, would require thought. She would have to get Henry on his own and was concerned as to how to do this. She had scarcely seen him since the move. She had no illusions about future drives in the country or of his making unaccompanied visits to Webster Street, even if invited. Especially if invited. Rosa would have to come too. She would ask them for a meal when Gaby and Rufus were out, as they often were. She should have asked them before. Rosa had been very kind to her. She would get out the silver.

'But I don't want to!'

'It's her birthday.'

'I don't care if it's her annunciation. I'm not going.'

'You are. We both are.'

'Rosa.'

'Henry.'

They stared at each other in the misty bathroom mirror. Red-nosed, creased and disillusioned, two old faces stared back. Rosa picked up the nail scissors, cut a few misparted grey hairs from the left side and whirled them down the basin.

Her back was towards him as she bent over, pink and shiny and familiar as his own. More so.

'It's Martin's birthday too.'

'Oh.'

She turned to him, her face serious. She didn't want him to get it wrong.

'I'm just telling you. I'm not trying to . . . not bully you or anything. I'll go anyway. I can make up some lie.'

Tears rushed to his eyes. 'Oh, my dear heart.'

It was some time since they had clutched each other naked and upright.

One of the pleasures of competence is the pleasure of getting it done, of having plenty of time in hand, of never having to scramble or rush. Bianca had set the table in the morning with the Worcester which remained. The silver had been polished,

225

the linen starched and she had done the flowers. The *blanquette* of veal had been made yesterday, whipped cream already glued the meringues, the coffee tray was laid. She had even found some proper dessert mints, elegant imported wafers of dark bitter chocolate with peppermint not given to ooze.

She sat upright in her wing-backed chair and gazed about the room. It was beautiful, this house, more beautiful than she could ever have hoped. She could have been in Titchfield, the wood was just as fine, her things as harmoniously placed as ever they had been. There were things to be done, certainly, the chintzes were worn, an ivory button handle had come off the bow-fronted commode, the longcase clock had yet to be set going. Some things were still packed owing to lack of space. But the feeling, the ambience, the mellowness was there. The glow of lives well lived and waited upon by others was evident in the deep sheen of the oak chest, the patina of the commode was there forever. Once things have that depth, that intensity of polish, only a quick buff up is required.

And Long Life is a godsend for silver.

Bianca realised she was having a Happy Birthday and would continue to do so when Rosa arrived. She was grateful to Rosa and, by extension, Henry, though she needn't go into that. Perhaps her birthday was not the night to bring up the question of the title. No.

The doorbell rang. It couldn't be them. Not at quarter past three.

Bianca, smiling and already into her blue, opened the door to excited strangers.

They introduced themselves. 'I'm Margie Dempster and this is Stephen.'

'How do you do.'

They wondered if they could just have another peep around. They realised that it was by appointment only, but

226

they were over this way on account of Stephen's mother and they happened to have seen Mrs . . . in the garden, and they were so excited about the place, they just wondered . . .

Stephen agreed. Margie reiterated. If she wouldn't mind too much could they slip round for a second, seeing they were passing, and wasn't it looking *lovely*.

Bianca's hand clutched the warm polished brass of the door knob. Her breath had gone, gone completely.

'I don't know what you're talking about,' she gasped.

'But we've made an offer. Conditional on finance. We signed on Monday.'

'There's been some mistake,' panted Bianca. 'Go away. Go away at once,' she cried and slammed the door.

'Ask Bettina!' Margie screamed back. 'Ask Bettina and then see, you silly old . . .'

They banged, they knocked, they rang the bell, they shouted.

Bianca stumbled to her chair, hid her ears with her hands. Still, still she could hear them shouting. 'Go away,' she begged. 'Please, please go away. Oh dear God, please.'

She picked up the blue cardigan beside her and pressed it to her trembling lips. She was shaking with fright. Cold, cold as ice. She must put things on, keep warm. That is what you do when you've had a shock. You keep warm. You treat for shock and work things out. You don't panic. It was just a muddle. Some stupid muddle. It would be all right, quite all right. Yes. She sat motionless clutching the cardigan, her eyes focused on the tiny washing instructions label, the rest of the world a blur.

Warm Gentle
Machine wash
Do not wring
Do not tumble
Acrylic

How could it be acrylic? She never bought acrylic. Never. She couldn't stand acrylic. She bought wool. Pure wool. Always. Always, always. She banged the crumpled thing to her eyes with shaking hands and sobbed her heart out.

But not for long. She would stop this nonsense. She would ring Bettina. Bianca walked to the kitchen, poured herself a glass of the water and drank it slowly as she gazed out the window to the emergent back garden. She put out a hand to steady herself against the wall which had once screamed *Fuck off, Fraser* and no longer did.

'Clarion Real Estate, Bettina speaking,' sang the voice. 'Can I help you?'

'Bettina, this is Bianca Lefarge speaking.'

'Sure is. I recognised your voice. Lovely day.'

'Bettina, two people have just banged on the door wanting to see the house.'

'Oh, that's *bad*. I hate that when it's appointment only. Really, some people. We told everyone, we said. And anyway who's come now when we've got a conditional.'

'What!'

'Like I said, offer conditional on finance. Margie and Steve Dempster. Lovely couple. Signed on Monday.'

'Who signed?'

'Well, him and Roof.'

'I'm sorry to have to tell you, Bettina,' breathed Bianca, her knees weak with joy, her heart singing, 'but there's been some mistake. Rufus does not own the title.'

'How d'y'mean?'

'The title is owned by Rufus's father. Mr Henry Felton.'

Bettina's voice lifted. 'Mrs Lefarge, I've seen it. I don't want to be snippy, but what do you think I am? Some sort of nutcase who can't recognise a title? Believe me, there's no glitches in this one. Rufus owns it and Rufus signed it and if you don't

228

mind, Mrs Lefarge, I'm a busy professional woman. Ask them. Ask Rufus.'

Panic seized her, panic and misery and heartbreak. She screamed down the telephone. 'You inveigled him, trapped him. I know my nephew. He's a good man, he loves me, he'd never, never . . . Oh, don't you tell me that, you . . . you. I've never liked you, hanging around, taking it all in, twisting Gaby and him round your little finger.'

Bettina gasped. 'Twisting Gaby? You must be joking. I'd as soon twist a python.' Her voice froze. 'As for *inveigling*. They didn't need any inveigling, Rufus nor Gaby, especially Gaby. I've never seen a sharper vendor. Keen as mustard. And frankly, Mrs Lefarge, I don't see why I should sit here being insulted by you, if you don't mind. Ask Rufus. Goodbye.'

Bianca put the receiver back in its cradle. Nothing, nothing in her whole life had been as bad as this. This was the worst. Andrew, the shoes, the horror, Justin's decline, all the insults and miseries of her life had been nothing compared with this. She was shaking all over as she tugged pale blue acrylic around her shoulders. She had nobody, nobody in the whole world. She knew that.

And nor do millions. Millions and millions and millions. Bianca squared her shoulders. She would get herself a gin. She would have a gin to help her think and she would work out what to do.

She walked slowly down the hall and reached for the bottle. It was virtually empty. Someone had drunk her gin. She saw them, Bettina, Phil, Gaby seated at the table, laughing, smoking, drinking her gin. Lifting glasses, clinking, congratulating themselves and each other. But not Rufus. Rufus had not been there. They had trapped him somehow. Inveigled. 'Rufus,' she moaned. 'Rufus.'

She poured the remaining gin into a kitchen glass, added a

slurp of water and drank it quickly. She would get some more. And cigarettes. She would work things out.

Webster Street, as Bettina had told them, was so handy. 'Slipper distance to the shops,' she had laughed.

The street was virtually empty, a sheet of newspaper sailed onto the road, was squashed by a woman cyclist in an orange parka who nodded. Bianca, her head throbbing, her heart torn, nodded back. The front door of a house opened, closed; cloud reflections drifted across the roof of its stick-on conservatory.

Jason, the young man with the bow-tie and the shaved head, greeted her with his usual enthusiasm.

'I want a large bottle of gin,' said Bianca. 'The largest you have.'

'Right on,' said Jason and moved to get it although it was self-service. Bianca knew this but she disliked carrying the naked bottle across yards of blue carpet to be decently cam-ouflaged at the counter—or rather dumped into a yellow plastic bag shrieking Liquorland. There is something about old women and bottles of gin. Something with which Bianca did not wish to be associated. Toothless drunken old hags in old prints selling their wares, *Drunk for a penny, blind drunk for tuppence.*

She concentrated on the carpet. It was two-toned with squiggles like a cross-section of the human brain Justin had once shown her. She stayed staring until the bottle was safely encased then slid the money across without looking.

She cradled the bag in her arms, held it to her chest. All around were bottles, bottles for miles. Bottles to help the thought processes, to calm, to clarify.

'There you go,' smiled Jason.

'Yes. Yes, thank you.' She stood motionless, her heart screaming for help, her eyes on his shaven head. 'What is that style of haircut called, Jason?'

230

Jason gave an embarrassed yelp. 'Aw, a Number One.'

She looked at him thoughtfully, stared at his well-shaped head, his neat ears. Stood cuddling gin among nuts and nibbles and Twisties in racks.

'Why is it called that?'

'They use a number one blade, see. The razor.'

Bianca nodded. So fit, so nimble, so kind. 'I see.' She stood silent for a moment, then gazed into his eyes. 'It looks very handsome,' she said.

Jason's shy feet moved again. 'Thanks.' He clapped his hands together in bonhomie and dismissal, dipped his head at her purchase. 'Yeah, well. That'll give you plenty of needle.'

'Thank you,' murmured Bianca.

'Good as gold,' said Jason.

Henry and Rosa went for a swim on the way to Bianca's. Henry had suggested it. He would pick Rosa up after work and they could slip down to the beach, why not. There would be plenty of time. He made many suggestions for shared pleasures now, kept an eye out, spotted mild treats, small breaks in the dailiness of life: a cafe with good polenta, a newly opened wine bar overlooking the container wharf, a film. They were both aware that this had been Rosa's province. She had always been good at treats and seemed amused by his endeavours, had looked him in the eye over an unexpected glass of riesling last Thursday. 'Are we bonding, Henry? Is that what we're trying to do? Rebond?'

'I hope so.'

She smiled, shook her head. In tolerance or mild negation, but not, please God, in rejection.

The swims after work were good. What could be more therapeutic than to lie in the sun, to relax with his wife after a day at the warehouse pretending all was well between himself and Rufus, a day spent tiptoeing around a son who walked on eggshells. What better than to lie beside her, to sense her presence as she padded through sand to flop beside him, to put out a hand to her wet thigh. 'Good?'

'Mmmn.'

'Warmer than yesterday?'

'A bit.'

'Good, good.' They would get there, they would get there in the end.

He had not told her about the change of title and must do so immediately. He opened his eyes to see her drying her wet head on an ancient beach towel of Carmen Miranda plus fruit. Rosa dropped it, put both hands to her mouth and yawned, her eyes on the frill of white surf edging blue and Rangitoto beyond.

'I wonder why the Maoris called it Bloody Head,' she said dreamily. 'We should climb it one day.'

There you are, you see. Straws in the wind, good omens waving. It would all be all right. He spoke quickly while it still was. 'I have changed the title to Webster Street. Made it over to Rufus.'

'Why on earth?'

An obvious question, and one not easy to answer. I did it to save you pain. I did it because our son exercised moral blackmail. I did it because I am who I am. The fact that you now know my secret anyway is because my pitch has been queered by your ex lover, the good, the loyal, Martin Fucking Brown, God rot his soul but don't bother. Martin Brown, of all people. An old man with half a gut, reeking of nicotine and a bore to boot. The very thought made him ill.

'Why didn't you *tell* me?' she cried into the silence.

Another difficult question, and equally impossible to answer. He dragged his mind back from betrayal. His voice was gentle as he sidestepped. 'Have you any objections?'

Rosa tossed her head. Drops of seawater fell on her freckled chest, her rounded arms as she swung towards him.

'Yes!' she cried. 'Yes, I do.'

'Such as?'

She gave a shuddering gasp. 'Don't you understand? No, you've never understood. You won't see. All his life I have worried about Rufus. I have worried whether perhaps he was . . .'

Was what? Feckless? Self-centred? Aren't they all. The young are meant to be. But was Rufus perhaps too sharp, too quick, too obsessed with instant wealth?

She could not say it. Loyalty as well as love forbade it. This was her secret. She was the only one who knew. And what did she mean, knew? There was nothing to know, nothing. Just that she loved Rufus and always had and always would. To tell, even to mention her fears was not only disloyal to him; suspicions, however vague, proliferate once shared, spread like bushfires and destroy. She had not even told Martin.

'It's Bianca,' she said finally. 'What if he, they, sell the house? You've made Bianca vulnerable, exposed to Gaby, of all people.'

'No. I made him put it in writing. He will not sell the house without consulting Bianca.'

Rosa shivered. 'Why did you do that?' she whispered.

'Because I'm not sure I trust him,' said Henry.

Her mouth dropped. At the statement, yes, but more, much more because Henry had made it. Henry, who had never been prepared to discuss his son, who knew Rufus would be all right, Henry *knew*. 'Oh, Henry,' she cried and flung herself at him.

'I didn't want to worry you,' he said over her shoulder to a gawking youth with a frisbee. Wet, salty, uncomfortable and uncomforted, she lay still.

'You'll have to tell her tonight,' she muttered.

233

'Yes.'

'How can you! How can you possibly?'

'I will.'

'It's her birthday.'

'You said.'

They picked up their sandy towels and trailed back to the changing sheds and cold showers and the rush hour.

Bianca sat upright in the wing-backed chair drinking gin. She had never put her feet up as Rosa did, had never flopped about and had no intention of starting now. She had made notes in her 3B1 notebook to clear her mind. There was much to think about. She would tell Rosa and Henry tonight of the perfidy of their son, what he had done, how he had done it. Though obviously it was Gaby. Bianca had never liked her, never. She had known, from the first moment she had seen her in those ghastly boots she had known, Gaby was sly, manipulative and not to be trusted. You had only to look at her. Those eyes too close together, too muddy. The eyes, she told her precariously balanced gin, are the windows of the soul.

She lit another cigarette, drank deeply. Oh, but gin was good. She looked at it, oily, beautiful and subtle to the tongue. The juniper berries, presumably, there was a picture on the label. But how do you know if you haven't tasted junipers? What did the tree look like, the bearer of these blue-black treasures? '*Oh ruddier than the cherry,*' she sang, '*Oh sweeter than the berry.*' There were no more words no more at all. She started again. '*Oh ruddier than the cherry,*' she sang and burst into tears.

This would not do.

She lifted her glass, lit another cigarette, opened her notebook once more and wrote slowly and carefully.

1. Tell Henry re Rufus.

2. Rosa to buy old villa.

3. Bianca to . . .

She sat up quickly, wiped ash from her blue front. How disgusting, she was a tidy smoker. Gaby had told her, she had said . . . what had she said? Something. It didn't matter. Nothing that terrible person said mattered. Person, not woman. Not woman, like Justin's woman. Justin against the light. '*Moon of* gladness *by night, strength and joy thou art to me*,' she sang, beating time with her cigarette like Miss Blennerhasset in senior choir. Though not really. Miss Blennerhasset hadn't had a cigarette. Bianca giggled, became serious. Miss Blennerhasset had had bad breath. Bianca couldn't be doing with bad breath. You could keep it. She giggled again, sobbed. There had been no gladness by night, no strength and joy at the end. Nothing.

Her notebook slipped to one side to lie beside the blue cardigan.

She noted with surprise that her glass was empty, stood up with stately care and walked down the wide hall to the kitchen, her hand checking the wall as she went. She poured the gin from the depleted open bottle, watched with approval as the water mingled. Oil and water don't mix but they do when necessary, they do when required to assist thought, to make plans. There was something, some reason, something to do with Henry . . . She would wait till she got back to her chair.

It had gone, the reason why Rosa would now have to buy the villa. Why she would be *duty-bound*. Bound by duty. Trussed. Men used to wear trusses. There had been advertisements in the *Auckland Weekly News*, strange little pictures at the side depicting appliances which could be sent for and which would arrive under plain cover. She would ask Henry, stupid old Henry. Henry, she would say, do men truss these days? Now that was funny, that was very funny. To truss or not to truss. To fuss or not to fuss. Trussy fussy.

She was dreamy now, dreamy and happy and strangely tired. She gazed around the room at the warm light flowing past calico curtains made by Rosa. Bianca had been disgusted at first (calico!) but they were cheap and there had been no fee for the making. Rosa had been only too happy to have been of some use. The curtains looked well, formed a muted backdrop for her things. Her things were here.

'Yes,' she whispered. 'Yes.'

'Fire engine,' said Rosa.

Henry, who had already pulled to the side of the road, nodded.

The engine shot past them, wailing its anguish into the distance as it spun around a corner in the direction of Webster Street.

'Bianca!' screamed Rosa.

He was ahead of her, speeding, cutting corners, hurtling after the thundering thing till it turned in to an adjacent street. Oh God, thank you, God.

Henry slowed for a second, but no more. 'Christ!'

The Webster Street house was well away, flames shooting skywards. They fell out of the car.

'Towels,' he yelled through the roar, 'get the wet towels. The hose.'

The Sex Pistols fan next door had already done so. Buckets were being filled, chain gangs begun. 'On the *door*,' yelled Henry, 'on the door.' He grabbed one of the wet towels, wrapped it around his fist and slammed it through the glass panel at the side of the door. Smoke billowed out as he unsnibbed the lock, the brass knob was red hot. He stumbled, stepped back and tried again. The door swung open, smoke and powdered plaster surged around them.

'Go away,' he screamed at Rosa's terrified face.

'Back,' yelled someone. 'Everyone back.'

236

The fan stood firm, continued playing the hose on Henry and the front door. Someone grabbed Rosa. 'Come back, you can't help.' Rosa punched the woman in the chest and dropped to her knees to follow Henry.

The fire engine arrived; efficient, well-trained men connected the hydrant and took control.

'Anyone inside?' they yelled at the youth.

'Yeah, two or three. Two old guys have just gone in.'

'In this lot? Jeeze!'

Bianca lay face down in the hall. The sitting room ceiling caved in as Henry and Rosa began dragging her out, showering them with plaster and burning debris. The three of them lay motionless beneath black smoke, drenched by water blasting from the firemen's hoses, surrounded by the roar of fire from the gutted sitting room and the creaks and tearing rumbles of the hall collapsing about them. The firemen saved them, picked them up bodily in their protected arms and carried them to safety like errant children beguiled by matches. They should not have gone in.

Bianca was dead.

Each cubicle in intensive care was equipped with its own ventilator, intravenous lines and ECG monitor. The lifesaving technology terrified him. Rufus knew about technology but not this stuff. These winking, blinking, green-eyed monitors appalled him, these ventilators, drips and draining bottles, these tubes in grey faces.

He came every day. He moved forward, breathless with fright, past people fighting for their lives. You don't get to intensive care unless you're fighting for your life.

Henry and Rosa lay in adjacent beds. Smoke inhalation had caused adult respiratory distress syndrome. They both had extensive superficial burns plus a certain amount of deep dermal burns, hands mostly. Less serious in Rosa's case. With

luck, the registrar had told him, they would recover. Rosa
certainly. They would be kept ventilated and endotracheal
tubes were essential at this stage as well as drips. 'So they can't
speak, of course.'

'No,' said Rufus. 'No.'

He had stood speechless between the two beds for days,
had watched the mouths around tubes, the blistered crackling
skin.

'Burns are always a bit of a shock,' smiled the registrar,
'but they're both heavily sedated.'

'Good. Good.'

The young nurse greeted him smiling. 'They've both been
extubated,' she said. 'They might even talk.' She touched his
arm. 'Ten minutes. Okay?'

He nodded. They didn't look any better, no better at all.
As always, he didn't know which bed to stand beside, which
parent to attend. Their eyes were shut. Henry's mouth a black
hole.

Rufus's eyes filled with tears. 'Dad?' he said eventually.
'Mum?'

He sat on the edge of the chair beside Rosa, weeping at
the sight of the olds. The half-dead olds. At Henry's swollen
and hairless head. At Rosa. Sweet Jesus, how had it all
happened, how had it come to this?

'Mum?' he said again. 'Dad?'

They opened their eyes together as though he had pushed
a button. Henry had no eyebrows; Rosa no lashes.

Rosa's cracked lips moved. He leaned forward.

'Gaby?' she whispered. 'Where's Gaby?'

'I don't know.'

Her eyes closed. The hand lying on the cover was bandaged. Hidden from sight. Not human at all.

He gave a compulsive sob. 'I'm sorry.'

Rosa's tongue licked. 'Bianca's dead.'

'I know, I know. Oh, my God, Mum. I didn't . . . You've got to believe me, Mum.'

Her head moved.

'*Mum.*'

Her bald eyes stared at him. 'Not now, Rufus. No. Not now.'

Henry held out an enormous bandaged hand. 'No, Rosa.' He gasped, tried again. 'It wasn't his fault. None of it. No.'

His eyes closed.

Catalonia

French and Spanish

Catalonia made to measure

Catalonia à la carte

Beautiful walks 18

A taste of Catalonia 26

Recommended eating...........................32

Wines and spirits.....36

Markets 42

Seashores and seabeds 46

Sporting activities ...52

Fairs and festivals 58

Regional history 64

Museums 74

Home decoration....82

Catalan culture........90

Family outings 96

Catalonia in detail

Roussillon 104

From Vallespir to Cerdagne 122

Costa Brava 138

Costa Dorada.........164

The Pyrenees.........182

Catalonia's interior....................196

Index 218

Catalonia made to measure

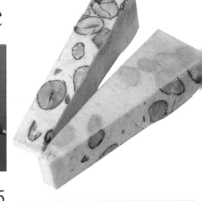

A weekend in Coullioure and on the Côte Vermeille

Begin with a gentle stroll in this delightful fishing port (pp. 120-121), which inspired both Braque and Matisse with its simple, sparkling colours. The short tour entitled 'the Fauvist way' (p. 76) is ideal to discover the port scenery. You can also visit the factories where anchovies, a local delicacy, are salted. After a charming lunch in Collioure, in the afternoon head to the Côte Vermeille (pp. 116-119) making sure to stop to enjoy the sea views and relax on the quiet beaches. In Banyuls (p. 119), a sailing port and seaside resort overlooked by terraced vineyards, take the time to taste the sweet local wine. From there, depending on your mood, you can walk the customs officers' trails, go back to nature at Cap Béar nudist beach (p. 119), or visit the Arago aquarium (p. 119). Return via Port-Vendres (p. 118), the ancient port of Venus, now a busy fishing spot whose main square has a pink-marble obelisk in memory of Louis XIV. Don't miss the port market, known as *la criée*, starting at 4pm, when freshly caught fish are sold from the boats. The auction is a lively and entertaining event, and Coullioure is renowned for its anchovies. (p. 120). The following day, take the cliff road along the rocky coast through the old village of Argelès-sur-Mer (pp. 116-117). Colourful markets enliven the village and the small museum at La Casa Albères recalls the traditional regional way of life. The long sandy beach of Argelès-Plage (p. 117) is the ideal place to stop for a swim and enjoy a relaxed family lunch. The eagle show at the Château de Valmy (p. 117), situated at the foot of the Albères hills, will entertain the whole family. You can spend the afternoon in the orchards and vineyards of the Roussillon plain, before returning to Collioure (pp. 120-121) for a sea trip or some regional wine tasting at the Maison de la Vigne.

A weekend
in Perpignan

The best way to dive into the Catalan world is a short stay in the capital of the kings of Majorca (pp. 104-107). Salvador Dalí once said that Perpignan station was the centre of the world; during the puritanical days of Franco, the Spanish would go there to watch *Last Tango in Paris* or *Emmanuelle*. Nowadays, French and Spanish Catalans alike promenade on the flowery banks of the River Bass and meet in Place Arago and Rue Mailly. A morning tour of the palace of the kings of Majorca will recall the glory days when Catalonia dominated the Mediterranean and beyond. After a quick look round the fine arts museum, where Hyacinthe Rigaud painted portraits of some of the most famous people in the world, enjoy a delicious lunch of anchovies wrapped in pastry and Banyuls wine on the terrace of the Casa Sansa.

In the afternoon, stroll in the Quartier Saint-Jean and admire the old bourgeois houses and private mansions around the cathedral. The old quarter houses several specialist shops. Don't miss the Maison Quinta with its attractive range of decorative items, including high-quality pottery and glassware. In summer, enjoy the Jeudis de Perpignan, celebrated with music and theatre or attend the International Festival of Photo Journalism. Don't be too shy to join the locals when they dance the *Sardana* in Place de la Castillet. The national Catalan circle dance is performed twice weekly at 5pm. The following day, join the locals in the rush to Canet-Plage (pp. 112-113), a popular beach in summer. If you prefer to avoid the crowds, head for Les Aspres (pp. 126-127).

Here, small sun-drenched villages, surrounded by delicately-perfumed wild plants, hide such architectural gems as the Serrabone priory or the ruins of a medieval château. Spare a moment to try a glass of Byrrh, a sweet aperitif with medicinal properties, made in Thuir (p. 126), the 'Byrrh capital'.

A weekend in Sitges and the Penedès

This area has a taste for festivals and wine.

On Saturday, you can head northwest to the peaks of the Alt Penedès (p. 210-211). Early birds can visit the renowned regional market in Vilafranca first. Early afternoon can be spent in the cellars of the Torres dynasty, discovering the secrets of wine tasting, with a detour to the wine museum, to see a splendid collection of glasses and bottles. In the evening, tasting the well-known Spanish sparkling wine, Cava, is a must. The second day can be spent in Sitges (pp. 172-173), one of the most popular coastal resorts in Catalonia, nestling between the Garraf massif and an attractive long crescent of sand. Pop into one of the lively bars that line the seafront. A souvenir of Barcelona's creative heyday, the Bodega de Gaudí is a remarkably beautiful modern wine cellar. This town likes to party and hosts such eclectic events as the gay carnival, a collectors' car rally and theatre and cinema festivals. Also, you can see the former home of the *Modernista* artist Santiago Rusiñol, now a museum celebrating the thriving days of Modernism. You can also drive to Vilanova to discover a unique collection of trains in the railway museum.

A weekend
in Cardona
and the Alt Llobregat

This is the place to discover pure industrial art. Situated midway between Barcelona and Andorra, Cardona is a good spot to choose as your base to explore the region, where you can stay in the medieval castle, said to be haunted. The former seat of the Dukes of Cardona is now a luxurious parador. The Dukes are buried in the nearby Romanesque church of Sant Vincenç. Wandering in the charming old streets of the town is the perfect way to spend the morning. In the afternoon, go on a family outing to the amazing salt mountain that made Cardona's reputation. Known locally as the Capital of Salt, the extraordinary mountain is 260 ft (80 m) high and 3 miles (5 km) around the perimeter. You can even venture down the shafts of the abandoned mine. A small museum displays some extraordinary objects made from salt. Round off the day in the Sierra de Castelltallat, where a carriage ride in the forest reserve will delight the whole family. The next day

can be dedicated to exploring the banks of the Llobregat river (pp. 202-204). Puig-Reig, once famous for its textile industry, still has the 19thC.

workers' housing estate, based on the English terraced style. You may want to treat yourself to a visit to the circus in Berga, the town famous for its monsters and demons festival, or descend into the depths of the coal mine in Cercs, followed by a visit to the pretty Romanesque church in Sant Esteve. You can also go upstream to the source of the Llobregat in Castellar de N'Hug, stopping at the former Clot de Moro cement factory, now a transport museum. A clear day is ideal for taking a ramble in the Cadí-Moixerò nature reserve, in the foothills of the Pyrenees.

A week
in Cerdagne
and the Núria valley

The warm air and colourful scenery of the Cerdagne valley (pp. 186-187) is a world apart in this area of the Pyrenees. At Llívia, a Spanish enclave in French territory, you'll find one of the oldest chemists' shops in Europe. At Puigcerdà, close to the border, there are many activities to enjoy: rowing on the lake, tasting the famous local pears or the renowned goose with turnips, acrobatics on the sophisticated ice rink or balloon trips. Continuing along the River Seger, you'll find some charming villages characteristic of the region. Stroll beneath the arches of the square in Bellver de Cerdanya before visiting the very pretty Santa Eugènia de Nerellà Romanesque church. Martinet is for food lovers, offering traditional country bread from Four Jordi and rustic cuisine from the Can Boix. At Lles there's a wide range of walking trails, as well as white-water sports for the more daring. Further west, a

stone's throw from Andorra, is the varied town of Seu d'Urgell (pp. 188-189), home to a beautiful Romanesque cathedral. Nearby, the town of Arsèguel has a small accordion museum and you can discover the traditional boats of Coll del Nargo. The second part of your stay can be spent in the Núria valley (pp. 184-185), east of Puigcerdà. Leave your car there and take the train to Ribes, where a rack-and-pinion train will take you on a bumpy climb up the mountain, ideal for a family outing. Stop briefly at Queralbs, a typical mountain village, making your way to the rocky sanctuary of Núria. The valley is known for

its skiing and is an ideal resort for the whole family, with beginners' and more advanced pistes. In summer, the bowl-shaped valley offers visitors a variety of excursions and activities, including archery and horse-riding and walks that skirt dramatic chasms. On your return trip, try to make time to visit Ripoll, 'the cradle of Catalonia'. It is home to the monastery in which the founder of the 500-year dynasty of the House of Barcelona is buried. The Monestir de Santa Maria, founded in 888 AD, was the power base and cultural centre of Guifré el Pilos (Count Wilfred the Hairy).

A week
in Barcelona

The capital of Catalonia inspires love at first sight, but takes a little longer to get to know (pp. 164-171) – at least four days for a first visit. The city itself is a flamboyant display of architecture through the ages, from the Roman remains of the Gothic quarter to the baroque gold decorations of the cathedral and the magnificent Modernist buildings of 'golden square' and the olympic village, built for the 1992 Olympic Games. Barcelona has long been cherished by artists, from the utopian Gaudí, who designed a fabulous garden city in Güell park, to Miró and Picasso, honoured by the city's museums and art foundations. The city has distractions for all ages, with numerous parks to explore, an aquarium, a zoo and a science museum for a family outing. The Ramblas are a city cliché, but a must. Go there to see the Boqueria market – lively, colourful and tasty. Walk around the port to see the statue of Christopher

Columbus and the former fishing district of the Barceloneta. Above all, pay homage at the temple of football, the stadium of Barça, a genuine institution. After your first encounter with this mythical and generous city, cool off at the coast at Sitges (pp. 172-173) or one of the numerous small ports along the Costa del Maresme (pp. 160-161). Or you can explore inland. Follow the Llobregat river to the famous mountain-top monastery of Montserrat, with its statue of La Morenetta (pp. 206-207). Thought by some to resemble a huge shipwreck, the isolated jagged massif, with its impressive pinnacles and deep gorges, is a wonderful setting for one of Catalonia's holiest places, and the monastery, surrounded by chapels and hermits' caves, is now home to Benedictine monks Enjoy a walk around the mountain

before making another essential pilgrimage to the land of Cistercian abbeys: Santes Creus, Vallbona de les Monges and Poblet are the three jewels of Romanesque art in Catalonia (pp. 212-213).

A week
in Font-Romeu

The French football team prepared for their eventual triumph in the 1998 World Cup at this health resort, 5,900 ft (1,800 m) above sea level, ideally located on a sheltered, sunny hillside with a beautiful panorama of pine forests (p. 134). There, you will find activities for all seasons: both cross-country and downhill skiing, swimming pools, horse-riding, archery, nine-hole golf courses, a fitness centre, tennis, squash, wall climbing, sauna, numerous excursions, canoeing, paragliding and mountain biking. You can rent furnished flats on a weekly basis from the tourist office. The resort is ideal for discovering the treasures of the French Cerdagne, which is a haven of freshness and sunshine. You can visit Eyne nature reserve, Dorres Roman baths, the solar oven in Odeillo (pp. 134-135), Lanoux lake, the panoramic view at Canigou peak, the Cerdagne museum in Léocadie, the abbeys of Saint-Martin-du-Canigou (p. 132) and Saint-Michel-de-Cuxa (p. 131), and the astonishing train ride from Villefranche-de-Conflent (p. 128). Come and discover the mountain region's year-round sunshine, its magnificent views and unforgettable excursions – a breath of really fresh air. Winter sports and summer games combine perfectly with the marvellous scenery.

you have a wide range of excursions to choose from. You can cycle on the seafront from Canet to Saint-Cyprien (pp. 114-115) and take a fitness run, hiking trail or horse ride around the small lake. Enjoy a day of fishing out at sea or a boat trip along the coast, or follow the ornithologists' trail around the small lakes of Canet and Saint-Nazaire. Treat yourself to a trip to Perpignan (pp. 104-107), once capital of the kingdom of Majorca, or an outing to the Byrrh cellars in Thuir (pp. 126-127). Finally, visit the charming medieval village of Castelnou (pp.126-127).

A week
in Canet-Plage

Sailors, sports enthusiasts and holidaymakers visit this lively coast throughout the year (pp. 112-113). Canet-Plage is the locals' favourite resort and very relaxing. They come for the beach, which stretches for miles, the aquarium, the unusual museums and the attractive local port. Little wonder that the town's symbol, found in the central Place de la Méditerranée, is a nude statue named La Fille de la Mer (Daughter of the Sea). You can easily walk the few miles to the old village of Canet-en-Roussillon, known for its wine and market-gardening industries and its fascinating château and ice well. Staying in Canet-Plage,

A week
from Tarragona
to the Èbre delta

egin your stay by
escaping to the biggest
theme park in Spain –
Port Aventura (pp. 176-177).
Discover Imperial China,
Mayan warriors, Wild West
Indians and Polynesian
dancers on a trip through
space and time. Afterwards,
you can appreciate more
ancient and historical marvels
in Tarragona (pp. 174-175),
sometimes described as 'the
balcony of the Mediterrranean'.
Now a major industrial port,
it's one of Spain's oldest cities,
preserving many remnants of
its Roman past as the capital
of Tarraconensis. The Romans
made it one of the most
elegant cities on the Iberian
peninsula, much lauded for its
climate and delicious wines.
The Roman remains are
splendid, the most beautiful
being the amphitheatre,
which sits regally on a hill
facing the sea. Nearby, there
are other traces of the Roman
occupation of Spain, like the
devil's bridge and the Scipion
tower. Then, leave civilisation
behind in the swamps of the

Èbre delta, Catalonia's
equivalent to the Camargue
(pp. 178-181). You can spend
at least two days in these
beautiful open spaces, a
paradise for both birds and
walkers. Flamingoes breed
here along with black-winged
stilts and herons. This is also
the ideal place to try fish,
seafood and the famous local
rice cooked in a Catalan
sauce. Find your way back to
civilisation by following the
course of the Èbre up to
Tortosa (pp. 216-217), which
is overlooked by the stately
outline of the Zuda fortress,
a reminder of the 8th-C.
Moorish invasion. Further
north is Tivenys (p. 216),
famous for its potteries, and
El Pinell de Brai, home to a
splendid Modernist wine
cellar, designed by one
of Gaudí's disciples.

Celebrate Picasso in Horta
(p. 217), a splendid mountain
village inhabited by goats and
wild boar. The sharp angles
and long straight lines of the
rocky scenery
inspired him
to produce
some of his
best cubist
works.

A fortnight
in Argelès-Plage

The Côte Vermeille (pp. 116-119), the inspiration of Fauvist and cubist painters, is ideal for relaxation or hiking, and the superb rocky seabed by the foothills of the Pyrenees is a gift for divers. Despite their busy tourist industries, the coast's small Catalan ports have preserved their traditional way of life, notably fishing by lamplight and the fish auctions. Argelès will give you

an insight into the secrets of the region, while you enjoy the resort's many activities. Visit the Mas Larrieu nature reserve, hike in the Albera range and ramble in Émilie (pp. 20-21) or to the tower of La Massane. Elne abbey (p. 115), found on the Roussillon plain, has a magnificent Romanesque cloister, floral friezes and stylised animals. On a Saturday, go to the local-produce market

in Céret (pp. 124-125), a village typical of the region, with enormous plane trees, perfect squares, medieval gates and a huge Baroque church. The village is also a temple to Cubism, home to a striking modern-art museum that contains works by Picasso, Braque and Chagall; see the same view once admired by Picasso from the shade of a plane tree on a terrace. As the day ends, look out over the sea as the charming port of Collioure (pp. 120-121) is bathed in delicate tones of crimson, and enjoy a moment to peacefully sit and dream.

A fortnight
in the northern
Costa Brava

the roads of the Empordanet region for a few days (pp. 148-151), between the sea and the countryside, and end your journey on the Spanish side of the Albera range (pp. 182-183), land of tortoises and prehistoric standing stones. Along your way, you'll experience the rich variety of the region's culture. Discover the fabulous legacy left by one of Catalonia's most celebrated painters, Salvador Dalí.

Born in Figueras in 1904, he died there in 1989 and is entombed nearby. Visit his museum-house in Port-Lligat (p. 141), his breathtaking Surrealist museum in Figueras and Gala's castle in Púbol (pp. 138 and 149). Figueras is also known for its toy museum – a paradise for children of all ages, with exhibits from all over Catalonia. There's also a colourful fruit and vegetable market on Thursdays.

Here, if the wind doesn't get you, the sun certainly will! It's simply scorching and attracts huge crowds. But leave behind the congested beaches and discover the hidden treasures inland or between two former fishing ports, now tourist resorts. For a different view of the Costa Brava, take the scenic walk from Cape Creus to the Sant Peres de Rodes monastery. Start off in Cadaqués (p. 140). This is the part of the coast that has been painted most often, having seduced countless artists since the beginning of the 20thC. Stroll through the streets lined with white houses, still untouched by property developers, and set out for Aiguamolls park (pp. 142-143), a haven for birds and walkers alike. Seek out the Greek and Roman remains of Empúries and discover the protected coast of the Medes islands' nature reserve (pp. 144-147). Saunter along

Catalonia à la carte

Beautiful walks

From hikes to family rambles, from a few hours to a few days, the region has everything for a beautiful walk.

Trails of discovery

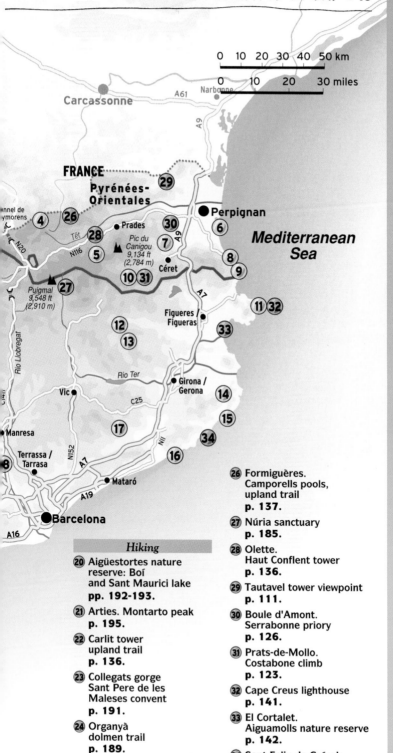

0 10 20 30 40 50 km

0   10   20   30 miles

Carcassonne

A61 Narbonne

A9

FRANCE
Pyrénées-Orientales
29

nnel de ymorens

4   26   ● **Perpignan**

Têt   ● Prades   30   6

28   7   *Mediterranean Sea*

N116   5   Pic du Canigou 9,134 ft (2,784 m)

N20   10   31   Céret   8   9

27   Puigmal 9,548 ft (2,910 m)   11   32

Rio Llobregat   12   13   Figueres / Figueras   33

Rio Ter   ● Girona / Gerona

Vic ●   C25   14

17   15   34

● Manresa   N152   16

Terrassa / Tarrasa   A7

8   ● Mataró   A19

●Barcelona   A16

Hiking

20 Aigüestortes nature reserve: Boí and Sant Maurici lake **pp. 192-193.**

21 Arties. Montarto peak **p. 195.**

22 Carlit tower upland trail **p. 136.**

23 Collegats gorge Sant Pere de les Maleses convent **p. 191.**

24 Organyà dolmen trail **p. 189.**

25 Lles. La Pera lakes **p. 187.**

26 Formiguères. Camporells pools, upland trail **p. 137.**

27 Núria sanctuary **p. 185.**

28 Olette. Haut Conflent tower **p. 136.**

29 Tautavel tower viewpoint **p. 111.**

30 Boule d'Amont. Serrabonne priory **p. 126.**

31 Prats-de-Mollo. Costabone climb **p. 123.**

32 Cape Creus lighthouse **p. 141.**

33 El Cortalet. Aiguamolls nature reserve **p. 142.**

34 Sant Feliu de Guíxols. Sant Elm hermitage **p. 154.**

Getting away from it all

RANDONNEE N°2 ° TOUR DU MASSIF MADELOC

Travelling through Catalonia, you'll encounter a wide variety of Nature's scenery and fragrances. Mountain lovers will adore the high peaks, pine woods, crystal–clear lakes and green valleys of the Pyrenees. For those who prefer the sea, the Côte Vermeille and Cape Creus are packed with hidden creeks and whitewashed fishing villages. Here, there are walks to delight the whole family. Follow in our footsteps and enjoy the magnificent landscapes, but make sure you have a good pair of walking shoes.

Following in the footsteps of shepherds

The traditional shepherds' path to the summer pastures still exists, starting at Prats Balaguer castle and running into the wild hills of the Cucurucull range. In the early 20thC., thousands of sheep would make this trip in July, spending the next four months in the higher meadows. Leave your car by the ruins of Prats Balaguer castle and set off along the legendary path. On reaching the dry-stone-walled house with the wild grass roof, you can return by following the track down through the forest. To get to the castle, take the N116 from Mont-Louis or Perpignan to Fontpédrouse. Here, at St-Thomas-les-Bains, you can take a dip in a natural hot springs jacuzzi. At the bottom of the valley, follow the signs for Prats Balaguer. The walk takes 2½ hours and is fairly easy.

Between sea and mountain

This week-long walk takes you over the mountains from creek to creek. The trail runs along the Albères range (p. 182) with its famous 14th-C. lighthouses, crossing cork-oak woods and deep valleys, before following the 'Fauvist way' to Collioure (p. 120). You can enjoy a glass of Banyuls wine and then head back, via Sant Pere de Rodes monastery (p. 138), which overlooks the Golfe du Lion. A remarkable series of *calas* will take you to Cape Creus

(p. 141), from where you follow the coast to Cadaqués (p. 140). The route ends with an encounter with legendary painter Salvador Dalí in Port-Lligat (p. 140) and his museum at Figueras (p. 139). Information: La Balaguère, Rte d'Argelès-Gazost, Arrens-Marsous, ☎ 05 62 97 20 21,

Cape Creus

𝐅 05 62 97 43 01.
One week trip: 3,580F.

Planning
your route
Maison des Pyrénées:
15, Rue Saint-Augustin,
75002 Paris.

Côte Vermeille

☎ 01 42 86 51 86.
Open Mon.-Fri.,
9.30am-6.30pm.
Ideal for organising
your trip, booking
accommodation,
and so on.

**Maison de la
Catalogne:**
4-8, Cour du
Commerce-Saint-André,
75006 Paris.
☎ 01 40 46 85 28.
Information on Spanish
Catalonia.

**Maison des Gîtes de
France:** 59, Rue Saint-
Lazare, 75009 Paris.
☎ 01 49 70 75 75,

𝐅 01 49 70 75 76
www.gites-de-france.fr.
A catalogue is available in the
UK from Gîtes de France's
official rep: Brittany Ferries,
The Brittany Centre, Wharf
Road, Portsmouth PO2 8RU.
☎ 0990 360 360
www.brittany-ferries.com

Gites de Catalunya:
Turisverd, Menric 7,
Pl. Sant Josep Oriol 4,
Barcelona. ☎ 93 412 69 84,
𝐅 93 412 50 16.

The conquerors
of the Pyrenees
Following a history of
impoverishment and
domination by Castile,
Catalan culture experienced
a spectacular revival in the
late 19thC. This awakening,
known as the Renaixença
(renaissance), owed much
to 'excursionism', an
intellectual movement
founded in 1876 that aimed
to reclaim Catalonia, particularly the Pyrenees,
for its people. Under the

leadership of the **Centro
Excursionista de Catalunya**
(CEC, Paradis ☎10 93 315
23 11) in Barcelona, this new
philosophy gave birth to the
nationalism of modern
Catalonia. Today, the CEC
has 5,300 members, or 'socios',
and operates as a leisure centre
and mountain club, offering
trips to the Pyrenees. They
have an office near the
cathedral, at the base of the
Roman columns. Why
not try a roped party
expedition?

Many faces of Catalonia

To those born under a wandering star, Catalonia offers a journey from capes to bays, from wooded hills to towering mountains. The azure Côte Vermeille, the giant guardian peaks of Carlit and Canigou, the gleaming lakes of the Pyrenees and the Èbre delta – it's all waiting to be discovered. Catalonia is a landscape of a thousand faces. To enjoy them all, climb aboard your magic carpet, guide in hand, and off you go.

Côte Vermeille

Sacred mountain

Mountain refuge and holy retreat, the Pic du Canigou (9,134 ft/2,784 m) has always captured the imagination. For Catalans on both sides of the border, it's simply the mountain. This volcanic cone between Conflent and Vallespir is only 37 miles (60 km) from the sea – the bridge between the Pyrenees and the Mediterranean. Throughout the ages, Canigou has commanded the respect of those who have worked in the mountain's shadow – shep-herds, coal miners and the iron men of Catalonia's forges. In the early 20thC., merchants would provide the resorts in Prats de Mollo and Vernet with ice from the glacier. These days, it's a busy playground for canoeing and white-water enthusiasts.

Parc National d'Aigüestortes

The Aigüestortes nature reserve, which covers 35,000 acres (14,000 ha) of the province of Lleida, was created in 1955 and is the only national park in Spanish Catalonia. You can go hiking, climbing or visit the rich Roman heritage of the Boí valley, and the park is also one of the most varied animal reserves in western Europe, with wild goats, brown bears and vultures among others. The glacial activity of the Quaternary era sculpted stout granite into crests and flattened soft slate. In the heart of the reserve are the twin needles called Les Encantats ('the enchanted ones'), which will delight hik-

Sant Maurici lake

LA GARROTXA VOLCANOES

The Volcans de la Garrotxa, a group of around 30 dormant volcanoes in the heart of Spanish Catalonia, is one of the most impressive sites in continental Europe. These giants entombed in ash, their names (Garrinada, Croscat, Roca Negra) inspired by fear, give the scenery of this 46-sq-mile (120-sq-km) area a timeless appeal. The wonderful scenery inspired many Catalan landscape painters and Olot, a small market town, has been the centre of an art colony since the founding of the Public School of Drawing in 1783. Today, the site is a popular local nature reserve and a fascinating place for adventure and study (p. 198).

ers. This hidden range is also home to some 300 lakes and ponds. The Sant Maurici lake, encircled by trees and mountains, lies beneath the twin shards of the Encantats. There's water everywhere and

La Garrotxa volcanoes

it gives its name to the park, 'aigües tortes' meaning 'tortuous waters'. During the early summer, walkers can enjoy the rhododendrons in the lower valleys and later the wild lilies bloom in the forests of fir, beech and silver birch.

If you visit in winter, the snow-covered peaks are ideal for cross-country skiing. Before setting off on your walk, check the park rules and regulations (p. 192).

Èbre delta

The Parc Naturel du Delta de l'Èbre covers around 12,000 acres (5,000 ha). The area was first governed by the Arabs, then the Cistercians and later the Hospitaller order of knights. In the middle of the 19thC., the construction of the Dreta canal assured the survival of both the region's developing agriculture and its 40,000 inhabitants. The main industries today are fishing and agriculture, with the region producing 98% of the rice grown in Catalonia. The 'ullals' (rice fields) of the 'masos' (estates) are often flooded in spring, becoming giant mirrors reflecting the

Fageda d'En Jorda forest

sky. If you decide to stay in this watery landscape, make use of the ferries which regularly cross the river. In Sant Carles de la Ràpita, order a rossejat, rice cooked in fish stock, with lamprey, eels or lobsters. The park is also a haven for birds, ideal for bird-watchers.

Open air, open country

For clear blue skies, fresh air and memorable walks, Catalonia is the perfect choice, with scenery that changes with the seasons and its abundance of animal and plant life. Follow the tracks of the acrobatic izard, the famous grouse or the cheeky marmot. Botanical experts and enthusiastic plant hunters can pursue their interest by scouring the valleys for medicinal herbs or beautiful wild orchids. You may be lucky enough to spot some of the rare butterfly species, particularly if you visit Catalonia between May and July.

Pyrenean flora

Plants struggle to survive at high altitudes and, as you climb, the changes in the vegetation are startling. Climate change through the ages explains the presence of certain other plants. The Pyrenees formed under a subtropical climate and some species managed to adapt to mountain conditions. In all, there are some 160 species that are indigenous to, or widely found in, the Pyrenees mountains.

Green steps

There are several distinct levels of mountain plant life. The **mountain stage**

Fritillary

(2,960-5,900 ft/ 900-1,800 m), fresh and humid, is home to beech and fir trees on the northern faces and Norway pine on the southern faces. There are also waterside plants, moors, meadows and masses of fallen rocks to be found, along with wood anemones, Pyrenean valerian, water saxifrages, fritillaries and the famous ramonde. The **sub-alpine stage** (5,900-7,900 ft/ 1,800-2,400 m) shelters pine forests, moors of ferruginous rhododendron, and some

Wood anemones

birch and rowan trees as well as many varieties of lily, iris and thistle. Higher still is the **alpine stage** (7,900-9,550 ft/ 2,400-2,900 m), where small willow trees cling to the rocks. The plants are smaller here, but their colours are quite vivid, with such varieties as campion, glacier buttercup, saxifrage, etc. Finally, highest of all is the **winter-flowering stage**,

Campion

Ferruginous rhododendron

Egret

but this is rather rare in the Pyrenees, and only a few lichens and algae manage to survive here.

Medes islands, a paradise for gulls and cormorants

Every morning, they fly to the plains of Empordà to catch worms, insects and mice. During the mating season, whilst using an elaborate language of

Vulture

Medes islands

A few miles from the coast, the Islas Medes are home to a variety of bird species, including bullfinches, blue blackbirds, hoopoes, rattle and peregrine falcons, grey herons and egrets. Some birds come here to nest in peace after fishing in the Ter valley. The most spect-acular island is home to a large colony of yellow-footed gulls – 8,000 couples mate here in March, April and May.

Rowan tree

ritual calls and postures to attract a mate, the birds are aggressive and protect their territory. The babies are usually born around mid-March and can fly five weeks later. They are grey in colour when born, and their plumage only develops after five years. You can visit the islands in a glass-bottomed boat and experience the huge and colourful range of marine life. There's even a good chance

you'll encounter the odd conger eel or barracuda. It's also a haven for scuba divers (p. 146).

LIME-BLOSSOM TEA — A MIRACLE CURE?

It was in Arles-sur-Tech in 1916 that François Domenach 'discovered' that lime-blossom tea could cure kidney stones, and ever since then the bark of the lime tree has been sold here as a remedy. Lime trees like humidity, growing well on riverbanks. When the sap rises, they are cut down and the bark is split lengthways (after 20 July, when the sap recedes, the bark sticks to the trunk and so the work is harder). The bark is then sent down to Serralongue and left to dry for a few weeks. It is then chopped into 6-inch (20-cm) pieces and brushed, shredded and shaped into sticks. This curative remedy, which is sold in brown paper bags in health shops, has been praised by, among others, Jean Cocteau and Jean Giono. Why not give it a try? It could be the answer to all sorts of aches and pains!

A taste of Catalonia

Cold meats, cheese, honey, jam, *touron*...
Catalonia has a wide range of delicacies to suit all tastes

Local produce

1. **Arties:** Tienda Juantxo (pâté) **p. 195.**
2. **La Seu d'Urgell:** Cadí co-operative (butter, cheese **p. 188.**
3. **Martinet:** Four Jordi (bread) **p. 187.**
4. **Bellver de Cerdanya:** Tupí de Cerdanya (pâté, cheese) **p. 187.**
5. **Ribes de Freser:** Can Rueda (cold meats) **p. 184.**
6. **Boule d'Amont:** Relais de Serrabone (foie gras, cheese) **p. 127.**
7. **Perpignan:** Roussillon snails **p. 106.**
8. **Collioure:** Société Roques (anchovies) **p. 120.**
9. **Cerbère:** La Roumaguère (cold meats) **p. 119.**
10. **L'Escala:** Casa Bordas (anchovies) **p. 145.**
11. **Pals:** Pals mill (rice) **p. 148.**
12. **Vic:** Can Vila and Ca La Teresona (cold meats) **p. 209.**
13. **Deltebre:** Cambra Arressora de Deltebre (rice) **p.179.**
14. **Amposta:** Duque (cold meats) **p. 180.**
15. **Lleida:** snails **p. 215.**
16. **Rupit:** Maria Carme (cold meats) **p. 209.**

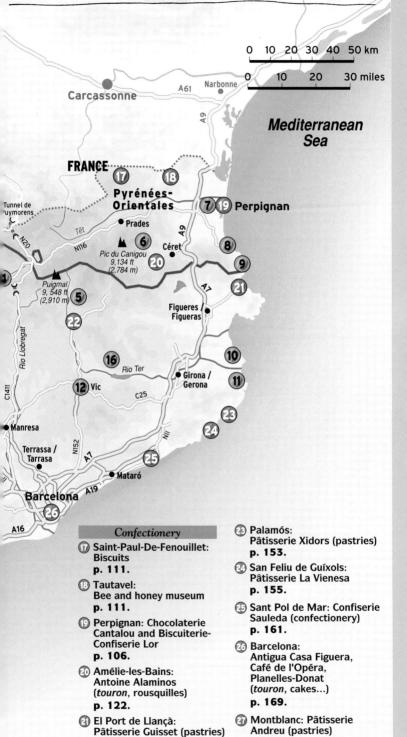

Carcassonne

A61 Narbonne

A9

Mediterranean Sea

0 10 20 30 40 50 km

0   10   20   30 miles

FRANCE

⑰ ⑱

Pyrénées-Orientales

⑦ ⑲ **Perpignan**

Tunnel de uymorens

N20

Têt

N116

● Prades

⑥

Céret

⑧

Pic du Canigou 9,134 ft (2,784 m)

⑳

⑨

①

Puigmal 9,548 ft (2,910 m)

⑤

A7

㉑

Figueres / Figueras

Rio Llobregat

㉒

C1411

⑯

Rio Ter

⑩

⑫ Vic

C25

Girona / Gerona

⑪

● Manresa

㉓

Terrassa / Tarrasa

N152

A7

NII

㉔

Barcelona

㉕

● Mataró

A19

㉖

A16

Confectionery	
⑰ Saint-Paul-De-Fenouillet: Biscuits **p. 111.**	㉓ Palamós: Pâtisserie Xidors (pastries) **p. 153.**
⑱ Tautavel: Bee and honey museum **p. 111.**	㉔ San Feliu de Guíxols: Pâtisserie La Vienesa **p. 155.**
⑲ Perpignan: Chocolaterie Cantalou and Biscuiterie-Confiserie Lor **p. 106.**	㉕ Sant Pol de Mar: Confiserie Sauleda (confectionery) **p. 161.**
⑳ Amélie-les-Bains: Antoine Alaminos (*touron*, rousquilles) **p. 122.**	㉖ Barcelona: Antigua Casa Figuera, Café de l'Opéra, Planelles-Donat (*touron*, cakes…) **p. 169.**
㉑ El Port de Llançà: Pâtisserie Guisset (pastries) **p. 138.**	㉗ Montblanc: Pâtisserie Andreu (pastries) **p. 212.**
㉒ Ripoll: Can Junyent (sweets) **p. 185.**	㉘ Tortosa: Pallerès **p. 216.**

A taste of the Catalan sun

Catalan cuisine is a delicate mixture of the products of both the sea and the mountains, like the region itself. The contrasting flavours of the Pyrenees and the Mediterranean are blended together in delicious and simple dishes. Basic ingredients are turned into hearty meals, cooked on the stove or *paradilla* (grilled) *à la planxa* (on an iron griddle). Catalonia generously shares its local produce, full of the flavours of the earth. Let yourself get carried away…

The art of blending flavours

Empordà, on the Costa Brava, is one of the main centres of Catalan gastronomy. Empúries, formerly a Greek and Roman colony, has preserved its ancient Arab and Jewish influences in its cuisine, which uses honey, lemon and cinnamon. The whole region has a long history of trade with countries of the Mediterranean and thus uses a wide range of spices from the Middle East.

The Mediterranean Influence

The influence of Arab physicians, who invented medieval gastronomy, can be found in Catalonia's sweet sauces scented with grilled almonds, in the *picada*, and in the flavours of cinnamon and bitter orange. However, this cuisine is also deeply rooted in Mediterranean culture, as demonstrated by the almost exclusive use of olive oil, and the importance of garlic and onion (especially in the *sofregit*) and of tomatoes, which were cooked here as early as the 16thC.

Escudella i Carn d'Olla

This is a rustic soup that takes its name from the *olla*, the Catalan stewing pot. From the late 13thC., the soup was made by combining three separate dishes: meat stock, which traditionally had been served as a starter; vegetables and meat – chicken or duck, leg of mutton or lamb and ham; and sliced *pilota* (a black pudding made from pork, onion, garlic, parsley, cinnamon, pepper, bread, egg and flour), with *fideus* (vermicelli), *cigrons* (chickpeas) or rice. From the 17thC.,

dry beans and potatoes imported from America were added to the recipe.

Here are some useful phrases for mealtime. A *bodega* is a wine bar, often decorated with barrels. Here, the wine is usually served by the glass, often accompanied by a choice of different cold meats. The *can* or *casa* is a simple restaurant offering a 'family atmosphere', with basic cooking, including stews and casseroles made from fresh local produce. *Chiringuitos* are found by the seaside and frequented by local fishermen, unlike *fondas*, which are roadside inns where the quality of the food may be 'pot luck'. *Granjas* offer dairy and farm products. Then there are the *horchaterias*, which specialise in drinks made from barley flavoured with almonds or groundnuts (*horchata de chufa*).

Throughout the ages, the dish has been adapted to living conditions and the local economy. *Escudella* was once prepared for large groups of guests, cooked continuously in the same *olla*, which was never washed, with fresh ingredients added to the leftovers from the previous day. It is the slow cooking that gives the dish its unique flavour – country fare that can be made with string beans, courgettes or garlic during the summer.

Cargolade

A convivial Catalan dish, usually served outdoors between May and September, with the traditional exception of July – as the locals say, 'Per juliols, ni dones ni cargols' ('In July, no women, no snails'). It's a simple recipe. In a shady place, build a fire using offcuts from the vines. When the fire is glowing, place the snails (around 50 per person) on a cooking rack over the fire. Remember that the snails need to be fasted for a fortnight, salted and placed in vinegar, then rinsed and left to dry. Season and then gently drip lard over the grilling snails. A glass of chilled red Corbières complements this dish perfectly. Traditionally, snails are served as a starter

and are usually followed by a selection of sausages and black puddings such as *butifarra*, a pork sausage, often grilled and served with beans. Catalan cuisine is varied and interesting and considered amongst the best in Spain. Bon appétit!

Sweet discoveries

Gourmets, bon-vivants, gastronomes, epicures, food lovers – whatever your choice of term, here are some sweet delicacies to be savoured or taken with you as you follow the festive Catalan way of life. There is a panoply of flavours to be enjoyed. Indulge yourself!

Autumnal sweets

Catalonia is a land of vibrant traditions. Every seasonal celebration has a sweet treat that brings the shop windows to colourful life. You'll be tempted by *tortell* during the feasts of Saint Antoine and Saint Paul, *bunyols* during Holy Week, *mona* at Easter and *coques* on Midsummer Day. On All Saints' Day, confectioners prepare the delicious *panellets*. This day symbolises the end of summer's abundance and, in the past, families would gather in the evening to say rosaries in memory of the dead while eating chestnuts (*castanyada*). The pasty consistency of the nut was supposed to prevent wandering spirits from entering the body. The locals now eat *panellets*, a confection of almond paste, coated with pine nuts, reminiscent of chestnuts, and drink sweet wine.

Touron – the secret of oriental flavours

There are many different legends surrounding the origin of the sweet delicacy *touron* or *turrón* (nougat). In the regional archives, is a letter from Queen Maria, written in Valladolid in 1453, asking the abbess Santa Clara of Barcelona to send some of her delicious *touron* as a gift for the king of Castile. During the plague in 1703 the confectioners' guild initiated a competition for the despairing population to create new sweets. Padre Torró is said to have invented *touron*

to bring comfort to the sick and plague-ridden people.

Time for tasting

It seems most likely that *touron* originated in the Arabic or Jewish culture in North Africa and would have been made as early as the

A CRUNCHY, LEMON-FLAVOURED TREAT

In Saint Paul-de-Fenouillet, squeezed between the last Catalan cliffs and the rocky Cathar country, the local speciality is *croquant à l'ancienne*, a crunchy, lemon-flavoured biscuit. It used to be eaten on feast days and is still made by local patisseries in the region. A treat really not to be missed (p. 111).

14thC. in the Xixona region. It's a flavour for gourmets to savour – a subtle blend of almonds, honey, cinnamon and pine nuts. *Turrón* comes in two main varieties: one white and hard, studded with whole nuts, and the other made from a soft paste of ground almonds.

It's quite delicious and makes an ideal gift to take home. It was once sold during the three months of the Christmas *ferias* and when these open fairs were abolished in 1850, the stallholders were forced into the porches of houses, where they can still be found today. There are two recommended shops to visit in search of this delicacy, one in Spain and one in France. **Planelles-Donat** in Barcelona (p. 169), and **Confiserie Lor**, in Perpignan (p. 106), which like its Spanish counterpart, is an address to avoid if you're on a strict diet!

Crema cremada, Mel i matò

Crema cremada (crème brûlée) is made with eggs, milk, sugar, flour and vanilla or cinnamon. In the Empordà region, it's eaten with very thin biscuits, called 'roscats'. The ramekins and kitchen blowtorches used in its preparation can be found in local ironmongers, where you can also buy a *porró*, the long-necked drinking jug. In this cattle-breeding region, it's not surprising to find desserts made from cream cheese – *Mel i matò* is easy to prepare and any gourmet will enjoy these curds covered with honey and sprinkled with flaked almonds. On Sunday, in front of the Montserrat monastery, there's a small market selling locally produced fruit and vegetables, where you can indulge in the sin of gluttony with the monks' blessings.

Recommended eating

Here are a few places where you can taste Catalan cuisine,
both traditional and modern.

① Artíes
Restaurant Urtau
p. 195.

② Espot
Casa Palmira
p. 193.

③ Esterri d'Àneu
Restaurant Bonabé
p. 188.

④ La Seu d'Urgell
Fonda Andria
p. 187.

⑤ Martinet
Can Boix
p. 187.

⑥ Castelnou
L'Hostal
p. 127.

⑦ Santa Pau
Cal Sastre
p. 201.

⑧ Besalú
Fonda Siqués
p. 201.

⑨ El port de la Selva
Ca l'Hermida
p. 138.

⑩ Cape Creus
Cape Creus bar-restaurant
p. 141.

⑪ Cadaqués
La Galiota
Es Baluard
p. 140.

⑫ Roses
El Buli
p. 143.

⑬ Sobrestany
Hotel del Caçador
p. 147.

⑭ Sa Punta
La Punta
p. 148.

Pico
de Aneto
11,182 ft
(3,408 m)

Pic
d'Esta
10,319
(3,145

ANDOR

Cataluña /
Catalunya

SPAIN

Rio Noguera

Rio
Segre

C1313

C1313

C25

N II

Lleida /
Lérida

Rio Segre

A2

N240

Ebro

Reus

Tarragona

Tortosa

A7

Mediterranean
Sea

0   10   20   30 miles

0 10 20 30 40 50 km

⑲ Sant Feliu de Guíxols

Eldorador Petit, Eldorado Mar
pp. 154-155.

⑳ Lorret del Mar

El Trull, Les Petxines
p. 159.

㉑ Arenys de Mar

El Posit de Pescadores
Hispània
p. 132.

㉒ Barcelona

Le Pinocho
p. 169.

Mediterranean Sea

㉓ Sitges

La Torreta
p. 173.

㉔ Vilanova i la Geltrú

El Peixerot
p. 173.

㉕ Tarragone

Les Voltes
p. 175.

㉖ Deltebre

El Cadell
p. 179.

㉗ El Poblenou del Delta

L'Estany
p. 181.

㉘ Sant Carles de la Ràpita

Le Miami Can Pons
Can Batiste
p. 181.

㉙ Cardona

Castle restaurant
p. 205.

㉚ Santa Maria de Queralt

Sanctuary restaurant
p. 203.

⑮ Bégur

La Fonda Caner
p. 151.

⑯ Peratallada

La Riera
p. 149.

⑰ Monells

El Monells
El Hort del Rector
p. 150.

⑱ Palamós

La Gamba
Port Reial
La Menta
p. 153.

Enjoy your meal!

Catalonia expresses its identity through its cuisine, a blend of the cultural and natural legacies of the Pyrenees and the Mediterranean. Like the region, the cooking is rustic and grounded in tradition, the dishes hearty and satisfying – wild rabbit with gambas, broad-bean stew, partridge with cabbage, cod in ratatouille, grilled snails and mushrooms – and there are so many other local flavours to enjoy.

Collioure and Escala anchovies

When tourists leave the shores of Collioure (Côte Vermeille) and Escala (Costa Brava), the fishermen go out on their search for anchovies. These little fish are harvested at night in September and October, from boats carrying a large lamp (the *lamparo*), and then they are salted as soon as they are unloaded. A few days later, they are gutted, topped and tailed, and then placed in spiral stacks in barrels, between layers of salt. They then pickle in their own juices for three months, before being put into tins or, for the most valued kind, jars, preserved in olive oil and salt. This regional speciality is still made according to the traditional process and employs some 200 families in Escala and three companies in Collioure. Anchovies are frequently used in Catalan cuisine, along with such derivatives as *anchoïade* (anchovy sauce) and olives stuffed with anchovies.

Calçotada

Among seasonal eating rituals, don't miss the *calçotada* if you happen to be in the Valls region (Tarragona) in the spring. Respect tradition by eating this dish with a napkin around your neck. Unpeeled spring onions (*calçots*) are grilled on blazing vine shoots in the open air. Then they are peeled quickly, leaving only the bulb, and eaten hot with the fingers, dipped in sauce. Catalans can be seen enjoying these enthusiastically, dressed in aprons and bibs. The secret lies in the sauce, the *salvitjada*,

which is a mixture of almonds, garlic, grilled tomatoes, olive oil, vinegar, salt, pepper, hot pepper, *bitxo* and mint leaves. In some villages, this spring ritual can last several days and with the *calçots* you can enjoy sausages with broad beans or lamb chops, and *crème catalane*. Try *calçotada* when it's the dish of the day in a restaurant and then you can complement your meal with Priorat wine, drunk from the *porro*. It's a superb way to enjoy participating in one of Catalonia's great culinary traditions.

Catalan *xatós*

The xató (pronounced 'chato') is typically served on Maundy Thursday, and is part of the popular holy-week carnival. The dish is a mixture of ingredients from the sea and the mountain regions, the traditional recipe varying from one village to another.

To make some for yourself, take a large bowl and mix together the leaves of a lettuce, 14 oz (400 g) of peeled and salted cod, 7 oz (200 g) of tuna in oil, 3.5 oz (100 g) of small green *arbequine* olives, 2 sliced semi-ripe tomatoes and 12 salted anchovies.

Dress the mixture with a vinaigrette spiced with 4 cloves of garlic, a pinch of chopped red chilli pepper and 1 oz (20 g) of grilled almonds. The tourist office publishes a brochure, '**Ruta del Xató**', listing local villages that specialise in this delicacy, which include Sitges, Vilanova and El Vendrell. In Sitges, a day-long guided tour is on the visitor's menu. It includes a gourmet meal as well as a lesson on how to make *xató* for yourself (information: ☎ 919 793 199). You can then go out and buy the ingredients locally and try it out on your friends at home.

FISHERMAN'S *BULLINADA*

Serves 6
3.3 lbs (1.5 kg) of fish (gurnard, anglerfish, eels, hog fish, etc.); 1.2 lbs (600 g) of potatoes; 1 onion; 1 sweet pepper; 3 cloves of garlic; mixed herbs (fennel, thyme, bay leaves); pinch of chilli powder, pinch of saffron and a knob of *sagi* (rancid lard!).
Fry the garlic, pepper and onion in olive oil in a pan until soft. Clean and dice the fish and add to the pan. Add some sea or salted water, the mixed herbs, spices, *sagi* and the peeled sliced potatoes. Leave to cook for 30 minutes on a medium heat until tender.

Wines and spirits

From Cava to Conca de Barberá, Muscat to Rivesaltes,
all places to add to your wine collection.

① **Tautavel**
Tautavel master
wine-makers
p. 111.

② **Rivesaltes**
Cazes estate
p. 109.

③ **Thuir**
Byrrh cellars
p. 126.

④ **Collioure**
Maison de la Vigne
p. 121.

⑤ **Banyuls-sur-Mer**
Robert Doutres,
Étoile co-operative cellar
p. 119.

⑥ **Capmany**
Bodegas Oliveda
p. 39.

⑦ **Masarac**
Mas Fita cellar
p. 139.

Pico
de Aneto
11,182 ft
(3,408 m)

Pic
d'Es
10,3
(3,145

ANDO

Garonna

Rio Noguera

C1313

SPAIN

**Cataluña /
Cataluña**

Rio
Segre

C1313

C25

N II

⑰

●Lleida /
Lérida

Rio Segre

A2

⑭

⑮

N240

Ebro

Reus ●   ● Tarragona

⑯

L'Espina
3,878 ft
(1,182 m)

Tortosa
●

A7

*Mediterranean
Sea*

A7

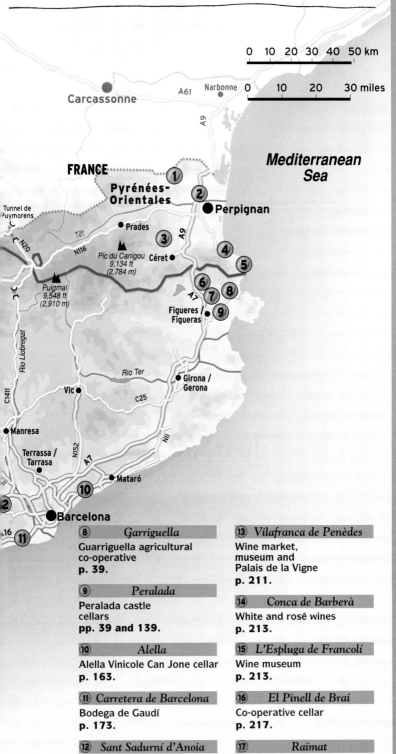

Carcassonne

Narbonne

Mediterranean Sea

FRANCE

Pyrénées-Orientales

① ② **Perpignan**

Tunnel de Puymorens

Prades

③ A9

Pic du Canigou
9,134 ft
(2,784 m)
Céret

④

⑤

Puigmal
9,548 ft
(2,910 m)

⑥

⑦ ⑧

A7

Figueres / Figueras

⑨

Rio Llobregat

Rio Ter

Girona / Gerona

C25

Vic

NII

Manresa

Terrassa / Tarrasa

N152

A7

Mataró

⑩

Barcelona

⑪

⑧ *Garriguella*	⑬ *Vilafranca de Penèdes*
Guarriguella agricultural co-operative **p. 39.**	Wine market, museum and Palais de la Vigne **p. 211.**
⑨ *Peralada*	⑭ *Conca de Barberà*
Peralada castle cellars **pp. 39 and 139.**	White and rosé wines **p. 213.**
⑩ *Alella*	⑮ *L'Espluga de Francolí*
Alella Vinicole Can Jone cellar **p. 163.**	Wine museum **p. 213.**
⑪ *Carretera de Barcelona*	⑯ *El Pinell de Brai*
Bodega de Gaudí **p. 173.**	Co-operative cellar **p. 217.**
⑫ *Sant Sadurní d'Anoia*	⑰ *Raïmat*
Codorníu cellars **p. 211.**	Raïmat estate **p. 215.**

Spanish Catalan wines
refined and subtle

There are six wine areas in Spanish Catalonia, but the heartland of the industry is the Penedès region, to the southwest of Barcelona. The cellars, using the latest technology to produce better wines, are well worth a visit. Also, don't miss the lively Saturday morning market in Vilafranca de Penedès or the superb, Modernist Cordoníu cellars, that ressemble a Bacchanalian cathedral, in Sant Sadurni d'Anoia. Take the scenic route, lose your way in the vineyards and taste wine from the bottle.

Penedès

This exclusive trademark applies to wine from a zone divided into three areas: coastal (Baix), central and, lastly, mountain (Alta), which includes some of the highest vineyards in Europe, at 2,600 ft (800 m). This region's chalky soil is ideal for growing vines. The vineyards on the coastal plain, located around Sitges and Vilafranca, produce strong, dark and slightly sweet wines. One of the major varieties of grape is *malvasia* (malmsey). The mountain vineyards produce light, charming white wines, made from *garnatxa* and macabeu grapes. The central area specialises in the production of the best sparkling wine in Spain, known as Cava.

How to choose

Most of the good wines of the region come from *garnatxa*, *ull de llebre* and *maçola* vines. With the addition of cabernet sauvignon grapes, the wine becomes tastier and more refined, the best examples being the Gran Coronas de Torres and the red from the Raïmat estate. There has recently been a revival of interest in the white wines.

Guariguella co-operative

They generally come from three grape varieties: macabeu, which brings an acid aroma and protects the wine against oxidation, *xarello*, which gives the wine body and colour and, *perellada* for a fresh and fruity flavour. For a few years now, some vineyard owners have added some noble grapes, such as chardonnay. In small quantites, they bring elegance and delicacy to the taste of the wine. The use of other grapes is mentioned on the label.

Empordà wine trail

The Empordà vineyards cover 3,000 acres (1,200 ha) of the Figueras plain to the north of Barcelona, where vines grow easily, owing to the exceptional sun, rare frosts, and chalky and humid soil.

In this area, you can visit some of the 26 cellars and co-operatives which bear the trademark. One of these is the Oliveda family's estate in Capmany (☎ 972 54 90 12), which produces some prestigious vintages, such as Rigau Ros Chardonnay, as well as excellent red, white and *rosado* (rosé) wines. Try not to miss the pretty medieval village of Peralada, where you can enjoy a wine-tasting at Peralada castle. All the wines here are aged in oak barrels, including the full-bodied Peralada Cabernet Sauvignon Tinto 1995 and the Gran Claustro 1995, which is renowned for its wonderful tasty aromas. As for white wine, the Peralada Sauvignon is a safe investment. You can end your wine trail by stocking up at the Guariguella co-operative (☎ 972 53 00 02), where you'll find unbeatable prices and a generous *porrròn*. A perfect end to a fascinating day for all lovers of wine.

THE SAGA OF CAVA
Cava accounts for the major part of the production of the Penedès area. Like Champagne, Cava is left to ferment a second time after bottling; however, it lost the right to call itself 'champagne' when Spain joined the EU in 1986. Cava is made with xarello, perellada, macabeu, chardonnay and monastrell grapes. A monk named Dom Pierre (1635-1715), who lived in Hautvilliers abbey, near Reims in France, was responsible for inventing sparkling wine. In 1872 Josep Raventós, who was working for a company named Cordoníu, in Sant Sadurní d'Anoia, made the first 300 bottles of Cava according the 'champagne method'. The wine quickly gained a strong reputation, but then, at the end of the 19thC., phylloxera, a deadly plant disease, destroyed 92% of the vineyards. Manuel Raventós purified the soil, replaced the damaged vines and asked the great architect Josep Puig i Cadafalch to build the cellars. These cellars, a temple to Bacchus, are a unique piece of Modernist architecture (p. 211). Raise a glass to the designer!

French Catalan
wines strong and full-bodied

The Roussillon region (eastern Pyrenees) is bathed in the sunshine and so offers a respectable choice of naturally sweet wines, Muscat and local wines. Full-bodied, strong, tasty and rich, these wines take their strength from the rays of the sun, needing only a few drops of rain each year. Take a journey through these sun-struck vineyards and, shaded under a trellised vine overlooking the sea, enjoy a glass of golden Muscat.

MAISON DE LA VIGNE ET DU VIN DE COLLIOURE **3**

ROUTE DES VIGNES

Naturally sweet wine or Muscat?

The VDN (Vin Doux Naturel) trademark, which refers to 'naturally sweet wine', is reserved for the products of four vines – Muscat, Grenache, Macabeu and Malmsey – grown in Languedoc-Roussillon and some other areas of the south of France. These wines are made by adding a purée of very ripe grapes to neat alcohol during fermentation and are a speciality of Roussillon because of the high sugar content of its grapes. To be labelled *rancio*, a VDN must age for at least two years in barrels exposed to the sun in the summer and kept warm in the winter. For a map of the Roussillon wine

circuit, telephone
☎ 04 68 51 31 81.

Rivesaltes
Among the VDNs, Rivesaltes is the Muscat of Roussillon. Made from Alexandria and small-seed Muscat grapes, it has been produced since the 13thC. and is one of the oldest sweet wines in Europe. The flame-coloured wine turns fawn as it matures,

becoming more sweet and fruity, and is drunk young, to accompany a dessert.

Banyuls
The vineyards of Banyuls are an essential part of the Côte Vermeille landscape. Planted on narrow terraces held in position by low shale walls, they produce a deep and dark, naturally sweet wine, which can age for up to 40 years. Its subtle flavour embraces the most delicate of aromas. For information on tasting and buying, see p. 119.

Maury
On the northern hills of Agly, 1 million gallons (45,000 hl) of this stocky and powerful wine are produced each year from black

RIVESALTES AND COMPANY

Rivesaltes wines are generally drunk as aperitifs or with a dessert, but they complement a remarkable variety of dishes. Try them with melon or with foie gras, or a lobster stew with an old Rivesaltes. Also, Muscat de Rivesaltes goes exceptionally well with Roquefort cheese. An open bottle can be kept for about 10 days – don't let those heavenly aromas go to waste.

Grenache grapes. The vineyards are located beneath the Château de Quéribus, in the Aude region of the eastern Pyrenees. The wine is garnet-red in colour when young and turns mahogany with age, acquiring a cocoa aroma.

Collioure

This trademark is given to the natural red wines of Banyuls, not to be confused with the sweet wine of the area. The grapes – red Grenache, mourvèdre, syrah and carignan – are grown over an area of 1,500 acres (600 ha) and give the wine its label, 'grenache de Collioure'. About 220,000 gallons (10,000 hl) of red wine are produced annually. Recently, some rosés have also appeared.

Côtes-du-Roussillon and Côtes-du-Roussillon-Villages

Fruity and rich in alcohol, these wines are also privileged with an AOC trademark, certifying their origin. Over many years, strenuous efforts

were made to improve the quality of these red (12°), white and rosé (11°) wines. The reds of the best villages bear the 'Côtes-du-

Roussillon-Villages' AOC, including Caramany, Montnet, La Tour de France, Vingrau and Lesquerde. The major grape variety has always been the carignan, which prospers in the shale soil of northern Roussillon, along the Agly coast. These wines have a pleasant aroma full of berries, a rich and pleasant tannin, as well as a long-lasting, fruity taste. The white wine, however, is not as good as the red or the rosé.

A Byrrh in Thuir

Seven medicinal plants, which give vitality and aid digestion, are used in the preparation of this very popular aperitif. Byrrh is based on wine, spiced with quinine and wine spirits, with cocoa and orange peel added to give the drink its pleasant taste. For information on visits to the Byrrh cellars, see p. 126.

Markets

Markets, rural or crafts fairs, perfect
for socialising as well as shopping.

① **Martinet**
Monday
p. 187.

② **Bellver de Cerdanya**
Thursday
and Sant Llorenc crafts
every day in August
p. 187.

③ **Llívia**
Saturday
p. 187.

④ **Puigcerdà**
Sunday
p. 187.

⑤ **Saillagouse**
Friday
p. 187.

⑥ **Osséja**
Thursday
p. 187.

⑦ **Alp**
Thursday
p. 187.

⑧ **Guardiola de Berguedà**
End September
to end October
p. 203.

⑨ **Castelnou**
Tuesday
p. 127.

⑩ **Perpignan**
Tuesday, Thursday,
Saturday and Sunday
p. 106.

Mediterranean Sea

FRANCE

Pyrénées-Orientales

⑩ Perpignan

• Prades

⑨

⑪

Pic du Canigou
9,134 ft
(2,784 m)

Céret •

③
④ ⑤
⑥
⑦
Puigmal
9,548 ft
(2,910 m)

⑧

Figueres /
Figueras •

⑫

Rio Ter

⑬ Vic

Girona /
Gerona •

⑭

⑮

⑯

• Manresa

Terrassa /
Tarrasa •

⑰

⑱ Mataró

⑲ Barcelona

Tunnel de
uymorens

Tết

N116

N20

Rio Llobregat

C1411

N152

A7

A19

A16

Carcassonne

A61   Narbonne •

A9

A9

A7

NII

C25

0 10 20 30 40 50 km

0   10   20   30 miles

---

⑮   *Palamós*

Monday-Friday
(afternoons)
p. 152.

⑯   *Sant Feliu de Guíxols*

Sunday
p. 154.

⑰   *Arenys de Mar*

Every day
p. 162.

⑱   *Vilassar de Mar*

Variable
p. 163.

⑲   *Barcelona*

La Boqueria
(Monday-Saturday),
stamp-collectors market
(Sunday)
p. 169.

⑪   *Port-Vendres*

Monday-Friday
from 4pm
p. 118.

⑫   *Olot*

Monday and Crafts market
four times a year
p. 199.

⑬   *Vic*

Saturday
p. 208.

⑭   *Llafranc*

Mid-August
p. 151.

⑳   *Deltebre*

Every day, 11am
p. 179.

Local specialities

From the mountains to the sea, in busy city squares or the heart of the valley, Catalan markets overflow with the produce of the region. Here you'll find olive oil, cold meats, mushrooms, cheese, Pyrenean honey, fruit from Roussillon and countless other locally-grown products with natural aromas and tastes to savour.

Olive oil, the oil of youth

The healthy, nutritional virtues of olive oil are well known. Introduced 2,500 years ago by the Greeks, the olive tree produces small black, dry, green, tender or juicy fruit. In Catalonia the olives are called *pomal*, *corconadella* or *rodonell*. At the Millas mill (Moulin de Millas, 4 Avenue Jean-Jaurès, Millas, ☎ 04 68 57 28 67), they are washed in spring water, ground by millstone, pressed and spun in a centrifuge according to the traditional method, producing a particularly aromatic virgin olive oil. The local co-operative increases its production each year (125 tonnes in 1998).

There is even a shop that celebrates the olive tree with a festival on 14 July.

A sun-drenched garden

The cultivation of fruit, along with the vine, is a major source of wealth in the Roussillon region, which enjoys exceptional amounts of sunshine. Peach orchards climb the foothills of Mount Canigou and extend across the fertile soil of the Riberal region, sheltered by the Alberes range, to the sea. The orchards of the eastern Pyrenees, covering 20,000 acres (8,000 ha), are the largest in France. In summer, Roussillon harvests yellow peaches, juicy white peaches, yellow nectarines and the larger red nectarines.

Roussillon gold

The word 'apricot' is said to come from the Arabic 'barcoq', which in turn derives from the Latin 'braecoquum', meaning 'to ripen early'. The apricot tree is one of the first to bloom in the spring. Rich in vitamins and minerals, apricots (Lambertin No.1

and Rouge du Roussillon)
are recommended for those
who suffer from anaemia,
sportsmen and just about
everyone else. So, eat up!

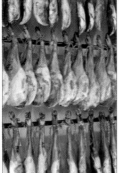

Mushrooms the size of a French beret!

Mushroom picking has
become very popular over
the last few years. It gives
townspeople an excuse to
escape to the countryside,
and connoisseurs delight in
hunting for the most delicate,
natural flavours. Mycology,
the study of mushrooms, is
widespread in Catalonia
and *boletaires* (mushroom
gatherers) even organise
special competitions. In the
autumn, there are gourmet
days and mushroom
exhibitions in Olot, Berga
and Seu d'Urgell. To get off
the beaten track, take part
in a mushroom-picking
excursion. After it has rained,
grab your penknife and a
straw basket and head into the
woods and fields of Montseny,
Empordà, Cerdagne or Capcir.
Determination and a keen
eye, along with your natural
instincts, will lead you to the
best spots for cep mushrooms,
rovellon (milk cap) and
rossinyol (chanterelle)
mushrooms, or even *tofones*
(truffles). In spring and
autumn, markets heave with
mushrooms and restaurants
invariably serve a selection
of delicious dishes such as

bacallà amb rabassols (cod with
morels). These specialities are
not to be missed and are a
highlight of the local cuisine.
Spoil yourself!

A DELIGHTFUL MORNING AT LA BOQUERIA

If you're staying in
Barcelona and are
an early riser, visit
La Boqueria market,
on the Ramblas,
one of Europe's most
spectacular food
markets (see p. 169).
A stroll through this
covered market is a
unique experience.
Taste *embutits*
(cold meats of the
Cerdagne), *fuet* (cured
sausage), Pyrenean
rhododendron honey,
goat's and sheep's
milk cheese with
pepper or herbs,
or curdled for *Mel
i Matò*. Cooked
vegetables are also
sold by weight
(chickpeas, haricot
beans and broad
beans), as well as dry,
salted cod and all
types of seafood. Let
yourself get carried
away by this colourful
slice of Catalan life.

Seashores and seabeds

Sandy or pebbly, wild or protected, naturist or otherwise,
Catalonia has many beautiful beaches.
And there are surprises waiting on the seabed...

Beaches

Garonna

Pico
de Aneto
11,182 ft
(3,408 m)

Pic
d'Estats
10,319 ft
(3,145 m)

ANDORRA

SPAIN

Cataluña /
Catalunya

Rio Noguera

C1313

Rio
Segre

C1313

C25

N II

Lleida /
Lérida

A2

Rio Segre

A2

N240

Reus

Tarragona

Ebro

L'Espina
3,878 ft
(1,182 m)

Tortosa

A7

13

**Mediterranean
Sea**

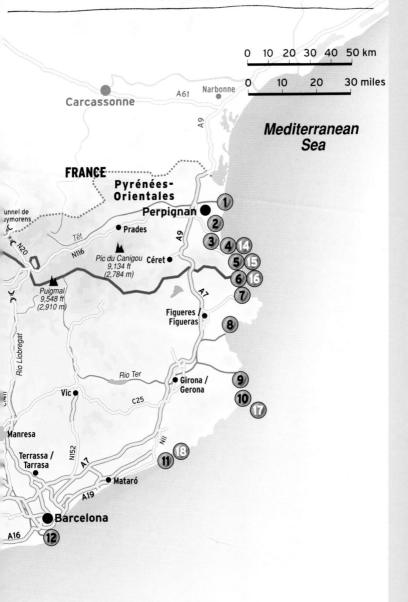

0 10 20 30 40 50 km

0   10   20   30 miles

Mediterranean Sea

Narbonne

Carcassonne

A61

A9

FRANCE

Pyrénées-Orientales

Tunnel de uymorens

Perpignan

N20

Têt

Prades

N116

A9

Pic du Canigou
9,134 ft
(2,784 m)

Céret

Puigmal
9,548 ft
(2,910 m)

A7

Rio Llobregat

Figueres /
Figueras

Rio Ter

Vic

Girona /
Gerona

C25

Manresa

Terrassa /
Tarrasa

N152

A7

Mataró

A19

NII

Barcelona

A16

1
2
3
4   14
5   15
6   16
7
8
9
10 17
11 18
12

Marine life

14 Collioure
   p. 121.

15 Cap Béar
   p. 118.

16 Banyuls
   p. 119.

17 Medes islands
   p. 146.

18 Tossa de Mar
   p. 157.

Beside the seaside

The coastline of Catalonia is shaped like a large amphitheatre opening onto a dramatic and stunning stage – that of the Mediterranean Sea. Its many delights await your discovery. Search out the coast's protected nature parks, the wonderfully rich marine life or the beaches (the nudist ones, if they takes your fancy). Alternatively, simply sail from port to port and enjoy the lovely scenery at your own pace.

Via Costa Brava

Tourists have been coming to the Costa Brava since the late 19thC. First came the well-to-do of Barcelona, followed by visitors from all over Europe and even the other side of the Atlantic Ocean. These days, some coastal towns – like Lloret, Tossa or Sant Feliu – can seem like English, German or French colonies. However, the Costa Brava still remains popular with the Catalans and the Spanish. Tourism accounts for 15% of Catalonia's income, most of it from beach resorts.

Beware of the tourists!

The reckless tourist boom of the 50s and 60s ignored the environment and disfigured the 380-mile (600-km) coastline. But the tourist trade declined in the 90s, as Turkish and North African resorts began to offer cheaper holidays. Besides, with the cost of living increasing at a pace, the Catalans had to rethink their approach – better standards, better quality service and better food for an increasingly demanding market. Despite the modern buildings, the coastline still has many pretty sights to offer: Cape Creus, Begur castle,

Palamós port, Sant Feliu vegetable market, the viewpoint in Lloret and, further south on the Costa del Maresme, Sitges, favourite resort of the gay population. However, avoid August if you want to enjoy what remains of the coast's nature life.

HOW SAND IS MADE

As the waves erode the foothills of the mountains, cliffs collapse and rocks of different sizes build up. The sea continues the process of erosion, dispersing the scree and shaping stones into pebbles. At the edge of the sea, as at the bottom of rivers, the waves and the currents ebb and flow endlessly. This process wears and polishes the chips of rock into round and smooth gravel. With time, the gravel gradually gets smaller and smaller... until it turns into fine grains of sand.

Medes islands' miracle

The seabed around the little archipelago of the Islas Medes, located a few miles from the Empordà coast, is of significant scientific interest and has been protected by law since 1983. Fishing is forbidden, but diving is allowed but regulated. Thanks to this protection, the islands have been miraculously preserved and people come from all over the world to dive here.

Sea life

The thick layers of colourful seaweed that cover the underwater rocks around the Islas Medes are characteristic of the shallower parts of the sea. This seaweed provides food for such creatures as sea urchins, mullets, winkles, octopuses, shellfish and others. Below 33 ft (10 m), you can find types of seaweed that have adapted to the lack of light and manage to flourish in the semi-darkness. Among the rocks, there are lobsters, hog fish, congers and groupers, all lurking quietly. Numerous purple urchins and trumpet-shells live at the bottom of the sea. Below 66 ft (20 m), you can see authentic coral and limestone seaweed reef. These miniature forests are home to 600 animal species. Finally, there are underwater caves full of life, thanks to the currents. There are endless riches to be found here and there's no better

way to discover this fascinating world than by scuba diving. However, some visitors may prefer to keep their heads above water and opt for a more comfortable voyage of discovery. Head instead for the aquarium in Barcelona (p. 171), where you can enjoy watching the fish at close quarters or choose the laboratory aquarium in the Arago reserve in Banyuls-sur-Mer (p. 119).

Fishing heaven

If you fancy a spot of trekking and trout tickling in the mountains or if your dreams on dark winter nights are of fly-fishing and capturing sardines by lamplight, then Catalonia is the place for you. Sea-faring fishing enthusiasts may long to be aboard a felucca or a 'lateen' boat. Just raise anchor in your mind and set sail for this glorious Mediterrranean region.

Lights in the sea

Lamparo fishing owes its name to the lamp that is fixed to the boat to lure sardines and anchovies to the surface. Like moths, the fish are attracted to the light and when the lamp is pointed at the sea it also illuminates the floating plankton which entices the hungry sardines. Blinded by the light, the fish can then easily be caught. This fishing technique was invented in Spain and was used first in Collioure in the 1940s, before its popularity spread along the coast.

In Catalonia, lamparo fishing generally takes place at night between April and September.

Bigger and bigger boats

Lamparo fishing originally used the traditional lateen sailing boat – the *catalane* – with nets pulled in by hand. This was then mechanised and, in 1959, little trawlers fitted with powerful engines, bigger nets and sensors appeared. Today, boats are 60-66 ft (18-20 m) long and the total circumference of

the nets can be as much as 1,300 ft (400 m). However, the miraculous catch still depends on the expertise and hard work of the *fogater* ('the lamp man').

The traditional Catalan boat

The traditional *catalane* boat was created in the shipyard of a small fishing port by three men, one of whom was a master carpenter. The building materials were taken from the local forests. Evergreen oak wood met all requirements.

The parts for the frame of the boat were carved lengthways into the wood. The rudder was carved in one piece from a plane tree and could be as long as 8.5 ft (2.6 m). The mast was made from a pine tree sent from the sawmills of Cerdagne. Once the body was finished and caulked, it was rigged. The mast, which was the same length as the boat, had to be fixed carefully at the centre of the deck, leaning at a 20° angle. The boat's stability depended on the accuracy of this process. The lateen sail was then fitted on the trailing aerial. The triangular shape of this sail, *a la trina* (three-pointed), gave the boat its unique shape, along with the rounded deck, which helped to drain water.

To each their own

The shape of the *catalane* changed according to the kind

of fishing for which they were used – the *sardinals* (30-36 ft/ 9-11 m) for sardines, the *ilaguts* (smaller fishing boats) and the hardy *bouares*, which set sail in pairs. An essential feature of Catalan scenery, the boats were immortalised by the painters Matisse and Derain in their work. In 1948 Derain said that 'Collioure without sails is like a night without stars'. You can admire the boats in the Barcelona maritime museum (p. 170) in which the sea-faring history of Catalonia is well documented.

THE ART OF FLY-FISHING

Fanatics say that taking up fly-fishing is like joining a religion. The rivers and lakes of the Pyrenees are full of trout, but to catch any you must be familiar with the technique, which originated in England. You also need to master the art of making these magnificent artificial insects, with feathers taken from cockerels, some thread and a certain amount of dexterity. They make fly-fishing into a real hunting art. For many anglers, this is the best way to fish; it certainly is one of the most noble, athletic and least deadly ways. Fly-fishing takes place from early spring to mid-September and demands an intimate knowledge of insect activity. It's important to understand the way mayflies, caddis flies and other insects move, and the times of the day they fly over the surface of the water, since trout live on insects. The success of your catch will depend partly on your knowledge, and more crucially on your sense of observation. The joy of fishing is more than just the number of fish that are caught; one single fish is reward enough for a day of patience. It's a subtle and complex art, as its enthusiasts will testify.

Sporting activities

Windsurfing, canoeing, paragliding, parachuting, mountain biking, horse riding, rafting, kayaking, skiing, ice skating...Catalonia has a lot to offer to sports fans. Also, see the map of hiking routes pp.18-19.

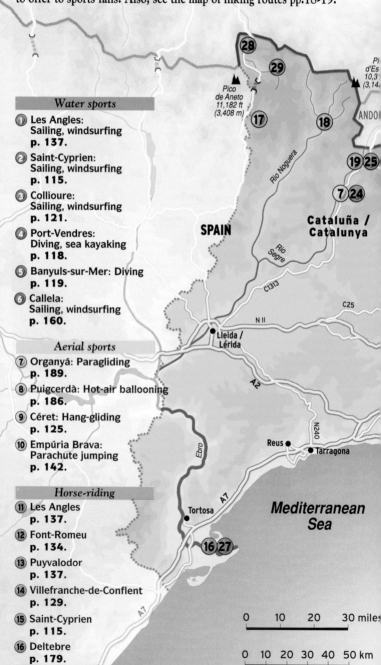

Water sports

① Les Angles:
Sailing, windsurfing
p. 137.

② Saint-Cyprien:
Sailing, windsurfing
p. 115.

③ Collioure:
Sailing, windsurfing
p. 121.

④ Port-Vendres:
Diving, sea kayaking
p. 118.

⑤ Banyuls-sur-Mer: Diving
p. 119.

⑥ Callela:
Sailing, windsurfing
p. 160.

Aerial sports

⑦ Organyà: Paragliding
p. 189.

⑧ Puigcerdà: Hot-air ballooning
p. 186.

⑨ Céret: Hang-gliding
p. 125.

⑩ Empúria Brava:
Parachute jumping
p. 142.

Horse-riding

⑪ Les Angles
p. 137.

⑫ Font-Romeu
p. 134.

⑬ Puyvalodor
p. 137.

⑭ Villefranche-de-Conflent
p. 129.

⑮ Saint-Cyprien
p. 115.

⑯ Deltebre
p. 179.

SPAIN

Cataluña /
Catalunya

Pico
de Aneto
11,182 ft
(3,408 m)

Pi
d'Es
10,3'
(3,14.

ANDO

Rio Noguera

Rio
Segre

C1313

C25

N II

Lleida /
Lérida

A2

Ebro

A7

N240

Reus ●

● Tarragona

Tortosa ●

*Mediterranean
Sea*

0	10	20	30 miles

0	10	20	30	40	50 km

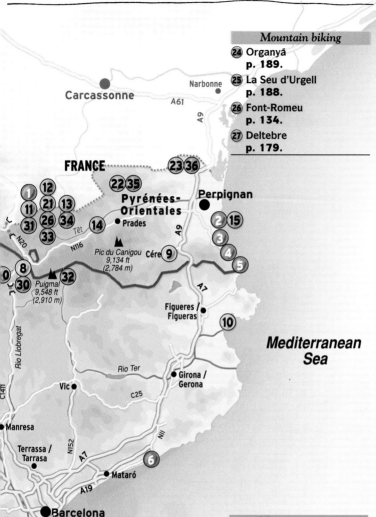

Mountain biking

24 Organyã
p. 189.
25 La Seu d'Urgell
p. 188.
26 Font-Romeu
p. 134.
27 Deltebre
p. 179.

Mediterranean Sea

Mountain sports

28 Bossót
p. 194.
29 Báqueira-Beret
p. 195.
30 Puigcerdà
p. 186.
31 Les Angles
p. 137.
32 Vall de Núria
p. 185.
33 Font-Romeu
p. 134.
34 Puyvalador
p. 137.
35 Saint-Paul-de-Fenouillet
p. 111.
36 Tautavel
p. 111.

River and lake sports

17 Boí
p. 192.
18 Llavorsi
p. 191.
19 La Seu d'Urgell
p. 188.
20 Lles
p. 187.
21 Font-Romeu
p. 134.
22 Saint-Paul-de-Fenouillet
p. 111.
23 Tautavel
p. 110.

Mountain and water sports

If you have a sudden, irresistible craving to indulge in snow-shoe trekking in a nature reserve or cross-country skiing with your family, then Catalonia is the place for you. The choice of activity doesn't stop there – it's a great place to experience that adrenalin rush on a windsurfing board or water-skis. A dream destination for sports enthusiasts in search of excitement, the area offers snow-covered mountains and deep blue seas in a landscape full of contrasts.

Mediterranean mountains

Between 4,300 and 8,500 ft (1,300-2,600 m) the Pyrenees offer one of the largest skiing areas in southern Europe.

Cerdagne, Capcir, Conflent, Mount Canigou and the Arán and Ter valleys have varied slopes suitable for all the family. A group of nine ski resorts in the eastern Pyrenees, known as the 'Catalan Snows', promote tourism that respects the natural splendour of the area's lakes, peaks and valleys – Capcir is nicknamed 'Little Canada'. One ski pass gives you access to all nine resorts and the multitude of pistes on offer.

NEW SNOW

The mountains get busier every year. Snowboarding, surfing, snow-shoe walking and cross-country skiing are just a few of the sports now on offer. The Californian influence is strong in the Pyrenees, bringing the 'new snow' sports developed in the 1980s. While mono-skiing never really took off, snowboarding is more popular every year. Other more or less recent disciplines are also gaining in popularity. The 'skwaal' is a long, shark-shaped board, longer than a snowboard, which demands quick and expert footwork. Curved skis are 'carved' – tipped at the front and splayed at the back – allowing spectacular curves but at the same time increasing the risk of avalanches. Ski hiking (with seal skin fitted beneath the skis) makes it easier to climb uphill but demands tremendous fitness and stamina. Finally, 'telemark', which originated in Norway, is an interesting cross between ski hiking and cross-country skiing. However, snow-shoe walking is the discipline that appears to have become a favourite with the greatest speed. It is not a 'sliding' sport and plays a key role in the recent diversification of winter sports. Hats and gloves on, and off you go.

resorts have a large number of clubs offering beginner's instruction or further training in windsurfing, surfing or sailing. The Catalan sailing federation (Federacio Catalana de Vela) has a busy watersports school based in the port of Barcelona, which organises races in all categories throughout the year.

Boats for all tastes

In Masnou, near Palamós, discover the *pati a vela*, a small Catalan catamaran, built without a bar and steered only by weight and balance, and by just one person. The town of Roses is the capital of windsurfing, lying at the head of a sweeping bay with one of the longest beaches in the area. It has

The more fashionable resorts

Some resorts, such as Font Romeu and Les Angles, have dedicated areas for snow-boarders called 'snowparcs', with specially designed pistes equipped with bumps, ramps and obstacles that make perfect challenges for those who enjoy jumping and and

acrobatic manoeuvres. On the Spanish side, the resort of Baqueira-Beret is the most elegant, regularly welcoming the Spanish royal family. Núria and Vallter 2000 are the furthest east and therefore enjoy the largest snowfall.

The wind in your sails

From Port Barcarès to Cerbère and from La Jonquera to the Èbre delta, Catalonia's coastal

become something of a mecca for lovers of water sports, just as Casteldefells is now the place to go, particularly in winter, if you're a 'hobie cat' fanatic. In the low season, boats can be rented with ease from one of the small clubs along the coastline, and you can head out to sea and enjoy the delights of the Mediterranean. Catalonia has it all and is just waiting for you to come and enjoy it.

For the love of football

A lthough rugby is the predominant sport in the southwest of France, from Béziers to Narbonne to Toulouse, football is unquestionably the sport of Catalonia. 'It's more than a club' is the slogan of FC Barcelona and its legendary football team is regularly watched by more than 100,000 devoted fans from all over the world. When 'Barça' wins a game, flags are raised and in the streets you hear car horns and songs everywhere. To start a conversation with a Catalan, just mention Barça – and get ready for a lively discussion.

Unmissable – Barça museum

The Barça museum (p. 170) has an international reputation and is the second most-visited museum in the city. The club's rich history is told through photos, trophies, records and audio-visual displays. The football club's

A century of history

The club was founded in 1889, at a time when Barcelona was beginning to assert itself as a great capital. The 1888 Universal Exhibition had successfully promoted the city, which then tried to join the European movement. The club, however, was founded by a Swiss, Hans Gamper. It's somewhat ironic to think that the colours of Barça, now so central to the Catalan identity, are actually those of the Swiss Vaud province and that most of its founding members were English or German.

The pursuit of freedom

During the dictatorship of Franco, whenever Barça played against Real Madrid, the club became a symbol of the region's hatred of the centralist regime. Its financial powers (the richest club in Europe, with a budget of 5,200 billion pesetas) and its political attitude during the dictatorship constantly attracted enmity. Nowadays it is a symbol of the Catalan spirit and of the region's desire for wider influence beyond the Pyrenees and ultimately, worldwide recognition.

biennial art festival displays work by painters, sculptors and writers inspired by the sport. Artists such as Dalí, Clavé, Miró and Subirach have given prestige to this institution, which is worth a visit even if you're not a football fan.

From north to south

Gamper's touch of genius was to have named the club after the city. In a way, to be a *socio* (member) is to become Catalan, and as such the

football club has been instrumental in the integration of immigrants from all over Spain. From the beginning, the founders regarded the institution as a unifying place where real fraternity should be respected. FC Barcelona's 108,000 members come from all social backgrounds and membership is handed down from father to son.

Nou Camp

Barça's present ground was inaugurated in 1957 and replaced the legendary Corts stadium, a single stone of which became the foundation stone of the Nou Camp, thus ensuring continuity. It was

conceived by three architects, Soteras, Mitjans and Barbon, and can seat 120,000 spectators, making it the second biggest stadium in the world.

Canaletes fountain

At the top of the Ramblas, by the Canaletes fountain, where strangers have been meeting since the 19thC., the fortunes of FC Barcelona are the subject of constant debate.

Conversations about the latest game against Real Madrid ignite the Catalans' passion for their home and a football commentary becomes a contest of eloquence. If you can read a little Castilian Spanish, buy any local daily paper (*La Vanguardia* or *El Periodico*) or get started on reading *Offside*, a novel by Manuel Vazquez Montalban and you'll soon be like one of the 4 million Catalans who can't go to bed on Sunday until they know how Barça has fared.

DON'T FORGET ABOUT RUGBY
Catalan sport is not, however, just about football. On the French side, rugby is king, with Perpignan one of the French Catalan cities where rugby fever runs highest. In fact, the final of the French championship in 1998, between Perpignan and Stade Français, is still

very vivid in everyone's memory here. The match, won by the Parisian team, featured the two Lièvremont brothers – Thomas, who was playing for Perpignan, and Marc, who was playing for Stade Français.

Fairs and festivals

Classical music, jazz, theatre, dance... Catalonia likes to celebrate.

Fairs

(1) Les: Eth Haro burning
p. 194.

(2) Isil: Midsummer's Day bonfires
p. 191 .

(3) Castellbò:
Cathar refugees' day
p. 189.

(4) Arsèguel: Accordion
festival
p. 189.

(5) Martinet:
Fiesta del Turista week
p. 187.

(6) Puigcerdà:
Fiesta de l'Estany
p. 186.

(7) Ribes de Freser:
Sheepdog
trials
p. 184.

(8) Prats-de-Mollo:
Beer festival
p. 123.

(9) Arles-sur-Tech:
Medieval festival
p. 123.

(10) Céret:
Féria, cherry festival
p. 125.

(11) Perpignan: Perpignan
Thursdays, summer
festival, Sanch procession
p. 107.

(12) Collioure:
Saint-Vincent festival
p. 121.

(13) Roses: Suquet festival
p. 143.

(14) Santa Pau: Bean festival
p. 201.

(15) Llafranc: Festa Major
p. 151.

(16) Calella: Beer festival
p. 160.

(17) Palamós: Maritime festival
p. 152.

(18) Tossa de Mar: Sant Pere day
p. 157.

(19) Santa Cristina:
24 July festival
p. 159.

(20) Mataró: Fiesta Mayor
p. 162.

(21) Argentona: Cántaro
international festival
p. 163.

(22) Cardona: Bull festival
p. 205.

SPAIN

Cataluña /
Catalunya

Pico
de Aneto
11,182 ft
(3,408 m)

ANDOR

Pi
d'Es
10,31
(3,145

Rio Noguera

Rio
Segre

C1313

C1313

C25

A2

Lleida /
Lérida

Rio Segre

Ebro

N II

A2

A7

Tortosa

Reus

Tarragona

Mediterranean
Sea

27

28

26

25

2

0 10 20 30 40 50 km

0 10 20 30 miles

FRANCE

Pyrénées-
Orientales

Narbonne

Prades

Tét

Pic du
Canigou
9,134 ft
(2,784 m)

Puigmal
(9,548 ft
(2,910 m))

Perpignan

Céret

Figueres /
Figueras

Rio Ter

Girona /
Gerona

Vic

*Mediterranean
Sea*

C25

Manresa

Terrassa /
Tarrasa

Barcelona

Mataró

Festivals

30 Perpignan:
Mediterranean festival
p. 107.

31 Prades:
Pablo Casals festival
p. 131.

32 Thuir: Catalan festival
p. 126.

33 Céret: Carnival
p. 125.

34 Peralada: International
music festival
p. 139.

35 Castelló d'Empúries:
Street entertainers'
festival
p. 142.

36 Palafrugell: Cuban
sea-song festival
p. 151.

37 Sant Feliu de Guíxols:
Monastery music
and theatre festival
p. 154.

38 Tossa de Mar:
Classical music festival
p. 156.

39 Sitges: International
theatre festival
p. 173.

40 Cantonigròs
p. 209.

23 Sitges: Carnival, Corpus Christi
p. 173.

24 Vilafranca de Penedès:
Chicken fair, acrobatics
p. 210.

25 Valls: Calçotada festival
p. 213.

26 Montblanc:
Medieval week
p. 212.

27 Lleida: Snail fair
p. 215.

28 Coll de Nargo:
Village fair
p. 189.

29 Berga: Festival of demons
p. 202.

Seasonal celebrations and traditions

Popular culture is still very much alive in Catalonia and, from the solstice to the equinox, traditional festivities turn villages into life-size theatres. You can watch parades of giant papier-mâché figures, the arrival of the three Kings, carnivals from out of a Fellini movie, endless Sardana dances and the incredible feats of the 'castell' acrobats – celebrations that bring colour to every day life. The origins of many of these festivals, meant to ward off superstition and disease, have been long forgotten, but the party still goes on. Try to arrange your itinerary to coincide with one or two of these festivals, and witness a fascinating part of Catalan life that will guarantee a memorable trip.

Bear festival, Prats-de-Mollo

First Sun. of Feb. holiday, followed by 3 days of carnival.
Information from the tourist office:
☎ 04 68 39 70 83.

In Eurasia, man and bear have always had an intense and ambiguous relationship. Since prehistoric times they have shared the same territory, often fighting for the same cave or prey. The Festa de l'Os originated in a curious medieval legend. It is said that a shepherd girl was once kidnapped by a bear, who tried to seduce her. The cries of the young girl alerted the foresters working nearby, who rescued her. Early in the afternoon on the day of the festival, after a barbecue and a few drinks, a couple of men disguise themselves as bears, wearing sheep's skins, fur hats and with their faces and hands covered in soot and oil. Armed with heavy bludgeons, they noisily enter the village and chase the villagers.

Sanch procession, Perpignan

A CIRCLE ROUND THE SEASONS

The Sardana, the traditional Catalan dance for all generations, is an ancient tradition and probably originated in Crete. After a few introductory steps, short steps on 8-measure alternate with long steps on 16-measure, repeated twice. In the end, participants join hands towards the centre of the circle. The *cobla* (orchestra) is made up of 11 musicians, including a *flabiol* (a flute played with one hand), a tambourine, two cornetins, a *fiscorn* (saxaphone), two *tibles* (wind instruments) and a *tenora* (oboe), the emblematic instrument of the Sardana. The style of the music is bitter and haunting. Put on the *vigatanes*, the traditional espadrilles made in Saint-Laurens-de-Cerdans, and join in the dance. Sardanas take place in Barcelona, at noon on Sunday, in the cathedral square, or at 6.30pm in Sant Jaume square; or in Perpignan, twice weekly during the summer around 5pm in front of the Castellet.

Hunters follow and pretend to shoot the intruders. At the end of the day, 'white bears' capture the 'brown bears' and shave them to turn them into men. An energetic circle dance, along with stories and legends about the terrifying bear, end the festivities. It's certainly quite a spectacle, and it would definitely be worth trying to arrange your trip to include this colourful fiesta.

capital of the kingdom of Majorca. The *Caparutxa*, the veil worn by the penitents, has a double meaning, symbolising both the shame of sin and, on a more practical note, the former mission of the members of the arch-brotherhood, who came to the aid of those sentenced to death. To protect the condemned from being stoned by the crowd on their way to the stake, the priests would surround them, dressed in the same way and wearing a hood. Protected by this anonymous guise, the victim was able to escape the punishment of the crowd. These days, the procession is organised by the Arch-Brotherhood of the Precious Blood of our Lord Jesus Christ, which was founded in 1416.

Christmas and Easter

On 13 December, which is the feast of Santa Llucia, the Christmas market is set up in the square in front of the cathedral in Barcelona. Nativity cribs are displayed, the figures presented in a setting made of corkwood and moss. The traditional *caganer* figure is quite a surprise – a shepherd relieving himself

Sanch procession, Perpignan

Good Friday

Information from the tourist office:

☎ 04 68 66 30 30.

The Procession de la Sanch ('blood of Christ') is a real sacrament of Catalan popular faith. This impressive ritual is 500 years old and takes place every year on Good Friday, in the streets of the former

on the ground, which symbolises the fertilisation of the earth. This time of the year is full of celebrations, including the *Pessebre Vivent* (nativity play), which takes

give a *mona* to their godchildren – a crown-shaped cake studded with 3-12 eggs, symbolising life, perfection, and renewal. On Maundy Thursday and Good Friday, scenes of the Passion of Christ are re-enacted in Gerona, Cervera, Esparreguera and Sant Viçent dels Horts.

New Year's Eve and the Epiphany

To celebrate the New Year, families and friends gather around a *postre del music* (musician's dessert), made with honey, dried fruit and *matò* (curds). On each of the twelve strokes of midnight, a grape is eaten for good luck. On the night of 5 January, children leave some *touron* and dried fruit for the three Kings – and bread and

'Noisy' carnivals

The *Carnestoltes* ('noisy carnivals'), which were forbidden during the Franco era, take place from Shrove Tuesday through to Ash Wednesday. Under the Franco regime many local and regional fiestas were banned and the carnival was considered to be amongst the most licentious and frivolous. Today it's celebrated with great gusto in Catalonia (and elsewhere). In the weeks preceding the celebrations, beautiful masks and costumes are sold in the shops. The festivites include masked balls and parades of floats in Sitges (28 miles/45 km south of Barcelona), Roses in the Empordà region and Vilanova la Geltru. To signal the end of the festivities, the traditional figure of Carnaval is burnt. On or after Ash Wednesday,

place in Báscara, a medieval village north of Gerona. Holy Week begins with Easter Sunday, when palm leaves are plaited into the shape of crosses, flowers or mythical birds and sold in village markets. Around the Mediterranean, palm trees are a common symbol of regeneration and immortality. On the same day, godparents

water for their camels. In the *Cavalcada dels Reis Mags* (Procession of the Three Kings), the Kings are said to walk from the sea to coastal villages and inland towns, bringing presents and sweets to good children, who give their wish list to their pages beforehand. The children who behaved badly during the year are given pieces of charcoal!

the 'Burial of the Sardine' takes place, a ritual in which a mock sardine, representing winter, is buried.

Sant Jordi and the Montblanc dragon

23 April

Sant Jordi (Saint George) is the patron saint of Catalonia. A popular figure in the Middle Ages, he was said to have slain

a dragon and the Catalan nobility incorporated him on their coats of arms during their fight to retake Catalonia from the Moors. He is celebrated on the 23 April with roses, his traditional flower, and books, because the remembrance of the death of the writer Cervantes has become associated with the festival over the years. Even the smallest village sells roses and books on their ramblas. Traditionally on this day, a man gives his partner a rose and receives a book in return.

Corpus Christi

This festival celebrates the Eucharist, a Christian tradition that replaced fertility rituals as early as 1264. The centrepiece on this occasion is the procession of the *caps grossos* ('large heads'/giants). In Berga, on 2 June, one of the most popular fiestas takes place. Giants, devils and bizarre monsters, including a fire-breathing wooden dragon, parade through the town during the Patum. In Sitges an old tradition is retained when the streets of the old town are turned into carpets of flowers on Whit Sunday, filling the town with colour and fragrance. Since the 13thC., in the cathedral cloister and the courtyard of the Casa del Ardiaca, the traditional *ou com balla* ('dancing egg') ritual has been respected – simply an empty egg, left to balance on a fountain. This ritual, combining the symbolism of water and rebirth, represents the Eucharist displayed in church.

'CATALAN CASTLES'

Various dates: 4-5 July, Festa Major de Terrass; 15 August, La Bisbal del Penedès; fourth Sunday of August, El Arboç (Baix Penedès).

In summer, the traditional *castell* (human-pyramid) displays have become a symbol of community, with everyone playing their part. The base, the *pinya* ('pine cone'), is formed by stout and robust men. Around them, taller men reinforce the foundation, and then the overall weight of the participants decreases as the tower grows. The *collas* (display troupes) wear white trousers, a colourful shirt and a black scarf around their waist and compete to build towers between five and nine levels high. The all-time record is a *castell* of 10 levels, with 700 participants! Traditionally, it is always a child who is placed at the very top (the *anxaneta*), who then waves at the crowd. This event originated in Valls, a village 12.5 miles (20 km) from Tarragona and there are now 56 groups and 11,000 regular participants. Valls is famous for the daring and skill of its *castellers*. The club, the Xiquets de Valls, is so renowned that there's a monument to them in the town, portraying the human tower, symbolising the role of the individual within the community as a whole. You can also see the *castellers* in action in Vilafranca del Penedès.

Regional history

From the Roman remains in Tarragona to Serrabone priory, discover the history and monuments of the eastern Pyrenees and Spanish Catalonia.

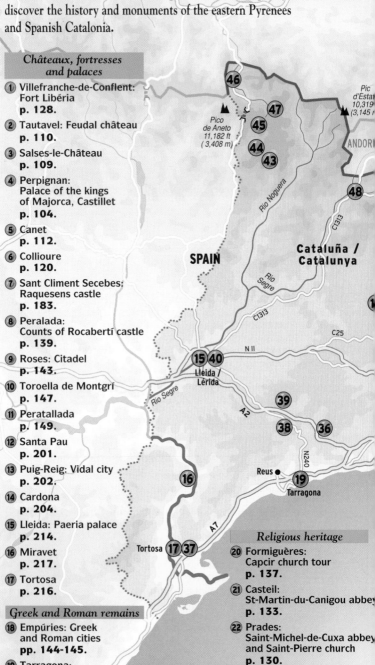

Châteaux, fortresses and palaces

1. Villefranche-de-Conflent: Fort Libéria
   p. 128.
2. Tautavel: Feudal château
   p. 110.
3. Salses-le-Château
   p. 109.
4. Perpignan: Palace of the kings of Majorca, Castillet
   p. 104.
5. Canet
   p. 112.
6. Collioure
   p. 120.
7. Sant Climent Secebes: Raquesens castle
   p. 183.
8. Peralada: Counts of Rocabertí castle
   p. 139.
9. Roses: Citadel
   p. 143.
10. Toroella de Montgrí
    p. 147.
11. Peratallada
    p. 149.
12. Santa Pau
    p. 201.
13. Puig-Reig: Vidal city
    p. 202.
14. Cardona
    p. 204.
15. Lleida: Paeria palace
    p. 214.
16. Miravet
    p. 217.
17. Tortosa
    p. 216.

Greek and Roman remains

18. Empúries: Greek and Roman cities
    pp. 144-145.
19. Tarragona: Roman remains
    pp. 174-175.

Religious heritage

20. Formiguères: Capcir church tour
    p. 137.
21. Casteil: St-Martin-du-Canigou abbey
    p. 133.
22. Prades: Saint-Michel-de-Cuxa abbey and Saint-Pierre church
    p. 130.
23. Artes: abbey church
    p. 123.

Pic d'Estat 10,319 (3,145 f

Pico de Aneto 11,182 ft (3,408 m)

ANDOR

SPAIN

Cataluña / Catalunya

Río Noguera

Río Segre

C1313

C1313

C25

N II

Lleida / Lérida

Río Segre

A2

N240

Reus

Tarragona

Tortosa

A7

**Mediterranean
Sea**

Off the beaten track

On either side of the Pyrenees, Catalonia hides unsuspected treasures: a sacred mountain, an area littered with medieval architecture, heavenly orchards, valleys of peaches and apricots, whitewashed fishing ports, lauze-roofed farms, religious refuges perched on mountain tops, and so on. Set out early on mountain paths and a rich and varied landscape unfolds beneath you.

Prats de Mollo

Catalan farmhouse

Shadows and light: Catalan architecture

From the steep foothills of the Pyrenees to the wild creeks of the coastline, Catalan houses reflect the shades of the scenery. Rural Pyrenean architecture was developed by farmers and shepherds according to the demands of the terrain and climate. The Roman infuence is strong throughout Catalonia and the Catalan farmhouse – a place to both live and work – is a descendant of Roman houses. Usually of solid appearance, with an open, paved courtyard, the kitchen, where families would gather around the fireplace, is the heart of these simple homes. In the mountains, the valley is cultivated while the houses are built on the sunny hillsides. In Catalonia, as

Santa Maria chapel, Formiguères

in the Basque country, isolated farmsteads can be found outside the villages. If you have the chance, a stay in a farmhouse that takes guests is highly recommended. It's a truly wonderful way of finding out about the Catalan way of life and its traditions at first hand.

Plaza Mayor, heart of the village

Almost all Spanish villages have a Plaza Mayor (main square) that is the heart of community life, the setting for markets, concerts and all festivities. Around the square you'll find the church and often arched galleries lined with shops and bars. Some beautiful family mansions can often still be found on the Plaza Mayor, bearing the arms of their former owners, the nobles of the village. Keep an eye out for them.

Cadaqués

A tour of some of the most beautiful villages

Ille-sur-Têt, just off the N116, 15 minutes from Perpignan, is a charming village that hides an exceptional religious and architectural heritage within its ancient walls. After crossing the stark granite scenery of the Fenouillèdes region, you come to **Bélesta**,

The château of Castelnou

Castelnou

a border village with delightful shady streets and squares planted with plane trees. **Thuir** is the capital of the Aspres region, famous for its Byrrh cellars and its lively squares and marble fountains. Overlooking the valley among black shale and red cork trees, 1 mile (2 km) down the road, is **Castelnou**, one of France's most beautifully preserved medieval villages, with its winding, pebble-paved lanes and steps. This heritage spot features a magnificent 10th-C. château that belonged to the counts of Cerdagne, distinctive rounded houses, a small Romanesque church, steep alleys and watchtowers. A little further on, at the gateway to the Conflent region, the fortified village of **Eus** clings precariously to a rocky outcrop. In the Vallespir region, the deep valleys are dotted with charming villages, including **Céret**, **Prats-de-Mollo** and **Arles-sur-Tech**. In the Capcir area, **Formiguères** is the former residence of the kings of Majorca, where you'll find lauze-tiled houses clustering around the 12th-C. church. It's one of the prettiest and best-preserved villages in the region, hardly changed since the kings stayed here to relieve their asthma.

CAIXA DE NUVIA

The 'bride's wedding chest' was an institution among Catalan families of the 16th-18thC. Generally made of walnut wood, it would be 4.5-ft (140-cm) long and 2-ft (60-cm) high. Soon, such chests became popular in the mountains as well as the valleys, and were found in farms as well as palaces. On the day of their wedding, couples would be given a chest containing their dowry, with a secret compartment for the bride's jewellery. In the 18thC., the chest was superseded in popularity by the dresser, and then by the wardrobe with a mirror – less mobile, but more useful. You can admire these wedding chests in the antique shops of Calle Banys Nous in Barcelona. Browsing around the other small but fascinating antique shops in Carrer de la Palla and Carrer del Pi in the Barri Gòtic is a great way to spend a morning.

On the hunt for Roman art treasures

Poblet monastery

After centuries of neglect, Romanesque art once again fascinates those who love simplicity and purity. Step by step, discover this world of secret abbeys and hidden hermitages – the beauty of Serrabone priory, Sant Pere de Rodes monastery, the imposing Cistercian monastery in Santes Creus, the Boí valley chapels, etc. From the Pyrenean slopes to the vineyards of Penedès, set out on a hunt for these wonderful hidden treasures.

Serrabone priory

The watchtowers

Romanesque art was the first artistic movement to reach throughout the Western world. It originated in the Middle Ages, at the end of the first millennium, after the downfall of the Carolingian Empire. Catalonia, which had always been open to European influences, started to build its own identity with numerous churches, abbeys and monasteries. Every Christian building on the Iberian peninsula depended on the progress of the Reconquista. The Moors had conquered Spain early in the 8thC. and were stopped in 732 in Poitiers, France, by Charles Martel. The Moors remained on the peninsula until the downfall of the Kingdom of Granada in 1492, but Catalonia was liberated relatively early on and so managed to preserve a greater part of its Roman buildings.

Romanesque churches

At the same time as the Counts of Catalonia rejected French sovereignty and turned their attention to the Reconquista, they established the notorious feudal and seigniorial system. At this time, gold was currency, the population was then expanding and Romanesque art was in its heyday. Catalunya Vella, north of the road to Aragon (Anoia, Segarra, Urgell), is where this style first appeared. But the splendours of Romanesque art did not reach Catalunya Nova (bounded by the Llobregat river) until 1149, when the Christian reconquest began. This explains why the finest Romanesque buildings are found in the Pyrenees – on either side of the border – La Seu d'Urgell, Santa Maria de Ripoll, Sant Climent de Taüll, Sant Miquel de Cuixà and Sant Marti del Canigò.

Poblet monastery

Santes Creus monastery

Many influences

The Lombard master craftsmen influenced the first examples of Romanesque art in Catalonia. The constructions were strict, functional and sometimes fortified to resist possible Saracen assaults. As the Reconquista progressed, the Roman style became furniture. Over 2,000 churches and around 200 castles are built in the style of this period, and the museums of Urgell, Vic, Gerona and Barcelona all have remarkable treasures on display.

Capital in Saint-Michel-de-Cuxa abbey

Saint-Martin-du-Canigou abbey

purer and more complex – Lombard stripes, blind arches and heavily carved portals were used to ornament the buildings. On top of the columns of cloisters, figures and Persian birds fighting, Kufa and Celtic writing are entwined. It's a solid and well-balanced form of art, which ahd an influence on all construction of the period (churches, monasteries, castles, seigniorial homes, bridges), as well as on painting, sculpture, gold work, illumination work and

On horseback, on foot or by car

If you are travelling by car, you can enjoy the **Cistercian road**, which winds its way through the Penedès vineyards to the Alt Camp. You will be amazed by the famous Cistercian monastery of Santa Maria de Poblet (spiritual centre and burial place of the Aragon and Catalan kings), and that of Santes Creus, with its fountain for ablutions. Visit the sister monastery and cloister of Vallbona de les Monges, the third of the 'Cistercian triangle' monasteries. If you want to get off the beaten track, try the secret–abbey trail of French Catalonia. A seven-day walking tour will enable you to visit some unique sites. For more information on this journey of discovery, contact: **Terres d'Aventure** (6, Rue Saint-Victor, Paris, ☎ 01 53 73 77 77) or **La Balaguère** (Route d'Argelès, Arrens-Marsous, ☎ 05 62 97 20 21).

From the Iron Age to industrialisation

I n the 1850s Catalonia became an important industrial centre, and had the world's third most important cotton industry. Thanks to the region's trading history and highly-skilled craftsmen, Catalonia was at the forefront of the Industrial Revolution. Between them, the founders of Modernity and of Modernisme created factories and warehouses that now go to constitute a fascinating industrial heritage.

Modernist cellar, El Pinell de Brai

Detail of tiling, El Pinell de Brai

A glorious past
As early as the Middle Ages, Catalonia was a successful commercial centre. After an economical and political recession lasting two centuries, the 18thC. sees Catalonia's revival and, in 1778, the port of Barcelona was authorised to begin trading with America. The main products were brandy, nails and light weaponry from the Catalan forge of Ripoll, high-quality paper from the mills of Capellades and, above all, printed calico. In 1832, Josep Bonaplata, an industrialist, established the first steam-driven factory in Barcelona. In 1848, the first Spanish railway was inaugurated

between Barcelona and Mataro. In 1888, Barcelona's mayor, Francesc de Paula Ruis I Taulet, used the Parc de la Ciutedella as the site of the World Fair, and this became the symbol of the industrial era. It also marked the advent of an architectural innovation – the new Modernista style.

Vic flour-mill

Sant Sadurni d'Anoia

Factory towns

Since coal was rare, water power was used, which is why the new textile factories were built along the major Catalan rivers, the Llobregat (p. 202) and the Ter. These factories, called *colònies*, were designed according to an English model as self-sufficient communities, with industrial buildings, bosses' houses and workers' houses along with all

CHARCOAL OR SOLAR ENERGY?

Below Font-Romeu, in the village of Odeillo, is the biggest solar oven in the world (☎ 04 68 30 77 86; see p.134). Discover the strange beauty of this high-technology device, which can produce temperatures as high as 3,880°C (7,016°F). Its power is described as 'stronger than 10,000 suns' and the nine-storey laboratory building has a huge curved mirror on one side which reflects the magnificent Pyrenees while helping scientists to research high-temperature issues. In Haut Conflent, you can mine the history of the regional coal industry, which declined after World War II. Leave from **Thuès-entre-Valls**.

Museu de la Ciencia in Terrassa

the other services required – schools, churches etc. Paternalistic rules prevented the social conflict and protest that affected large towns and cities, and the workers immediately spent their wages in the shops belonging to their masters.

Modernity and Modernisme

Catalan industrial heritage owes its singular style to Modernisme (p. 80). This artistic movement appeared at the same time as the Catalan

Renaixaça, a time of strong industrial growth, which owed a great deal to bourgeois investors, encouraged by the stable political climate. There are numerous magnificent examples of this period's marriage of art and commerce: the works of Domènech i Montaner, P. Falqués and Puig i Cadafalch in Barcelona; Gaudí's Colonia Güell in Santa Coloma de Cervello; the steam factories by L. Muncunill in Terrassa; the flour mills in Vic, Gerona and Manresa; and the spectacular Cordorníu cellars in the Casa Madre de Cava in Sant Sadurni d'Anoia (p. 211), where a vast quantity of sparkling wine is produced.

Vic flour-mill

Roman Catalonia

atalonia's history is marked by periods of high prestige and there remain some impressive souvenirs of this glorious past, particularly in the ancient imperial city of Tarragona. All along the Via Domitia and Via Augusta, the route to Carthage for the Roman legions, you can find the traces of this civilisation. The names of towns, the Catalan language, the region's heady wines and olive-oil dishes all testify to the lasting influence of 400 years of occupation. It's interesting to observe the influence the Romans had in many aspects of life in Catalonia. Tarragona, one of Spain's oldest cities, preserves several remnants of its ancient past. During the month of May, you can even act like a gourmet Roman and feast on ancient dishes.

Via Domitia

Roman city, Empúries

Three thousand years of Iberian history

Merchants from all around the Mediterranean were soon drawn to Spain by its natural resources and the splendid constructions made by the Iberians. As early as the 11thC. BC, Phoenicians established trading posts all along the Andalusian coast, and also founded Collioure. Then the Phoceans, a nation of Greeks hailing from Asia Minor, settled in Catalonia in 8th-6thC. BC. They founded ancient Empirion, now known as Empúries (p. 142), in 575 BC, before the Rhodians settled in the present site of Roses in the 7th C. BC. Trading developed rapidly and the cultivation of vines and olive trees was introduced.

Roman peace dividend

The Romans began to colonise Catalonia as early as 218 BC, following the Punic wars. Throughout the 2ndC. BC, from their base in Tarraco, the Romans exploited the country's resources and organised communities, forcing the natives to adopt their way of life. They founded new towns, linked together by an important road network, and also settled in the countryside. Under the Emperor Augustus, Catalonia

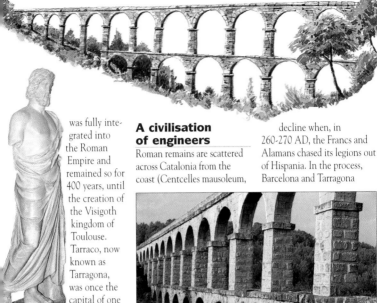

was fully integrated into the Roman Empire and remained so for 400 years, until the creation of the Visigoth kingdom of Toulouse. Tarraco, now known as Tarragona, was once the capital of one of the most important provinces of Hispania and remained so until the end of the Roman domination.

A civilisation of engineers

Roman remains are scattered across Catalonia from the coast (Centcelles mausoleum, Montbui and Badalona thermal baths) to the valleys of the Pyrenees. In Roman times, the towns were small replicas of Rome, linked together by a network of roads, such as the Via Augusta, which crossed the Pyrenees at Junquera and continued down to Alicante. Barcelona and many other towns were fortified, bridges were built (Martorell 'devil's bridge'), as well as aqueducts (Les Ferreres bridge) and triumphal arches (Berà, near Tarragona, in honour of one of Trajan's generals). The old city of Emporion became a popular spa, portrayed by its statue of Aesculapius, god of medicine, which dates from the 4thC. AD. The power of Rome was already in

decline when, in 260-270 AD, the Francs and Alamans chased its legions out of Hispania. In the process, Barcelona and Tarragona were devastated and only a few prestigious buildings remain. You can still see the extensive ruins of the Roman amphitheatre and the Praetorium, and nearby stands the Museu Nacional Arqueològic, which houses one of the most important collection of Roman artefacts in Catalonia (p. 175).

Devil's bridge, Tarragona

AN INVITATION TO DINNER WITH CASSIUS

In Roman times Tarragona was the capital of Tarraconensis and May is the month for feasting just like a Roman. Ancient gastronomic traditions are revived and savoured in taverns, bars and pastry shops all over the city. If you're feeling brave you can try such unusual dishes and combinations as turtledove boiled in its own feathers, stuffed sow's dug and fricassée of roses with pastries. Information from the tourist office in Tarragona:
☎ **977 245 203.**

Museums

Archaeology, sculpture, painting, popular traditions…
Whatever your interest, the museums of Catalonia
will illuminate your journey. See also p. 50.

Archaeology

① Tautavel:
Museum of prehistory
p. 110.

② Prades:
Museo Pablo-Casals
p. 130.

③ Empúries:
Museo de Arqueología
p. 144.

④ Ullastret: Museum
of the Iberian village
p. 150.

⑤ Gerona:
Monastery archaeological
museum
p. 196.

⑥ Tossa de Mar:
Museo Municipal
p. 156.

⑦ Tarragona: Museo
Nacional Archeológico
p. 175.

⑧ Lleida: Museum of history
and archaeology
p. 214.

Art and popular traditions

⑨ Esterri d'Àneu:
Vall d'Àneu ecomuseum
p. 190.

⑩ Arséguel:
Accordion museum
p. 189.

⑪ Llívia: Esteva pharmacy
p. 186.

⑫ Sainte-Léocadie:
Cerdagne museum
p. 135.

⑬ Saillagouse: Cerdagne
museum/charcuterie
p. 135.

⑭ Perpignan: Museum
of popular culture
p. 105.

⑮ Canet: Museum of toys,
boats and cars
pp. 112-113.

⑯ Argelès-sur-mer:
Museum of rural life
p. 117.

⑰ Banyuls: Mas Maillol sculpture
p. 119.

⑱ Saint-Laurent-de-Cerdans:
Espadrille museum
p. 122.

⑲ Castellfollit de la Roca:
Charcuterie museum
p. 199.

20 Gerona: Museum
of Catalan Jews
p. 197.

21 Palau-Sator: Museum
of rural traditions
p. 149.

22 Palafrugell:
Corkwood museum
p. 150.

23 Argentona:
Wine jar museum
p. 163.

30 Tossa de Mar:
Museo Municipal
p. 156.

31 Barcelona:
Modern art museum,
Aguilar palace, national
museum of Catalan art,
contemporary art
museum
pp. 165-170.

32 Montserrat:
La Moreneta museum
p. 206.

FRANCE Pyrénées-
Orientales **Perpignan**

Tunnel de
uymorens

Têt

Prades

Pic du
Canigou
9,134 ft
(2,784 m)

Céret

Puigmal
9,548 ft
(2,910 m)

Rio Llobregat

**Figueres /
Figueras**

**Mediterranean
Sea**

Rio Ter

Vic

**Girona /
Gerona**

Cl411

Manresa

**Terrassa /
Tarrasa**

Mataró

Barcelona

A16

| 0 | 10 | 20 | 30 miles |
| 0 | 10 20 30 40 | 50 km |

33 Sitges:
Museu del Cau Ferrat
p. 172.

34 Sarral: Museo del
Alabastro Sarral Imade
p. 213.

35 Horta de Sant Joan
p. 217.

Fine arts

24 La Seu d'Urgell:
Diocesan museum
p. 188.

25 Céret:
Modern-art museum
p. 124.

26 Saint-Cyprien:
Contemporary art centre
p. 114.

27 Cadaqués:
Museo Perrot-Moore
p. 140.

28 Figueras:
Teatro-Museo Dalí
p. 139.

29 El Far d'Empordà:
Museo de Arte Naïf
p. 143.

Others

36 Vielha:
Arán valley museum
p. 194.

37 La Pobla de Lillet:
Museo del Transporte
p. 203.

38 Olot:
Museo de los Volcanes
p. 200.

39 Gerona: museum of cinema
p. 197.

40 Sant Feliu de Guíxols:
museum of history
p. 154.

41 Cardona:
Josep Arnau salt museum
p. 204.

Many shades of art

Travelling around Catalonia, it's easy to understand why so many painters were moved to paint the pure and contrasting colours of the landscape. The geometrical shapes formed by the sky, the earth and the sea, the blinding light, the ochre earth, the copper-coloured vineyards, the blue-green oak and olive trees, the reflecting sea and the off-white scrubland are the perfect subject for the cubist or Fauvist painter, depending on your mood. Add to this the creative genius of such artists as Miró and the world is transformed.

Collioure and Fauvism

Henri Matisse (1869-1954) discovered Collioure (p. 120) in May 1905 and was joined there a month later by André Derain (1880-1954). This charming little port has been a magnet for artists since Matisse first settled here and his disciples were known as 'Fauves' (deer). The pure and arbitrary colours used by these two

masters of Fauvism shocked the public of the early 20thC. Matisse, still an apprentice when he arrived, came to Collioure every year until 1946, staying in a different house each time. Fauvism began with paintings such as *La Fenêtre Ouverte* (1905) and *Le Nu Bleu* (1907). Sometimes Derain would paint the same subjects as Matisse, such as the bell-tower in Collioure. Other artists followed, including Raoul Dufy and Juan Gris. As the sun sets and the landscape turns red, walk along the **Fauvist way** (leaflet available from the tourist office, see p. 121), which is illuminated with reproductions of the famous paintings of that movement.

Céret, a Mecca for Cubism

Pablo Picasso (1881-1973) spent three consecutive summers (1911-1913) in this little town perched on the side of a mountain. Georges Braque (1882-1963) joined him in the first year. There they worked together in perfect harmony, facing Mount Canigou and the Pyrenees. In their paintings, they used stencils of figures and letters clipped from the Perpignan newspaper – the prelude to an extensive use of collage. Painters loved to stop at the Capucins convent, the Grand Café or the arena. Two other cubist artists, Juan Gris and Auguste Herbin, were also working in Céret in 1913. Céret, nicknamed the cubist Mecca by André Salmon, became a pilgrimage centre and many other artists settled there. A museum in Barcelona, housed in a late-medieval palace (p. 166), is

dedicated to the first period of Picasso's work, which reflects the artist's encounter with Barcelona's bohemian way of life.

Barcelona – the Surrealist dream of Joan Miró

Born in Barcelona in 1893, in a little street in the heart of the old town, Joan Miró remained very much attached to Catalonia throughout his life. With his primal sketches and colours, he created a universal style. His planets, constellations and other flights of fantasy are an invitation to dream of the cosmos. At the Fundació Joan Miró in Barcelona (p. 168) you can discover his poetic works,

among lithographs, etchings, tapestries, ceramics, stage sets and masks. The works are displayed in natural light and not all the paintings are bright and colourful, notably the moving 50 black-and-white lithographs of the Barcelona series (1939-44), which depict the horrors of the Spanish Civil War. Miró also created many of the monuments in Barcelona. To complete your introduction to Miró, visit the ceramics museum in the Pedralbes royal palace (p. 165), and drink an explosive cocktail at Boadas (☎ 93 318 88 26), at the top of the Ramblas, one of the painter's favourite haunts.

ANTONI TÀPIES FOUNDATION IN BARCELONA

It is hard to separate the life and work of this artist, born in 1923. All of his work is suffused with a political commitment that links it profoundly with the social reality of the Franco era. Influenced by the Dada and Surrealist movements, his art is unrestrained and provocative. From 1956, he re-invented the world in his painting, using an astonishing sign language that evolved towards abstraction, using subtraction rather than addition. From his precious icons to his subtly coloured sketches, his work is poetic and powerful.

Dalí and Gaudí

Statue of Dalí, Cadaqués

A ntoni Gaudí, a generous visionary and utopian, personifies Barcelona to perfection. The bizarre spirit of Salvador Dalí, inveterate megalomaniac, still haunts the museum in Cadaqués and the Rachdingue, a Surrealist nightclub with a sulfurous reputation. These two iconoclasts, misanthropic or mythomaniac, embody the playfulness and fantasy of Catalonia.

Vilajuïga

Salvador Dalí – madman or megalomaniac?

Dalí was born in 1904 in Figueras, near Gerona. He mounted his first exhibition at the tender age of 15, going on to study fine arts at the Escuela de Bellas Artes in Madrid before travelling to Paris, where he was introduced to the Surrealists by Miró. He became the emblem of the movement, before falling out with its members. Unlike Miró or Picasso, Dalí never objected to the Franco regime. He moved to America during the

Spanish civil war and after returned to Catalonia with Gala, his wife and inspiration, who was once married to the

Dalí theatre-museum, Figueras

French poet Paul Éluard. At the end of his life, after Gala's death, he lived in his museum in Figueras (p. 139), alone and infirm. This bizarre monument to an eccentric artist is the most visited museum in Spain after the Prado, and should definitely not be missed. You can also visit other places haunted by Gala and Dalí: the whitewashed village of Cadaqués, Cape Creus with its apocalyptic landscape, and the unusual hermitage at Port Lligat in which the couple lived. Dalí died in his home town in 1989.

The 'dalirious' show goes on

In Vilajuïga, near Roses, in 1968, Salvador Dalí inaugurated a Surrealist nightclub in a farm owned by a French couple, Pierre Bessière and Marie Antoinette Mahé de Boislandelle, also known as 'Miette'. Dalí designed the logo and murals and soon the Rachdingue became the place for 'dalirious' nightlife in the touristic Costa Brava. The 'beautiful people' would come for extravagant,

La Sagrada Familia

facade was the east side, the Life of Christ. The building, still unfinished, has become the symbol of the ever-changing city of Barcelona. A fascinating, ambitious and controversial work, its final stage is scheduled to take place by the centenary of Gaudí's death in 2026. Today, the cranes wait idly for funds from the church's Japanese sponsors. As you climb one of the main towers, you'll see spires like rockets, which twist into reptiles' tails and explode into floral crosses.

bohemian parties, presided over by the Master himself. Today, a crowd of artists still gathers there for more 'techno' but no less extravagant pleasures. Not to be missed by the maestro's fans.

Port Lligat

La Sagrada Familia

'It's not a skyscraper, it's a mindscraper', Jean Cocteau once said of this building. One of Europe's most unconventional churches, the first stone of this temple dedicated to the Holy Family was laid in 1883. It's an expiatory church founded by donations and the architect Gaudí worked on the

symbolic, organic design of the Sagrada Familia for 40 years. He died, hit by a tram, in 1926 when the only completed

It's a symphony of stone and wind, which may be considered kitsch but is, undeniably, a unique and daring work of art.

GÜELL FAMILY

Juan Antonio Güell hosted all of Barcelona high society in the family's home of Pedralbes: aristocrats, grand bourgeois, nouveaux riches, and *indianos* of astronomical wealth. The Güell family belonged to the last category – the epitome of success, social revenge and prestige in the Spanish colonies. Back in Spain, they started textile businesses and built palaces and parks. Eusebi Güell, son of the family's great patriarch, commissioned Antoni Gaudí with numerous projects, including the stunning park which bears the Güell name, in the northwest of the Eixample quarter (p. 166).

Modernisme
exuberance and fantasy

Modernisme is the characteristic architectural style of Barcelona. Under the influence of this art movement, houses were built like sculptures, with gold and light-blue facades, and flowering chimneys. Modernisme was opposed to rhetoric, logic and order – imagination took control. Some scrap of innovative genius can be found on every street corner, making some Catalan cities quite extraordinary.

Running in the family

Modernisme was a movement which started at the end of the 19thC., with a close relationship to British Modern Style, the Belgian Style 1900, the German Jugenstil, the Vienna and Prague Sezessionstil, the Italian Liberty and the French Art Nouveau. It was unique in the way it tried to re-appropriate a broader movement: the Renaixança (1878) or 'rebirth' of Catalan identity. It was turned into a way of life by writers, musicians, poets, painters and architects.

The turn of the century

In the 19thC. people believed that science and progress would save humanity. At the end of the century, this positivist spirit underwent

Fortuny theatre

Casa Navàs, Reus

a deep crisis, which opened the way to anarchism and social violence. Subjectivity, irrationalism, a return to nature, and a new interest in oriental doctrines took over from order and reason. Modernisme objected to both intellectual snobbery and provincial bad taste. The movement was supported by nationalists as well as the new industrial

classes and therefore had a wealth of sponsors to pay for its dreams.

The roots of Catalan Art Nouveau

The origins of the movement were in Catalonia's glorious medieval era, as the crafts, the spirituality and the decorative taste of that time came back into favour. At the same time, in England, the pre-Raphaelites (1848), the Arts and Crafts movement (1888) and the

Symbolists were the new signs of a spiritual and society-orientated art. William Morris (1834-1896) brought handicrafts back into fashion and, in France, Viollet-le-Duc (1814-1879) conceived a passion for medieval design.

How to recognise the Modernist style

In the 19thC., architecture was eclectic and genres were blended together. One building could have Egyptian, Romanesque, Moorish and Greco-Roman influences all at the same time. Neo-Gothic art was also quite popular. Modernist architects were singular in the way they made

PATHS OF MODERNISME

The Generalitat de Catalunya (Passeig de Gràcia 105, Barcelona, ☎ 93 484 95 00) publishes some interesting suggestions for seeking out Modernisme throughout Catalonia. For information on Modernist tours of Barcelona, you can contact the tourist office (Plaza de Catalunya 17, ☎ 906 30 12 82).

use of these influences, with curved lines, asymmetry, energy, rich detailing and refinement characterising their work.

From street lights to shop signs

In Modernisme a creation was considered as a 'total work of art', including all the arts. So, cabinetmakers, workers in mosaic and ceramics, jewellers, ironsmiths, sculptors and master glassmakers all worked together. They were drawn by detail – everything was taken into consideration,

from a doorknob to a mosaic lining. The halls of Modernist buildings are often excellent illustrations of this luxurious ornamentation and attention to detail.

Talking shop

Barcelona still has some 200 shops and public buildings constructed in the Modernist era. You can imagine elegant ladies walking around the city, hobbling in their velvet or damask dresses, tying their ankles in order to avoid tearing their tight skirts as they move slowly along. Many shops have kept a window or a counter from this time. The extravagant decors were often inspired by nature, figures of women, or popular legends, with a sumptuous blending of the various colours of the materials used.

Discovering Modernisme in Reus

An out-of-the-way Catalan town, Reus – located near Tarragona – bears surprising witness to the skilful craftsmen and shrewd merchants of the late 19thC. Domenech i Muntaner, the noted architect, brought Modernisme to Reus and some poets held conferences in the town. You can now follow the Modernist way yourself by visiting such buildings as Casa Navàs, Rull and Gasull, Escoles Prat de la Riba, Teatre Fortuny, Celler del Raïms restaurant and, best of all, the splendid Pere Mata Institute. Information can be obtained from the tourist office in Reus (Plaça de la Llibertat, ☎ 977 34 59 43).

Casa Rull, Reus

Home decoration

Ceramics, jewellery, fabrics, pottery...
Catalan craftsmen will open their doors to you.

① **Perpignan:**
Sant-Vicens garden,
arts and crafts centre
(ceramics, tapestry)
Maison Quinta
(Catalan weaving)
pp. 106-107.

② **St Feliu d'Avall**
Marc Pujo tile factory
(terracotta)
p. 86.

③ **Sorède**
Micocouliers
(whips, walking sticks)
p. 89.

④ **Céret**
LV Richard Caritg
(Catalan corkwood)
Regional arts and crafts
centre (jewellery, ceramics)
pp. 84 and 124.

⑤ **Saint-Laurent-
de-Cerdans**
Toiles du Soleil (Catalan
weaving, linens, espadrilles)
Musée de l'espadrille
(espadrilles)
pp. 85 and 122.

Garonna

Pico
de Aneto
11,182 ft
(3,408 m)

Pic
d'Esta
10,319
(3,145

ANDOR

Río Noguera

**Cataluña /
Catalunya**

SPAIN

Río
Segre

C1313

C1313

C25

N II

● Lleida /
Lérida

Río Segre

A2

⑫

N240

● Reus

Ebro

● Tarragona

⑬

L'Espina
3,878 ft
(1,182 m)

● Tortosa

A7

**Mediterranean
Sea**

0   10   20   30 miles

A7

0 10 20 30 40 50 km

⑩ Arenys de Mar

Can Soler workshop
(espadrilles)
p. 162.

⑪ Barcelona

Miró foundation shop
(postcards, posters etc.)
BD Mallorca (furniture,
ornaments etc.)
Vinçon (furniture, ornaments
china etc.)
Ici et Là (tablecloths, wrought-
iron furniture etc.)
Hôma (lamps)
pp. 87 and 168.

⑫ Sarral

Alabastro Sarral Imade
museum shop
p. 213.

⑬ Tivenys

Picurt pottery workshop
p. 216.

⑥ Olot

Crafts market
(woodwork)
Art Cristia
(figurines and nativity sets)
p. 199.

⑦ La Bisbal d'Empordà

Can Marunys ceramics
workshop
p. 150.

⑧ Quart

Ceramics factories
p. 197.

⑨ Breda

Roca Auladell workshop
(cooking pans)
p. 159.

Catalan style

Mediterranean art is definitely in fashion these days when it comes to decorating a home. Catalonia preserves the traditional expertise of its craftsman while inventing new styles, collections of fabrics and colourful ceramic works. The colours are vibrant and warm like the Catalan earth, a blend of tradition and imagination. Barcelona's reputation as a fashionable city is second to none. If you have eclectic tastes, you'll love it; there are so many styles to choose from – colonial, country, high-tech, kitsch, ecology, surrealist…

Transformations

Like every country short of raw materials, such as Japan, Sweden and Switzerland, Catalonia has had to specialise in the transformative process, whether of textiles, glass, ceramics, leather, metal, wood, paper or the graphic arts. The innovations of Modernisme gave the companies in these industries an enormous boost. However, the roots of Catalan creativity run much deeper than this. When the New World was discovered, the dominant Castile district prevented Catalonia from trading with the Americas. Thus the region had to produce its own wealth and was forced to develop an artisanal and familial tradition that continued throughout the centuries, particularly in the textile industry.

Catalan fibres

Catalonia preserves its traditional textile industry, just as Roussillon and the Balearic islands have kept their ancient weaving frames. In Santa Maria del Cami, in

Arles-sur-Tech (Tissages Catalans, ☎ 04 68 39 10 07) or Saint-Laurent-de-Cerdans (Toiles du Soleil, ☎ 04 68 39 50 02), some manufacturers still make *llengos de Mallorca* and traditional patterned fabrics. The Majorca technique is called *ikat* and the half-cotton half-linen canvas is 2 ft (70 cm) wide. The most characteristic design is named *raxa*. This rough and stiff canvas mixes primal, contrasting colours. In French Catalonia, table linen (aprons, napkin rings etc.) is decorated with colourful strips or check patterns, lateen sails or *croix badines*, designs once embroidered on espadrilles.

A passion for wood
LV Richard Caritg
390, Av. du Vallespir, Céret
☎ 04 68 87 00 97
Open Mon.-Fri. 8am-noon and 2-6pm.
In Céret, Richard Caritg is the last surviving traditional cork manufacturer. From May to the end of July is the lifting season, when the slow-growing cork is harvested from the Albères orchards and the slopes of Mount Canigou. It takes between 12 and 15 years to mature. Once the sap has

risen, a worker cuts the side of the tree in different places and uses a *picassa* to lift the bark. Depending on the noise made (sharp or otherwise), he will decide whether to remove the bark. It is vitally important that the tree makes a 'singing' sound. The slice of bark is brushed, drained of sap and left to dry for a

---

JOIN THE DANCE
Did you know that espadrilles are still hand-made in Saint-Laurent-de-Cerdans? As natural style is back in fashion, don't miss this shop to complete your look before returning home. In the past, around 20 companies, employing some 600 people, specialised in the making of espadrilles. These shoes can be *basquaise* or *vigatane* (named after Vic, in southern Catalonia), and are used to dance the Sardana. The soles are made from jute and the fabrics used can be plain, striped or lacy. The former working co-operative has been turned into a museum (☎ 04 68 39 55 75) and you can visit the espadrille factory and the Toiles du Soleil textile workshop. the museum is open every day and makes an interesting trip, so get your dancing shoes on!

BD design shop, Barcelona

year in the open. The sap evaporates in the sun and the cork is then boiled for 30 minutes and kept for 3 weeks in a dark room before being cut by hand. In this way, Richard Caritg oversees and

monitors the whole process, from the tree to the bottle, supplying estates and châteaux with corks for wines that are laid down to age. Around 3 million corks are carefully made, destined for the most famous vintages. He also makes corks to the specific require-ments or pottery and ceramic artists, choosing bark from different trees accordingly.

A vibrant tile factory
Tuilerie Marc Pujo
Avenue du Languedoc, Sant Feliu d'Avall

D916, 6 miles (10 km) from Perpignan
☎ **04 68 57 82 27**
Marc Pujo owns the last *tuilerie* in southern France, the perfect stop if you're renovating your home or would just like to make it look brighter. His enamelled, baked-clay gutters, drainpipes and gargoyles add bright colours to the roofs and walls of houses on the Roussillon

plain. The dry clay is ground, kneaded, stamped out, and then hand-pressed. It is baked once, the enamel ladled on, and then baked a second time. With this method he produces some wonderfully vibrant colours, such as olive green, honey, cobalt blue, burnt umber or burgundy, that gleam with the craftsman's pride. Take a little of the Catalan sunshine home with you.

Made in Catalunya
Barcelona has a reputation for being at the forefront of innovative and contemporary design, and its fresh, young design artists create subtle, poetic and sometimes humorous objects. While you walk around this city, which has produced many artistic prodigies, do try to visit at least some of the following 'in' places.

BD (Mallorca 291, ☎ 93 458 69 09) is a harmonious blend of two rather different aesthetic concepts. This Modernist showroom was established by Domenech i Montaner (1895), to display an exceptional selection of 20thC. creations. Works include furniture by Mackintosh, Hoffman, Gaudí, Thonet and Mies van der Rohe, and decorative art by Andre Ricard, Ricardo Bofill, Oscar Tusquets and Mariscal. **Vinçon** (Passeig Gracia 96, ☎ 93 215 60 50) is another of Barcelona's many design institutions, housed in a fascinating Modernist setting. In 1929 Vinçon began to sell bone china from his native country, Germany, before starting to design pieces himself. You will find all sorts of objects here, from keyrings to sofas, designed by Pedro Miralles, Alicia Nunez, Mariscal and Nancy Robbins, among others. In the Born quarter, which is becoming increasingly fashionable, you'll

find two small shops which are also worth a visit. **Ici et Là** (Plaza Santa Maria del Mar 2, ☎ 93 268 11 67) opens onto a square cooled by

a Gothic fountain. It's simple and refined and offers a selection of small wrought-iron furniture, multi-coloured mosaic consoles and ethnic articles, as well as Catalan tablecloths. A few steps along, in a former coffee warehouse, **Hôma** (Rec 20, ☎ 93 315 27 55) sells bedside lamps and primitive ecological wall lights in natural 'jungle' materials,

EVEN THE SMOKE IS ORGANIC

In Barcelona, many shops have turned 'organic', offering a slice of country life in town and promising health, love, and happiness. The eco- and organic generation has opened shops and restaurants that guarantee the authentic origins of their products. You'll be offered *organicas* shirts made with cotton from Peru, gluten wheat balms, *tortillas paisanas*, recycled cardboard products, and even readings of the soles of your feet (which makes a change from palm readings!). On an unhealthy note, people smoke every-where in Spain. Giving disapproving looks to cigarette addicts is unknown and smokers continue to puff away in chemists' shops, on the metro, in restaurants and even in 'no smoking' areas. Get used to it!

such as raffia, natural wood and bamboo. A recycling flavour for your home. If you have eclectic tastes, you won't be disappointed by what's on offer in Barcelona. There are almost as many styles as there are shops!

Ici et Là design shop, Barcelona

A closer look at the Mediterranean elm

Riding whips, sticks, crops and walking sticks are all made from the same tree – the Mediterranean elm. Known principally as an ornamental tree in avenues and public gardens, it forms the raw material of an industry centred around Sorède, in the eastern Pyrenees, and Sauve, in the Gard region. Today, the Hermès fashion house, amongst others, has come to appreciate its fine expertise.

Some facts about the tree itself

The Mediterranean elm grows between sea level and 2,625 ft (800 m) in calcareous or siliceous soil where there is some humidity, light and warmth. Its wood, greyish white or dark green, is elastic and heavy, and it is composed of long malleable fibres. Once it has dried, it hardens and will not rot.

The *perpignan*

In the mid-17thC., a certain M. Massot established the first Mediterranean-elm whip

factory in Perthus. The whips, known as *massots* or *perpignans*, rapidly became popular, not just in France but also all over Europe. Around 1850, the first plantations appeared near Sorède, south of Perpignan, where the climate and irrigation were ideal, and the first crops and whips factory opened. A new industry was born.

Rise and fall

From 1920 to 1926, this factory employed 120 people and sold its products all over France, North Africa, and even in America. There were also factories in Argelès and Perpignan (which have now disappeared). The families that worked in the industry either grew the trees, harvested the wood or worked in the factories. However, the industry's workforce had declined from 400 in 1914, to just 6 by 1978.

WHIP SPEED

Did you know that the snapping sound made by a whip (as used by lion-tamers in a circus) is actually produced when the tip, the tuft, breaks the sound barrier? The wrist motion moves the whip tip at 1,377 ft per second (420 m/sec), and the speed of sound is 1,280 ft per second (390 m/sec).

From the tree to the whip

The tree must be at least 15 years old and any shoots on the trunk must have been pruned when young, to avoid any hitches in the wood. The wood is cut into strips, left to dry out for a year, and then sawn into 'carrats' – square sections. These sections are then straightened, if necessary, before being fed through a machine like a large pencil-sharpener, which gives them a cone shape.

A twisted handle

The originality is in the twisting, rather than plaiting, of the wood. The roughcast sections are split lengthways into four even strands, leaving a few inches at the end, which then forms a plain handle. Each strand is shaved into a cone shape and then bathed in steam to increase its flexibility. They are then hand-twisted around the handle, dried, varnished and decorated with leather.

An age-old skill rediscovered

As cars gradually replaced horses, the demand for whips collapsed. However, since May 1981, the Les Micocouliers workshop has happily managed to rescue this traditional skill from extinction. The only place where whips are still made by hand, their products now include western whips (for animal tamers in circuses) and walking sticks. Both the factory and the shop are open for visits. **Les Micocouliers**, 4, Rue des Fabriques, Sorède, ☎ 04 68 89 04 50. Open daily, 9am-noon and 1.30-4.30pm.

Hay-forks

This craft is all about the skill of the *réblaquaire*, the man who shapes the tree with a careful pruning process. When the tree reaches a height of 4 ft (1.2 m), it is regularly pruned so that the three shoots will form the prongs of the fork. The shrub is ready after five or six years. The forks are cut between November and March, and then barked, bent and finished.

Catalan culture

All the dates and places to remember to bring the spirit of Catalonia to your holiday.

Celebrations

1. Canigou:
   Midsummer's Day fair
   p. 132.

2. Thuir:
   'Thuir la Catalana' festival
   p. 126.

3. Perpignan:
   Sanch procession
   p. 107.

4. Argelès-village: Sardane dancing
   p. 116.

5. Céret:
   Sardane gathering
   p. 125.

6. Roses: Suquet festival
   p. 143.

7. Arsèguel:
   Catalan accordion capital
   p. 189.

8. Sitges:
   Sant Bartolomeu fair
   p. 173.

9. Vilafranca del Penedès:
   chicken fair
   p. 210.

Museums

10. Perpignan: Museum of popular arts and traditions
    p. 105.

11. Olot:
    Museum of nature art
    p. 199.

12. Gerona: Museum of history
    p. 197.

13. Berga: Plaza de Catalunya
    p. 202.

14. Mataró:
    Santa Maria basilica
    p. 162.

15. Barcelona:
    Modern art, contemporary arts and Barça museums
    pp. 165, 169 and 170.

16. Montserrat:
    Modern-art museum
    p. 207.

Garonna

Pico de Aneto
11,182 ft
(3,408 m)

Pi
d'Es
10,3
(3,145

ANDO

Rio Noguera

C1313

7

Cataluña /
Catalunya

SPAIN

Rio Segre

C1313

C25

N II

A2

Lleida /
Lérida

Rio Segre

A2

Ebro

N240

Reus ●

● Tarragona

A7

Tortosa ●

*Mediterranean
Sea*

0 10 20 30 40 50 km

0   10   20   30 miles

Mediterranean Sea

Carcassonne

A61 Narbonne

A9

FRANCE

Pyrénées-Orientales

Tunnel de
ymorens

Têt N116

Prades ②③

N20

Pic du Canigou
9,134 ft
(2,784 m) ①

Céret ⑤

Puigmal
9,548 ft
(2,910 m)

①⑧

Perpignan ③ ⑩

④

A9

A7

⑲

⑦

⑬

Rio Llobregat

Figueres /
Figueras

⑥

⑪

Rio Ter

Vic ⑳

C25

Girona /
Gerona ⑫

Manresa

Terrassa /
Tarrasa

N152

A7

㉑

④

N II

Mataró

A19

⑮㉒ Barcelona

A16

Catalan specialities

⑰ Bellver de Cerdanya:
Tupí de Cerdanya
p. 187.

⑱ Saint-Laurent de Cerdans:
Textiles
p. 123.

⑲ Cerbère: Cold meats
p. 119.

⑳ Vic: Can Vila and Ca La
Teresona delicatessens
pp. 208-209.

㉑ Sant Pol:
Sauleda confectioners
p. 161.

㉒ Barcelona: Planelles-
Donat confectioners
p. 169.

Others

㉓ Prades:
Catalan language school
p. 131.

㉔ Îsles Formigues
p. 151.

Parla català ?

In the 10thC., the Counts of Barcelona broke away from central control, becoming kings of Aragon in 1137. The arago-catalan state was one of the foremost powers of medieval Europe, reaching its peak in the 13th-14thC. with King Jaume I (1213-1276), who conquered land all around the Mediterranean. His son, Jaume II, inherited a kingdom that was culturally and economically rich, but he was unable to prevent the French crown from asserting its claim – the golden age of Catalonia came to an end. In 1659, the Treaty of the Pyrenees ceded Roussillon to France and Catalan pride didn't recover until the 19thC. Since then, an artificial, historical border has divided a region with a long-standing cultural identity.

A nation divided

On the French side of the border, **Northern Catalonia** encompasses the Pyrénées-Orientales département and its principal city, Perpignan. The Côte Vermeille and Collioure are wild and colourful; inland is the Albères range, which extends to the sea. The highest point of the French Catalan Pyrenees is the Pic Carli, at 9,583 ft (2,921 m) and the mountains are beautiful, particularly in the heart of the Conflent, Capcir and Cerdagne regions. On the Spanish side, **Southern Catalonia** covers more than 12,000 sq miles (32,000 sq km), extending from the Pyrenees to the River Èbre in the south and as far as Lleida in the east. The area is crossed by four mountain ranges. From north to south, the three coasts are the Brava, Maresme and Dorada. The only other area in Europe that unites the appeal of the high mountains and the sea is France's Alpes-

Maritimes region. Barcelona, with 3 million inhabitants, would like to be seen as the capital of the Mediterranean and it looks as if it may not be long before the title is granted.

Catalan language

Catalan is very close to the Occitan language of the south of France, both having Romance origins. It is spoken from Salses-en-Roussillon to Valencia, in Spain, in Andorra, in the Capcir region and even in the Balearic islands. During the most prosperous era of Catalan history (13thC.), the writer Raymond

Lulle made Catalan the language of aristocratic letters. Unfortunately, centralization dealt it a fatal blow, rather like the one suffered by the province's own 'langue d'oc'. In the 16thC., King Philip II proclaimed Castilian to be Spain's official language, to

Saint-Michel-de-Cuxa abbey

the detriment of all regional languages. However, Catalan remained the language of everyday life and was reborn in the 19thC. Since 1979, according to the statute of Catalan autonomy, Catalan has been acknowledged as the original language of Spanish Catalonia, and since 1983 it has been recognised as an official language, with the same status as Castilian. These days, some 7 million people speak Catalan fluently.

No bull

Did you know that Catalans are not interested in either *corridas* or castanets? The Catalans are not be confused with the Castilians, and even

less so with the Andalucians. You'll find mushrooms and Sardana dancing at their festivals, not bulls and Flamenco dancing. Although known for being shrewd businessmen, clever merchants and skilful craftsmen, Catalans are not widely admired in the rest of Spain – they are said to love money and work and to be unable to stop for a siesta. It's no surprise, then, that this region generates 25% of Spain's GDP. As a nation, they like to keep a balance between work and play. Watch out for the street signs and shop signs in Catalan. They are often easier to understand than the spoken language.

MUSIC FESTIVALS AND TRADITIONAL CUSTOMS
Every summer in Conflent, the churches Saint-Pierre-de-Prades and Saint-Michel-de Cuxa abbey echo to the soothing sounds of chamber music. In 1950 Pau Casals initiated this internationally famous festival, which takes place from 26 July to 3 August (further information from the tourist office in Prades – ☎ 04 68 05 41 01). On a completely different note, Lluçanès (Spanish Pyrenees) unites traditional customs and music all summer long (last weekend of May to early August), with excursions along the shepherds' paths, harvest and Mid-summers' Day feasts, parades of giants and *capgrossos*, traditional dances and *botifarradas* (tastings of local produce). The Solc festival won the first prize for popular culture in 1998. Further information from the tourist office of Sta Eulalia de Puig-Oriol (Lluça), ☎ 93 855 40 62.

Copas, tapas and company

It's not called *Bar*-celona for nothing. This city loves its bars and some are already household names, including the Suizo, Oro del Rin and La Luna. Some have avant-garde interiors, decorated with fairground bric-a-brac or home-brewing equipment, but there's many a tapas bar with a well-worn billiards table in the corner.

The city beats to every conceivable rhythm, so you should find something to enjoy whatever your mood or taste. Each district has its own distinct flavour and atmosphere. And you should be prepared for a good night out at least once in Barcelona. Here are a few suggestions of which establishments to visit to make your evenings memorable.

There's a wide range of varieties, ranging from cold meats and cheeses to tasty hot dishes. Some popular tapas include *escalivada* (aubergines and peppers pickled in olive oil), *calamares* (squid) and Escala anchovies with *embotits* (cold pork) from the Pyrenees, as well as the famous *fuets* (dried sausages) and *pernil serrano* (country ham).

A Catalan feast

Catalans will not invite you into their homes readily. As in many Mediterranean countries, social life takes place in the street. An invitation to *anar de tasca* or *ir de tapas* is already a mark of trust and acceptance. It means an evening of bar-hopping, not to get drunk but to socialise around some appetizing snacks (tapas) and a glass of local wine. The word 'tapas' is said to come from the lids put on wine glasses to keep flies away ('tapar' meaning 'to shut/obstruct'). Soon pieces of ham or cheese were put on these lids, as with oriental 'mezzes'. Originally free of charge, tapas generally have to be paid for nowadays.

Order at the bar

Tapas traditions mainly originate in Andalucia and the Basque country. But the

FUN AND GAMES

You can see just about anything in the bars of Barcelona, but games are particularly popular. The elderly play *manilla*, a Catalan tarot-card game, or *subbastat* for afternoons on end, using chickpeas and corn kernels as counting chips. In the bar Marsella, fortunes are told using tarot cards. With its somewhat dilapidated decor, Canodrom Pavello, plays host to the greyhound-racing enthusiasts from the nearby track. With snooker available at the Velodrom, and darts and Internet cafés opening up everywhere else, El Arquer has invented *copas y flechas*. For 1,200 pesetas, you can have a drink while brushing up on your archery, winning hearts into the bargain like a modern-day Robin Hood! All opening hours and addresses can be found in the listings magazine *Guia del Ocio*. Cycling enthusiasts can treat themselves to a *cocha menys* (Esparteria 3, ☎ 93 268 21 05) and discover the city by cycling and dining accompanied by a well-informed guide.

Catalans have their own distinctive customs. Orders for a *raciòn* or *media raciòn* (full or half-portion) are placed *a la barra* (at the bar). Tapas are eaten before meals and be careful not to talk too loudly, or you may find yourself mistaken

for a noisy Andalucian! You'll find at least one bar in even the smallest village, where locals gather to enjoy a drink, a chat and a few tapas. In general, everyone pays for themselves. You could offer to pay for a round, but remember Catalans have a reputation for being careful with their money, unlike the Andalucians.

A guide to the nightlife

Fashions in Barcelona nightlife change with dizzying speed. The busiest nights are Thursday, Friday and Saturday. In summer, the *carpas* (tents) set up at the port and the higher parts of the city are the trendiest locations for the season. First and foremost, if you want to do things the Catalan way, don't start too early. Nothing happens before 11pm and some nightclubs don't get going until 2am. If you're out all night, you'll

always find a bar with *chocolate con churros* or a bakery with crunchy *pa de coca* first thing in the morning. As you may have gathered, not much time is left for sleeping in Barcelona. This Catalan party is open to all, if you play by the rules. Prepare to enjoy yourself – you can always sleep when you get home!

L'arquer
TAPES, COPES y FLETXES

Family outings

Zoos, aquariums, museums, nature reserves, theme parks,
walks... everything for a successful family holiday.

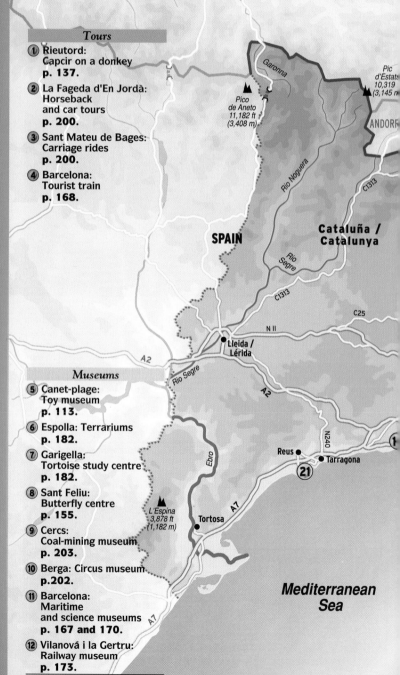

Tours

① Rieutord:
Capcir on a donkey
p. 137.

② La Fageda d'En Jordà:
Horseback
and car tours
p. 200.

③ Sant Mateu de Bages:
Carriage rides
p. 200.

④ Barcelona:
Tourist train
p. 168.

Museums

⑤ Canet-plage:
Toy museum
p. 113.

⑥ Espolla: Terrariums
p. 182.

⑦ Garigella:
Tortoise study centre
p. 182.

⑧ Sant Feliu:
Butterfly centre
p. 155.

⑨ Cercs:
Coal-mining museum
p. 203.

⑩ Berga: Circus museum
p.202.

⑪ Barcelona:
Maritime
and science museums
p. 167 and 170.

⑫ Vilanová i la Gertru:
Railway museum
p. 173.

Garonna

Pic
d'Estats
10,319
(3,145 m)

Pico
de Aneto
11,182 ft
(3,408 m)

ANDORR

Rio Noguera

C1313

**Cataluña /
Catalunya**

SPAIN

Rio
Segre

C1313

C25

N II

Lleida /
Lérida

A2

Rio Segre

A2

N240

Reus ●

● Tarragona

21

Ebro

L'Espina
3,878 ft
(1,182 m)

● Tortosa

A7

A7

*Mediterranean
Sea*

Theme parks

⑬ Saint-Cyprien: Aqualand
p. 115.

⑭ Roses: Aquabrava
p. 143.

⑮ Palamós: Aquadiver park
p. 153.

⑯ Lloret: Water World
p. 159.

⑰ Blanes: Pinya Rosa park
p. 159.

⑱ Palafolls: Marineland
p. 161.

⑲ Villassar de Dalt:
Isla Fantasia
p. 163.

⑳ Barcelona: El Tibidado
p. 167.

㉑ Vila-Seca: Port Aventura
p. 176.

Zoos and aquariums

㉒ Casteil: Animal park
p. 133.

㉓ Canet: Aquarium
p. 113 .

㉔ Argelès: Eagle displays
p. 117.

㉕ Banyuls-sur-Mer:
Marine nature
reserve
and Arago aquarium
p. 119.

㉖ L'Estartit:
Subacuatic Vision
p. 146.

㉗ Sobrestany:
Animal park
p. 147.

㉘ Barcelona:
Zoo and aquarium
pp. 166 and 171.

Something for the kids

Catalonia is full of exciting places for the whole family to visit. Although the Spanish birth rate is one of the lowest in Europe, children are treated as royalty and there's always something to interest even the most inquisitive minds, including rare-animal breeding farms, bird sanctuaries, boat trips, rack-and-pinion trains, aquariums and various natural wonders. Let your curiosity take over and make the most of the many attractions of Catalonia.

The legendary yellow train – 'Le Petit Train Jaune'

It's hard to imagine Cerdagne without its little yellow train, which is probably why this delightful mountain line still exists today. The 38.5-mile (62-km) track climbs 3,820 ft (1,165 m) using every device imaginable, including viaducts, 19 tunnels and more than 20 bridges – a real testament to the art of railway building. The train has remained virtually unchanged since the early 1900s. It runs over the River Tet and its gorges and through and around the mountain where it climbs, undulates and twists. It doesn't hurry (38 mph/60 kph) and the recent addition of open-topped carriages means you can enjoy a great view of the Cerdagne region between Vernet-les-Bains and Latour-de-Carol. So climb aboard for a very unusual train ride – the kids should love it. The trip is two and a half hours of pure delight and it's a wonderful way to discover Cerdagne, both ancient and modern (see Villefranche-de-Conflent p. 128).

Aquabrava, Roses (p. 143)

Walking with wolves

The Les Angles animal park (p. 137) is everything but a zoo. The animals are not kept in cages, but in vast, open enclosures. There is a wide range of Pyrenean and cold-climate fauna and with just binoculars and a stout pair of shoes you'll be ready to watch bears, wolves, wild goats, bison and reindeer. The 91-acre (37-ha) park is a real mini-safari. Younger children will

Aquabrava water park, Roses (p. 143)

Marineland, Palafolls (p. 161)

In the Port Aventura theme park (p. 176), now owned by Universal Studios, you'll discover the architechture, shops, local traditions and cuisine of five different countries. There's a small Mediterranean fishing village which pulses with the rhythm of popular songs. The exuberant vegetation of Polynesia conceals shipwrecks and tropical waterfalls. Behind the Great Wall is the splendour of the millennial Chinese Empire. In the jungle, you'll find the ancient Mexican pyramids, where you can enjoy corn pies with pimentoes and mariachi music. Finally, lost in the desert is Penitence, a Wild West town with miners, cowboys and cardsharps. Each zone has amazing white-knuckle rides as well as attractions suitable for younger children.

prefer the 1-mile (1.5 km) 'red' route, while others can follow the 'yellow' route (2 miles/3.5 km, 2.5 hours), to see wild sheep, ibex and wild goats. The bears are the stars of the park. They live as in the wild among real mountain streams and trees, so please avoid feeding them peanuts.

Under the volcano

At the foot of the dormant volcanoes of La Garrotxa (p. 198), a ride in a horse-drawn barouche is quite charming. The track runs through the Fageda d'en Jorda with its spiky basalt rocks, one of the prettiest landscapes of the volcanic zone. Many Catalan painters have been inspired by the stunning scenery, some of them based in a small art colony in Olot (p. 200). The quality of the light is quite remarkable and you could even take your own paints and sketchbook should you fancy trying to capture the scene. The area includes the most southerly beech grove in Europe, protected from the sea wind by a natural barrier formed by the Croscat, Puig de la Costa and Santa Margarida volcanoes. The GR2 path runs along the Roca Negra and Santa Margarida volcanoes, where you can descend into the crater and emerge on the opposite hillside leading to Croscat (2-hour trip). Soil, calcined rocks and hills of ash are all signs of the violence of past eruptions.

Catalonia in detail

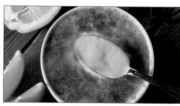

Costa Brava 138

Roussillon 104

From Vallespir to Cerdagne 122

Costa Dorada 164

The Pyrenees 182

Catalonia's interior 196

Catalonia in detail

In the following pages, you'll find all the information you need to visit Catalonia. The region is divided into tourist zones, each marked with a different colour so you can easily find your way around.

```
0   10  20  30  40  50 km
```

```
0     10      20      30 miles
```

Pic
d'Estat
10,319
(3,145 r

Pico
de Aneto
11,182 ft
(3,408 m)

Esterri d'Àneu

Caldes
de Boi

(5)

Llavorsí

ANDOR

Sort

La Seu
d'Urgell

Río Noguera

Gerri de
la Sal

C1313

Tremp

SPAIN

**Cataluña /
Catalunya**

Río
Segre

Ponts

Cardon

C1313

C25

Lleida /
Lérida

N II

A2

Vallbona de
les Monges

Sarral

Río Segre

A2

Santa
Creus

Villafranca
del Penedè

Montblanc

(6)

N240

Vilanova
i la Geltr

Reus●

● Tarragona

Ebro

El Pinell
de Brai

Cambrils
de Mar

(4)

L'Espina
3,878 ft
(1,182 m)

Tivenys

A7

● **Tortosa**

Deltebre

Amposta

Sant Carles de la Ràpita

*Mediterranean
Sea*

Carcassonne ●   A61   ● Narbonne

A9

Mediterranean Sea

Saint-Paul-de-Fenouïllet ○
① A9
○ Port-Barcarès
Saises-le-Château ○

FRANCE

Perpignan ●   ○ Canet-Plage

unnel de ymorens
②   **Prades ●** Têt   **Pyrénées-Orientales**
Font-Romeu ○   N116   ○ Saint-Cyprien-Plage
Pic du Canigou 9,134 ft (2,784 m) ▲   Argelès ○ Collioure
○ Llívia   **Céret ●**   ○ Port-Vendres
gcerda ○   Prats-de-Mollo ○   ○ Banyuls
Puigmal 9,548 ft (2,910 m) ▲   ○ Núria   ○ Cerbère
○ Queralbs   La Jonquera ○   ○ Portbou
○ Ribes de Freser

⑤   **Figueres / Figueras ●**   Roses ○   ○ Cadaqués
○ Ripoll   ○ Olot   Besalú

○ Berga   ○ L'Escala

○ Puig-reig   Rio Ter   **Girona / Gerona ●**   Torroella de Montgri ○   ○ L'Estartit
Pals ○
● **Vic**   ⑥   C25   Palafrugell ○   ○ Begur
○ Llafranc
③   ○ Palamós
Manresa   Tossa de Mar   ○ La Platja d'Aro
A7   ○ San Feliu de Guíxols
Terrassa / Tarrasa   N152   Pineda de Mar   Blanes ○ Lloret de Mar
tserrat ○   Sant Pol de Mar ○ ○ ○ Malgrat de Mar
Sabadell   **Mataró ●**   Arenys de Mar   Calella
A19

④   ● **Barcelona**
A16
tges ○

Perpignan, 'Fidelissima'

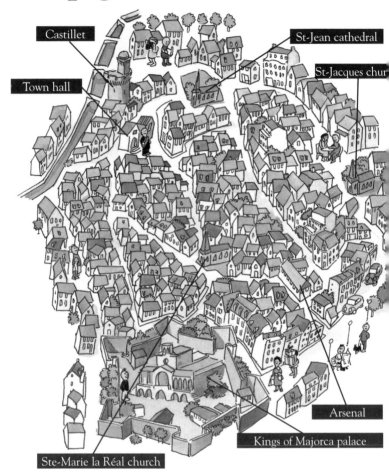

Castillet

St-Jean cathedral

St-Jacques chur[ch]

Town hall

Arsenal

Kings of Majorca palace

Ste-Marie la Réal church

'**P**erpinyà' is, first and foremost, Catalan. Squashed between the mountains and the sea, the economical and cultural capital of Roussillon owes its stormy history to this strategic location. Many different Mediterranean civilisations helped to form the city, which now takes its lead from Barcelona. Its raucous students, sunny squares planted with palm trees, excellent cuisine and delicious wines make it a lively and tasty destination.

Kings of Majorca palace
Rue des Archers
☎ **04 68 34 48 29**
Open daily, 10am-6pm
(5pm in winter).

Admission charge.
Perpignan's prestigious past is linked to the reign of the Counts of Barcelona and the expansion of the Catalan kingdom. The stately Palais

Spotcheck
F2

Pyrénées-Orientales

Things to do

• Visit a chocolate factory
• Sant-Vicens garden
• Festivals and celebrations

Within easy reach

Vallespir (15.5 miles S)
p. 122
Céret (18 miles S) p. 124
Les Aspres p. 126

Tourist office

Perpignan:
☎ 04 68 66 30 30

des Rois de Majorque, a 12th-14th-C. stronghold, overlooks the city. The gardens and the main courtyard are the principal sights – evidence of the splendour of former times. King Jean II of Aragon gave the city the nickname 'Fidelissima' ('the most loyal') when its citizens supported him against Louis XI of France in the 15thC.

Quartier Saint-Jean and the cathedral
Place Gambetta

The 14th and 15thC. **townhouses** and **patrician homes** of the Quartier Saint-Jean recall the city's prosperous times. Lose your way in the maze of back streets – the canopies and half-timbered facades of Rue des Marchands will lead you back to **Place de la Loge**, the historical centre of the town. The Loge de Mer ('sea house') was once the commodities exchange and the headquarters of the marine ministry. The original weathercock (1397) still graces this elegant building. On the square, the bronze *Vénus au Collier* ('Venus with necklace'), sculpted by Maillol, still presides over many Sardana dances. The

elegant patio of the **Hôtel de Ville** (town hall), once the seat of the local administration, is worth a look for its wrought-iron portals, painted beams and splendid Hispanic and Moorish ceilings alone.

Castillet – Musée d'Arts et Traditions Populaires
☎ 04 68 35 42 05.

Perpignan likes to party

Open daily exc. Tues. 15 June-15 Sept., 9.30am-7pm; 9am-6pm, rest of the year. *Admission charge.* This 14th-C. brick castle was first the city gate and, later, a prison. The long, open parapets and the pink dome of the

pinnacle give the building an oriental look. It houses the interesting **museum of popular arts and traditions**, named 'Casa Pairal'. From the terrace, the view of the city, the Roussillon plain, the sea and massive Mount Canigou is unrivalled. Nearby, the 14th and 15th-C. **Cathédrale Saint-Jean** (open 7.30-

Altarpiece, Saint Jean Cathedral

11.45am and 3-7pm) is one of the finest examples of southern Gothic art. The apses and the chapels of the 157-ft (48-m) nave hide wonderful retables. The painted and sculpted details are worth a closer look. Walk further along to the **Campo Santo Saint-Jean** (14th -C.), Place Gambetta, a cloister-cemetery with marble archways unique in France. The family vaults, recessed in the wall, are decorated with the coats of arms of the city's nobility. Return to the world of the living in the colourful Quartier Saint-Jacques. 'Jaumet' (local resident), Romany and North African communities share the area. Take in the atmosphere while sipping a mint tea on the terrace of a local café.

Castillet tower

Place Cassanyes hosts a lively market (Tuesday, Thursday, Saturday and Sunday), selling snails, smoked hams and herbs etc. Behind the Église Saint-Jacques (13th-14th-C. church) is the attractive, well-maintained **Jardin de La Miranda** (open 3-6.30pm), the garden sheltered by the bulwark of Saint-Jacques and its parapet of thin bricks (*cayroux*) and pebbles worn by the sea. The fragrances of the Mediterranean and tropical plants make this garden the ideal place to admire the city and the River Têt in peace. The Quartier Saint-Jacques was traditionally where gardeners would grow the typical Perpignan *hortas* (gardens), orchards of delicious fruit and the vegetables that are still produced in the agricultural plains.

Sweet delicacies for gourmet travellers

Here are two places to discover the tasty traditional sweets of the region. **Chocolaterie Cantalou** (2980, Avenue Julien-Panchot, ☎ 04 68 56 35 35. Film screenings and opening hours: July-Aug., Mon.-Fri., 2-5.45pm; rest of the year, Wed. pm). Here you can learn everything about the history of chocolate, the cocoa tree and the making of the drink, which used to be a royal privilege. Of course, you can also taste all the different chocolates – even with

orange blossom, for those with delicate nerves, or almonds for irritability. Any old excuse! **Biscuiterie-Confiserie Lor** (85, Rue Pascal-Marie-Agasse, ☎ 04 68 85 65 00. Open all year, Mon.-Fri. 9am-noon and 2-6pm). Video screenings and free tastings of *rousquilles*, *amandines* and soft, crunchy *touron* will unveil all the delicious secrets of these little gourmet sins.

Roussillon snails

9, Place de la Republique
☎ **04 68 34 47 65**
Open Tues.-Sun., 8am-12.30pm.
To cook your own *cargolade*, you can get the snails from this wholesaler (about 40F for 100 *petits-gris*). You can even buy the herbs to go with them and the special griddles for the barbecue.

Jardin de Sant-Vicens, arts and crafts centre

Rue Sant-Vicens
☎ **04 68 50 02 18**
Garden always open.
Free admission.
Created by Firmin Bauby in 1950, the Sant-Vicens garden was constructed around a traditional *mas* (country farm). Orange trees heaving with fruit, oleanders, Barbary fig trees, palm trees and agaves are all reminiscent of Arab Andalucia. Flower bushes, impatiens, gaillardes, daffodils and pelargoniums defy winter and vary with the seasons.

Concerts are held during the summer and there are exhibitions and sales of ceramics and tapestries in the crafts centre.

Maison Quinta
3, Rue Grande-des-Fabriques
☎ 04 68 34 41 62
Open daily exc. Sun. and Mon. am, 9.30am-noon and 2.30-7pm.

This two-storey shop, housed in a former mansion, is a must, not only for its decorative art and earthenware crockery, but also for the traditional fabrics, sold by the metre, or as tablecloths, napkins, table mats and pinafores. A large choice and good taste are guaranteed. After all this shopping, rest at **Casa Sansa** restaurant (3, Rue Fabrique-Couverte, ☎ 04 68 34 21 84, closed Sun. and Mon. lunchtime).

Festivals and Festivities
Complete listings and precise dates of events are available from most tourist offices.

Don't miss the Procession de la Sanch ('Blood of Christ' procession) on Good Friday – an institution for the Catalan faithful, when sacred relics and a crucifix are carried to the cathedral by the Brotherhood of the Holy Blood. The **Estivales**, a theatre festival, is held in June and July. The musical **Festival Méditerranéen** takes place in July and Aug. The **Jeudis de Perpignan** (Perpignan Thursdays) brings musicians and theatrical companies onto the streets and squares of the city. These are all lively and entertaining events, so try to catch one if at all possible.

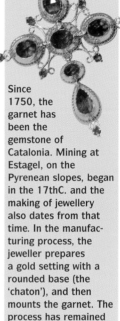

PERPIGNAN GARNETS

Since 1750, the garnet has been the gemstone of Catalonia. Mining at Estagel, on the Pyrenean slopes, began in the 17thC. and the making of jewellery also dates from that time. In the manufacturing process, the jeweller prepares a gold setting with a rounded base (the 'chaton'), and then mounts the garnet. The process has remained entirely unchanged for centuries, producing splendid jewellery. It's a strong tradition among many Catalan families to pass one or more pieces of garnet jewellery down from generation to generation. Some of the best jewellers include:

Gil and Jean Barate
(5, Rue Louis-Blanc, ☎ 04 68 34 37 68).

Michel Gourgot
(13, Rue Louis-Blanc, ☎ 04 68 34 67 79).

Jacques Creuzet-Romeu
(9, Rue Fontfròide, ☎ 04 68 34 16 94).

Jean Paulignan
(19, Rue des Augustins, ☎ 04 68 34 74 83).

Salses castle and lake

Salses was fortified early, owing to its strategic position on the border between Roussillon and Languedoc. Its pink-brick and stone château is a prime example of military architecture. Its heavy silhouette stands incongruously among the vineyards. Close by, the small lake of Leucate offers fishing and water sports. After taking to the water, relax with a dozen delicious oysters and a glass of the local white wine. What better way is there to enjoy yourself?

The history of the lakes

The Mediterranean waters reached their existing level some 3,000 years ago, when the Golfe du Lion (Lion gulf) was carved with deep indentations. Under the influence of the swell and sea winds, the alluvial deposits from coastal rivers formed stretches of sand called 'lidos'. This, in turn, led to the creation of large seawater lakes. Originally, these were open to the sea, but as the sandbanks grew they became closed off and fresh water from the rivers slowly replaced the seawater. The lakes increased

in size and opened paths to the sea, known as *graus* in the Occitan language. It was some time before the distrustful

locals began to settle on these temporary coasts.

Salses and Leucate lake

The Étang de Salses et Leucate, 9.5 miles (15 km) long and 2-3 miles (3-5 km) wide, with an area of 17,300 acres (7,000 ha), forms the border between Roussillon and Languedoc. A renowned mullet-fishing spot since ancient times, fisheries belonging to Lagrasse abbey first settled here in the Middle Ages. Thatched huts and flat-bottomed boats, which help laying nets in deep waters, can still be found today on the

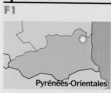
Île des Pêcheurs ('fishermen's island'). Many companies now operate fish arms (trout, dogfish, salmon etc.) around the lake, and to the north, Leucate oyster farmers have their beds. Sadly, however, the lake, rich in animal and plant life and a resting place for weary migrating birds, is highly endangered.

Salses-le-Château
☎ 04 68 38 60 13
Open June-Sept., 9.30am-6.30pm; low season, 10am-noon and 2-5pm. *Admission charge.*
This small town takes its name from two local salt-water springs (*salses*). The region was under Spanish government until the Treaty of the Pyrenees (1659) and it was the Spanish king, Fernando the Catholic, who ordered the construction of the town's powerful **fortress**. It was built between 1497 and 1506, when fortresses had to adapt

to new artillery, and the walls, 19-33 ft (6-10 m) thick, resisted many sieges and were designed to withstand attack from a new invention – gunpowder. After 1659, the château's strategic importance diminished and it was turned into a prison. It was restored by Vauban in 1691. On a clear day, the view of Mount Canigou and the sea from the terrace of the keep is quite breathtaking.

RIVESALTES, CENTURIES-OLD MUSCATEL
Located 3 miles (5 km) from Salses. Go via Rivesaltes and the Domaine Cazes (4, Rue Francisco Ferrer, ☎ 04 68 64 08 26), which has been a major Muscat producer for nearly 700 years. Other producers include Henri Desboeuf (Espira-de-l'Agli, ☎ 04 68 64 11 73) and Domaine Sarda-Malet (Mas Saint-Michel,Perpignan, ☎ 04 68 56 72 38).

Salses castle

Tautavel and Le Fenouillèdes

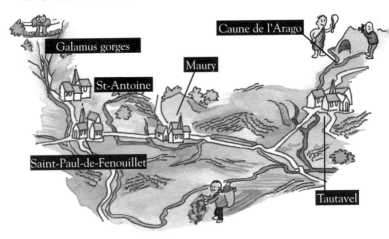

During your travels in the Languedoc region, you're sure to hear about Tautavel Man. He's a local celebrity in these parts, just like the French stars who have also settled here. However, Tautavel Man is no ordinary superstar. He was actually lived here around 450,000 years ago. One of the oldest Europeans, and possibly even your ancestor, his bones were discovered in a cave in 1971.

Tautavel

Historic gastronomy

Tautavel is located 18.5 miles (30 km) from Perpignan, in the Corbières range, the foothills between the Pyrenees and the sea. Once the hunting ground of prehistoric man, it is now covered in vineyards. After a walk round the remains of the **feudal château** (13thC.), you'll undoubtedly enjoy tasting some local products. In July and August you can eat a 'prehistoric' meal, including bison and reindeer (☎ 04 68 29 07 76).

Musée de la Préhistoire
☎ 04 68 29 07 76
Open Apr.-June and Sept. 10am-7pm; July-Aug. 9am-9pm; Oct.-Mar. 10am-12.30pm and 2-6pm. *Admission charge.*
Recently, the discovery in Spain of 36 human bones that were 800,000 years old stole the title of Oldest European

Tautavel, in the foothills of the Pyrenees

from Tautavel Man. He lived in the nearby Caune de l'Arago cave, and his skull was found in 1971. In this excellent museum, prehistory is brought to life by the use of diorama and computer simulations to tell the story of 450,000 years lived under the sun. In the shop you can buy *Rahan ou l'Homme de Tautavel* comics (75F) or replicas of prehistoric eating forks for snails (79F).

TAUTAVEL MASTER WINE-MAKERS

24, Avenue Jean-Badia
☎ **04 68 29 12 03**
Open daily 8am-noon and 2-6pm.

Free admission. At the Maîtres Vignerons de Tautavel, an interesting exhibition takes visitors through the vine and wine seasons and reveals the ancient tools and traditions of wine-makers. You can enjoy a wine-tasting of Muscats, flowery and fruity Rivesaltes, and the ruby Côte-du-Roussillon. Real enthusiasts should make a detour to Maury, on the road to Saint-Paul-de-Fenouillet, to visit Domaine Mas Amiel (☎ 04 68 29 01 02; open daily in summer, 8-6pm, by appointment Sat. and Sun.), or the Cave des Vignerons de Maury (128, Avenue Jean-Jaurès, ☎ 04 68 59 00 95; open daily, 9.30am-12.30pm and 2.30-7.30pm, until 6pm in winter). Perfect places to buy gifts for wine-lovers.

Bee and honey museum
☎ **04 68 29 40 36**
Opening hours according to number of visitors. Telephone in advance. *Admission charge.*
The Écomusée de l'Abeille et du Miel is, first and foremost, the story of André Huguet's passion for bees. Six huge

hives are spread over the botanical garden, revealing the secrets of apiculture. The visit ends with a free tasting of the different sorts of honey. You are bound to find original gifts among the museum's complete range of farm and craft products.

Far tower
To burn a few calories, climb the pebbly path of the Torre del Far, a medieval signal tower with a memorable view over the Pyrenees and the sea (not advisable in summer, as there's no shade).

Arboretum and cave
Before leaving Tautavel, visit the Arboretum de Gouleyrous (☎ 04 68 29 47 40), at the foot of the Grotte de la Caune d'Arago (open in high season, 9am-7pm), which is crossed by botanical paths planted with Mediterranean species. It's about an hour round-trip from Tautavel.

Le Fenouillèdes
Wild scenery
To the west of Tautavel, the wild land of Le Fenouillèdes is quite remarkable, with its limestone cliffs, forests and rivers. The Gorges de Galamus, 3 miles (5 km) from Saint-Paul-de-Fenouillet, are unusually beautiful, with the Ermitage de Saint-Antoine (hermitage) hiding in the rocky face. You can try the thrills of canyoning or climbing in the gorges by contacting Sud Rafting (☎ 04 68 20 53 73).

Spotcheck
E2

Pyrénées-Orientales

Things to do
• Musée de la Préhistoire
• Bee and honey museum
• Tautavel master wine-makers

Within easy reach
Les Aspres, p. 126

Tourist office
Tautavel:
☎ **04 68 29 07 76**

Sweet, crunchy treats
Biscuiterie Brosseau
7, Chemin de Lesquerde, 66220 Saint-Paul-de-Fenouillet
☎ **04 68 59 01 62**
Open Mon.-Sat., 9am-noon and 2-6.30pm.
Rousquilles, crunchy biscuits, almond cakes... there are just so many temptations here. If you pass Saint-Paul-de-Fenouillet, do try to take the time to stop at this inviting biscuit factory. From its foundation in 1890, the recipes for these sweet treats have been handed down through five generations of the Brosseau family. So, forget the diet for a day!

Canet-Plage
and the coast

On the Roussillon coast, Canet is the most popular resort for the people of Perpignan. The wild banks of the small lake are also a favourite stop for pink flamingos and migrating coots. The vast beach is ideal for water sports and the sailing port is perfect for a stroll. Unusual museums can be found along the way, and you can get close to sharks and Amazonian piranhas at the aquarium. If you fancy relxing in a café, there are plenty here to choose from.

Canet-en-Roussillon

A busy history

The 16th-C. **Église Saint-Jacques** is dominated by the church's enormous bell-tower. Visit the the picturesque ruins of the former **viscounts' château**

L'église Saint-Martin de Canet-en-Roussillon

(11th-14thC.) and the Romanesque **Église Saint-Martin** (11th-12thC.). Nearby, the unusual ice well (17thC.) is also of interest. In summer, a small train or tram links the village to the beach (information from the tourist office).

The bell-tower of the church, Canet-en-Roussillon

Canet-Plage

Strolling around the resort

This resort's popularity took off in the 1920s to 1940s, but the area was seriously damaged during World War II and had to be substantially rebuilt. Today, Canet-Plage stretches over 2.5 miles (4 km), from the mouth of the River Têt to the sandbar of the small lake. A walk around the sailing port is a delight. Boat trips are also possible and you can enjoy windsurfing or mini-golf (information from the tourist office).

Car museum

Les Balcons du Front de Mer (Canet S)
☎ 04 68 73 12 43
Open daily, 1 July-31 Aug., 2-8pm; 1 Sept.-30 June, 2-6pm, closed Tues. and end Dec.- beginning Feb. holiday.
Admission charge also allows entry to the boat museum
The **Musée de l'Auto** tells the history of the motor car from 1908 to the 1970s. All the major prestige car manufacturers have exhibits, including Citroën and Delage.

Fire engine in the car museum, Canet-Plage

of the pioneers of sailing. There's also a model-making workshop.

Toy museum
Place de la Mediterranee
☎ 04 68 73 20 29
Open daily 1 July-31 Aug., 2-8pm; 1 Sept.-30 June, 2-6pm, closed on Tues.
Admission charge.
Santa's favourite musem, the Musée du Jouet, displays some 3,500 toys collected from all over the world, from very ancient to modern-day.

There's something here for everyone, including electric train

Boat museum
Les Balcons du Front de Mer (Canet S)
☎ 04 68 73 12 43
Open daily, 1 July-31 Aug., 2-8pm; 1 Sept.-30 June, 2-6pm, closed Tues. and end Dec.- beginning Feb. holiday.
Admission charge also allows entry to the car museum.
The Musée du Bateau is a treat for all model enthusiasts,with models of the Pharaonic barge of Kheops, prestigious transatlantic liners, Catalan barges, the Clémenceau aircraft carrier, as well as a display of marine antiques that tell the story

Spotcheck
F2

Pyrénées-Orientales

Things to do
• Boat trips
• Car museum
• Boat museum
• L'Aquarium
• Canet lake walk

With children
• Toy museum

Within easy reach
Saint-Cyprien (9.5 miles/15 km S), p. 114.

Tourist office
Canet-en-Roussillon:
☎ 04 68 73 61 00

sets, lead soldiers, boats, board games, dolls and mechanical toys and models.

L'Aquarium
Blvd de la Jetée
☎ 04 68 80 49 64
Open daily 1 July-31 Aug., 10-8pm; 1 Sept.-30 June, 10am-noon and 2-6pm, closed on Tues. except school holidays.
Admission charge.
The aquarium has 300 species of marine life from all 5 continents. Colourful corals,

intimidating Amazonian piranhas, flamboyant tropical fish and fascinating sharks inhabit this surprising and exotic world. There's even a coelacanth, a living fossil found in the depths of the Indian Ocean. It's a quite fascinating, if not particularly beautiful, specimen.

CANET LAKE WALK
Information from the Scerem, Capitainerie du Port
☎ 04 68 73 58 73.

This easy 1.5-mile (2.5-km) walk around the shores of the lake, which starts at the sandbank between Canet-Plage and Saint-Cyprien, will introduce you to all the watery flora and fauna. Depending on the season, you'll see various bird species: grebes, seagulls, cormorants and

waders among the reed beds. The *sanils*, huts made of fine reeds, have been rebuilt on the banks. To end your trip, visit the farm of Mas Roussillon, 5 miles (8 km) from Canet, where there's an olive orchard, a bamboo plantation and an exotic garden.

Saint-Cyprien

a sea cure

This welcoming resort is geared up for your every need. Ideal for active family holidays, the setting and entertainment make it the perfect place for children aged 3-16. Saint-Cyprien is home to Michel Platini and Yannick Noah's Grand Stade sports school, an international golf course offering training sessions all year round and the resort is also a port of call for the sailing Tour de France. If you need a breather, you'll find peace and tranquility in the Elne cloisters in Saint-Cyprien-Village.

Vous êtes dans une Station KID

Vous y trouverez :
un environnement, un accueil, des activités et des aménagements adaptés aux vacances de vos enfants.

The old village

Saint-Cyprien-Village, around 2 miles (3 km) from the sea, is surrounded by vineyards. Thanks to the sponsorship of painter François Desnoyer (1894-1972), who frequently stayed in Saint-Cyprien, the **Fondation François-Desnoyer** was set up in Rue Émile Zola (☎ 04 68 21 06 96; open daily, 10am-noon and 3-6pm, July-Aug.; 2-6pm except Tues., rest of the year; admission charge). It displays paintings by Gauguin, Miró, Cézanne, Matisse, Braque and Picasso, and statuettes by Bourdelle and Maillol. The **Centre d'Art Contemporain** (☎ 04 68 21 32 07; has the same opening times as the Foundation) houses temporary exhibitions of contemporary art. A free shuttle (look for

the 'navette municipale gratuite'), links the village to the beach (or there is a path, if you would prefer the walk).

Saint-Cyprien-Plage
Trips by boat or train

Saint-Cyprien was established in the 1960s and soon became a popular resort. Capellans lake (L'Étang des Capellans) has an important sailing harbour (2,200 berths). You can take a trip on the lake on a shuttle that leaves from the seawater

fountain on Quai de la Pêche. You can also take a day trip on a boat from the sailing harbour on the *Roussillon* (☎ 04 68 21 44 91, Quai C)

or go fishing on the open sea on the *Quetzal* (☎ 06 09 54 78 12, purchase tickets, Quai H19). In addition, a guided tour of the resort is available

on the little train. Further information from the tourist office (☎ 04 68 21 01 33).

SPORTING ACTIVITIES TO SUIT EVERYONE

The 2-mile (3-km) beach at Saint-Cyprien offers many sporting possibilities. Catamarans and windsurfing are available at **Hawaii Surfing** (Route du Golf, ☎ 04 68 21 08 34), with facilities for children aged 5-6. **Udsist** sports centre offers sailing lessons for all levels, either with accommodation, or you can choose to visit on a daily basis (Quai Jules-Verne, ☎ 04 68 21 11 53). These lessons can be combined with horse-riding lessons at the pony club **Écuries du Mas des Angles** (☎ 04 68 21 15 87; open all year). Also, south of Saint-Cyprien, in a naturist spot near Mas Bertyrand, there's an enormous sports complex, the **Grand Stade**. You can play four racket games here: squash, tennis (Les Capellans, ☎ 04 68 37 32 00), badminton and table tennis.

L'Aqualand
Route d'Argelès
☎ 04 68 21 43 43
Open mid July-mid Sept., 9.30am-8.30pm. *Admission charge. Free for children under 3 ft 3 in (1 m).* Race down the river rapids, hurtle down the multi-slide, negotiate hairpin bends, descend into the breathtaking black tunnel in the scenic slopes... The biggest water-park in the region also has musical parades and clown shows as well as the exciting watery rides and attractions.

Elne
A prestigious past
A small, fortified village, Elne stands on a hillside amid vineyards and fruit trees. The Roman Emperor Constantine named the town, which was the capital of Roman Roussillon, after his mother, the Empress Hélène ('Elna'). The town was an episcopal

seat from the 6th to the 17thC. and boasts a stunning, and particularly well-preserved Romanesque cloister (☎ 04 68 22 70 90; summer open daily, 9.30am-6.45pm; winter open daily, 9.30-11.45am and 2-4.45pm; admission charge). Nearby stands the remarkable Romanesque **cathedral** (11thC.). The crenellated facade gives the monument the look of a fortress. It houses some fine tombs, including that of Ramon de Costa. Before you leave, visit the ramparts for a pretty view of the peach and apricot trees that cover the hill.

Côte Vermeille
from Argelès to Cerbère

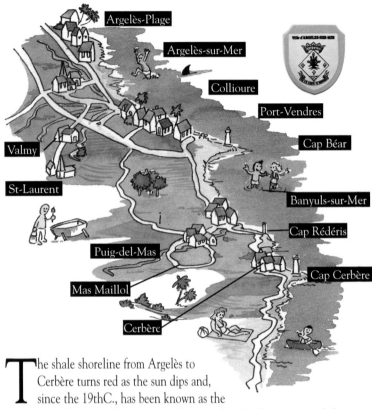

Argelès-Plage

Argelès-sur-Mer

Collioure

Port-Vendres

Cap Béar

Valmy

St-Laurent

Banyuls-sur-Mer

Cap Rédéris

Puig-del-Mas

Mas Maillol

Cap Cerbère

Cerbère

The shale shoreline from Argelès to Cerbère turns red as the sun dips and, since the 19thC., has been known as the 'Côte Vermeille' ('vermilion coast'). These profound colours attracted the Fauvist and cubist painters who immortalised this landscape. Here, the mountains meet the sea in deep creeks, where ancient fishing villages nestle. It's a real treat to spend some time in these Catalan harbours, where maritime traditions, like *lamparo* fishing and fish auctions, are alive and well. Relax under the trellised vines of a terrace, looking out to sea, and enjoy a glass of sweet Banyuls wine.

Argelès-sur-Mer
A colouful Catalan atmosphere

The lively old Catalan village of Argelès-Village enjoys year-round colourful markets and competitive games of boules under the plane trees. Sardana dances are held here every Monday from June to September. The Gothic **Église Notre-Dame-del-Prat** (14thC.) is beautifully furnished. Argelès-Plage, a popular beach, with its watersports is just 1 mile (2 km) away, and can be reached on a little train or a bus from June to September.

Museum of rural life and traditional skills

4, Plaça dels Castellans
☎ 04 68 81 42 74
Open Mon.-Sat. am,
9am-noon and 3-6pm.
Admission charge.
This museum, housed in the
Casa de Albères, displays
the history of rural life and
industry in the region around
Argelès, including agriculture,
the wine industry and the
manufacturing of whips,
espadrilles and corks.

Argelès-Plage

This town, which has over 60
camp sites and a dozen beach
and sailing clubs, has a winter
population of 7,000 that swells
to more than 20,000 in the
summer. If the splendid boats
in the harbour at the mouth
of the River Massane inspire
you to take to the water, try
a trip on a Catalan barge

Spotcheck
F2

Pyrénées-Orientales

Things to do

- Boat trips
- Sea kayaking and scuba-diving
- Walking trails
- Arago aquarium

With children

- Birds of prey display

Within easy reach

Vallespir, p. 122
Les Aspres, p. 126

Tourist offices

Argelès-sur-Mer:
☎ 04 68 81 15 85
Port-Vendres:
☎ 04 68 82 07 54
Banyuls-sur-Mer:
☎ 04 68 88 31 58

CHÂTEAU DE VALMY BIRDS OF PREY

1 mile (2 km) from Argelès
☎ **04 68 81 67 32**
Open daily,
end Mar.-beginning
Nov., 11-6.30pm.
(4 shows a day)
Admission charge.
At the Volerie des
Aigles,eagles, kites and
vultures fly freely in a
splendid setting in the
Albères foothills. The
birds take turns to
display their refined
skills in an exceptional
show, with the sea as
a backdrop.

(☎ 04 68 81 20 21). There are
also sea trips (three per afternoon in the summer) along
the Côte Vermeille, Collioure
bay (p. 120) and **Cap
Bear point** (Information
from the tourist office,
Pl. de l'Europe,
☎ 04 68 81 15 85).

Sorède
A rediscovered craft

CAT Les Micocouliers
4, Rue des Fabriques
☎ 04 68 89 04 50
Open Mon.-Fri. 9-
11.30am and 2-4.30pm.
For more than a century,
industry in Sorède was based
around the *micocoulier* tree
– the Mediterranean elm.
Flexible and robust, the tree
produces wood with long,
malleable fibres that, after
steaming, becomes hard and
does not rot. The manufacture
of whips, or *perpignans*, ceased
at the beginning of the 1970s,
due to the lack of demand.
However, in 1981 the
workshops of CAT saved this
old craft, re-establishing the

production of western whips (for lion tamers) and walking sticks. It is possible to visit the workshop.

Port-Vendres
An ancient harbour

Shipwrecks discovered in the harbour prove that sailors came here as early as the 7thC. BC. The Greeks would shelter here when bad weather struck on their route from Agde to Rosas (Costa Brava). The Romans are said to have

built a temple to Venus here, hence the name – Portus Veneris ('the port of Venus'). Port-Vendres depended on Collioure (train shuttle, p. 120) at the end of the period of Spanish domination in the mid-17thC. When Roussillon was ceded to France in 1659, this fishing harbour became a port of war, fortified by Vauban. King Louis XVI created the old harbour and a pink marble obelisk (17thC.) was erected in his honour. After a prosperous period of trading with Algeria (until the latter gained independence from France in 1962), the commercial activities of Port-Vendres became more modest. Now, the harbour is shared by *lamparo* fisherman, who use huge searchlights to attract unsuspecting anchovies, and pleasure yachts. The fish auction (Monday-Friday, from 4pm, when the trawlers return) is exclusively for professionals, but it's fascinating to watch.

Sea and sun

Pebble beaches and small, hard-to-reach creeks stretch the length of this rocky coast.

Next to Cap Béar is a small cove, very popular with naturists – accessible by a footpath starting behind the signal station. **Cap Béar** is the last spur in the Albères range, diving straight into the sea. On the 197-ft (60-m) cliffs there is a small road leading to the semaphore and lighthouse. For a quiet swim, make for the remote creeks on a sea kayak. If you fancy exploring the seabed to witness the rich marine life of the area, take a diving course at a local club. Information from the tourist office, 3, Quai Pierre-Forgas.

Along the farmhouse trail

This easy three-hour walk will allow you to discover the traditional mountain farmhouse (*mas*) of this region. When these were active farms, their owners

would live by agriculture, breeding, and forest crops. The trail takes you through a forest of chestnut and hazel trees, past the Notre-Dame-de-Vie hermitage and the

small Romanesque church, the Église Saint-Laurent-du-Mont, which hides behind a mimosa copse. Information from the tourist office: *Randonnées à Argelès-sur-Mer* (brochure 15F).

FOLLOWING
THE TRAIL OF
THE *GABELOUS*

From Banyuls, you can walk towards either Cap Béar or Cap Rédéris. These ancient coastal paths are now carved deeply into the ground. They used to be known as the 'customs officers' paths', the scene of the adventures of *gabelous* (customs officers), coastguards and smugglers. Formerly, the Catalan barges would sail along Cap Cerbère and unload their goods in natural caves. The population of Banyuls would make a good livelihood for themselves by smuggling salt and tobacco, and the path only fell into disuse after 1945. The walk around this lovely coastline is a delight. The tourist office publishes a topographic guide (30F) to help you on your way (Av. de la République, ☎ 04 68 88 31 58).

Banyuls-sur-Mer

Wine and sea

Banyuls is well known both for its sweet wine and its pleasant beach, located in a pretty bay surrounded by breathtaking scenery of narrow terraces kept in place by shale walls. The cultivation of wheat and olive trees used to be very lucrative, and honey was also abundant. Today, the town is a tranquil place. Dance a few steps, under the shade of centuries-old plane trees, on the dance floor in **Place Paul-Reig**, and visit the colourful houses of the **Quartier de la Pointe de l'Houne**. The view from the **Île Grosse** is unique and the nearby village of **Puig-del-Mas**, standing on a hillside, is quite charming. For a sailing trip, you can obtain information from the tourist office, Avenue de la Republique. Banyuls wine is sweet and spicy, and fortified with *eau de vie* during its lengthy fermentation. It's said that a fine Banyuls is the only wine that should be drunk with chocolate desserts. For **wine tasting** visit Robert Doutres, **Cave Coopérative l'Étoile**, and for wines try Domaines du Mas Blanc and de la Retoris, Hospices de Banyuls or Cellier des Templiers. (Route du Mas de Reig, ☎ 04 68 98 36 70; open daily, Apr.-Dec., 10am-7pm.)

Arago marine reserve and aquarium

☎ 04 68 88 73 39
Open daily, 9am-noon and 2-6.30pm, until 10pm in summer.
Admission charge.

On the edge of the rocky coastline, this sea nature reserve covers 1,600 acres (650 ha) from Île Grosse to Cap Peyrefitte. At this centre, unique in France, 25 scientists from the national science research centre, 10 teachers and 65 engineers conduct research on marine life in its natural environment.

The best way to learn about the species living in these creeks is to visit the aquarium of the Arago oceanographic laboratory. There you can see groupers, squid, anemones and scorpion fish swimming around the coral in 36 tanks, while staying safe and sound on dry land. It's possible to go diving in an authorised part of the reserve with Cap Carbère, ☎ 04 68 88 41 00.

Mas Maillol

Vallée de la Roume, 2.5 miles (4 km) SW of Banyuls
Open daily exc. Tues. and public holidays, 10am-noon and 2-5pm, low season; 10am-noon and 4-7pm, May-Sept.
Admission charge.

Aristide Maillol, one of the greatest sculptors of the 20thC., spent the last days of his life at this *mas* (mountain farmhouse). Born in Banyuls in 1861, he made his career in Paris but often used to come to work in his home town in autumn. He died in 1944 in a car accident, and was burried in the *mas*. *La Mediterranée*, a sculpture of warm curves, adorns his tomb.

Cerbère

Gourmet detour

This calm and pleasant village, located 2.5 miles (4 km) from the Spanish border, is known for its uncrowded pebbly beaches, small creeks as well as its border station. An ideal spot for a picnic whilst admiring the spectacular coastline, you can also stock up on wine, Barbary fig jam, Cerbère honey or Catalan cold meats, at La Roumaguère (☎ 04 68 88 41 72).

A tour of
Collioure

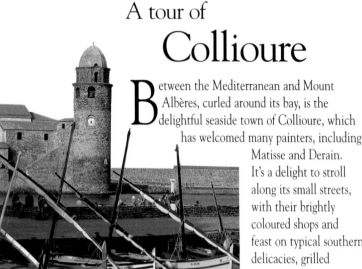

Between the Mediterranean and Mount Albères, curled around its bay, is the delightful seaside town of Collioure, which has welcomed many painters, including Matisse and Derain. It's a delight to stroll along its small streets, with their brightly coloured shops and feast on typical southern delicacies, grilled vegetables and marinated anchovies. If you're a fan of the latter, then this is the town for you. Renowned for its anchovies, you can watch the colourful fishing-boats along the quay, delivering their spoils.

A quick trip into the past

Cocoliberis, as it was known by the Romans, was occupied in turn by Visigoths, Saracens and the Carolingian French, and then, between the 12th and 17thC., it was successively part of the kingdoms of Aragon, Majorca and France, before finally becoming French in 1659. Its unsettled past has left it with many forts and towers, which you can discover following the **walks** marked by blue and white

signposts (information from tourist office, Pl. du 18-Juin). Long dependent on fishing (both Fauvist and cubist painters immortalised the colourful fishing-boats), especially **anchovies**, this traditional industry is still carried on today by a few small companies. Visit Société Roque, 19, Route d'Argelès (☎ 04 68 82 04 99; open every day), where their tempting products are on sale.

Royal château
☎ 04 68 82 06 43
Open summer, 10am-5.15pm, winter 9am-4.15pm, closed public holidays. *Admission charge.*

Built in the 12thC. on a Roman site, this castle was the residence of the kings of Majorca from 1276 to 1344. You can visit the basements, the parade ground, the main courtyard and the walls. The castle houses the Fondation de Collioure, which organises exhibitions all the year round, some of them focusing on local crafts such as whip-making or espadrilles. Opposite is the Templars' headquarters (*see below*).

The old town
The Église Notre-Dame-des-Anges (open 7.30am-noon, 2-6pm) is notable for the 17th- and 18thC. retables which adorn its side-chapels, and for its main altar, a fine example of Catalan Baroque and the work of the 17thC. Catalan sculptor, Joseph Sunyer. The church is a landmark and was painted by Matisse and many others. It was built in the 1680s to

DIVING AND SAILING

CIP de Collioure, 15, Rue de la Tour; ☎ 04 68 82 07 16. The international diving club (Club International de Plongée) offers two training courses, of one week or two days. For those who have at least the Level 1 certificate, it's possible to explore the underwater flora and fauna, as well as the wrecks of three ships sunk during World War II. The Club also offers training in yachting, and in Mediterranean-style sailing on a traditional Catalan boat. Accommodation can be provided in the centre of town.

replace the original church, destroyed by Vauban. Look out for the bell tower, a former lighthouse. St Vincent is the patron saint of Collioure and the festival in his honour (14-18 August) is very popular. There is a **pilgrimage** to Notre-Dame-de-la-Consolation and a bullfight (16 August), with fireworks in the evening, which attracts many tourists. From June to September, Collioure hosts many festivities, including sardine festivals, music events, folk-dancing competitions, firework displays, etc. (Information from the tourist office, ☎ 04 68 82 15 47, or the town hall, ☎ 04 68 82 05 66).

L'Hostellerie des Templiers, an art-lover's dream

12, Quai de l'Amirauté, opposite the castle, ☎ 04 68 98 31 10. Closed Sun. and Mon. in winter; hotel closed

The Templars' hostel

in Jan.; restaurant closed Nov.-Feb.
To find out more about the famous past of this village, ask Jojo Pous, an art-lover who owns this hotel and restaurant which contains a local museum. His father was a friend to such painters as Matisse, Maillol, Dalí, Picasso and Dufy, and gave them bed and board in return for the odd painting or drawing, so now the building is filled from cellar to attic with 2,000 works of art, as well as a *livre d'or* ('book of gold') containing drawings and watercolours.

Take a swim

The beaches are small, but there are enough of them for everyone to find somewhere to go for a dip in the sea. 'Nord' at St Vincent, near the church, 'Boramar', between the church and the castle, 'Port-d'Avall' and 'Boutigué' outside the old town, as well as the inlets of the Ouille and the Balette rivers, are all ideal spots to take a refreshing plunge. If you prefer, there's also a windsurfing school.

Spotcheck
F2

Pyrénées-Orientales

Things to do

• Collioure festivals
• Diving and sailing
• Boat trips

Within easy reach

Vallespir, p. 122
Les Aspres, p. 126

Tourist office

Collioure: ☎ 04 68 82 15 47

Boat trips and train rides

You can take a boat trip from the harbour. Information is available from Saint Laurent (☎ 04 68 81 43 88) and l'Albatros (☎ 04 68 82 56 77), both of which organise daily trips in the summer along the rocky coast. From the centre of town, take a ride on the miniature train (☎ 04 68 81 16 96; departs hourly between 10am and 10pm; admission charge), which travels to Fort St Elme via the vineyards above the town and then returns via Port-Vendres and the sea-front. The journey takes about 50 minutes. When you get back, you can take some refreshment at the Maison de la Vigne, Place 18-Juin (☎ 04 68 82 49 00), where you can try the local wines.

Fresh air in
Vallespir

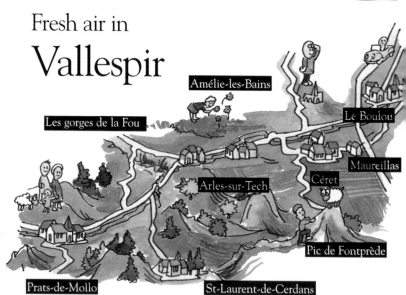

Amélie-les-Bains

Les gorges de la Fou

Le Boulou

Maureillas

Arles-sur-Tech

Céret

Pic de Fontprède

Prats-de-Mollo

St-Laurent-de-Cerdans

I f you feel like a change of air, head to Vallespir, a narrow, sun-lit valley of cork and oak trees, between the hot springs of La Preste and Le Boulou. Nature awaits you with all its delights. Climb into the freshness of the mountains, watch orchards and fields give way to chestnut woods and sheep pastures, and succumb to the charms of this natural environment, where Catalan traditions are still very strong.

Amélie-les-Bains
Source of health

The sulphurous waters of the spring have made this spa a place of pilgrimage since prehistoric and Roman times; the remains of a vaulted

Roman swimming pool are still visible in the hot baths. The spa rises on either side of the river Tech and is still a popular spot with those seeking treatment for **rheumatism** and **respiratory problems**. (Thermes d'Amélie-les-Bains; ☎ 04 68 87 90 00). After the baths, you can relax in a nearby coffee shop and treat yourself to one of the many Catalan cakes: **Antoine Alaminos**, Rue des Thermes (open 7am-1pm and 3.30-7.30pm in summer).

Saint-Laurent-de-Cerdans
Espadrilles and Catalan fabrics

A traditional centre of Catalan weaving, old-style espadrilles are still made here. You can inspect the materials (jute and hemp for the rope soles), see how they are made, and watch a video showing the history of the village as well as these fabric shoes, at the **musée de l'espadrille** (Rue Joseph-Nivet, ☎ 04 68 39 55 75, open May-Sept. daily 9am-noon and 3-7pm; Oct.-Apr. Mon. to Fri. 9am-noon and

ARLES SUR TECH – RICH CATALAN TRADITIONS

In its green valley, Arles keeps Catalan tradition alive with its many religious and secular festivals. Its medieval festival is a superb street event and there are also the festivals of its patron saints Abdon and Sennen (procession from the Rodella 30 July; information from the tourist office). The Église Sainte-Marie was founded by the French emperor Charlemagne in 778, and the abbey church's 13th-C. Gothic cloister has a sombre elegance, while a 4th-C. sarcophagus has the unique property of never running out of pure water. There's also a well-appointed sports centre, home to international basketball and a former Catalan weaving workshop which can be visited (p. 84-85).

2pm-6pm; admission charge). The museum is housed in a redundant textile factory. At the **Toiles du Soleil** (Le Village, ☎ 04 68 39 50 02; open Mon. pm to Fri. 8.30am-noon and 3-7pm, Sat. and Sun. 2.30-6.30pm), they produce authentic Catalan fabrics, including household linens such as tablecloths, curtains, blinds and sofas, as well as *razzeteurs* – handmade espadrilles with rope soles and laces (around 300F a pair).

Their shoes are very well made and are sold in shops throughout the region.

Prats-de-Mollo
Walks and celebrations

Around 2,000 ft (740 m) above sea level, Prats-de-Mollo is a pretty walled village, famous for its **bear festival** (Fête de l'Ours) in February, which is followed by three days of **carnival** (information from the tourist office), and its **hot baths**. Sardana dancing often takes place on the square outside the old walls. In 1984, nearly 6,000 acres (2,393 ha) of mountain ecosystem were turned into a nature reserve, in which rhododendrons, gentians and martagon lilies all cluster in the foothills of Mount Canigou. Many signposted paths, including a **botany trail** starting from the Chalet de las Conques (1.5 hours). From La Preste, the **Costabone** summit (7,888 ft/ 2,465 m) can be reached in eight hours if you are fit. It's a 10-mile (15-km) drive to Spain via the Ares pass. At Fort Lagarde, a citadel constructed by Vauban in

Spotcheck
E2

Things to do
- Medieval festival
- Museé de l'Espadrille
- Bear festival
- Fou gorges

Within easy reach
Perpignan, p. 132
Saint-Cyprien, p. 142
Côte Vermeille, p. 144
Collioure, p. 148

Tourist offices
Arles-sur-Tech:
☎ 04 68 39 11 99
Prats-de-Mollo:
☎ 04 68 39 70 83

1692, there are exhibitions of cannon-fire, horse-riding, fencing and acrobatics. (July-Aug. daily 2.30pm and 4.30pm, June 2.30pm except Wed., Sept. 3pm exc. Wed.)

Fou gorges
☎ 04 68 39 16 21
Open Apr.-end Oct., 10am-6pm.
Admission charge.
A breathtaking sight, more than 600 ft (200 m) from the top to the bottom in places, the Gorges de la Fou are the narrowest gorges in the world. Nearly 5,000 ft (1,500 m) of footbridges enable you to discover the succession of grottos and waterfalls cut into the mass of rock.

Église Sainte-Marie cloister, Arles-sur-Tech

Céret, a painters paradise

In the heart of Vallespir, clinging to the Catalan Pyrenees, is Céret, which can claim to be the capital of cherry trees and of the art of still-life painting. Since it has 310 days of sun each year, it produces the earliest-ripening cherries in France. It was this same sunshine that attracted Picasso, who was also seduced by the peaceful charm of the village. He invited his friends Braque, Masson and Dufy, and it became the Mecca of Cubism. Céret is full of different things to do: you can visit a museum, go hang-gliding or learn the local folkdance, the Sardana.

Musée d'Art Moderne

8, Boulevard du Maréchal-Joffre
☎ 04 68 87 27 76

Open daily July-Sept. 10am-7pm, Oct.-June 10am-6pm, Oct.-Apr. 10-6pm. Closed Tues. *Admission charge.*
Housed in a former convent, this beautiful little museum of modern art was founded in 1950 by the painter Pierre Brune and contains works by artists who stayed in the region, such as Cocteau, Dalí,

Miró and Picasso, as well as paintings by Juan Gris, Tàpies, Max Jacob and Matisse, and a collection of 28 terracotta bowls by Picasso. He painted the various *corrida* scenes during an intense five-day period, and subsequently donated the pieces to the museum in 1953. The contents of the museum are even more interesting if you take a stroll around Céret first and then see how many of the scenes you can recognise.

Métiers d'Art Saint-Roch

4, Bd de La Fayette
☎ 04 68 87 04 38
Open in winter 10am-noon and 2-6pm, closed Sun. and Mon. am; summer daily 10am-12.30pm and 3-8pm.
Once a church school, since 1967 this building has been in the hands of a number of craftsmen, who restored it and turned

PROMENADES DE PICASSO

'In 1911 the sculptor Manolo, on the run from Spanish military service and in love with French Catalonia, succeeded in bringing Picasso to Céret. [Picasso] lived in a large house within a grand garden, on the way to the forest, looking out on the Pyrenees. He got on with his work, while his pet ape got stuck into the jam jars. He was at Céret, in 1913, when he heard of the death of Don José, his father.' (Extract from *Promenades de Picasso*, Éditions du Chêne).

it into a regional arts and crafts centre. Some 15 creative artists show off their skills here: pottery, woodwork, jewellery, weaving, glassware, leatherwork, and painted silk. Some of them organise training workshops. To learn how to make clay models, work with moulds, the potter's wheel and oven and create enamelwork, contact Pierre Devis or Marc Delattre.

Non-stop party

At Céret, it's never long before the next celebration: fireworks for the feasts of **Saint Jean** (23 June) and **Saint Ferréol** (18 September), when you can take part in a 12.5-mile (20-km) run; the **Carnival** in February; a grand **Sardana dance festival** on Easter Monday; the **cherry festival** (Fête de la Cerise) at Whitsun; the **Mediterranean women's music festival,** held in mid-September; the **féria** in July, with its traditional bullfighting in the arenas

(a favourite of Picasso) – three days of free-flowing wine and fireworks. On Saturday visit the local market, with its array of fresh produce, including the plump cherries that grow in the orchards around the town, on sale from as early as April. For exact dates and times of the events held in Céret, contact the tourist office.

Pop your cork!

According to legend, it was in Roussillon that Dom Pérignon discovered the cork that could hold his untameable wine, Champagne. The cork tree actually grows wild over thousands of acres in Catalonia. It was used widely until the 1950s, when competition from Spain and Portugal grew too strong and the cork woods were abandoned, but now increased demand has led to their use once again. Free guided tour (Mon.-Fri., telephone in advance) of the Sabaté cork works, Espace Tech, Oulrich – ☎ 04 68 87 20 20.

Flying high, or feet on the ground

With its plains and hills, Céret is for free spirits. Hang-glide from the **Fontfrède peak** (3,355 ft/1,031 m) – contact the Delta Club (Aude et Po, ☎ 04 68 87 25 54) or M. Delseny (☎ 04 68 87 34 15). If you prefer to keep your feet on the ground, the tourist office has leaflets with sign-posted trails. The orange route to Saint-Ferréol hermitage, takes 2 hours leaving from the **Céret bridge** (14th-C. Pont de Céret), and the blue route to Fontfrède peak, leaves from Les Capucins, taking 4.5 hours through beech woods, heather moors and with a magnificent view of **Mount Canigou**.

Les Aspres
Byrrh and fabulous beasts

Corbère

Thuir

Prieuré de Serrabone

Castelnou

Boule-d'Amont

The region of Les Aspres, west of Perpignan, owes its name to the dryness of its pebbly soil. In the midst of the delicately-scented scrubland rises the magnificent priory of Serrabone, decorated with mythical beasts. Little villages scattered beneath the burning sun contain Romanesque churches or castle ruins. The food is tasty and, for an aperitif, try the local Byrrh.

Thuir

'Thuïr la Catalana'
Information:
☎ 04 58 63 45 86.
This celebration of the richness of traditional Catalan culture includes exhibitions, talks and games. The festival begins with a parade full of music and colour, including impressive giants. The festivities last for a week in July. It's worth trying to time your visit to coincide with the festivities. For exact dates contact the tourist office.

Byrrh cellars
6, Boulevard Violet
☎ 04 68 53 05 42
Open Apr. (exc. Sun.) May, June and Sept., daily 9am-11.45am and 2.30-5.45pm; Oct. (exc. Sat.) and July-Aug., daily

10-11.45am and 2-6.45pm. Closed first fortnight in Jan. *Admission charge for 45-minute guided tour.*
Thuir, capital of this region, is best known for its aperitif, 'Byrrh'. Seven of the herbs used in the making of this drink have medicinal properties and are considered good for the digestive system. Cocoa and orange peel are added to give a pleasant flavour. A visit to the Caves Byrrh will reveal the

story of the Violet brothers, who invented this sweet, quinquina-based wine in the 19thC. Bought 20 years ago by Pernod-Ricard, these cellars now produce a range of other aperitifs, such as Cinzano and Dubonnet and contain some 800 vats, one of them the largest oak barrel in the world.

Castelnou

Prieuré de Serrabone
☎ 04 68 84 09 30
Open daily 10am-5.30pm, closed 25 Dec., 1 Jan., 1 May and 1 Nov. *Admission charge.*
The tiny road to this priory clings to the side of the mountain, running through forests of oak and heather and is a spectacular route.

Serrabone ('good mountain') priory lies isolated in an area of great beauty, and is a fine example of local Romanesque architecture. Built in the 12thC. and inhabited by monks for nearly 200 years, it is noteworthy for its pink marble platform where carved

floral motifs and fabulous mythical animals intertwine, contrasting with the plain masonry of the church. Castelnou itself is a beautifully-preserved medieval village, with winding pebble lanes and steps.

A botanical trail

Leaving the church, follow the short path through sagebrush, absinth and rock rose, and the tiny 500-ft (150-m) vineyard which supplies the local wine. You can also visit an orchard of local fruit trees, such as figs, peaches etc., as well as a forest arboretum.

Boule d'Amont

Serrabone farm produce

☎ 04 68 84 26 24.
Open daily exc. Tues. Easter-end Oct.; summer, daily 11am-7pm.
On the way back from the priory, stop amid beautiful surroundings in the very heart of the Boulès valley at the Relais de Serrabone. Here you can buy such delicacies as duck, foie gras, goat's cheese, honeys, jams, herbs and wines, all direct from local producers. Boule d'Amont also has a charming 11th-C. church.

Val d'Amont inn

Auberge du Val d'Amont

CASTELNOU, A STOP FOR GOURMETS

From Thuir towards Castelnou.
(open in summer 10am-8pm)
The château is one of the finest historical sites in the area (*see picture below right*). Its golden houses, outstanding surroundings and good food make it a charming spot to take a rest. At Hostal, 13, Carrer de na Patora or Patio, 9, Carrer del Mig, you can taste the generous cuisine of Roussillon, such as *cargolades* (snails), meat grilled on vine shoots, stuffed squid, game and mushrooms – all washed down with local wines. There is a picturesque street-market in Castelnau on Tuesdays, 9am-7pm, from mid-June to mid-September.

Spotcheck
E2-F2

Pyrénées-Orientales

What to do
• 'Thuïr la Catalana' festival
• Byrrh cellars tour
• Excursions

Within easy reach
Perpignan, p. 132
Les Fenouillèdes, p. 138
Saint-Cyprien, p. 142
Côte Vermeille, p. 144

Tourist office
Thuir: ☎ 04 68 84 67 67

☎ 04 68 84 76 76
Rooms available by the week or the night; closed Jan.
From this guest house, set amid green and pleasant countryside, with the tiny nearby church containing gleaming Baroque retables, you can walk to Serrabone priory in 1.5 hours, or take the 2-hour sanctuary trail (mountain bikes for hire).

The Castelnau medieval château

Villefranche-de-Conflent the legendary yellow train

Hollowed out by the valley of the River Têt, the Conflent stretches from Mont-Louis to Prades and takes its name from the many rivers that come together here. As you go from shore to mountains (Canigou and Madres), the countryside changes from the market gardens and vineyards at Vinça, to the peach trees at Prades, and the apple trees in the Rotja valley, while the middle and high mountains have vast pastures for sheep-farming.

Stronghold and key to the region

Villefranche, a stronghold since its early days, dominates the valley of the Têt and its tributaries. At first, all you can see of the town are the walls and fortifications built by Vauban, Louis XIV's military architect, in the 17thC. He also built **Fort Libéria**, which stands on a hillside above the town and has a pretty view over the valley gorges. Among the narrow old streets is the **Église Saint-Jacques** church, with its Romanesque facade of pink marble from the nearby quarry. As you walk around you'll notice shop signs made of cast iron and a large thistle fixed to some old doors to act as a barometer. Many of the buildings in Villefranche are classed as historic monuments. It's almost like stepping back in time.

The little yellow train, 'the Pyrenean metro'
Information at Villefranche station (Gare SNCF)
☎ 04 68 96 56 62.

Fort Libéria, Villefranche-de-Conflent

CONFLENT ON HORSEBACK

Contact:
Éric Loux
La Cavale
66360 Mantet
☎ 04 68 05 57 59.
Only one road goes to Mantet, and it goes no further. This is the jumping-off point for peaceful horseback expeditions in the magnificent mountains, along quiet, almost forgotten, dappled trails, with the rustling of the shy wildlife among flowers found nowhere else, under a deep blue sky where eagles, vultures and sparrowhawks wheel. A weekend expedition includes overnight accommodation in a bed and breakfast establishment or a gîte. It's a great way to enjoy a hidden corner of the area.

Spotcheck

E2

Pyrénées-Orientales

Things to do

- The yellow train
- Canalettes caves
- Upper Conflent walking trails
- Conflent on horseback

Tourist office

Villefranche-de-Conflent:
☎ 04 68 96 22 96

A walking tour of the upper Conflent

From Olette you can embark upon a five- or six-day walking trail which takes you around the villages that cling to the valley slopes, such as Thuir-d'Evol and Escaro, and to the nature reserves of Mantet and Jujols, where you can take courses on the ecology of birds (☎ 04 68 97 05 90). This is a truely wonderful trek, signposted throughout, and can also be travelled on horseback if you prefer (further information from l'Aleco, Olette, ☎ 04 68 97 08 09).

The train runs all year round, with eight return journeys daily in summer, taking 3 hours each way (40 miles/ 63 km at a speed of 20 mph/ 30 kph) to the terminus of Latour-de-Carol (188F return). It's a fascinating journey, both for the landscape through which you pass (little villages clinging to the rocky hillside, narrow gorges, tiny valleys and waterfalls) and for the technical complexity of the railway itself, which has the highest station in France, at over 4,500 ft (1,500 m). The *Petit Train Jaune* (little yellow train) is often used by locals, especially in winter, when the roads are icy, and you can join them on this unusual ride on one of Europe's most scenic railways.

Le Conflent

Canalettes caves

On the Vernet road
☎ 04 68 96 23 11
Open Apr.-June 10am-noon and 2-5.30pm; winter, Sun. and school holidays, 2-5pm.
Admission charge.
The Grandes Canalettes are 30- to 400-million year old caves with spectacular rock formations. The temperature in the caves is 57°F (14°C), so dress warmly.

Ramparts, Villefranche-de-Conflent

Prades
focus of passions

Surrounded by peach orchards, this town of 7,000 inhabitants, a local administrative centre,

is also a centre for enthusiasts of various kinds. For the hardy, it's base-camp for expeditions to Mount Canigou; for lovers of Catalonia, the summer university is a focus of Catalan culture; cinema addicts will meet specialists here; the chamber-music enthusiast will love the Pablo Casals festival – and the little-known Saint-Michel-de-Cuxa abbey will dazzle all those who love Romanesque art.

Église Saint-Pierre

This church, the city's main historical monument, dates originally from Romanesque times, but only the marble and granite bell-tower (12thC.) survived rebuilding in the 17thC. The furniture and interior decoration, especially the largest Baroque retable in France, the work of Joseph Sunyer, make a prolonged visit worthwhile.

Musée Pablo-Casals

4, Rue Victor-Hugo
☎ 04 68 05 41 02
Open winter, Mon.-Fri. 9am-noon and 2pm-5pm; summer, Mon.-Sat. 9am-noon and 2-6pm. *Free admission.*
The Rue du Palais-de-Justice, with its pink marble pavements, gutters and old house gates with Catalan cast-iron locks, leads to this small museum dedicated to Pablo Casals, the distinguished Spanish cellist and conductor who first inaugurated a Bach festival here in 1950, which still continues today. On the first floor is a permanent exhibition of archaeology

and a reconstruction of an old-style Catalan kitchen. The museum is housed in the same building as the tourist office (☎ 04 68 05 41 02), which organises guided tours of the city on Wednesday mornings, and has information

SUMMER EVENTS

Pablo Casals, the famous Spanish cellist and conductor, went into exile in 1939 to avoid the Franco regime. He settled in Prades and gave concerts, attracting music-lovers from all over Europe, the profits going to support Spanish refugee artists. He was an eminent exponent of Bach and in 1950 he founded the Bach Festival. Casals refused to play in Spain while the country was under Franco's fascist rule, and died in Puerto Rico in 1973. During the Festival Pablo-Casals, the most eminent chamber musicians and orchestras play each year (26 July-13 August, ☎ 04 68 96 33 07).

Catalan summer university (Université Catalane d'Été) holds beginners and advanced courses in Catalan, as well as lectures, workshops and free entertainment every evening in the church square (15-24 August, ☎ 04 68 05 41 02).

Prades film festival (Ciné-rencontres de Prades), hosts film-studies led by specialists and showings of full-length and short films in the presence of filmmakers, actors and technicians. Discussions and analyses of videos (third week in July, ☎ 04 68 05 20 47).

Romanesque days (Journées Romanes) have lectures and guided tours on Romanesque art in Catalonia (first fortnight in July, Abbaye Saint-Michel-de-Cuxa, ☎ 04 68 05 41 02).

Spotcheck
E2

Pyrénées-Orientales

What to do
• Music festivals
• Catalan summer university
• Prades film festival
• Romanesque days

Within easy reach
Le Fenouillèdes, p. 110

Tourist office
Prades: ☎ 04 68 05 41 02

cloister has been rebuilt in New York. The abbey has now been largely restored, and has returned to life now that a group of Benedictine monks from Montserrat are once again living there. The 12th-C. **cloister**, with its column chapters of pink marble sculpted with flower and animal motifs is a masterpiece of local medieval art. The Bach festival is staged mostly in the monastery in late July-early August.

about trips to Mount Canigou (refuges, guides, routes, maps, hiring mountain-bikes and 4x4) as well as about caving, canyoning and white-water rafting.

Abbaye de Saint-Michel-de-Cuxa
2 miles (3 km) S of Prades on the D27
☎ 04 68 96 15 35
Open daily (exc. Sun. am) 9.30-11.50am and 2-5pm (summer 6pm).
Admission charge.
The monastery, which was very important from the 9th to the 17thC., was sacked during the French Revolution at the end of the 18thC. and the ruins pillaged by unscrupulous art merchants – part of the

Cloister, Saint-Michel-de-Cuxa abbey

On the Canigou trails

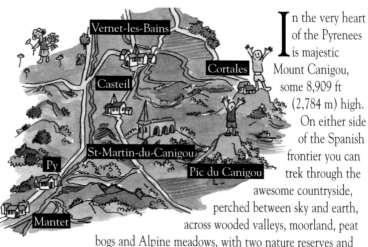

I n the very heart of the Pyrenees is majestic Mount Canigou, some 8,909 ft (2,784 m) high. On either side of the Spanish frontier you can trek through the awesome countryside, perched between sky and earth, across wooded valleys, moorland, peat bogs and Alpine meadows, with two nature reserves and the astounding Saint-Martin abbey to explore.

Canigou
Sacred mountain of Catalonia
In the 18thC., cartographers thought that the Pic du Canigou was the highest in the Pyrenees, even in the whole of Europe. It has been the inspiration for many legends, supported by several air-travel disasters, which gave it the reputation of swallowing up aeroplanes. In recent times the riddle has been solved – the high concentration of manganese and iron made

the mountain into a natural magnet. For Catalans the mountain is legendary. It's at the heart of the age-old ceremonies and traditions of the feast of Saint-Jean; on the night of 24 June, Catalans on both sides of the frontier take the 'fire of Saint Jean' from the summit of Canigou and use it to relight all the fires in the surrounding countryside. Cross-shaped bouquets of St John's Wort, verbena and walnut leaves are hung in houses to bring good luck.

Climbing the mountain
Climing is possible from mountain-huts along the GR10 from Mariailles (☎ 04 68 05 57 09)

or from Cortalets (☎ 04 68 96 36 19). Four-wheel-drive vehicles can take you as far as the chalet at Cortalets, but the road is a difficult one for ordinary cars. From Vernet-les-Bains: Transport Taurigna, ☎ 04 68 05 63 06; taxi from the station, ☎ 04 68 05 62 28. From Prades: M. Colas, ☎ 06 14 35 70 65, M. Casadessus, ☎ 06 11 76 01 88.

Vernet-les-Bains
Getting back in shape
The hot springs of this town, said to cure rheumatism and respiratory problems and a favourite of Rudyard Kipling before World War II, will get you back on your feet after your trek. People still come here to drink the

waters. On the first Sunday in August, the town organises a race up Mount Canigou, open to all. The mountain surroundings are really glorious. Before you set off on your trek, the tourist office at Vernet-les-Bains will be able to tell you where to sleep and get supplies, and has two leaflets giving all the information you need.

Abbaye Saint-Martin-du-Canigou

After Vernet-les-Bains, take the D116 to the village of Casteil. From there, you can climb a ramp up to the abbey (around 30 minutes walk). Alternatively, Garage Villacèque will take you there by jeep.

Garage Villacèque:
☎ 04 68 05 51 14.
Abbey: 04 68 05 50 53.
Guided tours at 10am, noon (11.30am and 12.30pm Sun. and Holy days), 2pm, 3pm, 4pm, 5pm in summer; 15 Sept.-14 June 10am, noon, 2.30pm, 3.30pm,

4.30pm. Closed Tues. from 1 Oct. to Easter. *Admission charge.*

The crenellated bell-tower was built in 1007, and rebuilt after earthquake damage in 1428. Later the abbey went into decline and was abandoned and left in ruins, until its restoration by a Christian community, who came to live here in 1952. The abbey is perched on a cliff some 3,500 ft (1,090 m) high and in the cloister you can see impressive column-chapters of pink and white marble.

Parc Animalier du Casteil

☎ 04 68 05 54 08
Open daily in summer, 1-7pm; winter, Wed., Sat. and Sun., 1-7pm, and daily in school holidays. *Admission charge.*
The 7.5-acre (3-ha) Casteil wildlife park is home to a number of animals – lions, bears, apes and llamas – all of them donated to the park for safekeeping. There's a teaching programme on the Pyrenean bear for children.

PY AND MANTET NATURE RESERVES

Variety is the watchword in these two nature reserves (17,500 acres/7,000 ha), located on the northwest spurs of Mount Canigou, 3,000-8,500 ft (1,000-2,700 m) above sea level. At this height you'll find birch, hazel, beech, pitch pine and turf, with large tracts of fescue and spikenard. This variety of vegetation is ideal for foxes, boar, martens, squirrels, badgers, wild cats and wild goats. The royal eagle and the capercaillie are also found here. Four signposted trails leave from the village square at Mantet and the car park at Py.

Cerdagne plateau
sun, sun and more sun

Font-Romeu

Odeillo

Planés

Bourg-Madame

Eyne

Llo

Ste-Léocadie

Lying west of the Roussillon Pyrenees, the Cerdagne is a plateau 3,850 ft (1,200 m) above sea level, which opens onto valleys of meadows and cultivated fields. Surrounded by granite mountains, and with its flora dominated by pitch pines, this upland plain is a haven of fresh air which also enjoys maximum sunshine, which is why a giant solar furnace has been installed here. Nature is kind and the air is clear; here you might catch sight of marmots and wild sheep among the rare edelweiss and angelica.

Font-Romeu

Sporting paradise

A popular ski resort and base for many high-mountain treks among the forests, this spot is also renowned for the relief of asthma. Its sunshine and altitude (5,750 ft/1,800 m) led to the building of a Grand Hotel here at the beginning of the 20thC., now divided into self-catering apartments. The area's wide range of excellent sporting possibilities include kayak and white water canoeing, paragliding, horse-riding, golf, climbing, mountain biking, skating, skiing, and trekking to Pradella lake or La Calme rock. If it's sporting facilities you're looking for, Font-Romeu is the place for you. Even France's Olympic team members train here. For more information, contact the Mountain and guides office – ☎ 04 68 30 23 08.

Temple of the sun, Odeillo
2 miles (3 km) from Font-Romeu
☎ **04 68 30 77 86**

EYNE VALLEY AND NATURE RESERVE - SPORT AND ADVENTURE

The Réserve d'Eyne covers nearly 3,000 acres (1,177 ha), beginning at more than 5,000 ft (1,700 m) above sea level, and is rich in rare species of mountain flora and fauna. This area has been famous among scientists since the 18thC. and botanists flock here each spring. In winter there's a ski resort, Eyne 2600, on the slopes of the Cambras-d'Azé. Like many local villages, such as Llo and Planès, Eyne contains a pretty little Romanesque church with a charming Baroque altar-piece. The 11th-C. church in Planès is very unusual because of its triangular shape and is well worth a visit. Cal Païis a particularly charming and welcoming hotel with a wide range of open-air activities. It's highly recommended for all the family (☎ 04 68 04 06 96).

Open daily in summer, 10am-6pm (7.30pm July-Aug.); winter (Oct.-May), daily 10am-noon and 2-6pm. *Admission charge.*
This is the sunniest spot in France, so in 1968 the biggest solar furnace in the world was built here, to conduct research into high-temperature materials and processes. Temperatures reach 5,400°F (3,000°C) thanks to its huge

Llo village

mirror, which is bigger than the Arc de Triomphe. There's an exhibition and video showing how it all works.

Saillagouse
6 miles (9 km) from Font-Romeu

Musée-Charcuterie de la Cerdagne
☎ 04 68 04 71 51
Open July-Aug. daily exc. Mon.; winter by appt.
The Cerdagne plateau has been famous for its cold meats since Roman times, and Bernard Bonzom will guide you through this museum of traditional pork-butchery, including a drying-room where 700 hams hang. You can buy

Spotcheck
D2

Pyrénées-Orientales

What to do
• Trekking, horse-riding, mountain biking
• Visit the solar furnace
• Cerdagne museum of pork-butchery

Tourist office
Font-Romeu:
☎ 04 68 30 68 30

home-made products here, or eat traditional meals such as *boles de picolat.*

Sainte-Léocadie
3 miles (5 km) from Bourg-Madame
Musée de la Cerdagne
☎ 04 68 04 08 05
Open daily in summer, 10am-1pm and 3-7pm; daily in low season, 10am-noon and 2-6pm, except Tues. Closed mid-Nov. to mid-Dec.
Admission charge.
This museum, housed in the beautiful 18th-C. farmhouse of Cal Mateu, contains exhibits on such aspects of local life as shepherds and their flocks, working in the fields, pig farming and the little yellow train. It also has the highest vineyard in France (over 4,000 ft/1,300 m above sea level) and more than 400 bottles are sold at auction every year.

Capcir plateau
wild beauty

This little-known Pyrenean plateau, at an altitude of around 4,500 ft (over 1,400 m), is a paradise for outdoor enthusiasts. It caters for serious skiers in the winter and hikers in the summer and its lakes and pine copses, as well as the traditional little villages, will make you want to make your stay last a little longer.

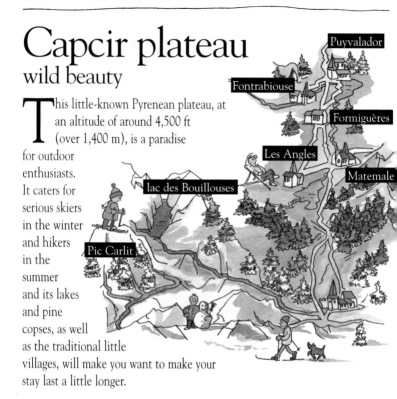

An upland glacial valley

The isolated plateau of Capcir is the upper valley of the Aude, a small area that measures around 8 miles (13 km) from north to south and the same from east to west. It's the perfect spot to get away from it all. From the Quillane pass (5,623 ft/ 1,714 m) to the village of Puyvalador, it forms a bowl hollowed out by glaciers between the Carlit and Madrès mountains. Once a land of pastures and forests,

it has come to life again thanks to its **ski resorts** (Les Angles, Matemale, Puyvalador, Formiguières) and its popular **hiking trails**. Artificial lakes and dams have also been built.

Carlit circuit

This high-altitude hike reaches an altitude of 7,763 ft (2,426 m). It's divided into four stages, all equipped with mountain refuges. It's a magnificent trek, not too difficult, well-signposted and clearly described in the guidebook *Grandes Randonnées*

en Pyrénées Orientales, which should be available in local tourist offices. Start your journey at the **Refuge des Bonnes Heures** at the Lac des Bouillouses (6,560 ft/ 2,050 m), 66210 Mont-Louis (☎ 04 68 04 24 22). Half-board in a dormitory costs 190F (Closed Oct.-Nov.). A less strenuous way of taking the tour is with **Rando Confort**'s Tour du Carlit (information from Pyrénées-Roussillon, Perpignan, ☎ 04 68 66 61 11). **La Pastorale**, based at Porta in Cerdagne, organises horse-treks (☎ 04 68 04 83 92).

Les Angles

Sport, or a bit of relaxation?

The Lac de Matemale, situated on a plateau known as 'little Canada', is some 5,000 ft (1,650 m) high, surrounded by a vast pine forest. The lake has a fully equipped beach and offers windsurfing and sailing (**Club Nautique de l'Ourson**, ☎ 04 68 04 30 77). You can also try pony- or horse-back

PUYVALADOR – CAPCIR ON A DONKEY

Rieutord
5 miles (7 km)
NW of Formiguères
☎ **04 68 04 41 22**
Open June-Oct.
At Puyvalador you can go for a one-day trip with a donkey to carry your luggage or the children, or you can take a trip lasting several days, You can even leave the children with Claudine and Bruno while you go for a more demanding trek. The children will be quite safe and they'll learn about mountain life with an officially recognised course. In winter, you can take the opportunity to go cross-country skiing or snowshoe trekking.

trekking (**Les Crinières Blondes**, ☎ 04 68 04 43 71) or hikes lasting several days (**Équisud**, ☎ 04 68 04 43 62). Trout-fishing is available at the Lac de Balcère, and in winter you can go skiing (**École de Ski Français**, ☎ 04 68 04 47 82. For cross-country skiing contact Centre Guy Malé, ☎ 04 68 04 31 05 or Compagnie des Guides, ☎ 04 68 04 39 22).

Wildlife park
☎ **04 68 04 17 20**
Open daily June-Aug., 9am-7pm; winter, 9am-5pm.

Admission charge.
At just under 5,500 ft (1,800 m) and in natural surroundings, the two circuits (2.5 miles/3.5 km and 1 mile/1.5 km) will enable you to observe the wildlife of

the Pyrenees – goats and sheep, boar, ibex, bear and wolf.

Formiguères

A breath of fresh air
Home to the summer palace of the kings of Majorca in the 13th-14thC., this village has both fresh air and history, including the Romanesque Sainte-

Spotcheck
D2-E2

Pyrénées-Orientales

What to do
• Carlit circuit
• Sailing
• Horse-riding
• Fishing

With children
• Capcir on a donkey

Tourist offices
Formiguères:
☎ **04 68 04 47 35**
Les Angles:
☎ **04 68 04 32 76**

Marie church (13thC.) and the ruins of a **castle** (9th C.) where King Sancho of Majorca died in 1232. The tourist office offers a tour of churches of the region. West of Formiguères is a lakeside trek at the **Étangs de Camporells** – 6,750 ft (2,240 m) high – which you can reach on foot (4 hours from Formiguères) or by chairlift. The **Fôret de la Matte**, planted by French statesman Colbert in the 18thC., is home to deer and has many footpaths. The **Pic de Madrès** has superb views. For fossil lovers the **Grotte de Fontrabiouse** (open 15 June-15 Sept., 10am-7pm; admission charge) is a cave with some extraordinary rock formations (it does get very cold in the cave though, so take a sweater).

Around Sant Pere de Rodes the treasure hunt

In the Rodes range, north of the Cape Creus peninsular, the massive bulk of the Sant Pere de Rodes monastery stands facing the sea. Nearby, El Port de la Selva and Llançà are picturesque old fishing villages, while inland, Figueras honours the eccentric artist Salvador Dalí, who was born there in 1904. Here he founded the Teatro-Museo Dalí in 1974, an interesting and unusual place, housed in his home town's former theatre.

Teatro-Museo Dalí, Figueras

El Port de la Selva

With its feet in the water

This village shelters from the north wind at the end of a tiny curving cove. The Tramontana wind can be fierce, but tends to rage mainly in winter. The natural harbour retains its old fishermen's houses with their whitewashed walls. A coastal path beside sea caves leads from the S'Armella lighthouse to the tip of Cape Creus. At the Ca L'Hermida restaurant (L'Illa 7, ☎ 972 38 70 75; open Apr.-Sept. daily except Sun. evenings and Mon.; menu prices from 3,000 ptas), seafood lovers will be able to try the unique experience of *llagosta à la catalana* (lobster cooked in chocolate).

El Port de Llançà

5 miles (7 km) NW of El Port de la Selva on the G1612
Come for a swim

Fish are sold here every afternoon in the covered market and for sun and sea lovers, there are fine beaches nearby. Llançà is also known for its *llances*, lance-shaped

almond sweets, which you can buy at the Guisset bakery in the main square (☎ 972 38 02 72; open 8am-1.30pm and 4.30-8.30pm). Dominating the centre of this square is the 'tree of freedom', a huge plane tree decorated with the town's coat of arms.

El Port de la Selva

Sant Pere de Rodes

10 miles (15 km) S of Llançà on the N260, then the G1610 towards Roses

Monastery

☎ 972 38 75 59
Open daily exc. Mon.,
10am-7.30pm,
June-Sept., 10am-1pm
and 3-5pm, Oct.-May.
Admission charge.

Sant Pere de Rodes monastery

In the heart of the Rodes hills, at 1,600 ft (520 m), the 10th-C. Benedictine Sant-Pere-de-Rodes monastery is a masterpiece of Catalan Romanesque art. At the top of the mountain, there's a magnificent view from the ruins of Sant Salvador castle – west over the Golfe du Lion and the Cape Creus peninsular and east to the first spurs of the Pyrenees.

Peralada

Castle of the Rocabertí counts

The Rocabertí family, Counts of Peralada, built this castle in the 14thC. on the ruins of an earlier castle. It is in a mixture of Gothic and Renaissance styles, reworked in medieval style in the 19thC. Located in the outhouses of the Del Carmel covent, the castle museum (☎ 972 53 81 25; guided tours 10am, 11am, noon, 1pm, 4.30pm, 5.30pm and 6.30pm; admission charge) displays beautiful medieval column-chapters, but the best

thing in its collection is a magnificent display of ceramics and old glass.

Place your bets

Reflected in the waters of a small lake, the two large crenellated towers of the castle, which also appear on local wine-bottles, mark the entrance to the casino (slot machines 11am-5am; gaming room 7pm-5am). The Festival Internacional de Música takes place each year in the grounds (18 July-24 Aug., ☎ 972 53 81 25).

Figueras

12 miles (20 km) SW of Llançà

A temple to Dalí

Teatro-Museo Dalí
Pl. Gala-Salvador Dalí 5
☎ 972 51 18 00
Open 10.30am-5.15pm
June, 10.30am-7.15pm
July-Sept. and 10pm-12.30am, 24 July-29
Aug.; 10.30am-5.15pm
exc. Mon. Oct.-May.
Admission charge.
This museum is apparently the largest in the world devoted to Surrealism. Housed in the former municipal theatre, it's as bizarre as the artist himself.

Toy museum

Museu de Juguets de Catalunya
Sant Pere 1
☎ 972 50 45 85
Open Mon.-Sat.
10am-1pm and
4-7pm; Sun. and
public holidays
11am-1.30pm.
Closed Tues. in winter.
Admission charge.
Here you'll find toys from all over the world, in particular a superb

collection of robots, puppets and teddy bears, as well as a Meccano Eiffel Tower.

PERALADA WINES

You can buy these wines in the castle, with the Castillo Peralada label. Try the Blanco Pescador, the Cresta Rosa, or the Tinto Cazador. Those with large budgets may like to try the aromatic Gran Claustro 1955. The wines of Mas Fita (Masarac, Perala-da-Vidarnadal, 1 mile/2 km away, ☎ 972 50 20 41) are also worth trying. Since 1992 it's been possible to buy completely organic white, rosé and red Torlits (700 ptas a bottle), and a young Fita Novell (650 ptas a bottle).

Cape Creus
the end of the world

This is where the Pyrenees meet the Mediterranean, at a steeply sloping headland which is the easternmost point of the Iberian peninsula, and feels like the end of the world. Accessible only on foot or by boat and now a national park, the cape has remained unsullied by property developers. Cadaqués is a pretty little village much favoured by the artists in the early 20thC., with its fine beaches and lovely atmosphere. Port-Lligat owes its fame to Dalí, who settled here in the 1960s.

Cadaqués

The artists' town
Undoubtedly the most painted and photographed place in the Costa Brava, Cadaqués, with its whitewashed houses and alleys climbing up the hill, certainly invites the visitor to take a stroll. It's dominated by the large Baroque church, the Església de Santa Maria.

In the early part of the 20thC. the town attracted a renowned group of artists – not only Dalí, but Picasso, Éluard, Breton and García Lorca. It has managed to preserve much of the charm that originally captivated these creative spirits. Even today, it's the artists who make sure that the town does not fall victim to developers.

A panorama of painting
Museu Perrot-Moore
Vigilant 1
☎ 972 25 82 31
Open daily 10.30am-1.30pm and 4-8pm, July-Aug., 4-8pm except Sun., Sept.-July.
Admission charge.

This art museum contains an interesting collection of paintings from the 15thC. to the present day, specialising in works by the German masters, such as Dürer and Cranach, and modern Cubist and Surrealist paintings.

Gastronomic art
La Galiota (Narcís Monturiol 9, ☎ 972 25 81 87; open mid-June to mid-Sept. and the week before Easter) offers Dalí's favourite meal (cheese and chicken soufflé with apples) for 2,500 ptas. Or, on a different level, there's the **Es Balua** restaurant (Riba Nemesi Llorenç 2, ☎ 972 25 81 83; 3,500-4,000 ptas; open daily 10 June-4 Oct., weekends only, rest of the year) offering such delicious dishes such as seafood croquettes and fish and rice ragout.

CAPE CREUS
BAR-RESTAURANT
☎ 972 19 90 05
Open 1-8pm
weekdays, 1-11pm
weekends.
Around 2,500 ptas.
**This restaurant at the
very end of the
peninsula, facing the
sea, stands ready to
welcome famished
walkers. As you gaze
out to sea, tuck into
chicken curry with
ginger or a *Fin del
Mundo* steak – you
deserve it after all
your efforts. Good,
comforting food and
an ideal location.**

Port-Lligat
1 mile (2 km)
N of Cadaqués
Dalí country
At the end of a peaceful cove,
where the last few fishermen
of Cadaqués come to anchor
their boats, lies Port-Lligat.
It became famous thanks to
Dalí, who lived here with his
wife Gala from the 1960s
until her death in 1982 when
the artist left the town.
However, the memory of him
still lingers on.

Dalí house-museum
Rive de Port-Lligat
☎ 972 25 80 63
Open mid-Mar. to
beginning Jan. Closed
Mon. from end Oct.
By apptmt only.
Dalí's 'house' is
actually a row of old
fishermen's cottages
that he and his wife
Gala renovated over
the years. Only part
of it is open to visitors,
and numbers are
restricted with only
eight people allowed
in at a time. A stuffed

polar bear still stands guard in
the vestibule, and giant eggs
crown the roof. What else
would you expect?

Gala's boat
Rive de Port-Lligat,
in front of Dalí's house
☎ 617 465 757
*1,000 ptas per person.
(Trips every hour)*
In 1955 Dalí discovered a
battered old fishing boat at
Milagros, which he had
repaired and named Gala,
after his wife. Arturo, the
owner of the boat, took her
out fishing in it every day, and
fans of the eccentric Dalí can
climb aboard for a sea trip.

Cape Creus
4.5 miles (7 km)
N of Cadaqués
Protected area
With an area of more than
34,000 acres (13,860 ha), this
is Catalonia's largest nature
reserve, either on land or at
sea. Walkers should beware
of the north wind, which
blows fiercely on this exposed
ground and can chill even the
hardiest outdoor enthusiast.
A number of well-maintained
roads and paths make it
possible to traverse the coastal
cliffs or venture into the
interior of the peninsula,
which is home to more than

Spotcheck
F3

What to do
• Fishing-boat trips
• Cape Creus walking

With children
• Dalí house-museum

Tourist office
Cadaqués: ☎ 972 25 83 15

250 species of birds, while the
surrounding seabed is rich in
sponges and coral.

A trail to 'the end of the world'
Two hours on foot.
Take the *camí antic*, on the
north side of Cadaqués,
towards Port-Lligat. From
there, follow the S'Alqueria
beach and the Es Jonquet
cove. Further on, a side-road
leads to Guillola bay, passing
the Mal Paso bridge
and taking you
straight to 'hell bay'.
The last part of the
trail is the most
difficult, since the
coastline rises very
steeply as far as Cape
Creus lighthouse, but
getting to 'the end of
the world' makes it all
seem worthwhile.

Els Aiguamolls nature park

and the last marshlands of the Empordà

A iguamolls means 'marsh' in Catalan, and the Aiguamolls nature reserve lies between the mouths of the Muga and Fluviá rivers, opposite Roses bay. Spread over nearly 12,400 acres (5,000 ha), this reserve is a paradise for birds and birdwatchers and in its waters, both fresh and salt, there are a host of fish.

A paradise of natural beauty

The Empordà marshlands once extended much further, between Roses and the River Ter, south of Empúries, but the needs of farming and uncontrolled expansion of tourism in the Costa Brava reduced them drastically. Luckily, in 1983 a nature reserve was created to protect the varied wildlife, which includes teals, herons, pink flamingos and storks.

PARC NATURAL
AIGUAMOLLS DE L'EMPORDÀ

9.30am-2pm and 4.30-7pm, Apr.-Sept. Halfway between Castelló d'Empúries and Sant Pere Pescador, El Cortalet is the information centre for the reserve, the ideal place to organise your visit and pick up guide-sheets to the signposted trails that take in the most interesting places. It is also home to a centre for the reintroduction of storks and otters into the natural environment.

El Cortalet

☎ 972 45 42 22
Open 9.30am-2pm and 3.30-6pm, Oct.-Mar.,

RESERVA NATURAL INTEGRAL

SILENCI

A walk in the park

The signposted trails start from El Cortalet. The longest (marked red, 5.5 miles/9 km)

covers the whole of the reserve. Another (white and green, 2.5 miles/ 4 km) goes to the sea. A third (green and red, 2.5 miles/3.7 km) leads to the En Túries shallows. The best view is from the Senillosa observatory, near the El Matà shallows. Returning towards Roses bay, you come across one of the last unspoilt beaches in Catalonia. Roses is a Greek foundation on the north end of the gulf.

Castelló d'Empúries
2.5 miles (4 km)
N of El Cortalet

Troubadour country festival

This inland medieval village celebrates its links with its past history at the **Tierra de Trobadores Festival** (information, ☎ 972 15 62 33), which takes place each year around 11 September. Jesters, tumblers, troubadours (travelling musicians) and courtly ladies throng the streets, proud knights fight tourneys

and a lively medieval market takes you back in time to the atmosphere of a 12th–14th-C village.

Empúria-Brava
3 miles (5 km) W of Castelló d'Empúries
Chocks away!
Aérodrome
☎ 972 45 01 11
Built on former marshlands (a network of canals unites the houses), the Empúria-Brava marina was created entirely for tourists and so its amenities are bang up to date. You can, for example, try a **parachute jump** (ages 16 and up), or take a **mini-plane flight** (three passengers) to Cadaqués (20 mins, 4,500 ptas per person) or the Medes islands (30 mins, 6,000 ptas per person). Prepare to take off if you're feeling adventurous.

NAIVE ART MUSEUM
El Far d'Empordà
☎ 972 52 57 29
Open daily 10am-8pm, June-Aug., 10am-7pm, Sept.-May.
Admission charge.
In 1958, in the Modernist El Molí de la Torre building, the French industrialist André Laporte opened this Museo de Arte Naif to show his own collection of naive art, the first piece of which he had bought in a Paris flea market. This art museum has no great masters, but offers an eye-catching collection of unknown treasures.

largest fishing port, the old quarter of this town still has remains of the **citadel** built by Charles V in the 16thC. to defend against Turkish attacks. On the Cala Monjoi, 5 miles (8 km) from the town, is one of Spain's best

Aquabrava water park
Les Garrigues, Carretera de Cadaqués
☎ 972 25 43 44
Open 4 June-14 Sept., daily 10am-7pm.
Admission charge.
A giant water park for the young and not-so-young,

where you can hurtle down the slides and flumes, go kamikaze tobogganing, ride the River Run or go for a trip along the Amazon. For the less energetic, there's the Kids Lagoon and the Rio Tranquillo, or just soak up the sun around the Oasis swimming-pool. Don't miss the Aqua Burger, where you can eat your lunch with your feet in the water.

Roses
6 miles (10 km) NW of Castelló d'Empúries
Fish feasts
A famous seaside resort as well as northern Catalonia's

restaurants, **El Bulli** (☎ 972 15 04 57; closed Mon.-Tues. and Nov.-Mar.). And if you're in Roses on 29 June, there's a festival in honour of *suquet* (Catalan stew), one of the glories of Catalan cuisine.

Empúries' ancient remains

Near L'Escala, south of the Gulf of Roses, stand the Greek and Roman ruins of Empúries. In commemoration of its ancient glory, the Olympic flame was brought here from

Athens in 1992 to start its journey to Barcelona to inaugurate the Olympic Games. Empúries testifies to the prestige of the conquerors who once dominated the shores of the Mediterranean.

The Phocaean colony of Empúries

The Greek colony of Empúries (in Greek *emporion* means 'trading-post') was founded around 600 BC by the Phocaeans, who had already founded Marseille. The first settlement, **Paliápolis**, or 'old city', was built on a little island, today joined to the mainland and the site of the small, walled village of **Sant Martí d'Empúries**. Here the Greeks built a temple to Artemis, the goddess of the moon and of hunting.

A new era of prosperity

Across from their island, the Greeks built another town on the mainland, called **Neapolis** or 'new city'. It became an ally of Rome during the Second Punic War (218-201 BC), and

a century later the Romans built a third city on the hill overlooking the Greek town. Empúries then flourished in a new age of prosperity until the end of the 3rdC. AD. The Arab invasion in the 8thC brought about its final decline.

The ruins
☎ 972 77 02 08
Open daily 10am-8pm spring-summer, 10am-7pm autumn-winter.
Admission charge.
The archaeological site consists of two areas: the Greek Neapolis and the Roman city. The site has been completely excavated, and the

Greek ruins are mixed in with more recent buildings. The **archaeological museum** (Museo de Arqueología; same opening hours as the ruins), housed in a 17th-C. convent, contains a sizeable collection of Greek and Roman objects discovered in the course of the excavations; the best exhibit is the beautiful Roman **mosaic** depicting Iphigeneia.

Greek city
Walking along the seafront that links Sant Martí and L'Escala (1 mile/2 km), you'll find the remains of the Greek harbour wall, enlarged by the Romans. On the land side is

the entrance to the remains of Neapolis. Near the **Agora** (sacred square) stood the **Temple of Asclepius**, god of medicine. The statue of the god you can see here is a copy – the original is in the archaeological museum in Barcelona. Archaeologists have also uncovered the remains of a market, part of the city wall, and the ruins of an early Christian basilica from the 4th C., to the left of the entrance, near the beach.

Spotcheck
F3

What to do
• Empúries Greek and Roman remains
• Swimming in the sea

Tourist office
L'Escala: ☎ 972 77 06 03

Roman city

It was the Roman army, under the command of Scipio Africanus that landed here in 218 BC and began the Roman colonisation of the Iberian peninsula. The Roman city, on the site of the former army camp, was surrounded by a wall, part of which has now been uncovered. Inside, you can see the splendid **mosaic floors**, and the remains of the **Forum**, the centre of civic life. There's a small museum on the site where you'll find examples of how it might have looked.

Swimming into history

If you want to swim in the same place as the Greeks and Romans, you have a few beaches to choose from. North of Sant Martí is the start of the Gulf of Roses beach, the longest in the Costa Brava.

To the south are the beaches where the Greeks and Romans landed, the Playa del Moll Grec and the Playa del Convent, and also the Playa del Portitxol.

L'Escala

As early as the 2ndC. BC, Cato the Elder wrote of the fierce north wind that blows at L'Escala: 'When you talk, it fills your mouth. It can even knock down a man in armour or a loaded cart'. At the southern edge of the Aiguamolls de l'Empordà nature reserve, L'Escala used to rely on mackerel, sardine and anchovy fishing, but its main industry today is tourism.

It has some fine beaches and is popular with the local inhabitants.

L'ESCALA ANCHOVIES
Casa Bordas
Carretera L'Escala-Orroils
☎ 972 77 00 85
Open daily 9am-1pm and 2.30-7pm; closed Sun. pm in winter.
Salted anchovies, a speciality of L'Escala, used to be prepared for family consumption only, but now the tourist trade has led to increased commercial production. The quality has not suffered, however, and they are still just as delicious. At the Casa Bordas you can watch the different stages of the salting process and buy the finished product, to enjoy with local bread, tomatoes and olive oil. This is a typical Catalan snack (350 ptas for a small jar, 1,000 for a large jar).

Medes islands
underwater beauty

Opposite Estartit, the old fishing port of Torroella de Montgrí, less than 1 mile (1.5 km) from the Empordà coast, stand the steep-sided Medes islands. They are an outcrop of the limestone mountains of Montgrí and the largest of Catalonia's marine nature reserves. The protected seabed is a paradise for scuba-divers.

Disputed islands

These seven little islands and a few reefs, with a total area of just over 50 acres (21.5 ha), have often been fought over through the centuries. They were first occupied by the Greeks, who had a cemetery on Meda Gran, the largest of the islands. In the Middle Ages, they became a bolthole for pirates, before the French built a fort there, which later fell into the hands of the British. Today two lighthouses

to divers, are a magnificent sight. The seabed once attracted coral-gatherers and is home to more than 1,300 different kinds of marine plant and animal life, including the peaceful grouper-fish, which is the nature reserve's emblem.

Protected islands

The temptation to explore these beautiful islands and discover the marine life on the seabed is strong. However, it must be resisted, for nowadays,

boats are strictly controlled and access to the islands is limited. For a boat trip, contact the Estartit tourism office (Passeig Marítim 33, ☎ 972 75 19 10).

On board the Nautilus

**Subacuatic Vision
Passeig Marítim 23,
Estartit
☎ 972 75 14 89**
Trips every 30 mins, lasting 1.5 hours, 10.30am-7.30pm; in winter as required. *Adults 1,850 ptas, children aged 4-11 1,350 ptas.*
Experience the world of *20,000 Leagues Under the Sea*, in one of the three glass-bottomed catamarans, called Nautilus and run by the Subacuatic Vision company.

Estartit port

stand on Meda Gran: the first dates from 1866, and the second, built in 1930, runs on solar power.

Islands of mystery

Even before the sea separated the islands from the mainland, the water had already begun its long work of erosion, cutting a maze of tunnels and shafts in the rock. These spectacular caverns, accessible

this is a highly protected site. Fishing and landing – in fact, touching anything whatsoever – are all strictly forbidden. You need a permit to dive, private

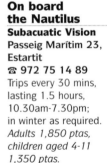

You'll discover such wonderful underwater sights as coral, bass, conger eels, barracudas, grouper-fish – all without even having to get your feet wet! It makes a wonderful trip for all the family.

La Casa de la Vila

Torroella de Montgrí
*3 miles (5 km)
SW of Estartit*
A museum for the islands
Classed as a historical monument, the old town contains fine medieval buildings. On the main square with its arcades is the 14th-C. **Casa de la Vila**. Behind the Baroque facade of **San-Genís** church is a typical example of Catalan Gothic architecture. At the **Museo del Montgrí y Baix Ter** (Casa Pastors, Calle Major 31; open 10am-2pm and 6-9pm Mon.-Sat., 10am-2pm Sun. and public holidays; closed Mar.; free admission) you can learn about the

history of the Medes islands and see the local archaeological remains.

Montgrí castle
Route signposted from the Carrer Fatima; 1 hour.
Go on foot to this imposing fortress, standing on the summit of the mountain of the same name. It was begun in 1294 by the Count of Barcelona, but was never finished. Nicknamed 'the dead bishop's ring', the castle wall is a massive structure some 70 ft (23 m) high, with a tower at each corner. A spiral staircase leads up to the rampart walk, from which there is a wonderful view of the Medes islands.

Spotcheck

F3

What to do
• Scuba–diving

With children
• Excursion in a glass-bottomed boat
• Sobrestany wildlife park

Tourist office
Estartit: ☎ 972 75 19 10

SOBRESTANY WILDLIFE PARK
☎ **972 78 84 94**
Open daily 9am-9pm in summer; 9am-1pm and 3-6pm Mon.-Fri., 9am-6pm Sat.-Sun. in winter.
Admission charge.
This 100-acre (40-ha) animal park, 5 miles (9 km) west of Torroella de Montgrí, has typically Mediterranean plant life and is home to 35 different kinds of animals. It's worth making a pit-stop in the village of Sobres-tany, where the Hotel del Caçador (☎ 972 78 84 19; closed Wed.) specialises in delicious game dishes. You'll spend around 3,500 ptas on a meal and the menu includes partridge, hare and wild boar dishes.

Empordanet region between the beach and the countryside

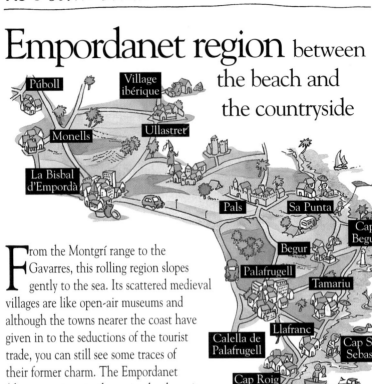

From the Montgrí range to the Gavarres, this rolling region slopes gently to the sea. Its scattered medieval villages are like open-air museums and although the towns nearer the coast have given in to the seductions of the tourist trade, you can still see some traces of their former charm. The Empordanet (the name given to the region by the writer Josep Pla) is compact and easy to travel around, so it is a good spot for a family holiday.

Pals

A traditional village

Pals, located 3.5 miles (6 km) inland, is completely different from the overcrowded coastal area. It's a delightful hilltop **medieval village**, with houses of ochre stone along the sloping streets. In a shady square at the top of the village is the Romanesque church,

next to a bell-tower, from which you can see below you the whole of the Empordanet, the Medes islands and Mount Canigou.

Pals rice

You can buy this rice at the pretty 15th-C. mill located 2 miles (3 km) east of the village (☎ 972 63 67 06 ; open Mon.-

Fri. 9am-1pm and 3-7pm, 135 ptas for 2.2 lbs/1 kg). In the nearby village of Sa Punta, the **La Punta** restaurant (☎ 972 66 73 76; open every day) serves a delicious local rice and seafood dish called *arrosejat*. It's a classic rice dish and is served with fresh local produce, naturally.

The beach

This beach of smooth sand extends some 6 miles (10 km) from Estartit to the Espinuda headland, barely interrupted by the mouths of the Ter and Duro rivers. You can still see the masts of Radio Liberty, an

American radio station that broadcast pro-Western programmes to the Eastern Bloc during the Cold War.

Palau-Sator

5 miles (8 km) NW of Pals on the G11650, then the G1651

A museum of farming life

Museo de las Eines de Pagès

☎ 972 63 50 06

Open Tues.-Sun. noon-8pm in summer; weekends and public holidays in winter. *Admission charge.* The village still has medieval remains, including a **castle-keep** and the church of **Sant Julia de Boada**, one of the finest pre-Romanesque buildings in Catalonia. The little **museum** of **rural life** illustrates the local way of

life and agricultural tools used in the area before the international tourist trade took over.

Peratallada

2 miles (3 km) SW of Palau-Sator on the G1651

Back to the Middle Ages

Set in hilly country, this little town takes you on a journey back in time as you enter via an old **stone bridge** and an ancient gate. Cut from the rock in medieval times, much of the town still dates back to that period, including the

Spotcheck

F3

What to do

- Ullastret prehistoric village
- La Bisbal potteries
- Cape Sant Sebastià walks
- Cape Roig gardens

With children

- Swimming in the sea at Pals
- Formigues islands boat trip

Within easy reach

Gerona (12 miles/20 km NW of Palafrell), p. 196-197

Tourist offices

Palafrell:
☎ 972 30 02 28
Pals: ☎ 972 63 61 61

Gourmet country

The castle restaurant (☎ 972 63 40 21; closed Feb., Sun. evenings in summer and Sun. evenings and Mon. in winter; 3,500-6,500 ptas) specialises in regional cuisine. **La Riera** (Voltes 3, ☎ 972 63 41 42; closed Wed. in winter; 2,500-

---

DALÍ CASTLE-MUSEUM

Púbol castle

5 miles (8 km) NW of La Bisbal on the C255

☎ 972 48 82 11

Open Tues.-Sun. noon-8pm, in summer; weekends and public holidays noon-6pm, in winter. *Admission charge.* **This museum forms part of the Dalí 'triangle' (*see also* the Museum at Figueras on p. 139 and the artist's house at Port-Lligat on p. 141). Dalí bought this 14th-C. castle for his wife and inspiration, Gala, and he came here only at her invitation. She was buried here after her death in 1982.**

Peratallada castle

pretty **Romanesque church**, with arcaded bell facade, and the castle (11th-15th C.), where classical music concerts are held each summer.

4,500 ptas) is also good. It serves very tasty dishes, including duck with parsnips and pears. The cuisine is simple, delicate and well worth trying.

Ullastret

3 miles (5 km)
NW of Peratallada
Prehistoric village
Open daily exc. Mon.,
10.30am-1pm and
4-8pm in summer,
10am-2pm and 4-6pm
in winter.
Admission charge.
About 1 mile (2 km) from the
medieval town, there is a vast
archaeological site containing
the remains of one of the
oldest Iberian villages in
Spain, which reached the

height of its prosperity in the
6th C. BC. It was discovered
in 1937 and excavated from
1947 onwards. The **site
museum**, in the old chapel of
Sant Andreu, shows objects
found during the excavations.

Monells

5.5 miles (9 km)
SW of Ullastret
on the C252 via Corça
Old village
The best part of the village is
undoubtedly the main square
(Plaza Major), with its 15th-
and 16th-C. porched houses.
But also, don't miss attractive
Oli square and Arcs
('arches') street. If you are
tempted to stay longer, have a
meal at **Monells** (Vilanova 11,
☎ 972 63 01 41; open daily
exc. Sun. evenings in summer,
only Fri. and Sat. evenings in
winter). Specialities of the
house are snails *à la grotesca*
and *bacalao* in honey. Also

worth trying is **El Hort del
Rector** (Església 2, ☎ 972 63
03 96; open daily exc. Mon.,
closed 15 Sept.-15 Oct. and
winter evenings exc. Fri. and
Sat.; approx. 3,500 ptas),
which offers you a choice of
nearly 120 different cod
dishes.

La Bisbal d'Empordà

*3 miles (5 km) E of
Monells by the C255*
**A village
of potters**
For more than 500 years this
village has been a centre of
pottery production,
specialising in black ware in
the 18th and 19th C., then
branching out into garden
pottery, jars and yellow-brown
varnished ware. To learn
more of the history of the
potteries, visit the **Museo de
Terracota** (☎ 972 64 20 67;
open

July-Sept. 10.30am-1.30pm
and 4.30-8.30pm; admission
charge). To buy samples of
the local wares, visit the **Can
Marunys** workshop (Padró
120-122, ☎ 972 64 28 51;

Monells old village

open Mon.-Fri. 8am-1pm and
2.30-6.30pm; closed 15 Aug.-
15 Sept.), where prices are
reasonable (250 ptas a plate)
and tradition is maintained.

Palafrugell

*7.5 miles (12 km) E of
La Bisbal on the C255*
Cork museum
Museo del Suro
Tarongeta 31
☎ **972 30 39 98**
Open Tues.-Sat.
10am-1pm and 5-7pm
in summer, 5-8pm in
winter (10.30am-1.30pm
weekends).
Admission charge.
Some 3 miles (5 km) from the
sea, this little village is a
favourite with those on
holiday in nearby villages,
who come here to do their
shopping. Once it was a centre
for the production of corks.
That is all ancient history
now, but the little museum
brings it all back. It's a good
base for several beaches and
pretty coves,
and is close to
Calella de
Palafrugell and
Llafranc.

**Calella de
Palafrugell**
Formerly the fishermen's
quarter, it's now a seaside
resort. The most striking part
of the town is the **Carrer de
les Voltes**, with its white
arcades opening onto the

beach. This is where, on the first Saturday of July, the **Habaneras festival** takes place, devoted to the songs that the sailors brought back from Cuba in the 19th C. If you miss the festival, you can still listen to habaneras while sipping a *cremat* (coffee with rum flambé) at **La Vella Lola** in Port Bot, or at **Rick Art**, near the church.

Cape San Sebastià

The cape San Sebastià pokes out between the beaches of

CAPE ROIG
GARDENS
1 mile (2 km)
SE of Palafrugell
☎ **972 61 45 82**
Open 9am-8pm
in summer, 9am-6pm
in winter.
Admission charge.
In the 1920s a
Russian colonel
discovered Cape Roig
and built a villa here.
Helped by hs wife, he
planned this botanical
paradise, which
currently contains
more than 700 exotic
species. From the
top, there's a good
view over Cape Planes
and the Formigues
islands; below, lies
Cala d'en Massoni,
where the colonel's
wife liked to swim.

Tamaríu and Llafranc. On its heights is a lighthouse built in 1857, and the lookout tower and 18th-C. hermitage make a pleasant destination for a walk with a wonderful view of the sea and the coast. At Llafranc don't miss the

Llafranc beach

Boig market, which takes place in mid-August, at the same time as the **Festa Major**. Tamaríu is a very pretty spot with a lovely seafront.

Formigues islands

Formigue means 'ant' in Catalan. The islands are in Calella bay (15 mins by boat) and the sea around them is full of fish, but dangerous. These tiny islands have played their part in history. In August 1285 the French, under Felipe III, fought a sea battle with the Catalan forces of Roger de Lluriat just off the coast. The French lost the battle, which turned out to be one of the most important of the Middle Ages.

Begur
5 miles (7 km)
NE of Palafrugell
Begur – a town with a view
This little inland town stands at the foot of its impressive **castle**, which was built on a conical rock. From the top there is a fine **panorama**, sweeping from Pals beach and the coves of the shore to the Medes islands.

In good weather, you can even see the Gulf of Roses coast on the horizon. This is hunting country, famous for its rabbits and partridges, as well as snails, and of course the various dishes made with **Pals rice**, which you can taste at the **Fonda Caner** (Pi i Ralló 14, ☎ 972 62 23 91; closed Wed. in winter; 1,500-3,500 ptas).

The beaches of your dreams

Sa Riera, Aiguafreda, Sa Tuna and Fornells are famous coves cut into the steep cliffs of Cape Begur. The azure-blue coves are a real delight. Further south is Aiguablava, a bay of smooth sand, quite shallow, surrounded by cliffs and woods, hidden between the Es Muts headland and the

Sa Riera beach

Cabres and Ses Failuges rocks. You can walk along the curve of rocks and sea, or climb to the Aiguablava parador and stroll in its gardens with their view over the sea.

Palamós,
the smell of the sea

Palamós has always relied on fishing (its fishing fleet is the second largest in northern Catalonia) and has not been overtaken by the tourist industry. So it remains quiet and picturesque, unlike its neighbour Platja d'Aro, a noisy and brash international tourist centre. Palamós has excellent sailing facilities, and the Platja de la Fosca is a particularly good spot for all the family to enjoy.

The port, a breath of sea air

To take in the maritime atmosphere, stroll in the picturesque Cala S'Alguer district or along the sea front. In the evening, it's worth waiting for the sun to set over the bay; in the afternoon, the

fresh fish auction takes place near the harbour wall, at the Pósito de Pescadores. Perched on a headland, the old part of the town overlooks the port and is a pleasant place to take a stroll.

Sea festivals and music

On 16 July, sailors' processions take over the streets of the port for the **Vierge del Carmen festival**. In July and August there is a series of concerts, the **Temporada de Verano** (information and reservations: ☎ 972 60 23 30), as well as two festivals of traditional sea music, the **Festival de la Canción Marinera** and the famous **Muestra de la Habanera**, typical of the Costa Brava.

A feast of Palamós prawns

Information from the chamber of commerce and tourism.
☎ **972 31 35 33.**

Palamós prawns are officially recognised as exceptional and during May and June no less than 18 restaurants in the town and 4 in the nearby village of Sant

Antonio de Calonge celebrate this local speciality with a *menu de gamba* for 3,500 ptas, enabling you to try the numerous prawn dishes. You'll be offered a plate of prawns, along with *pa amb tomàquest*, slices of bread coated in tomato and seasoned

S'AGARÓ, PEACE AND TRANQUILITY

Near Platja d'Aro, S'Agaró is a charming oasis of tranquility. The construction of its dream appartments was started in the 1920's. You'll love the turn-of-the-century architecture, which in 'touristy' Costa Brava, is not all that common. The buildings have managed to integrate harmoniously with the environment.

with olive oil and anchovies. Make sure you try *fideos rossejats*, a delicious dish of fine pasta cooked in fish stock and served with a garlic mayonnaise.

Fresh fish

Bass, grouper, angler-fish, bream, turbot, lobster and rockfish all come straight from the sea to the restaurants of the port, such as **La Gamba** (Pl. Sant Pere 1, ☎ 972 31 46 33; open daily exc. Wed. lunchtime in summer, all day Wed. in winter; closed Nov.; special set menu 4,800 ptas) which specialises in local prawns and a delicious dish of chicken and lobster with black rice. **Port Reial** (Pass. del Mar 8, ☎ 972 31 85 99; closed Nov., Sun. evenings and Mon. evenings in winter) specialises

in turbot stew, and **La Menta** (Tauler i Servià 1, ☎ 972 31 47 09; open daily exc. Wed. lunchtime; closed Nov., Sun. evenings and Wed. in winter; approx. 4,500 ptas) tempts its guests with a delicate dish of prawns or a plate of fried squid with fresh seasonal vegetables.

A little taste of France

Pâtisserie Xidors
24.5 miles (39.5 km) from Palamós, on the Palamós-Gerona road
☎ 972 31 46 49
Open daily 9am-10.30pm in summer, daily exc. Mon., 9am-9pm in winter; closed 2 Nov.-4 Dec.
This patisserie excels in delicious French pastries and all kinds of savoury and sweet delicacies are available, either to eat in the tearoom or buy in the shop next door to take away. Their ice-cream is wonderful too!

Walking along the coast

Whether you feel like a gentle stroll, or a healthy hike, and however long or short you want your walk to be, it's bound to take you along the Camino de Ronda. Also known as 'Pirate Road', this is where, not so long ago, the villagers would take it in turns to watch out for pirates. This interesting coastal road starts at the Cala de la Fosca, crosses the Cala S'Alguer and finishes up on the sands of the Cala Castell.

Spotcheck

F4

What to do

• Fish-market and prawn dishes
• Walking on the coast road

With children

• Aquadiver water park

Within easy reach

Gerona (22 miles/36 km NW of Palamós), p. 196-197

Tourist office

Palamós: ☎ 972 31 43 90

Platja d'Aro
4.5 miles (7 km) S of Palamós on the C253

Gallons of fun

Aquadiver water park
Carretera de Circumval
☎ 972 818 732
Open daily 1 June-30 Sept., 10am-7pm (closed when it rains). *Admission charge.*
A giant water park for young and old alike, with a swimming pool with wave machine and slides and flumes for all ages, including an exciting tunnel nearly 33 ft (10 m) long. If this all seems too much there's also a cool pine-grove, in which to stretch out and relax.

Sant Feliu de Guíxols
a taste of Italy

The people of San Feliu have the blood of merchants from Genoa and Pisa flowing through their veins; this port was once a hive of Italian traders, sailors, coral gatherers, cork manufacturers and fishermen. In the past, the town was ruled by the Benedictines in their monastery; these days, however, it's the tourist trade that rules, as in most parts of the Costa Brava.

The monastery
Dating from the 10th C., the monastery lies near the entrance to the town, on the

great Monastir square. It's a vast complex, including a **fortified church** (open Mon.-Sat. 8-11am and 8-11pm, Sun. 8.30am-noon and 7-8pm), a **cultural centre**, a **history museum** (open Tues.-Sat., 11am-2pm and 6-9pm in summer, 11am-2pm and 5-8pm in winter, Sun. 11am-2pm all year) and the **tourist office** (☎ 972 82 00 51). Beacons were once lit at the tops of the Corn and Fum towers, to warn of the arrival

of pirates. The porch of the Ferrada gate is the symbol of the town and is worth taking a look. The town hosts a festival of music and drama in July-August.

Other sights
Despite the growth of tourism and the abundance of new development, there are still some fine Art Nouveau buildings. The cafés retain their *fin-de-siecle* atmosphere, as do the Constancia casino, the Casa Patxot (near the Rambla del Portalet), and the large buildings along the Sant Pol beach. You can hunt for

genuine bargains among the stalls of the **Sunday market** on the Paseo del Mar and the Plaza del Mercat. Just outside Sant Feliu, on the road to Gerona, is the unique Pedrata standing stone, with a fine view over the bay.

Hermit houses
You won't have to spend any money but you will have to climb up to a great height, either on foot or by car. From the Sant Elm hermitage there is a **fine panorama** over the bay. For 13.5 miles (22 km), the coast road to Tossa del Mar gives you a spectacular view of cliffs and coves at each and every turn. Between the Vallpresona and Saliane coves, lies the **Sant Grau** hermitage. It was the home of a hermit who used to warn his fellow citizens of the imminent arrival of pirates.

Eldorado – for lovers of good food
For those in search of gourmet delights, there's a choice of two Eldorados. **Little Eldorado**

was the first on the scene, serving such original dishes as rice with prawns, anchovy stew and cod in olive oil (Rambla Vidal 23, ☎ 972 32 18 18; set menu 3,650 ptas). **Eldorado Mar**, facing the sea, is newer and less expensive, with a simple seafood menu (President Irla 15, ☎ 972 32 62 68; closed Oct.-June; set menu 1,575 ptas).

Sweet-tasting corks
La Vienesa
Rambla Vidal 33
☎ **972 32 01 81**
Open daily 8am-2pm and 4-9pm. Closed Sat.-Sun. in winter.

Cork production here has long been just a memory, but a memory that's preserved in this patisserie

which sells cork-shaped chocolate biscuits known as *trefins* (from 1,000 ptas a box). You can also buy delicious Sant Feliu *beignets* (doughnuts) (3,000 ptas for 2.2 lb/1 kg). It's a veritable paradise for the sweet-toothed and a good place to buy gifts for those not fortunate enough to be with you.

Adults 800 ptas, children 500 ptas.
Just before you arrive at Llagostera you'll find this shop selling flowers and decorative plants. It also has other interesting attractions – a room full of live exotic butterflies and another with a butterfly exhibition.

Butterfly centre
16 miles (25.5 km) on the Comarcal road, C250
☎ **972 83 04 62**
Open Mon.-Fri. 9am-1pm and 4-8pm, Sun. 10am-2pm in summer; Mon.-Fri. 9am-1pm and 3-7pm, Sat. 10am-1pm and 3-7pm, Sun. 10am-1pm in winter.

WATER, WATER EVERYWHERE

Caldes de Malavella is the most famous hot springs in Spain. The healing waters come out of the earth at 60°C (140°F) and its beneficial properties have been famed since Roman times. There are two spas to choose from: Prats (Pl. Sant Esteve 7, ☎ 972 47 0051) and Vichy Català (Paseo Dr Furst 32, ☎ 972 47 00 00). The famous water here is also bottled and sold throughout Spain. You can take the waters, stroll in the gardens of the spas, or visit the ruins of the ancient Roman baths. Enjoy a family spa and refresh your spirits (you need to telephone in advance).

Tossa de Mar

sun, sea and sky

Thoroughly picturesque, surrounded by magnificent cliffs and little inlets, Tossa de Mar makes you want to stay that little bit longer. The crenellated towers and walls of the old town recall its turbulent past and you can enjoy a stroll in the narrow alleys of the whitewashed lower town. All around there is feverish development, since Tossa de Mar is one of the most popular tourist resorts on the Costa Brava.

Vila Vella, the old town

Tossa de Mar is visible for miles around, with its medieval town wall (12th-14thC.) and its crenellated towers and ramparts. A little higher, on the headland, is a lighthouse and the ruins of a Gothic church (14th C.). The site of the annual **classical music festival** that takes place between mid-July and early August, it also offers the best view over the entire village.

Tossa de Mar is certainly one of the prettiest towns on the Costa Brava. Vila Vella, the old town, is a network of alleys and stone houses and has been declared a protected national monument.

Tossa in Roman times

In Roman times, Tossa was known as Turissa and in 1914 **ancient Roman remains** from the 1stC. BC were uncovered in the Els Ametlers district.

The excavations are not yet open to the public, but the fascinating objects that have been unearthed are on display in the **Museo Municipal** (Vila Vella, Antiguo Palau del Batlle, ☎ 972 34 01 08; open 9am-9pm in summer; admission charge). Particularly worth seeing is the multi-coloured mosaic which is inscribed with the name of the owner of the house in which it was found.

Sea trips

Take a boat trip and get a fresh view of Tossa and the surrounding coastline. Tickets are on sale at the ticket booths at the main beach. You can take a trip to Blanes (9.50am and 4.45pm, two hours return, 1,250 ptas) with Crucero

Nordeste (☎ 972 30 04 93), Crucetours (☎ 972 34 26 92) or Viatges Marítims (☎ 972 36 90 95). Two boats, *Fondo de Cristal* (☎ 972 34 22 29) and *Panoramic* (☎ 972 30 04 93) will take you on a trip to the Givarola cove, where you will be able to discover the seabed caves of the north coast (10am-6pm, departure every hour, 1,100 ptas).

A colony of artists

In the 1930s, Tossa de Mar, then a quiet fishing village, attracted a number of

painters, including such notables as Marc Chagall, Jean Metzinger and André Masson. Several of their works, including *The Violinist* by Chagall (1934), can now be seen in the municipal museum, which is housed in the Palau de Batle.

Made in Hollywood

In 1950, Hollywood stars took over from the painters. Ava Gardner and James Mason both stayed here while filming. The beautiful Ava created her own drama by falling in love with a bullfighter, which made her boyfriend of the time, Frank Sinatra, somewhat jealous. The village still has a souvenir of this episode – a lifesize statue of Ava Gardner. There's no monument to the bullfighter though – Tossa claims to be the first 'anti-bullfighting' village in Spain.

Sant Sebastià pilgrimage

In order to fulfil a 17th-C. vow to thank Saint Sebastian for saving them from the plague, every year on 20 January the

people of the village send a man, the 'pilgrim of Tossa', together with a band of followers, on a two-day, 37-mile (60-km) hike to Santa Coloma de Farners.

Blanes and Lloret
gateway to the Costa Brava

This is where the Costa Brava really begins – at Blanes, by the mouth of the River Tordera, and Lloret de Mar, tourist capital of this part of the coast, where holidaymakers come in their droves in search of sun and fun. At one time the saying was 'romantic Blanes, classical Lloret', but that's history now, although you may find some traces of truth in the saying if you look hard enough.

Blanes

'Romantic Blanes'

From the rocks of the **Palomera**, which plunge sharply into the sea between two long strips of sand, there's a wonderful view across Blanes bay. On the top of the hill you'll find the ruins of **Sant Joan castle**, from where there's another panoramic view, south towards Blanes and its beaches and north towards the coastal mountains. The colourful local fiesta which takes place on 26 July ends with a giant firework display.

Sea views

Between the Santa Anna headland and the Palomera stretches the beautiful Passeig Marítim, which overlooks Blanes and its beach, with the sea on one side and the old town with its maze of little streets on the other. To escape the crowds and find unspoiled beaches, take the road that runs alongside the sea in the direction of Lloret and seek out the hidden coves, such as La Forcanera, the Cala Sant Fransesc, the Santa Cristina beach and La Boadella.

Marimurtra gardens

Passeig Karl Faust 10
☎ 972 33 08 26
Open daily 9am-6pm
(7pm Aug.).
Admission charge.
Located on the Santa Anna headland, these botanical gardens can be reached either by the steps that start from Marià Fortuny street, or by the *carilet*, a minibus that leaves from Catalunya square. The gardens boast more than 3,000 species of plants from the Mediterranean, America, Africa and Australia. At the

BREDA COOKING POTS

12.5 miles (20 km)
NW of Breda
on the B512
This village is famous for its *ollas*, the traditional earthenware cooking pots that date back to the 16thC. Their survival was assured by the establishment of a potters' guild in the town in 1777. In the Roca Auladell workshop (Sant Sebastià 20, ☎ 972 87 01 82; open 9am-3pm and 4-7pm), they make all types of traditional pots and saucepans for simmering meat and vegetables, with prices ranging from 200-800 ptas.

bottom of the cliff stands a pretty temple in the shape of a rotunda, with a water-lily pool.

Pinya Rosa park

On the B682, turn right towards the Santa Cristina hermitage.
Open daily 9am-6pm.
Admission charge.
This park faces the sea and is a fine blend of vegetation and ornamentation. There are more than 7,000 cactuses, pretty plant arrangements and many pleasant paths with stone steps, fountains and pools, as well as swings for the children and benches for parents.

Lloret
4 miles (6 km)
NE of Blanes

'Classical Lloret'

These days, Lloret is just a classic tourist centre, with a few good seafood restaurants. **El Trull** (Cala Canyelles, ☎ 972 36 49 28; open daily; approx. 4,500 ptas, set menu

1,650 ptas) offers live lobsters for the grill, as well as *fideos* with seafood and swordfish *a la brutesca* in a pretty garden setting. At **Petxines** (Jacinto Verdguer 16, ☎ 972 36 41 37; open daily except Mon. and Thurs. 20 Nov.-20 Mar.; approx. 5,000 ptas, set menu 1,575 ptas) the unforgettable speciality of the house is *bacalao* with yoghurt, curry and dried fruit. However, if you suddenly fancy a plate of fish and chips, you'll find no difficulty in finding one!

Come to the fiesta

The hermitage of Santa Cristina, between Lloret and Blanes, celebrates the patron saint of the town on 24 July, carrying her statue in a procession to the hermitage for a mass, before returning her to the little chapel where she rests. On the same day, in the main square, you can see the dance of the *almorratxes*, at the end of which each man sprinkles his beloved with perfumed water.

Spotcheck
E4-F4

What to do
• Marimurtra gardens
• Fiesta of Santa Cristina

With children
• Pinya Rosa park
• Water World

Tourist offices
Blanes:
☎ 972 33 03 48
Lloret del Mar:
☎ 972 36 57 88

Water World

0.8 mile (1.2 km)
on the Vidreres road
☎ 972 36 86 13
Open 10am-6pm May and 16-30 Sept., 10am-6.30pm June and 1-15 Sept., 10am-7.30pm July-Aug.
Admission charge.
This is a classic opportunity for some good clean family fun, offering a huge range of activities (most of them involving water). Choose from a giant toboggan ride, a wild water trip or mini-golf, amongst other adrenalin rushes. And what's more there's a free shuttle to and from the Lloret bus station, leaving you with no excuse not to enjoy Water World.

The Maresme

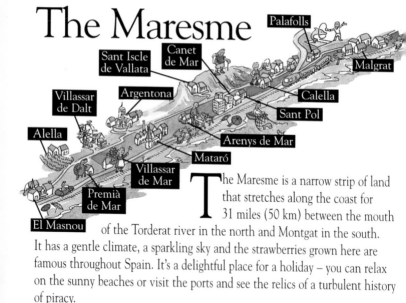

Palafolls

Sant Iscle de Vallata

Canet de Mar

Malgrat

Villassar de Dalt

Argentona

Calella

Sant Pol

Alella

Arenys de Mar

Villassar de Mar

Mataró

Premià de Mar

El Masnou

The Maresme is a narrow strip of land that stretches along the coast for 31 miles (50 km) between the mouth of the Torderat river in the north and Montgat in the south. It has a gentle climate, a sparkling sky and the strawberries grown here are famous throughout Spain. It's a delightful place for a holiday – you can relax on the sunny beaches or visit the ports and see the relics of a turbulent history of piracy.

The first train

Spain's first railway was built here in 1848, running between Mataró and Barcelona. Today its modern successor, with its comfortable, air-conditoned carriages, offers an unbeatable view of the Mediterranean coast on the journey from Barcelona to Blanes.

Calella

A little bit of Bavaria

The upper Maresme is the tourist heartland and Calella is its pulse – loud, buzzing, international and always awake. You don't come here for relaxation, but for fun on the beach or in the countless restaurants and cafés, clubs and discos. Calella is a

favourite resort for Germans and a huge **beer festival** is held here every October.

Sea-side
Club Nàutic Calella
Zona Platja
☎ 93 7661 852
or 609 33 2966
Open daily 8am-8.30pm, all year.
If you want to get away from the crowds, take to the sea. The inexperienced or lazy can take a trip in a crewed boat (8,000 ptas a day, lunch included, 4,000 ptas half-day). You can also take classes in sailing or windsurfing (17,000 ptas for 10 hours, over a two-day period).

MARINELAND WATER PARK AND ZOO
Malgrat road, Palafolls
☎ 93 765 48 02
Open daily 10am-7pm, 22 Mar.-2 Nov.

Admission charge.
This is a marine zoo and water park where old and young alike can have great fun swimming in fresh water, admiring the skills of the dolphins or listening to the birdsong in the bird pavilion, a sanctuary devoted to our feathered friends.
If you're particularly interested in wildlife, you can learn about the life of dolphins and the birds of prey of the Montnegre forest. The tour lasts three hours and costs 2,500 ptas.

Sant Pol
2.5 miles (4 km) SW of Calella

Port of call for sweet lovers
Sauleda confectionery
Manzanillo 20
☎ 93 760 09 01
Open daily 8am-2pm and 5-8.30pm.
Closed Tues. in winter.
Built at the foot of an old hermitage, Sant Pol is a typical fishing village, retaining some of its old charm, especially for lovers of sweets. At the Sauleda confectioners you'll find a delicious *touron* made with

hazelnuts, pine-seeds and honey (800 ptas each) and *cocas dulces* flavoured with apple (2,000 ptas for 2.2 lb/1 kg) or aniseed (1,700 ptas for 2.2 lb/1 kg).

Take a forest detour
The village of **Sant Iscle de Vallalta**, 4 miles (7 km) from Calella, is one of the gateways to the Montnegre range. From here, you can climb on foot to the highest points of the coastal chain, the Great Turó or the Montnegre de Ponent (2,300 ft/760 m), where you'll get a splendid view of the surrounding countryside. All around, houses have sprung up like mushrooms, but the **Montnegre nature park** remains unblemished. Here the Mediterranean and Atlantic vegetation is preserved, with its fine birch, cork-oak, hazel, chestnut and pine trees.

Canet de Mar
3 miles (5 km) SW of Sant Pol

A Modernist paradise
In the 1970s Canet was a haunt of rockers and hippies, but those days are long past and now the town is best known for its Art Nouveau buildings. The architect Lluís Domènech left his mark on many houses in the town; especially noteworthy are **Casa Roura** (1884) located

Spotcheck
E4

What to do
- Water sports
- Forest walks
- Canet Modernist architecture
- Arenys espadrilles
- Alella wine tasting

With children
- Barcelona-Mataró railway line
- Marineland water park and zoo
- Marine life treatment centre
- Isla Fantasia amusement park

Tourist offices
Calella de la Costa:
☎ 93 769 05 59
Arenys de Mar:
☎ 93 792 17 83
Mataró: ☎ 93 796 01 08

in Sant Domènec street, and **El Ateneo** (1888) in Ample street, while his son designed **Casa Domènech** and the **Fábrica Jover**. You can even visit the offices of the architect himself at the **Casa-Museo Domènech i Montaner** (Riera Gavarra 4, ☎ 93 795 46 15; open Tues.-Thurs. 10am-1pm, Sat. 11am-2pm; admission charge).

Arenys fishing harbour

Hand-made lace and espadrilles
Museo Frederic Marès de la Punta
Església 43
☎ 93 792 17 84
Open daily 11am-1pm and 6-8pm exc. Sun. and Mon. am.
Admission charge.
This museum specialises in hand-made lace, for which Arenys is famous. If you're looking for something a little more affordable, visit the **Can Soler** workshop in the upper town (Rambla Fransesc Macià 53, ☎ 93 795 05 10; open daily exc. Sun. 9am-1.30pm and 5-9pm), where many different kinds of espadrilles are hand-made (from 3,000 ptas).

Arenys de Mar
5 miles (8 km)
SW of Sant Pol
Fish and seafood galore

Arenys de Mar is the biggest fishing port on the Maresme coast and every day the fishing boats draw up to the harbour wall to sell their catch. At the **El Pòsit de Pescadors** (☎ 93 792 12 45; set menu 2,300 ptas, à la carte 5,000 ptas) you can watch the activity in the harbour while enjoying fish or seafood. The **Hispània** (Camí Real 54, ☎ 93 791 04 57; open daily exc. Sun. evenings and Tues.; closed Oct.; à la carte 5,000-6,000 ptas) offers excellent Catalan cuisine, including Montserrat tomatoes with sweet onions, chickpea balls and clam *suquet* (stew).

Mataró
6 miles (10 km)
SW of Arenys del Mar
Capital of the Maresme
This industrial town with its marina is not the most

exciting of spots, but it does contain several highlights, one of which is the retable of the **Los Dolores chapel**, a fine example of the Catalan Baroque style, in the Santa Maria basilica. Another is the **Missa de los Santes** ('saints' mass'), celebrated on 27 July from 10am to 2pm during the Fiesta Mayor (24-29 July).

Argentona
2.5 miles (4 km)
NW of Mataró
Town of *cántaros*
Situated in the heart of the Corredor range, Argentona sparkles with the sound of its 200 fountains. Legend has it that Sant Domènec's fountain has miraculous properties. However, this little town is mostly famous for its *cántaro* **festival** (Feria Internacional del Cántaro), held on 4 August. This is a competition involving the lifting of filled wine-jars (the *cántaros*), some of which can weigh nearly 450 lbs (200 kg). The little

Argentona's fountain of miracles

museum of wine jars (Museo del Cántaro, Pl. Església 9, ☎ 93 756 05 22) exhibits over 3,000 of every style and period. It's an unusual place, full of fascinating history.

Vilassar de Mar

3 miles (5 km)
SW of Mataró
City of flowers

In Vilassar de Mar, carnations certainly reign supreme. If you're a plant lover, head for the Vilassar flower and ornamental plant market (Nacional II, 0.4 miles/0.6 km; open daily 3-6pm). It's a feast for the eyes (and nose).

Gourmet stop
Ca L'Espinaler
Camí Real 1
☎ 93 759 15 89
Open daily exc. Sun. Apr.-May, 8am-4pm and 5-10pm.
A great place to stop for an aperitif in the evening. Try a glass of the delicious house vermouth, accompanied by a wide range of tapas – the anchovies in oil or fresh anchovies marinated in vinegar (1,000-2,000 ptas) are especially good. Treat yourself after a busy day on the road.

Premià de Mar

2 miles (3 km)
SW of Vilassar de Mar

ISLA FANTASIA
Finca Mas Brasso
Vilassar del Dalt
Motorway A19, Exit 6
☎ 93 751 45 53
Open daily 10am-7pm, Sat. night 2am-5am.
Admission charge.
A giant water park, with all sorts to see and do, including flumes, slides, pools and sports for those who like to work out while getting their tan. There's also restaurants and a disco. Fun for all the family.

Animals in peril
Centro de Recuperación de Animales Marinos de Catalunya (CRAM)
Camí Real 239
☎ 93 752 45 81
Tour 11am, first Sat. of the month; 1 hour.
Admission charge.
At first sight you could be forgiven for assuming that Premià de Mar is just like any other seaside resort, with its beaches, seaside houses, cafés and restaurants. However, you would be wrong because it's also home to the Fundación CRAM, which takes care of wounded sea animals, such as tortoises, dolphins, and, on occasion, even whales and sharks. Animal lovers will enjoy it.

Alella

3.5 miles (6 km)
W of Premià de Mar
Sun-drenched winery
Alella Vinícola
Can Jonc
Rambla Àngel Guimerà 62
☎ 93 540 38 42
Open Mon.-Fri. 8am-1pm and 3-6pm.
Free admission.
The inland town of Alella bathes in the sunlight that ripens the grapes for its rich and fruity white wines. Its noted vineyards are privileged with an exclusive trademark.
Alella Vinícola Can Jonc, which was founded in 1906, is the oldest winery in the town and, after your visit to the cellars and a wine tasting, you might be tempted to buy a few bottles of the Marfil blanc demi-sec, sec or rosé (525 ptas a bottle) or the Marfil Chardonnay (1,190 ptas a bottle).

Barcelona

Squeezed into the narrow gap between the Mediterranean and the Sierra Collserola, Barcelona has spread north as far as the River Besós and south to the Llobregat. This is a vibrant, cosmopolitan, late-night city, with an enticing mixture of the historic and the modern. Here you can do almost anything you want – admire great art in the gallerys, have an exciting night out in the clubs, search for antiques in dusty old shops or lose yourself wandering in the beautiful streets. Just take your time, open your eyes and enjoy the surprises that will come your way.

The Barri Gòtic

The 'Gothic district' is the oldest part of the city and, although it owes its name to the many 12th- to 15th-C. buildings, it actually dates back to Roman times. A wonderful city to explore on foot, on Saturday and Sunday there are guided tours organised by the tourist office (Plaza de Catalunya 17, ☎ 93 304 34 21; 950 ptas). If you're walking on your own through the historic Barri Gòtic, start at **San Jaume square**, built over the Roman forum. The name 'Jaume' (James) refers to the church that once stood here. The

square is dominated by the Palau de la Generalitat, seat of the provincial government, and the town hall, the Casa de la Ciutat (visits Sat. and Sun. 10am-2pm; free admission).

City of Augustus

Just by Sant Jaume, in a medieval building that houses the Centro Excursionista de Catalunya (Calle del Paradis 10; free admission), stand four Roman columns from the Temple of Augustus. Fixed in the earth, a millstone marks the highest point of the former Mount Taber, on which the Roman city, called Barcino, was built in the 3rdC. BC.

The cathedral

Open daily 8am-1.30pm and 4-7.30pm.
Free admission.
The cathedral was begun in 1298 under James II and

GREEN THOUGHTS

If the flowery contours of Art Nouveau is not enough for you, go and refresh your lungs and your spirits in one of the city's parks. The largest are **La Ciutadella**, to the east of the city, almost at the sea, and **Montjuïc** park, to the southwest. The **Parc Joan Miró** (Calle Aragó 1) and the

nearby **Parc de l'Espanya Industrial**, on the site of a former textile factory in the Sants district, are worth a visit. The **Parc del Laberint d'Horta** and **Parc del Castell de l'Orneta** are more suitable for play, with activities that both old and young can pay to take part in (information from the tourist office).

completed in the 15thC., but the fine Gothic facade, though designed in 1408 by the French architect Charles Galtès, was only built in fact at the end of the 19thC. Inside you can admire the elegant naves, the carved-wood decoration of the choir stalls and the Gothic and baroque altars in the side-chapels. Lifts take you onto the roof (open Mon.-Fri. 9.30am-12.30pm and 4-6.30pm, Sat. 9.30am-12.30pm; admission charge). The delightful cloister offers a cool oasis with its orange, magnolia and palm trees. There's also a fountain, decorated with a statue of St George, which provided fresh water.

French-style gardens

The French landscape gardener Claude Forestier laid out two gardens at historic points of the city. The first, which is centred round a waterfall, is on the parade ground of the **Parc de la Ciutadella**, an 18th-C. fortress that was replaced a century later by a public park (metro L1, Arc de Triomph station, or L4, Barceloneta-Ciutadella station; open 9.30am-7pm). The **Palau Reial de Pedralbes** gardens surround a royal palace built at the start of the 20thC., which now houses the pottery museum (Museo de Cerámica; metro L3, Palau Reial station; open Tues.-Sun.

Spotcheck
D4

What to do
• Barri Gòtic guided tour
• Sagrada Familia
• Snapshot of Spain
• Strolling on the Ramblas
• Boqueria covered market
• Maritime museum
• Barça football stadium and museum

With children
• Parks with games and fun fairs: Horta maze, Oreneta castle, El Tibidabo
• Zoo
• Güell park decorations
• Science museum
• Aquarium

Within easy reach
*Costa Brava (N),
pp. 138-163
Costa Dorada (S),
pp. 172-181
Montserrat (25 miles/
40 km NW),
pp. 206-207*

Tourist offices
Passeig de Gràcia:
☎ 93 238 40 00
Plaça de Catalunya:
☎ 93 304 31 21

10am-3pm; admission charge). It houses some unique pieces, including enamel decorations by Miró and Picasso.

Museum of modern art

Parc de la Ciutadella
☎ **93 319 57 28**
Open daily exc. Mon.
10am-7pm, Sun.
10am-2.30pm.
Admission charge.
This is part of the Catalan
national museum of art,
housed in the former arsenal.
Here you can see the art
conceived and created in
Barcelona from the turn of the
20thC. through to the 1930s,
including orientalist works by
Mariano Fortuny, fine portraits
of gypsy women by Isidre
Nonell, landscapes by Joaquim
Mir and, in the decorative arts
section, the first Art Nouveau
furniture, all curves and loops.

Zoo

Parc de la Ciutadella
☎ **93 225 67 80**
Open daily 9.30am-
7.30pm, May-Aug.,
10am-5pm, Oct.-Feb.,

10am-6pm, Mar., 10am-
7pm, Apr. and Sept.
Admission charge.
Here, among other things,
you can watch the trained
dolphins and say hello to
Copito de Nieve ('Snowflake'),
the only albino gorilla in the
world.

A museum for Picasso

Montcada 15-19
☎ **93 319 63 10**
Open Sat.-Tues. 10am-
8pm, Sun. 10am-3pm.
Admission charge.
The Aguilar palace, a fine
late-medieval building,
exhibits the early works of
one of the greatest, most
innovative and most
productive painters of the
20thC. Picasso came to
Barcelona in 1895 at the age
of 14 and stayed here until
1904. It was here that he
attended his first painting
classes, at the Llotja school

of fine arts. Particularly
noteworthy are the works of
his pink and blue periods,
his free interpretation of
Velásquez's *Noblewomen*, and
his ceramics and engravings.

Modernist park

**Parc Güell, Calle Nou
de la Rambla 3-5**
*Metro L3, Lesseps
station*
Open Mon.-Sat.,
10am-2pm and 4-8pm.
Güell park, north of the very
desirable Eixample district,
was designed by Gaudí, the
Modernist genius. This
fantastic, labyrinthine park
follows the natural shape of
the ground. There's a stairway

in the form of a multicoloured
dragon, leading to a square
overlooking the city and the
sea. You can view the countryside from the long, undulating
bench and imagine what it
would be like to live in a little
house in the middle of the

park. Laid out at the orders of Gaudí's patron Euesebi Güell, this park was supposed to contain a garden-city, but the only structures built were the two at the entrance, one of which houses the Gaudí museum.

La Sagrada Familia

Mallorca 401
☎ 93 455 02 77
Open daily 9am-8pm in summer, 9am-6pm in winter.
Admission charge.
This unique church, dedicated to the Holy family, was built to fulfil a vow and is financed by donations from the public. It's the best known of all Gaudí's works. The first stone was laid in 1883 and Gaudí worked on the building for 40 years, but it was left unfinished when he was killed by a tram in 1926, having completed only the Nativity facade. The building is an exuberant flight of fantasy, its

eight towers twisting up into the sky. Today the cranes stand awaiting further funding.

Passeig de Gràcia

At the end of the 19thC. work began on the construction that was to give birth to the district called Eixample (literally 'the widening'). The Passeig de Gràcia quickly became the most fashionable avenue in the heart of this wealthy quarter. Surrounding it is the Cujadrado de Oro Modernista ('Modernist golden square'). Don't miss the Manzana de la Discordia, where you can see the work of the three leading lights of the movement: Domènech i Montaner (Casa Lleó Morera, No. 35), Gaudí (Casa Batlló, No. 43), and Puig i Cadafalch (Casa Amatller, No. 41); and also the famous 'Pedrera' or

Casa Milà (No. 92), with its wave-like undulating decor.

Science museum

Teodor Roviralta 55
☎ 93 212 60 50
Open Tues.- Sun.
10am-8pm. Closed Mon.
Admission charge.
A museum for all the family at the foot of Parc Tibidabo, with games, workshop and lots of explanations that make understanding science child's play.

EL TIBIDABO

Plaza Tibidabo 3-4
☎ **932 11 79 42**
Open daily noon-10pm in summer (noon-1am Fri. and Sat.), Sat. and Sun. noon-8pm, rest of the year.
Funfair: adults 2,400 ptas, children 600 ptas.
This park is Barcelona's lung, where children come to run in the fresh air. At a height of 1,500 ft (500 m) above the sea, and just west of the city, you'll find a wonderful view over the city and the Mediterranean. The funfair was opened in 1908. To get there, take the metro to Tibidabo station, then the Tranvía Blau (350 ptas) which takes you, not too speedily, to the funicular railway (400 ptas). The view is particularly spectacular at dusk.

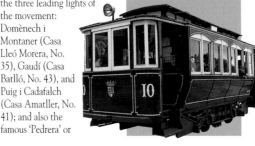

All roads lead to Montjuïc

A **tourist train** serves the Olympic hill (weekends and public holidays 11am-10pm; charge; 1 hour). It leaves from the Plaza d'Espanya and takes you to the National palace, the Miró foundation, the Olympic stadium and the Poble Espanyol. From the Paral-lel terminus of metro line 2, a **funicular railway** climbs the hill as far as the gates of the Miró foundation. Finally, the cable car (funicular terminus; charge) takes you effortlessly to Montjuïc castle. At the top, there is a panoramic view of the city and the port.

Olympic Montjuïc

Montjuïc was the site of the 1992 Olympic Games, for which the district (which was traditionally the Jewish quarter – the name meaning 'Jews' mountain') was extensively, not to say expensively, transformed. You can visit the magnificent **Olympic stadium** (Sant Jordí palace, open 10am-6pm), the Olympic gallery with its documents on the 1992 Olympics (☎ 93 426 06 60; open Mon.-Sat. 10am-2pm, until 8pm, June-Sept., Sun. 10am-2pm; admission charge) and the Picornell swimming pools (☎ 93 423 4041; open 9am-9pm; admission charge).

A snapshot of Spain

El Poble Espanyol
Marqués de Comillas, Parc de Montjuïc
☎ 93 325 78 66
Open Mon. 9am-8pm, Tues.-Thurs. 9am-2pm, Fri.-Sat. 9am-4pm, Sun. 9am-midnight.
Admission charge.
Giving a bird's-eye view of Spain, this 'Spanish village' gives a summary of traditional Spanish architecture. It was constructed for the Universal Exhibition of 1929, and you can see a glass-blowing, pottery, inlaid metalwork from Toledo, typically Spanish cafés and restaurants, brick and tiled houses from the Aragon countryside, and recreations of some of the famous Torres de Avilá – 88 granite towers that flank the walls of the Castilian city.

Catalan national art museum (MNAC)

Palau Nacional, Parc de Montjuïc
☎ 93 423 71 99
Open Tues.-Sat. 10am-7pm, Thurs. until 9pm, Sun. until 2.30pm; closed Mon.
Admission charge.
This museum has an extremely fine collection of Romanesque, Gothic, Renaissance and Baroque art,

including some of the finest Romanesque frescoes in Europe. Opposite the national palace, which was also constructed for the Universal Exhibition of 1929, stand the light-and-water fountains of Gaietà Buïgas.

Miró foundation

Plaza Neptú, Parc de Montjuïc
☎ 93 329 19 08
Open Tues.-Sat. 11am-7pm (8pm, July-Sept.), until 9.30pm Thurs.; closed Mon.
Admission charge.

The colours and shapes of Miró's work, though seemingly simple, astonish and enthrall the spectator. Watch out for the characteristic moons, women, birds and stars in his magical canvasses. The originals are priceless, but you can buy postcards and posters, framed or unframed, in the shop (2,000-3,500 ptas for a poster).

Las Ramblas

Until the 14th C. the Ramblas was a watercourse that flowed down from the Sierra Collserola. Today this avenue carries people who stroll along between the Plaza de Catalunya and the port. This is the beating heart of Barcelona, with crowds milling among the 140-year-old plane trees. Many different sorts of people gather here: traders in books and magazines, people selling jewellery and T-shirts, human 'statues', frozen under the trees for the strollers' enjoyment, musicians, poets, dancers and acrobats. The upper part of the avenue belongs to the bird and flower sellers, the lower part is painters' territory. Hire a chair (50 ptas) and enjoy the street show.

The Boqueria

Rambla 85-89
Open daily exc. Sun.
6am-9.30pm.
Even if you don't want to buy anything, take a stroll through the Boqueria, Barcelona's late 19th-C. covered market. Feast your eyes on the architecture, with the great Art Nouveau steel and glass gate, and the rows of fruit and vegetable stalls; listen to the cries of the fishmongers and the customers bargaining; enjoy the atmosphere and smell of the market. At the bar of **Pinocho** you can try Catalan-style tripe, braised veal, soup of the house or the fish of the day (open 6am-5pm; approx. 1,500 ptas).

For food lovers

The **Antigua Casa Figuera** (Rambla 83, ☎ 93 301 70 27; open 8.30am-9pm), founded in 1820 and now known as **Escribà**, can be recognised by its extraordinary Art Nouveau facade. This bakery is famous for its delicious pastries and chocolates. Opposite the Liceu, and open at all hours, the **Café de l'Opéra** (Rambla 74, ☎ 93 302 41 80) offers more than 200 different sorts of tea and, with its faded late 19th-C. decor and animated atmosphere, is a charming venue. Another Barcelona classic is the Xixona nougat sold at **Planelles-Donat** (Portal de l'Angel 7 and 25, ☎ 93 317 34 39; open Mon.-Sat. 10am-2pm and 4-8pm; 1,300 ptas a slab) – the best sweetshop in town.

Royal square

Built around 1850, on the site of a demolished Capuchin convent, the Plaça Reial is an oasis of calm after the hustle and bustle of the Ramblas. But make no mistake – the *cerverías* under the arcades of the square are very much part of Barcelona's bustling nightlife. The lampposts are an early work of Gaudí. On Sunday mornings there's a stamp and coin market between the palm-trees and Gaudí's street lights.

Museum of contemporary art

Museo de Arte Contemporáneo de Barcelona (MACBA)
Plaza dels Àngels 1
☎ 93 412 08 10
Open summer Mon.-Sat. 10.30am-8pm, Thurs. until 10pm, Sun. 11am-7pm; winter Mon.-Fri. noon-8pm, Thurs. until 9.30pm, Sat. 10am-8pm, Sun. 10am-3pm.
Admission charge.

In this dazzling white building designed by Richard Meyer you'll find more than 1,500 contemporary works of art from all over the world, with an emphasis on Catalan art since 1945 and external influences on local artists. This modern construction is in stark contrast to the facades of the old buildings nearby. It's also known as MACBA for short.

The port

At the foot of the Plaza Portal de la Pau, climb onto one of the little boats, known as *golondrinas*, anchored at the jetty. You can hear all about Barcelona's nautical history while travelling to the Olympic port (adults 1,275 ptas, children 550 ptas) or the Rompeolas (adults 485,

children 250 ptas). A swing-bridge over the water will take you to the **Maremagnum**, a modern shopping complex with shops, cinemas, cafés, bars and restaurants.

Drassanes and the maritime museum

Av. Drassanes
☎ 93 301 18 71

BARÇA – NOU CAMP

Av. Arístides Maillol
☎ **93 496 36 00**
Open Mon.-Sat. 10am-6.30pm, Sun. 10am-2pm.
Admission charge.
This shrine to football is the home of Barcelona's legendary team, which was founded in 1899 by the Swiss Hans Gamper and is supported regularly by more than 100,000 fans. Discover the rich history of the club in the Barça museum and imagine what it's like to be part of the roaring crowd in the Nou Camp stadium, the second largest in the world. In the museum shop, you can buy a range of souvenirs including the club's 100th-anniversary jersey (12,000 ptas).

Open daily 10am-7pm in summer, 10am-6pm Tues.-Sun. in winter. *Admission charge.*
The Drassanes, the old royal dockyards, were built between the 13th and 17thC. In these giant structures, some more than 330 ft (100 m) long, shipworkers could work on up to eight vessels at a time. One of these buildings now houses the Museo Marítimo, the museum of Catalonia's seafaring history, with a full-size replica of a Royal galleon.

Columbus' finger

Lift to the viewing gallery
☎ 93 302 52 24
Open daily 9am-8.30pm June-Sept., 10.30am-1.30pm and 3.30-6.30pm, rest of year. *Admission charge.*
At the foot of the Ramblas, in the Plaza Portal de la Pau, stands the monument to Christopher Columbus, commissioned for the Universal Exhibition of 1888. Perched on a column nearly 200 ft (60 m) high, the famous sailor and explorer points his finger towards the Mediterranean, turning his back on the New World he once

discovered. Perhaps he's homesick. From the top, the view is very impressive.

The seafront

Between **Barceloneta**, a former fishing district dating from the 18thC., and the brand new **Olympic port**, the seafront is full of bars and restaurants, with the two worlds, old and new, being linked by the Passeig Marítimo. On the beach at Barceloneta, 10 years ago you could still have eaten at the *chiringitos*, little family-run eating places sheltering under simple wooden canopies, near the bathhouses.

Aquarium

Moll de Espanya
del Port Vell
☎ 93 221 74 74
Open Mon.-Fri. 9.30am-9pm, until 9.30pm weekends, until 11pm, July-Aug. *Admission charge.*
One of the largest collections of Mediterranean sea life in the world is to be found in the aquarium's 20 pools and tanks, as well as many tropical species. A 260-ft (80-m) transparent tunnel allows you to walk among sharks, and in the Explora zone children will enjoy discovering the exciting world of the seabed.

Sitges and the Costa Dorada

Not so long ago, driving from Barcelona to Sitges was a nerve-wracking affair, not only because of the congestion, but because of the hairpin bends of the Garraf mountains as well. Luckily, since 1992 things have improved immensely; there's now a motorway and tunnels, and the trains run more frequently. This means that visitors have no problem getting to Sitges, one of Catalonia's most popular resorts, a paradise for holidaymakers with its sun, sea and sand.

Modernist festival
Museu del Cau Ferrat
Fonollar
☎ 93 894 03 64
Open Tues.-Fri.
9.30am-2pm and 4-6pm,
Sat. until 8pm, Sun. and
public holidays
9.30am-2pm.
Admission charge.
Modernist artists loved Sitges.
Between 1892 and 1899 the
Catalan Santiago Rusiñol
organised five Modernist
festivals here. The house
the painter used to live in
(actually two 16th-C.

fishermen's cottages, decorated
in a highly coloured 'neo-
Medieval' style) is today the
Museu del Cau Ferrat
('museum of wrought iron').
It contains paintings and
drawings by Picasso, Utrillo,
Zuloaga and others, as well as
wrought-iron ware and
ceramics which once belonged
to Rusiñol.

Maricel
☎ 93 894 03 64
Open summer 9.30am-
2pm and 5-7pm Mon.-

Fri., 9.30am-9pm Sat.-
Sun.; winter 9.30am-
2pm and 4-6pm, until
8pm Sat., 9am-2pm Sun.
and public holidays.
Admission charge.
This former hospital dating
from the 14thC. was reworked
in Modernist style by the artist
Miguel Utrillo. It's made up
of two buildings linked by a
bridge that crosses over
Fonollar street: one is the
Maricel de Terra, which faces
the Cau Ferrat museum, and
the other is the Maricel del
Mar, which houses a pretty

GAUDÍ'S BODEGA

15.5 miles (25 km) on the Barcelona road (C246)
☎ 93 632 00 19
Open Thurs.-Sun. 1.30-4pm and 9-11pm.
In 1985, at the request of his patron the Count de Güell, Gaudí built a very beautiful Modernist wine cellar on the coast. The Celler Güell or Celler de Garaff, today renamed the Gaudí-Garraf bar-restaurant, is worth the detour.

museum with a mixture of 19th-and 20th-C. paintings and sculptures (including José Maria Sert's World War I frescoes) and Gothic mosaics and a fine 15th-C. church retable.

Festivals all year long

In February, during the week of the **carnival**, Sitges becomes the 'gay capital' of Europe. In March, the **international vintage-car rally** takes places between Barcelona and Sitges, with drivers, of course, in vintage costume. At **Corpus Christi** everyone tries to outdo their neighbours' floral decorations, with carpets of flowers in the streets and carnations every-where. The town looks, and smells, splendid. You can also attend the **international theatre festival** in June, the fiesta of **Sant Bartolomeu** in August, with its folk dances and parades of giants, and the **international festival of fantasy cinema** in October (information from the tourist office, ☎ 93 894 42 51).

Royal 'xató'
La Torreta restaurant
Port Alegre 1
☎ 93 894 52 53
Open daily exc. Tues.
Taster menu 3,500 ptas.
Xató is a local speciality that looks like a big 'castle' of endive, salted anchovies, cod and olives. It's served with a sauce made from almonds, hazelnuts, pimentos, well-seasoned with salt, pepper and other condiments. There's a celebration of this local dish every year in February during international *xató* day. Try it at **La Torreta**, where the seafood dishes are particularly delicious.

Vilanova i la Geltrú
3 miles (5 km)
SE of Sitges
Seafood and a railway museum
This is the fourth-largest fishing port in Catalonia. Wander along the seafront and try the local delicacies such as *cremal* (a sort of stew of fish in garlic) and the *bull de tonyna* (dried and smoked tuna), at the **El Peixerot** restaurant (Paseo Marítimo 56, ☎ 93 815 06 25; approx. 4,500 ptas). You can complete your relaxing stroll with a visit to the **railway museum** (Museo del Ferrocarril, Pl. Eduard Maristany; open 10am-3pm Tues.-Sun., until 7pm Sat.; free admission last Sat. of the month).

Spotcheck
D5

What to do
• Visit the Modernist buildings
• Try *xató*
• International theatre and fantasy cinema festivals

With children
• Railway museum
• Fiesta of Sant Bartolomeu

Tourist office
Sitges:
☎ 93 894 50 04

Tarragona
All hail the Romans!

The ancient Tarraco was founded in 218 BC to serve as military base for Scipio's armies and played an important role in the Roman conquest of the Iberian peninsula. Today its role is different – it is a rapidly expanding tourist resort, thanks partly to the development of tourism in the Costa Dorada.

Roman circus
☎ 977 24 19 52
Open Tues.-Sat.
10am-8pm, Sun.
10am-2pm, in summer;
Tues.-Sat. 10am-1pm
and 4-7pm, Sun.
10am-2pm, in winter.
*Admission charge
(also gives entry to the
military and history
museums).*
Built in the 1stC. AD, the circus was used for chariot races. When intact it was very impressive; the arena itself being 1,000 ft (325 m) by nearly 400 ft (115 m), and it's still one of the best-preserved Roman buildings in the city.

Amphitheatre
Parc del Miracle
☎ 977 24 25 79
Open Tues.-Sat.
10am-8pm, Sun.
10am-2pm, in summer;
Tues.-Sat. 10am-
1pm and 4-7pm,
Sun. 10am-2pm,
in winter.

Situated east of the city, you can reach the amphitheatre via the Passeig de las Palmeras, a vast terrace which looks out over the Mediterranean. The amphitheatre was built at the beginning of the 2ndC. AD, and with its views over the sea, must have been a fine place to watch gladiators fight. In the arena are the remains of a Romanesque church (12thC.) dedicated to the first Christian martyrs.

In the footsteps of the Romans
Passeig Arqueológic
Avenida Catalunya
☎ 977 24 57 96
Open Tues.-Sat.
9am-9pm, Sun.
9am-3pm.
Admission charge.
The town's Roman remains can be seen among other, later constructions. Explore the old

AQUALEÓN SAFARI
Finca Les Basses,
Albinyana
22 miles (35 km)
NE of Tarragona
on the N340 as far
as El Vendrell,
then the C246
☎ **977 68 70 57**
Open Mon.-Fri.
10am-7pm and
Sat.-Sun. 10am-8pm,
19 Sept.-31 Oct; clo-
sed 1 Nov.-11 Apr.
Admission charge.
Zebras, rhinos,
elephants, tigers and
lions, all roam free,
together with more
than 300 species
of birds, to delight
young and old in this
safari park. You can
take your own car
into the area
reserved for the
herbivores or climb
aboard the
Safari-bus to
go and take a
look at the
carnivores.
There's also
a water
park of
more than
30 acres
(12 ha).

ramparts, built in the 3rdC.
BC, and now renamed the
Passeig Arqueológic; you can
follow the trail, admiring the
ramparts' huge stone-block
construction, and wander
through the ruins of the forum
and the maze of streets in the
upper town.

National archaeological museum
Plaza del Rei 5
☎ **977 23 62 09**
Open Tues.-Sat.
10am-8pm, Sun.

10am-2pm, in summer;
Tues.-Sat. 10am-1pm
and 4-7pm, Sun.
10am-2pm, in winter.
Admission charge.
The museum contains a
collection of objects found
in the town and the
surrounding area, with
fragments of statues including
a head of Minerva and a bust
of Pomona, pieces of Roman
architecture, ceramic, glass
or metal objects and coins.
The museum also owns the
finest collection of mosaics
in the whole of Catalonia,
including the mysterious

Berà arch

mosaic of the Medusa (2ndC.)
and the a mosaic of fish.

Roman remains outside the walls
A couple of miles (3 km)
north of Tarragona, near the
A7 motorway, you can find
another Roman structure, the
1st-C. **Devil's bridge**, an
impressive aqueduct nearly

Devil's bridge

Spotcheck
C5

What to do
• Visit the Roman remains

With children
• Safari at Aqualeón

Within easy reach
Poblet, Vallbona de les
Monges and Santes Creus
monasteries (25 miles/
40 km N), pp. 212-213

Tourist office
Tarragona:
☎ **977 23 24 15**
or **377 24 50 64**

700 ft (217 m) long and with
a maximum height of nearly
90 ft (27 m), which brought
water from Francolí to
Tarragona. Don't miss the
Tower of the scipions, a
funerary monument 30 ft
(9 m) high (4 miles/6 km NE
of Tarragona on the N340), or
the **Berà arch**, a monumental
gate on the Via Augusta that
linked Cadiz with Rome (12.5
miles/20 km from Tarragona
on the N340).

Eating Roman-style
Les Voltes
Trinquet Vell 12
☎ **977 23 06 51**
Closed Sun. evenings
July-Aug.
Approx. 3,500 ptas à la
carte; dish of the day
1,500 ptas.
Have a Roman feast under the
arches of the circus, between
the remains of the arena and
the galleries. You should try a
romescalda, a ramekin of fish
and seafood in a sauce of garlic,
grilled hazelnuts or almonds in
olive oil and, for the strong-
stomached, a very hot pimento.

Port Aventura
around the world in a day

The largest theme park in Spain, and the second largest in Europe after Disneyland in Paris, Port Aventura is now part of the Universal Studios group. Opened in 1995, it receives nearly 3 million visitors a year. Only a mile or so (2 km) from Salou, on the Costa Dorada, it's a great place for a family to have a break and take a fabulous world tour without leaving the shores of Catalonia.

Getting there

Salou is 7.5 miles (12 km) from Tarragona and 68 miles (110 km) from Barcelona by the A7 motorway. Take exit 35 at Vila-seca and you'll find the entrance to the park just past the toll. There are also little trains and buses from Salou or, if you're feeling more energetic, it's a 10-minute walk from Europe square in Salou.

Timetable and prices
Universal Studio's Port Aventura
Avenida Pere Molas
1 mile (2 km), Vila-seca
☎ 97 777 90 00
Open mid-Mar.-end Oct.: 10am-8pm 15 Mar.-15 June and 15 Sept.-30 Oct.; 10am-midnight 15 June-15 Sept.

Adults: 4,300 ptas for one day, 6,300 ptas for two consecutive days, 8,200 ptas for three

non-consecutive days, 3,300 ptas 7pm-midnight. Children and over-65s: 3,200 ptas for one day, 4,900 ptas for two consecutive days, 6,400 ptas for three

non-consecutive days, 2,000 ptas 7pm-midnight. Free admission for children under four years old.

Crazy bird

El Pájaro Loco, or Woody Woodpecker, a cartoon character created by Walter Lane in 1940, is the Port Aventura mascot. He wanders freely around the park, so you can meet him anywhere and any time, playing the fool or ready for a family photo. He promotes the various attractions, and he's hard to avoid or resist.

Five corners of the world

Five different exciting and exotic destinations await your discovery: the **Mediterranean**, **Polynesia**, **China**, **Mexico**, and the **Wild West**. You travel in space and time, having chosen to explore each area on foot, by train or by boat. Amid fantastic backdrops, with fierce cowboys, friendly fishermen, Chinese emperors and Mayan warriors, you'll find more than 30 fabulous rides, 25 fantastic shows, 18 restaurants from all over the world (as well as fast-food joints), sideshows and souvenir shops.

But it's not all show...

Of course the backdrops are recreations of the architecture of China, Mexico etc., but the Polynesian plants do come from the other side of the world, and the Chinese acrobats are really Chinese and were trained in Beijing. The Native Americans who entertain you by dancing and singing by the Colorado canyon have actually

come from the other side of the Atlantic. The actors of Port Aventura are there to make the illusion complete, but they are so sincere that you end up really wanting to believe them.

One adventure after another

The acclaimed star of the park is the **Dragon Khan**, in the Chinese section – the largest

rollercoaster in Europe, with 8 loops that are travelled at a speed of 70 mph (110 kph). It's an unforgettable experience – if you can handle it – but it's not for the faint-hearted. (The roller-coaster does not operate in high winds.) The **Stampida**, in the Wild West section, is less heart-stopping. The best water

rides are the **Tutuki Splash** (Polynesia), the **Silver River Flume** and the **Grand Canyons Rapids** (Wild West). In another style, **Fiestaventura** (Mediterranean) is a water show with fireworks, symbolising the park's five zones. The latest attraction for 2001 is **Tempo del Fuego** (Mexico), an exciting adventure set in an Aztec temple.

Spotcheck
C5

Within easy reach
Tarragona (7.5 miles/ 12 km S), pp. 174-175

Tourist information
Universal Studio's Port Aventura:
☎ 97 777 90 00

AQUÒPOLIS
Paseo Pau Casals 65 La Pineda, Vila-seca
☎ 977 37 16 40
Open 10am-6pm, 12-31 May and 1-10 Oct.; 10am-7pm, June-Sept.
Admission charge.
Less overwhelming than Port Aventura, but perfect for a hot day, this water park really does have its feet in the water. It's 2 miles (3 km) from Salou, right by Port Aventura, facing the La Pineda beach. It provides all the usual sorts of water-park activities: pool with wave machine, water slides, flumes, paddling pool for small children, solarium etc.

Èbre delta
the Catalan Camargue

At the southernmost point of the Catalan coast, the Èbre delta pushes out into the sea. This flat land was taken over by marshlands and rice fields in the 19thC., but two canals have drained it and made it habitable. It's outside the usual tourist circuit and is a vast stretch inhabited by birds, fish and bulls, and with long sandy beaches, lagoons and little fishing ports. Far from the crowds, you can explore this region on foot or by bicycle.

A paradise for birds...

...and bird-watchers, as thousands of birds stop in the delta during their winter migration to the warm south. Nearly 180,000 water birds, mainly duck, stay here while awaiting the return of spring. And there are about 100,000 birds that choose to live here, belonging to 300 different species, which represents some 60% of the species found in Europe. Take your binoculars and seek out one of the hides scattered around the park. You'll spot herons, avocets and even a flamingo or two.

Land of mosquitoes

If you want to admire the natural riches of the delta, you have to do battle with the mosquitoes, which abound in this humid area. Malaria was endemic here until the mid-20thC., but the mosquito population has been much diminished by fumigation.

Nevertheless, you'll want to bring repellants, citronella oil and creams to keep the pesky insects at bay, as well as soothing lotions to ease the pain if you do get bitten.

Deltebre

Gateway to the park

This is the 'capital' of the delta. Originally, there were two villages, Jesús i Maria and La Cava, which joined forces to form the little town of Deltebre. Here you'll find the **park information centre** (Ulldecona 22, ☎ 977 48 96 79; open Mon.-Fri. 10am-2pm and 3-6pm, Sat. 10am-1pm and 3.30-6pm). In order to better under-stand the ecosystem

Characteristic delta house

of the delta, you can join one of the centre's organised tours or visit the ecomuseum (admission charge).

WALKING, RIDING AND CYCLING

The more athletic visitors will enjoy themselves here. You can hire bicycles by the day (Hilario Pagà, Goles de l'Èbre 301, ☎ 977 48 05 49; Torné, Sant Blai 3, ☎ 977 48 00 17) or fish either in fresh water or in the sea (Enrique Navarro, Capità Cortés 3, ☎ 977 48 10 50 or 689 47 48 07; 22,000 ptas for one person, 33,000 for four people). If you prefer to let someone else do the work, try a horse-back ride. It'll take you places where your car just can't go. Hípica Delta (☎ 93 588 32 01; open 4-9pm in summer, according to the weather in winter) organises three-hour excursions (4,500 ptas each), night-trips on full-moon evenings or 40-minute rides on leading reins (3,750 ptas).

The king of rice

Marketed under the name 'Arros del Delta de l'Èbre', delta rice makes up one-fifth of the entire Spanish production – that is, about 100,000 tons (100 million kg) of rice, grown and harvested by seven co-operatives. At the **Cambra Arrossera de Deltebre** you can learn all there is to know about growing rice and the different ways of cooking it (Ave Goles de l'Èbre 4, ☎ 977 48 04 76; open Mon.-Fri. 9am-noon and 3-7pm).

Fresh fish galore

The fishermen of Deltebre moor their boats at the mouth of the river, on the left bank, where you can find pleasant and inexpensive restaurants. Try, for example, **El Cadell** (Ramón y Cajal 29, ☎ 977 48 08 01; open daily exc. Mon.; set menu 1,300 ptas, taster menu 2,500 ptas), a good place to taste the fish of the day, a *xapadillo* of eels, delta rice and many other local delights.

Fish market

Fresh out of the water, the catch is taken to the Pósito, or municipal 'storehouse', at Deltebre (Benavente, ☎ 977 48 10 26), where it's

Spotcheck
B6

What to do
• Watching the wildlife
• Fishing
• Wandering in the delta

With children
• Boat trips

Within easy reach
Tortosa and the Èbre valley (9.5 miles/ 15 km NW) pp. 216-217

Information
Èbre delta information centre:
☎ 977 48 96 79

sold in open market at 11am. It's an important moment in local life and worth trying to attend, with all its theatre, noise and entertainment supplied by the chiselled-featured fishermen, and its lively and characteristic atmosphere.

Boat trips

There are many different ways to enjoy the waters of the delta. Olmos (Unió 165, ☎ 977 48 05 48) and Garriga (Verge del Carme 40, ☎ 977 48 91 22) both offer return trips to the mouth of the river (600 ptas), or across the Èbre (60 ptas), if you want to take a shortcut or simply to get to know the delta from the water. The Creuers Delta de l'Èbre company (☎ 977 48 01 28 or 608 13 35 82) organises 45-minute **mini-cruises,**

BUDA ISLAND

This is the ecological reserve of the delta, a mini-paradise where 300 species of sea bird live. You can visit part of the island, on

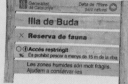

Generalitat de Catalunya — Delta de l'Ebre parc natural

Illa de Buda

✕ **Reserva de fauna**

○ ⓘ Accés restringit
✕ Es prohibit pescar a menys de 15 m de la riba
Les zones humides són molt fràgils.
Ajudem a conservar-les

condition that you obey the strict rules of this highly protected sanctuary. **Delta Guía** organises 90-minute guided tours (Mallorca 61, ☎ 977 46 80 54; open Wed., Sat. and Sun. in summer 10am-noon; 450 ptas each, minimum 30 people).

leaving from Buda island on the tip of the peninsula, and **day trips**, leaving from Amposta harbour, on the restaurant ship Santa Suzanna (3,300-6,000 ptas depending on the menu chosen).

beds of mussels and oysters. Amid the dunes and sandbanks, long stretches of beach and the burning sun, earth and sea are hard to distinguish as they shimmer in the heat.

and is an easy way of travelling from the left to the right bank. In the **Museo del Montsià** you can find out about the history and geography of the delta, and it also has sections on the cultivation of rice and the folk art of the Tortosa region.

Gourmet treat

Duque delicatessen
Avenida Catalunya 115
☎ 977 70 42 29
Open 9am-1.15pm
and 5.30-8.30pm.
Amposta's speciality is the **baldane**, a sort of rice- and onion-based *butifarra* – the local version of the unique Catalan sausage.

The left bank

The search for the natural beauty of the left bank leads you from the Garxal lagoon to the Canal Vell lagoon, from the Riumar beach to the banks of the Marquesa river. The Fangar peninsula looks out over the sea, its bay sheltering

Amposta
9.5 miles (15 km)
W of Deltebre
**Èbre delta
museum**
Museo del Montsià
Gran Capità 34
☎ 977 70 29 54
Open Tues.-Sat.
11am-2pm and 5-8pm.
Admission charge.
The Amposta suspension bridge is the last bridge before the river mouth,

*Sant Carles
de la Ràpita*
6 miles (10 km)
S of Amposta
A taste of the sea
Running parallel with the Èbre canal, the road ends in Sant Carles, the third-largest fishing port

in Catalonia, the perfect place to try fish, seafood (especially the delicious lobsters) and shellfish, not forgetting the *arroces marineros* (rice dishes cooked with fish or seafood). The **Miami Can Pons** (Avenida Constitució 35-37, ☎ 977 74 05 51; set menu 2,100 ptas, taster menu 5,500 ptas) is an excellent restaurant. The food at **Can Batiste** (Sant Isidre 204, ☎ 977 74 23 08; closed Sun. evenings; set menu 1,300 ptas, taster menu 3,000 ptas) is cheaper and also very good. Amposta and Sant Carles de la Ràpita are both good spots to choose as a base for exploring the delta.

Encanyssada lagoon

Poble Nou del Delta

**7.5 miles (12 km)
E of Sant Carles**

**A newcomer
to the delta**

This little village was created out of nothing in the 20thC., to bring farmers from all over Spain to cultivate the unused lands. Originally named Villa Franco del Delta, in honour of the Spanish

dictator, it was renamed when democracy was restored. With its white houses and its streets planted with palm trees, it looks like an African oasis.

Encanyssada
lagoon

*0.5 mile (1 km)
N of Poble Nou*

Amid bulrushes and rice-paddies, this lagoon is a perfect place to watch birds. The **Casa de la Fusta** houses an information centre and an

ornithological museum (☎ 977 26 10 22; open daily exc. Mon. 10am-2pm and 3-6pm). At the **L'Estany** restaurant (☎ 977 26 10 26)

you can hire bicycles or stop and taste the local cuisine: wild duck (1,200 ptas), eel in its own juice (1,200 ptas), frogs' legs (800 ptas) or sea anemones (800 ptas).

Beaches
and marshlands

From the Trinitat salt-flats, on the tip of the peninsula of the Banya, to the Gola de Migjorn, the river mouth south of the Èbre, there are endless stretches of sand, empty and untouched, interrupted only by the built-up Eucalyptus beach. To the north of the Trabucador, an isthmus 2.5 miles (4 km) long by 330 ft (100 m) wide, lies the Tancada lagoon, home to a large population of pink flamingoes.

Albera range

The Albera is the last outcrop of the eastern Pyrenees, the land of stone-age menhirs and dolmens. Once, smugglers ruled the mountain paths; in 1939, however they became the routes into exile for the republicans who managed to escape at the end of the Civil War. Since 1936 the Albera has been classified as a national nature conservation area, and it has become a sanctuary for the Mediterranean tortoise, a peaceful guest in this once turbulent region.

PAR. NATURAL DE L'ALBERA
Departament d'Agricultura,
Ramaderia i Pesca

An artificial frontier

The upper course of the River Llobregat separates the Albera from the Pyrenees chain, forcing it to turn towards the sea. To the south, the Empordat plain comes to an end at the foot of this range, whose highest point, the Puig Neulós, is only 4,143 ft (1,263 m). Since 1659, when the Treaty of the Pyrenees ended a war between France and Spain, the Albera range has marked the frontier between the two countries, as France took control of

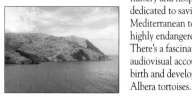

Roussillon and the Cerdagne region, which are culturally part of Catalonia.

Garigella
Tortoise sanctuary
Centro de Reproductión de la Tortuga
☎ 972 55 22 45
Open daily 10am-1pm and 4-7pm; closed Nov.-May.
Admission charge.
This tortoise 'reproduction centre', near Garigella, is both nursery and hospital, and is dedicated to saving the Mediterranean tortoise, a highly endangered species. There's a fascinating audiovisual account of the birth and development of the Albera tortoises.

Espolla
7 miles (11 km) NW of Garigella on the G1603
Tortoises prepare for freedom
At Espolla you'll find the information centre for the Albera nature conservation area (Amadeu Sudrià 3, (☎ 972 54 50 79; open Mon.-Fri. 8am-3pm, Sat.-Sun. 10am-1pm and 4-6pm in summer, and Mon.-Fri. 8.30am-2pm, Sat.-Sun. 3-5.30pm in winter).
Nearby are the terrariums

where the healthy tortoises are kept after they leave the reproduction centre. When they are three years old they are released back into the wild to live in their natural environment, in the scrubland under the cork trees of the Albera.

Spotcheck
F2

What to do
• Prehistoric stone trails

With children
• Tortoise sanctuary and terrariums

Within easy reach
Sant Pere de Rodes (15.5 miles/25 km SE), pp. 138-139
Figueras (12.5 miles/ 20 km S) pp. 138-139
Cape Creus (28 miles/ 45 km E) pp. 140-141

Information
Albera nature-conservation area information centre:
☎ 972 54 50 79

Prehistoric stones

This area is full of prehistoric stones: there are 115 dolmens and 15 menhirs, all properly accounted for and linked by a number of paths. Dolmens are

particularly abundant around Els Estanys, a lagoon that is also a refuge for birds. To see the stones properly, it is best to get a map from the information centre at Espolla, which also organises enjoyable half-day tours.

Sant Climent Secebes
2 miles (3 km)
S of Espolla
Requesens castle
To visit, telephone in advance:
☎ 972 19 30 81.
Admission charge.
This is a good destination if you're planning a walk. At Vilatolí de Dalt, 1 mile (2 km) from Sant Climent, an unpaved, 5-mile (8-km) track

leads to this fortress. It was built in the 11thC., and much restored at the end of the 19thC. by the Peralada family. It was the scene of fierce fighting between the Counts of Empúries and the Counts of Rosselló. If this walk is too long for you, there's a shorter route from Castellops, which leads past the little dolmen at the Medàs pass.

Port-Bou

This frontier post beside the sea is where the German-Jewish philosopher Walter Benjamin killed himself in 1940. He was attempting to flee the Nazi occupation of France, but he was convinced he had been betrayed by his guide and he took his own life. There's a monument to him at the entrance to the municipal cemetery, standing on a hill with the sea as a backdrop.

GOING INTO EXILE
The Grup d'Acció leader Salinas Bassegoda (☎ 972 53 51 52) offers you an unusual kind of pilgrimage. For 12,800 ptas (two days half-board) you can follow the routes taken by the Spanish republicans to escape the Franco regime at the end of the Spanish Civil War (1936-1939). In 1938 the Spanish republican government had been forced to retreat from Madrid to Barcelona, and then had to move again, to Figueras, in January 1939. After the nationalists took Barcelona in February, those still opposed to Franco fled to Nazi-occupied France.

Núria valley
family skiing

On the southern slopes of the eastern Pyrenees, among mountain peaks that are more than 9,000 ft (3,000 m) in height, the Núria valley offers the most entrancing scenery. In the past, devout pilgrims would climb on foot up to the sanctuary of the Virgin of Núria. Nowadays the valley is a nature park, and it's families that climb the hills, carrying their skis, or riding on the cog-rail train. Nature, however, still reigns supreme, despite the inevitable effects of the increase in tourism.

LA CABANA
DELS PASTORS
RESTAURANT

Ribes de Freser

8.5 miles (14 km)
N of Ripoll on the N152
Get ready for the off

The train to Núria leaves from this little village. Before you depart, however, visit the **Can Rueda** (Balandrau 1, ☎ 972 72 72 09; open 9am-1.30pm and 5-8pm) and buy some outstanding local farmhouse pâté, known as *pa de fetgfe* (900 ptas for 2.2 lb/ 1 kg) or some white 'bull', a sort of black pudding made with pig's tongue (1,000 ptas for 2.2 lb/1 kg). If you are here in September (on the first

Cog-rail train

☎ **972 73 20 44**
Every hour 8.15am-5.15pm, stops at Ribes-Vila, Queralbs and Núria.
Return journey: adults 2,150 ptas, children 1,175 ptas.
Situated on the Barcelona-Puigcerdà line, Ribes is where you change for Núria. From there, the cog-rail train takes you effortlessly through spectacular countryside to the top. The *cremallera* takes 43 minutes to travel 8 miles (12.5 km) across viaducts and tunnels, waterfalls and cliffs, climbing 3,000 ft (nearly 1,000 m) along the way. It's an extraordinary journey. Watch out if you suffer from vertigo!

Queralbs

4.5 miles (7 km)
N of Ribes de Freser
A real mountain village

You can get there by train or car, on a tarmac road with hairpin bends for 4.5 miles (7 km). The charming Romanesque church of **Sant Jaume** (13thC.) has a fine marble portico and sculpted column-capitals, which, by themselves, would make this picturesque mountain village worth a visit.

Sunday of the month) you can attend the **sheepdog trials** (Concurso de Habilidad con Gos d'Atura) and watch the dogs round up the sheep in record time.

RIPOLL

This is where Catalonia originated. In the Romanesque monastery (12thC.) lies Guifré el Pilós (Wilfred the Hairy), founder of the Barcelona dynasty. The Santa Maria west gate, last remnant of the original monastery, is a wonderful example of Catalan Romanesque sculpture. Ripoll also attracts food-lovers as it's here you can try *caricias* – boat-shaped pastries made of almonds and sugar (Can Junyent, Sant Pere 14, ☎ 972 70 07 66; open 8am-8pm).

Núria
5 miles (8 km)
N of Queralbs

Sanctuary

To reach the sanctury, either take the cog-rail train or climb straight up on foot – though it's a bit of a clamber. At the top, you'll find this peaceful place, built in 1883 on the site of an 11th-C. hermitage. For

centuries, shepherds and other locals have come here to pray to the Virgin of Núria, the patron saint of shepherds of the Pyrenees.

Vall de Núria

Between 6,400 and 7,400 ft (1,950-2,250 m), the ski slopes of the Vall de Núria, including beginners' slopes, are ideal for families. From the sanctuary, a cable car will take you to the inn at the summit of the Aliga, from where there is an outstanding view of the valley. On the plateau you'll find all the usual ski-resort amenities, including hotels, restaurants, shops and ski lifts.

Mountain of beauty

Whether you want to relax, get involved in sporting activities or enjoy the night-life, the Núria valley has it all, though this means that this beautiful area has become a bit of a tourist park. There's archery (1,500 ptas an hour), rowing on the lake (800 ptas an hour), horse-riding (3,000 ptas for 90 minutes), trips to Puigmal (9,600 ft/ 2,914 m), a children's play

Spotcheck
D2-E2

Things to do

• Trips on foot or horseback
• Archery
• Rowing
• Try the local savoury delicacies

With children

• Cog-rail train

Within easy reach

Cerdagne (18.5 miles/ 30 km W of Ribes) pp. 186-187
Vic (20 miles/32 km S of Ripoll) pp. 208-209
Garroxta (25 miles/40 km E of Ripoll) pp. 198-201

Tourist office
Ripoll: ☎ 972 70 23 51

area and a picnic area. You can also enjoy lovely walks around the edge of vertiginous chasms. The choice is yours.

Cami valley

The Cami Vell is a good route back down to the pretty stone village of Queralbs. The road follows the course of the Núria and you pass two spectacular waterfalls: the Salt de la Cua de Cavall and the Salt del Sastre. On either side, you'll be treated to spectacular views over the glacial valleys of Fontnegra and Fontalba. The river cuts its way among impressively wild rock formations, such as the Totlomón.

Cerdagne
garden of the Pyrenees

The Cerdagne valley ('Cerdanya' in Spanish), crossed by the River Segre that rises in France, is an open and gentle space in the heart of the Pyrenees, between the high mountains of Cadí and Andorra. Its warm, dry air makes it a favourite holiday destination.

Llívia

Medieval pharmacy
Dels Forns 10
☎ 972 89 63 13
Open Apr.-Sept.
10am-1pm and 3-7pm,
Sun. 10am-2pm;
rest of the year
10am-1pm and 3-6pm,
Sun. 10am-2pm.
Admission charge.
Llívia is a tiny part of Spain entirely surrounded by French territory. The most interesting thing in the town is the 15th-C. **Esteva pharmacy**, the oldest pharmacy in Europe, now a museum housing ancient clay pots and apothecary's instruments. In addition, you can find out about the **local plant life** from dioramas projected onto the nearby Berna de Sot tower.

Puigcerdà
4.5 miles (7 km)
NW of Llívià
A little taste of yesteryear
On its terrace overlooking the Segre river, Puigcerdà has become one of the most

popular tourist destinations in the Pyrenees. You can take a boat trip on the lake, floating among the birds and weeping willows. On the last Sunday in August, the vibrant **lake festival** (Festa de l'Estany) enlivens the peaceful shores,

concluding with a grand and colourful firework display. It would be a shame to miss it.

Cerdagne panoramic viewpoint
Although Puigcerdà is surrounded by mountains up to 10,000 ft (3,000 m) high, at just 4,000 ft (1,200 m) it still dominates the valley and, from the Ayuntamiento, you will discover a **unique view** of the verdant land of the Cerdagne. While you're there, try the **goose with turnips** and the famous **Puigcerdà pears**. It's a popular resort in winter.

Acrobatics on ice
Puigcerdà was the first town in Spain to take up winter sports and is very well equipped. Try its skating rink, which has hosted ice-hockey competitions since 1958 (☎ 972 88 02 43; open Mon., Tues. and Fri. 6-8pm, Sat. 5-9pm, Sun. noon-2pm and 4-8pm; closed Aug.-Oct.; adults 850 ptas, children 750 ptas).

Cerdagne hot-air ballooning
Globus dels Pirineus
Alp airport
6 miles (10 km)
S of Puigcerdà
☎ 972 14 08 52
Lift-off 7am or 8am;
lasts a half-day.
20,000 ptas per person, four or more people 18,000 ptas each.
A **hot-air balloon ride** is an unforgettable experience.

MARKETS AND SUMMER FESTIVALS IN THE VALLEY

The Cerdagne has lots of colourful markets selling excellent local produce, notably on Monday in Martinet, Thursday in Alp, Bellver and Oceja, Saturday in Llívià and Sunday in Puigcerdà. August is the month for festivals: a music festival at Llívià, the week-long 'Fiesta del Tourista' at Martinet, a handicrafts market at the 'Feria de Sant Llorenc' at Bellver, and a gathering of accordionists at Alp on 23 August. Details available from the regional tourist office, ☎ 972 14 06 65.

The flight lasts 75 minutes, but allow the whole morning because the balloon has to be prepared beforehand and you'll have lunch when you land.

Bellver de Cerdanya

12.5 miles (20 km) SW of Puigcerdà on the N260

Picturesque buildings and fine food

Bellver de Cerdanya is worth visiting for its porticoed square, the Santa Maria de Talló church (12thC.), and the pretty Romanesque church, Santa

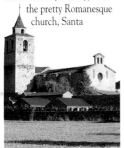

Eugènia de Nerellà, with its Pisa-style leaning bell-tower. Don't miss the **Tupí de Cerdanya** delicatessen, a real Aladdin's cave for the gourmet, selling mushroom pâté, cheeses, conserves, oils, vinegars and fruits preserved in alcohol. There's also a garden with aromatic plants

(Plaza Born, ☎ 972 51 04 94; open 10am-2pm and 4-8pm exc. Sun. Apr.-May and Mon.).

Martinet

5.5 miles (9 km) W of Bellver on the N260

Unforgettable flavours

The **Four Jordi** bakery makes proper rural bread, as well as

madeleines and *cocas* with diced bacon (Segre 57, ☎ 972 51 50 31; closed Wed.). The **Can Boix** restaurant serves excellent local cuisine, including *trinxat con rosta* (cabbage and potatoes minced with bacon), *platillo ceretà* (mutton with beans and wine), or Segre trout with almonds (km 204.5 on N260, ☎ 972 51 50 50;

closed Wed. in winter; taster menu 4,900 ptas).

Lles

6 miles (10 km) N of Martinet

Fun at the top

From Martinet, a twisting road will take you up to the ski resort of Lles. Here in summer, you can hike to the Pera lakes (7,500 ft/2,300 m). Or you can learn to kayak at one of the valley's many water-sports schools. Try Ribals Aventura i Esports, Routre de Lles, km 1, ☎ 972 51 52 14 (beginner's course costs 7,000 ptas, including lunch).

La Seu d'Urgell
the prince-bishop's land

etween Andorra and the Cerdagne, at the meeting of the Segre and Valira rivers, lies the pretty town of La Seu d'Urgell. Its bishop is, together with the president of France, co-ruler of Andorra. Its most popular saints control the weather: Sant Ermengol is the patron saint of rain, Sant Ol is for sunshine. In such good company you're sure have fun, whether you prefer outdoor pursuits or a spot of culture indoors.

La Seu d'Urgell
Romanesque tour

Santa Maria cathedral and the neighbouring cloister (open 10am-1pm and 4-7pm in summer, noon-1pm weekdays in winter) are fine examples

of Catalan Romanesque, with their wonderful sculpted decor. Don't miss the capitals in the cloister, carved with bizarre human and animal heads. Next to the cloister, Sant Miguel church (11thC.) is the oldest building in the town. Every year (end July-beginning Aug.) there's a dramatic recreation in living form of the **retable of Saint Ermengol**, one of the town's patron saints. The diocesan museum (open 10am-1pm and 4-6pm Mon.-Fri. July-Sept., noon-1pm in winter) is worth a visit for its 11th-C. illuminated manuscript, the *Beatus*.

Testing the Olympic waters
Parc Olympique del Segre
☎ 973 36 00 92
Rafting:
4,400 ptas an hour;
Kayaking:
1,300 ptas an hour;
Rowing:
1,300 ptas an hour;
Mountain biking:
800 ptas an hour,
1,600 ptas half-day.
This park was originally built for the 1992 Olympic Games, and has hosted canoeing championships. You can test your abilities on calm or wild water, according to your preference and your skill. You can also go mountain biking, roller skating and ballooning.

Fresh mountain produce
Sociedad Cooperativa Cadí
Sant Ermengo l 37
☎ 973 35 00 25
Open 8.30am-1pm.
After watching an interesting video on cattle breeding, you can visit the shop, which is full of delicious goodies such as super-fresh butter (185 ptas for 4.5 oz/125 g), all different

MAGIC MOUNTAIN
At Organyà Mount Cogulló rises up, offering the ideal spot for hang-gliding. Orgunyà Turístic (Casa de la Vila, ☎ 973 38 22 08; organises flights for beginners. The package includes a flight in a two-person glider, a horse-ride or a trip on the river rapids, a visiting to the village and half-board at the hotel (10,000-12,000 ptas for the weekend). You can also travel the dolmen trail on foot or by mountain-bike (17 miles/27 km of mountain road, looping from Organyà to Cabó and Favà then back to Organyà; allow 1 day for trip). It's a great place for sports enthusiasts.

Ruta dels Dólmens

kinds of cheese (around 1,400 ptas for 2.2 lb/1 kg) and fromage blanc (white cheese) (180 ptas for 2.2 lb/1 kg). Continue your gastronomic tour with a visit to the **Fonda Andria** (Joan Brudieu 24, ☎ 973 35 03 00) for a taste of the oxtail with mushrooms or boar stew or even the unmissable local quince pâté with cheese.

Castellbò

5.5 miles (9 km) W of La Seu d'Urgell, La Beseta road
Cathars
The Cathars were known as the 'perfect ones', but were considered heretics by the Catholic Church and hunted down. They believed that earthly pleasures were evil and lived very austere lives. Their beliefs were popular in Lombardy, in southern France and in Catalonia. Every year, on the second weekend in August, at Castelbò, the Cathars who took refuge in the Urgell highlands are commemorated with a variety of lectures, seminars, concerts, dances and spectacles in the ruins of the old priory of Santa Maria de Costoja.

Arsèguel

8 miles (13 km) E of La Seu d'Urgell on the N260
The sounds of the accordion
Every year on the first Saturday in July all the accordionists of the Pyrenees gather at Arsèguel, known as the accordion capital of Catalonia. There's even an **accordion museum** (Pl. del Castellot, ☎ 973 38 40 87). If that doesn't appeal to you, you can take a visit to the Isern family's **wool workshop** (☎ 973 38 40 09; open 9am-2pm and 4-7pm; admission charge), where you can stock up on everything from socks (200 ptas) to blankets (6,000 ptas) to keep warm on those chilly winter nights.

Coll de Nargó

16 miles (26 km) S of La Seu d'Urgell on the N260
Lumberjacks
The *raiers* were lumberjacks who made the felled trees into temporary rafts, to sail down

the Segre river to the sawmills. The last such journey took place in 1932, but this village has a fascinating museum dedicated to the raiers (located in the old church of the Rosary, ☎ 973 38 30 48; visit by appointment). On the third Sunday in August, during the local fiesta, two raiers recreate the old traditions of the industry and the crowds enjoy the spectacle from the banks of the river.

Noguera Pallaresa
Water sports heaven

Alós d'Isil
València d'Àneu
Isil
Esterri d'Àneu
Son del Pino
Espot
Escaló
Llavorsí
Rialp
Sort
Défilé de Collegats

U pstream from Escaló is the Noguera Pallaresa area, including 31 miles (50 km) of wild water that has been a magnet for lovers of sports such as kayaking and rafting for the last decade. This has been a goldmine for the local tourist trade, which previously relied solely on the winter snow of Pallars Sobirà, where you find Super Espot, a renowned ski resort.

Esterri d'Àneu
9.5 miles (15 km) N of Escaló on the C147
A village for gourmets

Upstream from Esterri d'Àneu, the waters of the Noguera Pallaresa get wilder, so build up your strength by trying the local specialities. In the **Tienda Can Teixidó** (Major 19, ☎ 973 62 63 86; open Mon.-Sat. 9am-2pm and 5-8pm, Sun. 10am-2pm), stock up on cold meats: *secallona* (dry sausage; 2,300 ptas for 2.2 lb/1 kg), *xorís* (flat sausage; 2,500 ptas for 2.2 lb/1 kg) or pâté (850 ptas for 2.2 lb/1 kg). If you can stomach a meal before the white water, the **Restaurante**

Bonabé (Carrer del Esports, ☎ 973 62 62 03; open daily exc. Mon.) offers a good selection of local recipes.

Vall d'Àneu museum of regional life and industry
Open daily 10am-2pm and 5-8pm.
Admission charge.
This museum extends over five sites. The original museum is at Esterri d'Àneu (Rue Arnau, ☎ 973 62 64 36) and has an exhibition of local life at the beginning of the 20thC. Then there's the **Àneu sawmill** outside Alós d'Isil (9.5 miles/15 km N of Esterri), the Romanesque church of **Sant Just i Sant Pastor** at Son del Pino (2.5 miles/4 km W of Esterri, via València d'Àneu), the **Espot hydroelectric power station**

(7.5 miles/12 km S of Esterri) and the **Sant Pere de Burgal monastery** (12thC.) at Escaló.

....

Isil

*5 miles (8 km)
N of Esterri on the C147*
Saint-John's fires

At Isil, as in most of the villages of the Pallars, the summer solstice is celebrated with great gusto. The festival takes place on the night of the feast day of Saint-John (23-24 July). Down from the mountain come 50 *fallaires* with their lighted torches (*falles*). At around 2am, they form a procession into Isil, where girls offer them bunches of wild flowers, pancakes and wine, then the torches themselves are burnt on a huge bonfire in the village square.

....

Llavorsí

*11 miles (18 km)
S of Esterri on the C147*
Wild water champions

There are 8.5 miles (14 km) of white water that separate Llavorsí from Rialp, and this is where most visitors end up, especially those who want to experience white-water rafting. You can also take a trip on a kayak, speedboat or water-bob. From 19 to 25 July the Rally Turístico Internacional del Río Noguera Pallaresa organises

kayaking and rafting competitions (information: ☎ 973 62 00 10).

For amateurs
☎ 973 62 10 02
Activities mid-Apr. to end Oct.

The Pallars adventure-sports association (Asociación de Empresas de Deportes de Aventura del Pallars Sobirà) offers a wide range of activities. You can make the famous descent from Llavorsí to Rialp by raft (4,000 ptas per person) – though children can only go halfway as it gets too difficult for them. For true sports lovers, there are multi-sport weekends on offer.

....

Sort

*2.5 miles (4 km)
S of Rialp on the C147*
Local '*tupi*' cheese
Coopérative Formatges Tros de Sort
Ch. De Vernedes
☎ 973 62 13 87
Open daily 8am-2pm and 4-6pm (by appointment).

The Sort *tupi* is a sheep's milk cheese preserved in local brandy. This local co-operative will tell you all about this and other local cheeses such as *tou roi*, a cow's milk cheese somewhere between a Camembert and a Munster (700 ptas for about 1 lb/500 g).

COLLEGATS GORGE
18.5 miles (30 km) S of Sort on the N260
This narrow gorge, cut in the limestone rocks by the waters of the Noguera, is one of the most impressive in Catalonia, with spectacular views of the red and ochre cliffs tumbling towards the waters below. From the Les Morreres car park, a little road leads to the ruins of the Sant Pere de les Maleses convent (6 miles/10 km round-trip).

Aigüestortes y Estany de Sant Maurici national park
born under a water sign

This, the only national park in Catalonia, is on the northern edge of the province of Lleida. It takes its name from its two outstanding features: the natural labyrinth of Aigüestortes in the southwest and the Sant Maurici lake in the northeast. The park is the largest glacial zone in Europe.

National park

Entry: via Caldes de Boí in the east, Espot in the west. Car park and information point at each entrance (open 9am-2pm and 4-6.30pm June-Sept.).

Within an area of 35,000 acres (14,000 ha), this park preserves some of the most beautiful landscapes in the Pyrenees: glacial lakes, a river and waterfalls, horseshoe valleys and peaks close to 10,000 ft (3,000 m). Wild lilies and rhododendron adorn the undergrowth, while beavers and otters play by the water. Entry to the park is free, but cars are not allowed. A rough-country taxi takes visitors from Espot to the Sant Maurici lake and from Caldes de Boí to Aigüestortes.

Boí valley

This is a good destination for a short expedition, with its mountainous landscapes and its 11th and 12thC. churches. The elegant simplicity of the bell-towers is typical of the

Sant Climent church, Taüll

first phase of Catalan Romanesque art. The church of **Santa Eulalia**, at Erill la Vall, has the best Lombard-style tower in the region. **Sant Climent** and **Santa Maria** at Taüll are also worth seeing. The murals that once decorated the interiors of these two churches can now be found in the Catalan art museum in Barcelona.

Organising your stay

Go to the **National park house** at Boí (Pl. Treió,

☎ 973 69 61 89; open 9am-1pm and 3.30-7pm), to gather information and route suggestions. The park has four refuges. The most athletic visitors may want to try something adventurous, like descending a ravine for a horseback ride in the valley, or taking a four-wheel drive trip and ravine descent with a guide (8,500 ptas a day). Information from the Patronato Vall de Boí, ☎ 973 69 40 40.

Caldes de Boí

This village has been known for its **hot springs** since Roman times. About 4,500 ft (nearly 1,500 m) up, it has 37 springs, renowned for their medicinal virtues, and 4 naturally warm baths. There are two hotels for those who want to take the waters, but you can also stroll in the gardens and visit the springs, which are not far from the River Noguera de Tort.

Caldes de Boí, Isard fountain

Excursion to Aigüestortes

Three-hour round-trip.
The path follows **Nicolau brook**, between Boí and Caldes de Boí. It's a relatively easy walk, and quite suitable for all the family. The first stopping-point in the park is **Llebreta lake**, at an altitude of 5,300 ft (1,617 m). Further on, you pass the **Toll d'en Mas waterfalls**, before reaching the **Aigüestortes plateau** (6,000 ft/ 1,850 m), a maze of brooks,

mountain streams and bogs (Aigüestortes literally means 'twisting waters'). If you want to continue, it will take four hours to reach **Sant Maurici lake**, by way of Llong lake and the Portarró d'Espot, from where there is a splendid view over Aigüestortes. Some of the finest scenery is around the lake.

....

Espot
12.5 miles (20 km)
E of Caldes de Boí
Espot valley
The mountain village of Espot on the eastern edge of the park stands at an altitude of 4,200 ft (1,320 m), north of the ski station of Super Espot. There is an **information centre** here too (Prat de la Guàrdia 4, ☎ 973 62 40 36; open 9am-1pm and 3.30-7pm in summer, 9am-2pm and 3.30-6pm exc. Sun. Apr.-May and public holidays in winter). Before you set off on the 3-mile (4.5-km) tarmac road that leads to the park, build up your energy at the **Casa Palmira** (☎ 973 62 40 72) – the menu includes onion soup, rabbit with prunes and Catalan cream (1,350 ptas).

ENCHANTED PEAKS

A crown of mountains is reflected in the icy-cold glacial waters of the Sant Maurici lake – in particular, the twin peaks of the Sierra dels Encantats ('enchanted ones'), the symbol of the park, which reach 9,012 ft (2,747 m). The story goes that they are really two men who were turned into mountains because they preferred to go hunting instead of attending Sunday mass. How cruel the ancient gods could be!

Spotcheck
B2-C2

Things to do
• Boí valley Romanesque churches
• Walking expeditions in the park

Within easy reach
Arán valley (37 miles/ 60 km NW of Espot) pp. 194-195
Noguera Parallesa E of Espot pp. 190-191

Tourist office
Espot: ☎ 973 62 40 36

Sant Maurici trail
From the car park, it takes about an hour to climb to **Sant Maurici lake** (6,200 ft/ 1,900 m). From there, it's 90 minutes to the **Atmiges refuge** (☎ 973 25 01 09; open 1 June-3 Sept.; 80 places), on the banks of the lake of the same name. Returning back down towards the south you'll reach the **Negre lake** (4 hours round-trip from Sant Maurici), the largest lake in the park. The summits of Muntanyó (9,520 ft/2,903 m) and Ereixe (8,734 ft/2,663 m) are reflected in its dark waters. Nearby is the **Josep Maria Blanc refuge** (☎ 973 25 01 08; open 1 June-3 Sept.), with 30 beds for weary walkers.

River Garonne in the Arán valley

a little bit of France in Spain

Les
Bòssost
Beret
Vielha
Salardú
Báqueira
Artíes
Tredòs
Pic Montarto

T he River
Garonne begins its
long journey towards
the French Atlantic coast in the
Aran valley and, indeed, the river is the only natural exit from the valley.
Because it was isolated for centuries, the valley has preserved its language
(Aranais, related to Occitan) and its customs. This country of majestic
mountains, forests and pastures receives a lot of snow, which makes it a
favourite haunt of skiers and trekkers.

Les

*15.5 miles (25 km)
NW of Vielha
on the N230*
Festivities
With its Roman and 19th-C.
baths, Les has a proud past,
but today this town is known
for a beautiful traditional
celebration – the **burning of
Eth Haro**. On the feast of
Saint Peter (29 June),
a pine trunk is placed in
the church square and
left there all year
until it is burnt
on the following
Saint John's
day (23 June).
The celebrations
include bonfires,
firecrackers,
fireworks and
dancing.

Bòssost

*6 miles (10 km)
S of Les on the N230*
A Gascon village
With its promenade, edged
with plane and lime trees,
and a dialect resembling
that of southern France,
Bòssost seems like a
little bit of Gascony.
Indeed, the village is
linked to France by
a winding road to
Bagnères-de-
Luchon via the
Bòssost gateway
(7,345 ft/
2,239 m).
Don't miss
the 12th-C.
Romanesque
church Era
Assumpcion
de Maria.

Vielha

**Capital of the
Arán valley**
Located in the old part of
town, don't miss the **San
Miqèu** church (12th-13thC.),
with its fine barrel-vaulted
nave and famous wooden bust
of the Christ of Mijaran.
The **musèu dera Vall d'Arán**
teaches visitors about the
history and culture of the
valley, as well as the geology
of the Pyrenees (Major 26,
☎ 973 64 18 15; open Tues.-
Sat. 10am-1pm and 5-8pm,
Sun. 10am-1pm in summer;
Tues.-Sat. Apr.-May, Sun.
10am-1pm in winter;
admission charge). At
Vilamòs, you can visit the
Casa Joanchiquet, a 19th-C.
Aranais house, which reveals
the history of local life.

For the athletic

Palacio de Hierro
Avenida de Garona 33
☎ 973 64 28 64.
Swimming pool:
weekdays 8am-9.30pm,
Sun. and public holidays
11am-9pm.
Skating rink:
weekdays 5.30-8.30pm,
Sun. and public holidays
noon-2pm and 4.30-9pm.
Admission charge.
The Palacio de Hierro is a vast
sports complex, with an ice
rink, two heated swimming
pools, a solarium, gymnasium,
sauna, massages and a bar.
Organised activity weekends
include rafting, skating and
ravine descents.

Artíes

4 miles (6.5 km)
E of Vielha on the C142
Hill-walks
and a local
tipple

This typical
local village,
with its stone
houses and
Romanesque
church, is not
far from
Montarto peak
(9,300 ft/
2,830 m), a
hill-walkers'

Miel de flores,
El Valle de Arán
Miel de fleurs,
Le Val d'Aran

PILGRIMAGE TO MONTGARRI
In the Plat de Beret
plains, to the north
of Báqueira, the
sanctuary of
Montgarri welcomes
pilgrims every year on
2 July. It's a famous
pilgrimage that
recalls ancient times
when villagers and
shepherds taking
their sheep up into
the meadows to graze
went to the sanctuary
to say their prayers.

favourite. There's an easy
6-mile (10-km) walk to the
Colomers ring of mountains.
While you're here, visit the
Tienda Juanxto for its local
delicacies: pâtés, honey,
blueberry liqueur and, above
all, *aigua de nodes*, a walnut-
based alcohol (Centra
Comarcal 142, 7A,
☎ 973 64 45 24; open
daily 9.30am-2pm and
5-9pm; closed Sun.
in winter). A drop of
aigua de nodes will
keep you warm on
your walks.

Aranais cooking
Restaurant Urtau
Plaza Artau 2
☎ 973 64 09 26
*3,000-3,500 ptas
per head.*
Artíes is famous for its
delicious regional cuisine and
you should certainly try the
game dishes (partridge, boar)
served at this restaurant.

Salardú

2.5 miles (4 km)
E of Artíes on the C142
Capital of the
upper Arán

Lying at the entrance to the
valley, coming from the La
Bonaigua gateway, Salardú is

Spotcheck
B1

Things to do
- Arán valley walks
- Skiing at Báqueira-Beret
- Musèu dera Vall d'Arán

With children
- Swimming and ice skating
- Burning of Eth Haro festival

Within easy reach
Noguera Parallesa
(37 miles/60 km SE of
Vielha). p. 190-191

Tourist office
Vielha:
☎ 973 64 09 79

an old fortified town, with
houses of stone and shale.
The Sant Andreu church
contains a fine Romanesque
sculpture, the **Majestat de
Salardú** (12thC.).

Báqueira-Beret

4.5 miles (7 km)
E of Salardú on the C142
Finally, snow

Once Báqueira and Beret
were two distinct villages, but
now they have joined together
to become one of the most
popular winter sports resorts in
Spain, a favourite of the
Spanish royal family.

Monumental Gerona

Those who live in Gerona may have the highest quality of life in Spain, but they choose to be discreet about it. Viewed from the outside, the city is like a sleeping beauty, slowly waking up to modern life but without turning its back on its glorious past. The old quarter, on the right bank of the River Onya, is absolutely marvellous. The chief town of northern Catalonia, Gerona is compact, a joy to walk around and full of charming surprises.

'City of a thousand sieges'

Roman 'Gerunda' became 'Djerunda' when the Moors occupied it in the 8thC., before the Franks recovered it under Charlemagne and made it a resolutely Christian city. Gerona has earned its nickname – 'city of a thousand sieges' – having been besieged 13 times between 1295 and 1809. Later, it was given the title of 'three times immortal' for having resisted Napoleon's troops on three occasions.

Eiffel bridge

The city is something of a record-breaker – 4 rivers converge here and it has 11 bridges. One of them is the work of the Gustave-Eiffel company, before they built the famous tower in Paris. The Peixateries Velles' bridge spans the Onya and ends on the Rambla de la Llibertat, one of the city's main shopping streets.

Catholic Gerona
Cathedral and museum
☎ 972 21 44 26
Museum open 10am-8pm exc. Sun. Apr.-May and Mon. in summer, 10am-2pm and 4-7pm in winter.
Admission charge for the museum.

Religious buildings dominate the old quarter of Gerona. First of all there is the cathedral, which overlooks the city from the top of a long flight of steps. Inside you'll find one of the most spacious of all European Gothic naves. The cathedral museum, accessible at one side of the building, contains great masterpieces of religious art, including the beautiful tapestry of the creation, an 11th-C. embroidery which colourfully retells the history of the world.

Sant Pere de Galligants monastery
☎ 972 20 26 32
Same opening hμours at the cathedral museum. *Admission charge.*
This former Benedictine monastery, a masterpiece of Romanesque art (12thC.), now houses the archaeological museum containing, among other exhibits, gravestones which were found in the old Jewish cemetery. It also houses a Roman grave, uncovered at the excavations at Empúries (*see* p. 144-145).

QUART'S TRADITIONAL POTTERY

This village, some 3 miles (5 km) from Gerona, still produces ceramics according to a tradition dating back to the 16thC. The pottery is mostly black, with very simple decoration. You can also find classic green pottery. In the Bonadona workshop (Carretera de Gerona 125, ☎ 972 46 90 02; open Mon.-Fri. 8am-1pm and 3-8pm), you can buy some fine pieces for your home: jugs (from 700 ptas), pots (from 3,500 ptas) and jars (1,500 ptas). The ceramics make lovely gifts to take home.

very popular in the Middle Ages. They were closed in the 15thC. and turned into a convent. Now visitors can see them restored to their original form as an authentic medieval bathhouse.

The Jewish quarter

The narrow De La Força street leads to the former Jewish quarter, built in the Middle Ages. This maze of lanes, alleys and tiny squares is one of the best-preserved medieval sites in Europe. In the 13thC., there was a famous cabalistic school here. You can visit the Centro Bonastruc ça Porta, with its **museum of Catalan Jewish history** (Sant Llorenç, ☎ 972 21 67 61; open in summer Mon.-Sast. 10am-8pm, Sun. 10am-3pm; admission charge).

Moorish bathhouse

Els Banys Arabs de Gerona
Del Sac 4-5
☎ 972 21 32 62
Open Mon.-Sat. 10am-7pm, Apr.-Sept., until 2pm, Oct.-Mar.; all year Sun. 10am-2pm.
Admission charge.
This is a recreation of the 12th-C. Muslim baths,

Spotcheck
E3-F3

Things to do

• Visit the old town
• Bonadona pottery workshop
• Cinema museum

Within easy reach

*Empordanet region (12.5 miles/20 km SE), p. 148-151
Palamós (22.5 miles/ 36 km SE), p. 152-153
Sant Feliu de Guíxols (20.5 miles/33 km SE), p. 154-155
Figueras (25 miles/40 km N), p. 138-139*

Tourist office

Gerona: ☎ 972 22 65 75

Cinema museum

Sèquia 1
☎ 972 41 27 77
Open daily 10am-8pm in summer; Tues.-Fri. 10am-6pm, Sat. 10am-8pm, Sun. 11am-3pm in winter. Closed Mon. all year.
Admission charge.
Back to the 20thC., with this museum of the early days of cinema. Among the 30,000 objects in the former Tomàs Mallol collection you can see the projector used by the Lumière brothers when they first showed a moving picture in public, and a 30-ft (9-m) film in which each frame is individually coloured.

Garrotxa volcanoes and the surrounding area

The Zona Volcánica de la Garrotxa nature park gives you a fascinating insight into the former volcanic activity on the Iberian peninsula. Some 30 cones, a number of now extinct craters and about 20 basalt lava flows make up this unique landscape. The gentleness of the climate, the variety of vegetation, especially in the Fageda d'en Jordà nature reserve, and the picturesque villages nearby make this a pleasant place to explore.

Besalú

14.5 miles (23 km) SW of Figueras on the N260

Gateway to the volcanic zone

With its small sloping streets and tile-roofed houses, the former capital of the County of Besalú is a picturesque village on the road that leads to the volcanic zone. From its medieval origins it has preserved a splendid old town centre, reached from a **fortified bridge** (11thC.), which spans the Fluvià river.

The old village centre

The historic heart of the village is hidden behind the remains of the ramparts. Right by the river you'll find the old Jewish

quarter, with the **Mikwa**, a building which was dedicated to ablutions and purificatory ritual bathing. Just off the main square the church of **Sant Viçenc**, with its mixture of Romanesque and Gothic styles, has extremely fine sculptures, especially on the doors and capitals. The remains of the church of **Santa Maria** (12th C.) are located at the top of the hill. **Sant Pere** church is a masterpiece of Romanesque art, decorated with lions and floral motifs sculpted in relief around the frontage.

Castellfollit de la Roca

8.5 miles (14 km) W of Besalú on the N260

A lofty village

On the edge of the volcanic zone, this village is built on a rocky spur, a former volcanic flow, some 200 ft (60 m) above the river. The old church stands on the edge of the cliff. A little **butchers' museum** shows how sausages are made and contains a collection of traditional tools and old machinery (Carretera Gerona 10, ☎ 972 29 44 63). When you visit you can finish by sampling the wares and, if

you want to stock up, there's a **market** every Saturday in the Plaza Major.

Olot

5 miles (8 km) W of Castellfollit on the N260

The capital of Garrotxa

At Olot you enter a land of sleeping volcanoes. The town itself contains four craters within its urban limits: Biseroques, Garrinada, Montolivet and Montsacopa. From its heights, the latter, at just over 300 ft (94 m), provides a magnificent panorama over Olot and the volcanic zone. At the top is the former Sant Francesc de Paula hermitage (17thC.). This was turned into a fortress by Napoleon's troops, who added two defensive towers.

Casa Gaietà Vila, Olot

El Firal

This is the very heart of the town, a tree-lined walk where the inhabitants go at the end of the day to stroll and take the air. The place is very lively on Monday, which is **market** day. Take a look at Olot's two Modernist buildings, the

Casa Gaietà Vila and the Casa Solà Morales, designed by the architect Domènech y Montaner and ornamented with frescoes and sculptures by Eusebio Arnau.

Casa Solà Morales, Olot

A great school of landscape painting

At Olot, because of the splendour of the countryside, landscape painting is king of the arts. The town is famous

for its painting school founded at the end of the 19thC. by the painter Joaquim Vayreda (1843-1894), who was much influenced by the French-Barbazon school, which insisted on the importance of open-air landscape painting. The Olot school attracted painters from all over Catalonia, and there's a vast collection of their work in the **Museo Comarcal de la Garrotxa** (Hospici 8, ☎ 972 27 91 30; open daily 11am-2pm and 4-7pm; admission charge).

Volcanic park information centre

Parc Nou
☎972 26 62 02
Open 10am-2pm and 5-7pm July-Sept. and 4-6pm Oct.-June
The information centre for the Zona Volcánica de la Garrotxa nature park is located in the En Castanys tower, an Italian-style building built in the 19thC. There you'll find all the information you need to prepare for your visit: services available, itineraries, road conditions, weather forecasts. In the basement the **Museo de los Volcanes** contains a geological collection (☎ 972 26 67 62; same opening hours as the information centre; closed

Sun. Apr.-May and Mar.; admission charge).

Volcanic zone
3.5 miles (6 km)
E of Olot on the G1524 towards Banyoles
Fageda d'en Jordà
A beech forest on a sea of lava – it's well worth a look. With its many little hills, the Fageda d'en Jordà nature reserve is a good place for a family excursion. Around 2.5 miles

(4 km) along the Olot-Banyoles road, another road leads into the beech wood. At the car park you can hire a horse-drawn carriage for a romantic ride in the countryside (☎ 972 68 03 58; daily 10am-2pm and 4-7pm; 800 ptas each, 400 ptas for children under six).

Batet de la Serra
This village is perched on a high plateau of basalt rock crowned by the Pujalòs volcano. The furrows that cut deep through the stone

fascinated the painters of the Olot school. The scenery is peaceful, with century-old oak woods, scattered farms, cultivated fields, the occasional flock of sheep and stone walls lining the roads. As if that wasn't enough, there's an unforgettable view of the whole volcanic zone and the eastern Pyrenees to the north.

Le Croscat
This is the biggest volcano in the peninsula – a cone 500 ft (170 m) high with a crater 2,000 ft (600 m) by 1,000 ft (300 m). It's also the youngest of the volcanoes; its first eruption took place around 17,000 years ago. These days, after 20 years of quarrying for the building trade, it's full of excavations on all sides. At the top you can see the remains of a former military tower built in the 19thC. during the Napoleonic occupation of the region.

Croscat quarry
Accessible on foot from the Can Passavent information centre (4.5 miles/7 km E of Olot on the G1524; 2 miles/3 km round-trip to the quarry).
☎ 972 68 03 58
Visit every hour 1 0am-6pm; one hour. *Admission charge.*
You can visit the inside of a volcano through the former **Croscat quarries**. From the Lava campsite, a little train of wooden carriages on rubber wheels takes you for an

astonishing journey across a landscape of hardened lava. The sizeable bumps that you see from time to time are huge solidified gas bubbles.

Santa Pau
*6 miles (9.5 km)
E of Olot on the G1524*
The bean festival

In the heart of the volcanic zone is the **picturesque village** of Santa Pau. Take in its old castle (13th-14thC.), its pretty Gothic church and, above all, its square surrounded by arches. Santa Pau is also famed for its beans, *fesols*, honoured every 21 January with a festival that brings chefs and gourmets to the village square. Beans figure all year round on the menu of the **Cal Sastre** (Placeta dels Balls 6, ☎ 972 68 04 21; open lunchtime Tues., Wed. and Sun., lunchtime and evenings Thur., Fri. and Sat.), served with pigs' trotters, snails, or *butifarras* (Catalan sausages).

Volcano hermitage

A short walk (2 miles/3 km) takes you from Santa Pau to the Santa Margerida volcano, the biggest in the Garrotxa (0.8 mile/1.2 km diameter). It's an easy descent into the interior of the crater, where you may be surprised to discover a 15th-C. hermitage that was rebuilt in 1865.

A trip in a hot-air balloon

Leave from
Santa Pau
Reservations:
☎ 972 68 02 55.
Open all year.

Maximum five passengers, 20,000 ptas.
If the idea of discovering the world of volcanoes from a great height in just 90 minutes appeals, then this trip is for you. You'll fly

VOLCANIC CUISINE

The powerful but tasty cuisine of the area uses country ingredients: potatoes, fesol beans, pork, snails, maize, chestnuts, turnips, and mushrooms in season. Try it at one of the restaurants of the Grupos Volcánico for less than 3,000 ptas: for instance the **Fonda Siqués** restaurant at Besalú (Companys 6-8, ☎ 972 59 01 10; open daily in summer; closed Sun. evenings and Mon. in winter). Enjoy a taste explosion!

over the Garrotxa volcanoes while sipping a glass of Cava (sparkling wine) and whetting your appetite with *cocas de llardons* (Catalan potted minced bacon). Lunch awaits you after your flight, with bread and tomatoes, local meats, Santa Pau fesol beans and Catalan sausage. What a way to spend a day!

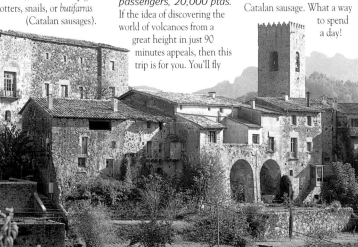

Upper Llobregat

Guardiola de Berguedà

Castellar de N'Hug

La Pobla de Lillet

Cercs

Santa Maria de Queralt

Berga

Puig-Reig

The upper course of the River Llobregat runs through an idyllic landscape. A few former industrial towns remind the visitor that the region relied for a long time on the profits from its textile industry, but the true nature of this part of Catalonia is revealed in the wild splendour of the limestone scarps and thick woods of the Cadí-Moixeró park.

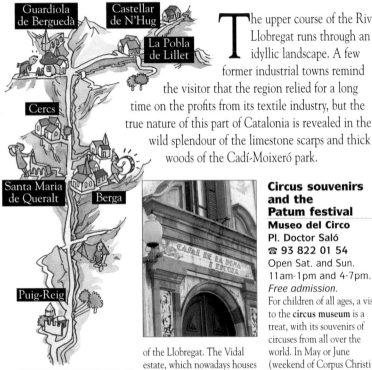

of the Llobregat. The Vidal estate, which nowadays houses a museum, bears witness to those times, when, as in English model towns, workers and their families lived on estates provided by their employers.

Puig-Reig

Vidal workers' estate
☎ 93 829 04 58
Guided tour Sat. and Sun. from 11am.
Admission charge.
Puig-Reig, situated beneath the ruins of a medieval castle, is famous for its industrial past. With its six *colonias* (workers' estates), it's the largest of the industrial 'textile towns' set up in the 19thC. on the banks

Berga
9.5 miles (15 km) N of Puig-Reig on the C1411
Home of the 'berguedana'
This town, the capital of the Berguedà, is like a history book, with its sculpted fresco in the **Plaza Catalunya**, depicting in 38 panels the major events of Catalonia's past. Berga is mainly known for its former textile manufacturing industry and the invention in the 17thC. by two local children (the Farguell brothers) of the *berguedana*, a machine that revolutionised cotton-working.

Circus souvenirs and the Patum festival
Museo del Circo
Pl. Doctor Saló
☎ 93 822 01 54
Open Sat. and Sun.
11am-1pm and 4-7pm.
Free admission.
For children of all ages, a visit to the **circus museum** is a treat, with its souvenirs of circuses from all over the world. In May or June (weekend of Corpus Christi) the **Patum** takes place, one of the most popular festivals in Catalonia. The main event is a procession of demons and monsters. The *patum* itself is a giant eagle made of sculpted wood that spits out fire.

Santa Maria de Queralt
2 miles (3 km) W of Berga
Catalonia's balcony
Perched 3,850 ft (1,174 m) up, the sanctuary of Santa Maria de Queralt provides a **magnificent view**, north to the Cadí range and its limestone cliffs and south over the plain of Berguedà. There's just one restaurant here (open daily July-Aug.; closed Mon. low season; 1,800-2,000 ptas), serving authentic peasant cuisine.

Cercs

4.5 miles (7 km)
N of Berga on the C1411

The underground train

Cercs is an old mining town. In the **mining museum** (Museo de las Minas, ☎ 93 824 81 87; open Tues.-Sun. 10am-6pm in summer, 11am-2pm in winter; admission charge), you can take a miniature train through the galleries of the former coalmine. South of the town, between Cercs and Berga, a medieval bridge spans the Llobregat and leads to **Sant Quirze de Pedret church** (10thC.), a fine example of pre-Romanesque art.

Guardiola de Berguedà

15.5 miles (25 km)
N of Cercs on the C1411

Mushroom market

Guardiola, located in the heart of the **Cadí-Moixeró nature park** celebrates the

mushroom each year with a huge mushroom market (**Mercat del Bolet**). This village is also the starting point for various treks up into the Pyrenees. The most vigorous visitor can attempt to climb **Mount Pedraforca** (starting from Saldes, 12 miles/20 km west of Guardiola).

Sant Llorenç monastery

0.5 mile (1 km)
N of Guardiola

This Benedictine monastery, lying between Guardiola and Berga, was founded in 898AD. Its Romanesque church has an interesting crypt. Enthusiasts for the old and beautiful can push on as far as Bagà (1 mile/2 km north), where the beautiful **Romanesque church of San Esteve** awaits them. Each year this village stages a medieval play, **La Rescate de la Cien Doncellas** ('redemption of the 100 virgins'; information and reservations: ☎ 93 824 40 13).

La Pobla de Lillet

5.5 miles (9 km) E of
Guardiola on the B402

Industrial heritage
Museo del Transporte de Catalunya
☎ 93 825 71 13
Open daily 11am-2pm, Sat. only in winter.

Spotcheck
D3

Things to do

• Visit the Vidal workers' estate
• Medieval play
• Patum festival

With children

• Circus museum
• Visit the old coalmine

Within easy reach

Cerdagne (12.5 miles/20 km N of Cadí-Moixeró), pp. 186-187
Vic (17 miles/27 km SE of Berga), pp. 208-209
Núria valley (25 miles/ 40 km NE of La Pobla de Lillet), pp. 184-185

Tourist office

Berga:
☎ 93 822 15 00

Admission charge.
From La Pobla de Lillet, the road follows the Llobregat to its source (take the BV4031 on the left). On the way back towards Castellar de N'Hug, the **Clot de Moro**, a former cement factory, is now the **Catalonia transport museum**, housing 150 old vehicles in a fine piece of industrial architecture.

SOURCE OF THE LLOBREGAT

The river has its origin at Castellar de N'Hug, 7 miles (11 km) north of La Pobla de Lillet, at an altitude of more than 4,500 ft (1,400 m). A climb of nearly 2,000 ft (over 500 m) leads to the source itself. From this impressive height, you can take in the Cadí-Moixeró nature park. Every year on the last Sunday in August there are **sheepdog trials** here (Concurso Internacional de Gossos d'Atura), when the dogs show their skills.

Cardona
medieval castle and salt mountain

Cardona, a small industrial town amid the forests of the lower Pyrenees, has two treasures. Its salt mountain, a glassy mass that shines in the sun, and its medieval castle, which has been a four-star hotel since 1976. Sunday, market day, is lively. In September, during the Festa Major you can see the extraordinary bull running.

Salt art
Museo de Sal Josep Arnau
Pompeu Fabra 4
☎ 93 869 23 47
Open Mon.-Fri. 11am-2pm and 3-7pm, Sun. 11am-2pm and 5-7pm.
Admission charge.
This little museum set up by Josep Arnau in 1934 has a collection of salt crystals and objects made out of salt, including the unmissable model of Cardona castle.

Castle and church
☎ 93 868 41 69
Open 10am-1pm and 3-6pm in summer, 10am-1pm and 3-5pm in winter; closed Sun. Apr.-May and Mon.
Admission charge.

This former home of the Counts of Cardona is an impressive 11th-C. citadel, rebuilt in the 18thC. It stands at the top of a 1,700-ft (546-m) hill, with the village at its feet, along the banks of the River Cardoner. Within the castle walls is a fine example of Catalan Romanesque art, **Sant Viçenc church** (11thC.), with an elegant **crypt** under its choir. Orson Welles shot some scenes of his film *Truth and Lies* here.

A fussy ghost
Parador de Cardona
☎ 93 869 12 75
Double room 15,000-17,500 ptas; no charge for children under 14.
The castle has been turned into a 'parador' (a fine, relatively inexpensive hotel operated by the Ministry of Tourism). It's claimed that, as in all self-respecting castles, there's a ghost. The spectre haunts room 712 on the top floor, and apparently only appears to women.

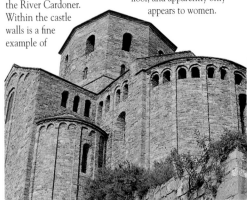

Eat like a king
You simply must treat yourself to a royal feast in the castle restaurant, where, during the hunting season, you'll be served partridge, boar or rabbit, all carefully and deliciously prepared. If there are mushrooms, so much the better. For dessert, try the *panets* of Sant Ignasi (set menu 3,500 ptas).

Corre de Bou, bull running
Information:
☎ 93 869 10 00
On the second Sunday in September there's the 600-year-old 'Corre de Bou', Cardona's biggest festival. The main square becomes the arena, in which the locals try to chase and dodge the bulls. The *cargolera* is the key to the event, installed in a large basket and left to the mercy of the animal, which repeatedly charges, pushing him into the centre of the crowd. It's an exciting and colourful event, and you should really try to take in the festival if at all possible.

Magic mountain

2 miles (3 km) SE of Cardona on the Mine road
Salt mine
In the 2nd C. the Roman writer Aulus Gellius recorded the existence of this unique phenomenon, a salt mine

more than 250 ft (nearly 80 m) high and 3 miles (5 km) in circumference. Worked since Roman times, the mine became less important with the discovery of potassium at the start of the 20thC. and finally stopped its operations in 1990.

Spotcheck
D3

Things to do
• Bull running festival

With children
• Salt mine
• Horse-drawn carriage ride

Within easy reach
Montserrat (31 miles/ 50 km SE), pp. 206-207 La Seu d'Urgell (47 miles/75 km NW), pp. 188-189

Tourist office
Cardona:
☎ 93 869 27 98

ECOLOGICAL CARRIAGE RIDES

Paisatge i Aventura
☎ 93 836 00 60
(telephone in advance).
Excursions leave from Casa Les Planes, Sant Mateu de Bages (15.5 miles/ 25 km S of Cardona on the C1410).
One day trip, 2,600 ptas per person, six people minimum; four people for two days, 34,000 ptas. Meals at the farm: 1,500 ptas. Half-board for children under 8.
You can explore the scenery of the Sierra de Castelltallat, a protected nature site south of Cardona, in horse-drawn carriage. This hilly country, whose highest point is 3,000 ft (900 m) about sea level, has many cool glades of beech trees and conifers.

'Journey to the centre of the Earth'
Recinto Mina Nieves
☎ 93 869 24 75
Open 10am- 6pm in summer 10am- 2pm winter. Guided tour lasting 2 hours (reservation required)
Admission fee

The interior of this mine is riddled with galleries and stalactites and stalagmites abound. You can even cross one of the galleries in a buggy, which is just as well, as it's over 800 ft long (270 m)and 240 ft deep (80 m). Deep in the mine's workshop there are salt carvings on display, made by a former miner.

Montserrat,
the Mecca of Catalonia

Mount Montserrat, with its sea of sharp, strangely shaped rocks, is not only a site of great natural beauty close to Barcelona, but also a much-loved place of pilgrimage. Many people come to the Santa Maria basilica to honour La Moreneta, a statue of the Virgin and child who holds a globe in her hand. While some come for religious reasons, others are attracted by the grandeur of the countryside, for the monastery stands surrounded by good hiking and climbing country.

Montserrat by road

25 miles (40 km) NW of Barcelona

You can get here from Barcelona by car or train. Those with least time should take the A18 motorway towards Manresa – taking the Montserrat-Sant Vicenç de Castellet exit. You can also take the N11, then the C1411, which follows the River Llobregat and has good views of the mountain and the rocky outcrops.

Montserrat by train

If you prefer public transport, trains go to Montserrat daily from 8.30am. Leave from Plaça d'Espanya station, line R5; stop at Montserrat-Aeri station, then take the cable car to the mountain. With the combined *Tot Montserra* ticket, you pay only once for the train journey, the Sant Joan and Santa Cova funiculars, entry to the monastery and lunch in the cafeteria. Information and purchase in any FGC (Ferrocarriles de la Generalitat de Catalunya) station.

A magnificent monastery

The Benedictine monastery was founded in 1025 and enlarged in the 12thC. As its reputation spread

internationally, new buildings were commissioned to accommodate pilgrims and scholars seeking the excellent theological training. Things went downhill in the 19thC., when Napoleon's armies destroyed a major part of the monastery. The current buildings, rebuilt from 1844 onwards, are not particularly interesting, but they do contain some fine objects.

La Moraneta and the museum collections

Basilica: open 7.30am-7.30pm
Chapel of the black Virgin: open all year 8-10.30am and noon-6.15pm (and 7.30-8.30pm in summer).
Museum: 10am-7pm in summer, 9am-6pm in winter.

La Moraneta, the famous black Virgin of Montserrat, is located in the 14th-C. basilica (restored in the 19thC.). Legend has it that the statue was carved by St Luke and

brought to Catalonia 50 years later by Saint Peter, but in reality dates from the 12thC. Originally pale in colour, over time it has darkened and is now the patron of Catalonia. The museum, on Santa Maria square, is in three sections: the **modern museum** (19th- and 20th-C. Catalan painters), the **Pinacoteca** (classic Spanish, Flemish and Italian paintings), and the **archaeological museum** (Mesopotamia, Egypt and Palestine).

COLLBATÓ CAVES
21.5 miles (35 km) from Barcelona on the N11
☎ **937 77 03 09**
Open weekends 10.45am-1pm and 4-6pm, daily exc. Mon. in Aug. Guided tour: 1 hour. *Admission charge.*
Opening into the heart of Montserrat mountain, these grottoes were first discovered in the 14thC. Their exuberant shapes were an inspiration for Gaudí's famous Sagrada Familia (see Barcelona, p. 164). In 1934 they were illuminated by Carlos Buigas, who created the fountains at Montjuïc in Barcelona.

Holy cave
One hour on foot from De la Creu square.
The **Santa Cova** is supposedly where shepherds discovered the statue of the virgin of

Montserrat one morning in April 880. A chapel was built here in the 17thC to commemorate the discovery. On the Santa Cova road, the Rosario Monumental is a **Modernist monument** by Gaudí and Llimona.

Sant Joan funicular railway
Leaving from De la Creu square
Before you take the funicular, don't miss the performance, in the basilica, of the charming little singers of the **Escolania**, one of the oldest children's choirs in the world (daily at 1pm and 7.10pm). The Sant Joan funicular climbs nearly 800 ft (250 m) in 7 minutes. At the top, at nearly 3,500 ft (more than 1,000 m), the panoramic view is superb, over Catalonia as far as the Pyrenees and the island of Majorca.

Things to do
- Visit La Moraneta
- Holy cave and the Modernist monument
- Mountain walks

Within easy reach
Barcelona (25 miles/40 km SE), pp. 164-170
Cardona (31 miles/50 km NW), pp. 206-207

Tourist information
Monastery:
☎ **93 835 02 51**

Mountain walks
From the upper station of the Sant Joan funicular there are several mountain trails. In 20 minutes you can get to the Sant Joan hermitage, or in 50 minutes to that of Sant Miguel. The route that leads

to the Sant Jeroni lookout point is longer and much more difficult, taking around an hour over rough ground. Finally, for experienced climbers there are the sheer-sided rocks. Be careful – there's a danger of falling, because the stone is very crumbly.

Vic
in search of the real Catalonia

Vic is a very Catalan town. It was here that the revival and defence of Catalan culture, against the unifying, homogenising tendency of the centre, began in the 19thC. The town is rich in medieval heritage and is renowned for its excellent local sausage and cold meats. For those seeking outdoor pleasures, the area offers the nearby Collsacabra and Guilleries ranges and Montseny mountain.

Vic
Bishops' city

In 716 the Moors destroyed the old city of Ausona. A hundred years later, Count Guifré the Hairy installed a bishopric and the city rose again from the ashes. In 1038 the **Sant Pere cathedral** was built (open 10am-1pm and 4-7pm). Only the bell-tower and crypts are original, but the current neo-classical cathedral (end of the 18thC.) contains fine frescoes by the painter

José Maria Sert (1874-1945). In the nearby **bishop's palace** (Palau Episcopal) there's a wonderfully rich collection of Romanesque and Gothic art (☎ 93 885 64 52; open daily 10am-1pm and 4-7pm exc. Sun. pm in summer; closed pm in winter; admission charge).

Colourful market

The little streets of the upper city all converge at the Plaça Major, with arcades sheltering bars and restaurants. On Saturday, the square is taken

over by the colourful and picturesque market. On the eve of Palm Sunday one of the biggest agricultural markets in the country takes place here.

Land of the sausage

Just like good winemakers, the pork butchers of Vic have their own quality trademark – the 'Denominación de Calidad

Llonganissa'. *Llonganissa* is a long, firm and finely textured cured sausage, *somalla* is spicy and quite dry, while *butifarra* and *fuet* are long and dry. Other varieties of the local

embutidos are also made in Vic, and include white, black, raw and egg-flavoured sausages. You'll find them at **Can Vila** (Pl. Major 34, ☎ 93 886 32 59; open Mon.-Fri. 8am-1.30pm and 4-8pm, Sat. 8am-2.15pm and 4-8pm; closed 15-31 July) or **Ca La Teresona** (Argenters 4, ☎ 93 886 00 28; open 9am-1.30pm and 4-8pm exc. Sat. and Sun.).

Sant Martí Sescorts
*9.5 miles (15 km)
NE of Vic on the C153*
Sau artificial lake

This spectacular site, surrounded by cliffs, consists of the water retained by the **Sau dam**, which drowned the little village of Sant Martí. Its lonely church spire can still be seen rising out of the water. On the bank stands the imposing Vic-Sau parador (☎ 938 122 323; open May-Sept.; 2,500 ptas), a perfect place to stay while taking in the idyllic surroundings. From **Tavertet**, a pretty village perched on top of the plateau, there's a magnificent view. Nearby the **Sant Pere de Casseres monastery**, founded in the 10thC., is a wonderful example of Catalan Romanesque architecture.

Cantonigrós
*15.5 miles (25 km)
NE of Vic on the C153*
A folk music festival, steeped in tradition
**Information:
☎ 93 886 20 91.**
In this village, on the Collsabra plateau, folk singers and dancers from all over the world meet in mid-July for a festival that celebrates regional folk music. It's certainly appropriate that this

Spotcheck
E3

Things to do
• Saturday market
• Vic sausages
• Sau dam
• Folk festival
• Montseny nature park walks

Within easy reach
*Ripoll and the Núria valley (20 miles/32 km N), p. 184-185
Berga and the Noguera Pallaresa (37 miles/ 60 km NW), p. 190-191*

Tourist office
Vic: ☎ 93 886 20 91

festival is staged in Catalonia, which has held on so strongly to so many of its own customs and traditions.

Rupit
4.5 miles (7 km) NE of Cantonigrós on the C153
A fairy-tale village

Built entirely of stone, this village stands in the middle of a forest of boxwood and green oak and, with its 16th- and 17th-C. houses and paved streets, it looks like an illustration from a book of fairy tales. You're strongly advised to make your trip to Rupit on a weekday rather than at the weekend when it is overwhelmed by hordes of visitors. Follow the road that goes alongside the stream to the magnificent Salt de Sallent waterfall. At Maria Carme's, you can buy delicious *butifarra* and a liqueur of herbs and orange blossom sold as *Aromas of Rupit* (Pl. Bisbe Font 2, ☎ 93 852 20 78; open daily 10am-2pm and 5-9pm in summer; closed Tues. in winter).

MONTSENY NATURE PARK
Montseny is the highest peak of the Catalan pre-littoral chain. From Vic, you get there via Seva

**(N152 south as far as Tona, then left towards Seva). The road goes to the top of the park, Turó de l'Home (5,615 ft/ 1,712 m), where there is a great view over the coastal plain to the Mediterranean.
If you want to go trekking, you can get ideas and information from the Can Casades information centre at Santa Fe (☎ 93 847 51 13), which also organises accompanied tours of the mountain. It's advisable to consult the experienced staff before heading out on a major trek.**

Alt Penedès
still or sparkling

The Penedès region, south of Barcelona, is a wine-producing area with its own 'appellation' (trademark). The best grapes grow in the *comarca* of the Alt Penedès, with its roughly 200 wineries and 40 *bodegas*. The little town of Vilafranca del Penedès is famous for its still wines, while Sant Sadurní is the Spanish capital of production of the sparkling wine known as Cava.

Vilafranca del Penedès
19.5 miles (31 km) SW of Barcelona on the N340
A great market
The Saturday-morning food market is quite an institution, with more than 400 stalls selling Penedès hens, chickens, ducks and turkeys, all nice and fat. The **chicken fair** (Feria del Gallo) on the 'rambla' Sant Francesc during the week before Christmas is the biggest poultry market in Catalonia.

Wine museum
Museo del Vino
Pl. Jaume 1
☎ 93 890 05 82
Open Tues.-Sat.
10am-2pm and 4-7pm,
Sun. 10am-2pm;
June-Aug. 9am-9pm;
closed Mon.
Admission charge.

Here you can learn about the history of wine since ancient times or admire the collection of bottles and glasses in the most astonishing and remarkable shapes. It's on the ground floor of the Vilafranca museum, which has a number of interesting collections: sacred art, Catalan painting, more than

1,000 pieces of pottery from the 16th to the 19thC., and a whole section dedicated to ornithology.

Human 'castles'
A *casteller* is a human pyramid up to six stories high, with a young child, the *anxoveta*, on top. Catalans enjoy forming human towers, particularly during fiestas, and they are a great attraction. When the little person on the top makes his or her customary wave, the solidity of the stack is tested. This form of acrobatics is popular throughout the Penedès and Tarragona regions, especially at Valls, where it originated. On the feast day of Sant Felix, during the Fiesta Major of Vilafranca (29 August-2 September) you can see the best *colles* (troupes) in Catalonia compete.

The Torres dynasty

☎ 93 817 74 87

Tour of the cellars and shop: Mon.-Sat. 9am-6pm, Sun. 9am-1pm. *Free admission.*

With vineyards in California and Chile as well as Spain, this *bodega* has earned a world-wide reputation. The headquarters is located at Pacs del Penedès, 2 miles (3 km) from Vilafranca (BP2121). You can visit the legendary cellars before making your purchases in the shop: the very popular red Sangre de Toro (600 ptas a bottle) or Gran Corona Réserve 1995 (1,400 ptas a bottle) or, among the whites, the Fransola (1,500 ptas a bottle).

PENEDÈS BARRELS
Casa José Torner Caellas
Amalia Soler 64-66, Vilafranca
☎ 93 890 02 49
Open Mon.-Fri. 8.30am-3pm and 4.30-9pm.

An original, but rather cumbersome, idea for a present – one of the barrels that this company has been producing since 1759. Worth visiting, if only to admire the wares, in oak or chestnut, with impeccable finishing. A 2-gallon (10-litre) barrel is 10,000 ptas.

y *el Vi* wine-tasting centre. It's a good place to spend three hours (morning or afternoon) becoming more of a wine buff.

Sant Sadurní d'Anoia

7.5 miles (12 km) NE of Vilafranca on the C243a

Spotcheck
D4-D5

Things to do
• Market and chicken fair at Vilafranca
• Barrel workshop
• Wine sampling
• Penedès Modernist buildings

With children
• Human castles

Within easy reach
*Sitges (15 miles/24 km SE of Vilafranca), p. 172
Santes Creus, Poblet and Vallbona de les Monges monasteries (40 miles/65 km W), pp. 212-213
Barcelona (21.5 miles/35 km W), pp. 164-170*

Tourist office
Vilafranca del Penedès:
☎ 93 892 03 58

amid beautiful grounds (Av. Jaume Cordoníu, ☎ 938 18 32 32; open Mon.-Fri. 9am-5pm; admission charge). Inside you'll find two fine examples of Modernist industrial architecture – the grand cellar or main hall, and the reception hall. Don't leave without trying a bottle of the house Cava. Take home a bottle (or two) of Anna Cordoníu (1,200 ptas a bottle).

Vine palace
Can Sadurni

N340 towards Avinyonet, then right on the BV2415 to San Perre de Molanta.
☎ 93 892 00 89
Visit: 2,500 ptas, including samples; free for children.

By appointment only. This 17th-C. farmhouse is home to the *Aula de la Vinya*

Sparkling *Cava* country

Many vineyards produce this famous sparkling wine, but the two kings of *Cava* remain the estates of Freixenet and Cordoníu. The latter, which commenced production in 1872 and is said to be the world's largest producer of the sparkling wine, owns the **Casa Madre del Cava**, set

Cordoníu estate

Santes Creus, Poblet, Vallbona de les Monges

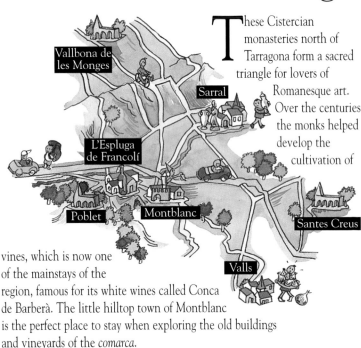

Vallbona de les Monges

Sarral

L'Espluga de Francolí

Poblet

Montblanc

Santes Creus

Valls

These Cistercian monasteries north of Tarragona form a sacred triangle for lovers of Romanesque art. Over the centuries the monks helped develop the cultivation of vines, which is now one of the mainstays of the region, famous for its white wines called Conca de Barberà. The little hilltop town of Montblanc is the perfect place to stay when exploring the old buildings and vineyards of the *comarca*.

Montblanc

Medieval town
The old town shelters within the 14th-C. walls and its narrow, winding lanes climb the hill, at the top of which is the Santa Maria church. Starting on 23 April there's a **medieval week** in honour of the patron saint of Catalonia, Sant Jordi. It's a lovely little town, with its river spanned by a Gothic bridge.

Sweet treats
Andreu pastry shop
Major 55
☎ 977 86 01 35
Open daily exc. Wed. 9am–2pm and 4–9pm; closed July.
Here you can buy the delicious almond and sugar pastries for which Montblanc is famous.

Santes Creus

12.5 miles (20 km) E of Montblanc on the A2, then the T200
Monastery
☎ 977 63 83 29
Open 15 Mar.–15 Sept. 10.30am–1.30pm and 3–7pm; until 5.30pm, 16 Sept.– 15 Jan., until 6pm,

16 Jan.–15 Mar; closed Mon.
Admission charge.
This is the oldest monastery of the three, founded in 1150. Its buildings date from the 12th to the 18thC. Don't miss the Gothic **great cloister** and the nearby **church**.

Vallbona monastery

Vallbona de les Monges
15.5 miles (25 km) N of Montblanc on the C240
Monastery
☎ 973 33 02 66
Open Tues.-Sat. 10.30am-1.30pm and 4.30-7.15pm, Sun. 2-4pm in summer; in winter, just afternoons; closed Mon.
Admission charge.
This establishment was set up in 1157, but it was not until 1175 that it became a Cistercian nunnery. The church is in Romanesque and Gothic styles (13th-14thC.) and the chapter-house shelters the tombstones of the abbesses.

L'Espluga de Francolí
3.5 miles (6 km) W of Montblanc on the C240
Wine museum and caves
This is an important centre of wine production with a tradition going back to the 11thC. The **wine museum** (Av. Rendé i Ventosa, ☎ 977 87 01 61; open Mon.-Fri. 9.30am-12.30pm and 3-6pm, weekend 10am-2pm; admission charge) is a good way to get to know the local wine.

There are some interesting geological formations in the **Font Major caves** (Av. Catalunya, ☎ 977 87 11 66; open 10.30am-1pm and 4.30-7pm).

Poblet monastery
2.5 miles (4 km) S of L'Espluga de Francolí
☎ 977 87 02 54
Open daily 10am-12.30pm and 3-6pm, until 5.30pm in wnter; 10am-1pm weekend.
Admission charge.
This is one of the true treasures of Catalonia and has been classified by UNESCO as a world heritage site. The monastery, founded in the mid-12thC., is surrounded by 14th-C. walls. In the abbey, be sure not to miss the fabulous **alabaster retable** and the **royal pantheon**. The beautiful **Gothic cloister** beside the church is a real masterpiece.

Valls
13 miles (21 km) SE of Montblanc on the N240
Calçot country
Calçots, a speciality of Valls, are small sweet onions that are grilled over charcoal. On the last Sunday in January there's a festival in their honour, the 'Calçotada', when they are cooked and served with *chuletas* (lamb cutlets) and *butifarra* (chargrilled Catalan sausages).

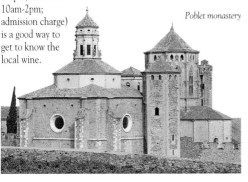

Poblet monastery

Spotcheck
C4-C5

Things to do
- Wine tasting
- L'Espluga wine museum
- Valls calçotada festival

With children
- Font Major caves

Within easy reach
Tarragona (25 miles/39 km S of Montblanc), p. 174-175

CONCA DE BARBERÀ
Since 1989 this little wine-making area to the north of Tarragona province has had its own trademark. In the past, most of its production went for Cava, but now it produces delicious rosés and white wines that are fruity and not too alcoholic.

Sarral
5.5 miles (9 km) N of Monblanc on the C241
Marble museum
The discovery of marble at Sarral led to the development of craft production. Visit the **Sarral marble museum** (Museo del Alabastro Sarral Imade, Conca 51, ☎ 977 89 01 58; open daily 10am-1pm and 4-7pm, Sun. by appointment; admission charge) and then make your purchases at the museum shop.

Lleida
fruits, flowers and snails

Lleida (also known as Lérida) is the capital of the only Catalan province with no access to the sea, and is covered with snow at the first frost. Nevertheless, its orchards, vineyards and olive groves are the envy of the surrounding plain. The Seu Vella cathedral stands on a high outcrop and dominates the city. It's visible from afar and is one of the city's symbols, the other being the snail that is the king of local cuisine.

Lleida

Seu Vella cathedral
☎ 973 23 06 53
Open Tues.-Sat.
10am-1pm and 4-7.30pm,
Sun. 10am-1.30pm.;
closed Mon.

In the middle of the remains of the Arab fortress (la Suda) lies the 13th-C. cathedral, Seu Vella (as opposed to Seu Nova, the newer, 18th-C. cathedral). It has an impressive octagonal bell tower (more than 200 ft, nearly 70 m in height). From the top (admission charge) there's a fine view of a sea of fruit trees and vineyards. The plain is irrigated by canals constructed by the Arabs, who invaded the region in the 8thC. On the way down, visit the cathedral with its carved, story-telling capitals.

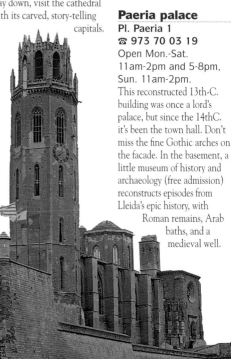

Restoration work began in the 1940s and the nave looks remarkable. You can take a lift from Seu Vella to the Plaça de Sant Joan in the town below.

Paeria palace
Pl. Paeria 1
☎ 973 70 03 19
Open Mon.-Sat.
11am-2pm and 5-8pm,
Sun. 11am-2pm.
This reconstructed 13th-C. building was once a lord's palace, but since the 14thC. it's been the town hall. Don't miss the fine Gothic arches on the facade. In the basement, a little museum of history and archaeology (free admission) reconstructs episodes from Lleida's epic history, with Roman remains, Arab baths, and a medieval well.

A festival for snails

May is Lleida's month of festivity. For a week starting on 11 May, there's the feast of Sant Anastasi, with a spectacle in the streets that pitches Moors against Christians. Then, on the penultimate Sunday of the month, there is the 'snail gathering'

('Aplec del Cargol'), when more than 250,000 visitors assemble in the Camps Elisis park to enjoy dishes of snails à la *llauna* and tempting local desserts.

Snail worship

Snails à la *llauna* is the most popular way of eating these delectable creatures in this area. They are placed open end uppermost on a tin plate and left to cook for 11 minutes over an open, wood fire. Then add a touch of salt, a few red and black pimentos, and a dash of olive oil, are added and the snails are ready to be eaten. Other variations on the recipe include snails à la *gormanda* and snails à la *butesca*, which are served in sauce with rice and rabbit or rice and cod. There is also the *cassola de tros,* a rich mixture of snails, pork, rabbit, red pepper and cognac. Take your pick!

Eating à la carte

For a change from snails, try some of the other local specialities. Especially recommended is the *escalivada de la huerta* (red peppers, aubergines and onions in oil and served cold with salad and vinegar) or try the *esqueixada,* a delicious variant on the *escalivada* dish made with cod.

Raïmat

8.5 miles (14 km) NW of Lleida on the N240

Raïmat estate
Domaine de Raïmat
☎ 973 72 40 00
Guided tours Sat.-Sun. at 10.30am, 11.30am and 12.30pm, by appointment other days.
Visit the Raimat estate wher a remarkable range of wines is produced. It's a good place to taste the local vintage, **Coster del Segre**. The whites and rosés, light and fruity, are drunk young, whereas the reds have more body and bouquet. Two good tips: the Chardonnay blanc (4,500 ptas a bottle) and the Cabernet-sauvignon (6,600 ptas a bottle). You can also buy a good Cava (sparkling wine) – Raïmat brut (5,700 ptas a bottle).

Spotcheck
B4

Things to do
• Visit the old town
• Snail cuisine
• Sant Anastasi and snail festivals
• Wine tasting
• Olive oil theme park

Tourist office
☎ 973 27 09 97

EVERYTHING YOU ALWAYS WANTED TO KNOW ABOUT OLIVE OIL...
Olive oil theme park
N240, km 71 (between Borges Blanques and Juneda)
☎ 973 14 00 18
Open Mon.-Fri. 10am-2pm and 4-7pm, weekend 10am-7.30pm.
Admission charge.
In a former property of the Knights Templar (13th C.), there are 13 rooms which trace the secrets of the production of olive oil – first cold pressing, extra virgin oil, acidity etc. There's a very fine Roman olive press (the biggest in the world) and a 1,000 year-old olive tree.

On the banks of the Èbre
between the mountains and the sea

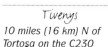

S outhwest of Tarragona, the River Èbre flows gently towards the sea, between the delta that bears its name and the Els Ports de Besiet mountains. This is the southernmost part of Catalonia, a rich and attractive region of varied landscapes, with olive, almond and fruit trees and vines.

Tortosa

Last city before the sea

South of the city is the Èbre delta and the sea. Tortosa was conquered in 714 by the Moors, who built an imposing fortress, **La Zuda**, which is now a parador, castillo de la Zuda. Even if you don't intend staying at the hotel, do try to make time to visit it for the stunning view. Below the fortress is the fine **Gothic cathedral** (14thC.), built on the site of a mosque. It has an impressive interior and several lovely chapels.

Moon cakes
Pallarès
Sant Blai 17
☎ 977 44 15 41
Open 9am-2pm and 4.30-9pm; closed Sun. pm, Mon. and Tues.
Pastissets are the great Tortosa speciality, dating back to the 11thC. – half-moon shaped cakes with angels' hair.

Unforgettable Èbre observatory
Observatorio geofísico
☎ 977 50 05 11
Tours Fri. 4pm and first Sun. of the month at 11am; closed Aug.
Free admission.
A little over a mile (2 km) from Tortosa, this observatory was founded by the Jesuits at the end of the 19thC. and is a centre for research into the physical characteristics of the earth.

Tivenys
10 miles (16 km) N of Tortosa on the C230
El Assut de Xerta dam
This water works, 960 ft (310 m) long and 75 ft (24 m) wide, was constructed by the Muslims in 1411. It spans the river from one bank to another, between Xerta and Tivenys, and was originally intended to divert the water in order to irrigate nearby land and promote cultivation in the surrounding area.

A tradition for ceramics
Tivenys pottery is heir to a long tradition. In the shop attached to the Picurt workshop (Romella 53, ☎ 977 49 60 12; open 9am-1pm and 3-7pm exc. Sat. and Sun.), you can buy attractive objects to take home. Choose from a selection of decorative ceramics (amphoras from 2,800 ptas; jars from 300 ptas) to lovely tableware, which would make charming gifts.

Tortosa cathedral

PICASSO AT HORTA

Picasso often said, 'All I know, I learnt at Horta'. This mountain village occupies a magnificent site, fit to inspire one of the 20thC.'s most extraordinary painters. Picasso stayed there for 9 months at the age of 16, and then came back in 1909, when he was 26. The massive blocks at Horta reappear in some of his cubist works. If you need convincing, take a look at the reproductions, numbering some 260, exhibited at the Picasso centre (Antic Hospital, ☎ 977 435 333; open Tues.-Sun. 11am-1.30pm; admission charge). Before you leave, don't forget to go and see the whimsical murals of goats and boars at Els Ports de Beseits (5 miles/8 km S of Horta). Picasso fans are in for a treat.

Benifallet

9.5 miles (15 km) N of Tivenys on the T301

Underground wonders

☎ 977 42 62 31
Open daily 10am-2pm and 4-7pm.
Admission charge.
On the left bank of the river, Benifallet has some splendid caves known as the 'Coves d'Aumediella'. The most interesting and beautiful geological formations are to be found in the Meravelles and Del Dos chambers.

Miravet

12 miles (19 km) N of Benifallet on the C230

The Templar castle

☎ 977 40 71 34
Open 4-7pm, 1 June-30 Sept., 10am-1pm and 3-6pm, rest of the year.
Admission charge.
Miravet is a picturesque hilltop

village. Visit its castle (15 mins on foot from the village), one of the finest examples of Templar architecture in Catalonia. Standing on a precipice, it affords stunning views. Afterwards enjoy a stroll in the old town. There are eight potters' workshops in El Raval dels Terrissers.

Miravet castle

El Pinell de Brai

2.5 miles (4 km) N of Benifallet on the C235

Shrine of wine

☎ 977 46 20 05
Open Mon.-Fri. 9am-1pm and 3-7pm, Sat.-Sun. 11am-1pm and 3.30-6pm (4.30-7pm in summer).
Admission charge.

Spotcheck

B5-B6

Things to do

• Èbre observatory
• Tivenys pottery
• El Pinell de Brai Modernist winery
• Horta

With children

• Benifallet caves

Within easy reach

Èbre delta (9.5 miles/ 15 km SE of Tortosa), p. 178-181

Tourist office

Tortosa: ☎ 977 51 08 22

This wine producing co-operative is not to be missed, both for its wines and for its Modernist architecture. It was built in 1922 by Cèsar Martinell, one of Gaudí's disciples. On the facade there is a ceramic frieze by Xavier Nogués, depicting picturesque scenes of farm work and wine making.

Miravet village

INDEX ● **219**

This guide was written by Alberto Cañagueral and MARIE-ANGE DEMORY, with additional help from CHRYSTEL ARNOULD, CAROLINE BOISSY, ÉLISABETH BOYER, ANNE-GAËLLE MOUTARDE, DAMIEN SAINT-PRIEST and LAURENT SCHMIDT.

Illustrations: RENAUD MARCA

Illustrated maps: STÉPHANE HUMBERT-BASSET

Cartography: © IDÉ INFOGRAPHIE (THOMAS GROLLIER)

Translation and adaptation: Y2K TRANSLATIONS (Email: info@y2ktranslations.com)

Additional design and editorial assistance: SOFI MOGENSEN, JANE MOSELEY and CHRISTINE BELL

Project manager: LIZ COGHILL

We have done our best to ensure the accuracy of the information contained in this guide. However, addresses, telephone numbers, opening times etc. inevitably do change from time to time, so if you find a discrepancy please do let us know. You can contact us at: hachetteuk@orionbooks.co.uk or write to us at Hachette UK, address below.

Hachette UK guides provide independent advice. The authors and compilers do not accept any remuneration for the inclusion of any addresses in these guides.

Please note that we cannot accept any responsibility for any loss, injury or inconvenience sustained by anyone as a result of any information or advice contained in this guide.

First published in the United Kingdom in 2001 by Hachette UK

Distributed in the United States of America by Sterling Publishing Co., Inc. 387 Park Avenue South, New York, NY 10016-8810

A CIP catalogue for this book is available from the British Library

ISBN 1 84202 099 4

Hachette UK, Cassell & Co., The Orion Publishing Group, Wellington House, 125 Strand, London WC2R 0BB

Printed in France by I.M.E. - 25110 Baume-les-Dames

Spanish handy words and phrases

Castilian Spanish is widely spoken in Catalonia although Catalan is probably slightly more prevalent. Spanish is certainly easier to pronounce, but be aware that you will see Catalan on menus, signs etc. Our handy words and phrases are in Castilian Spanish.

A basic guide to pronunciation

Spanish is not a difficult language to pronounce, but there are certain things you should know. An accent on a letter shows where the stress of the word should fall. If there is no accent, each syllable is given equal emphasis.

VOWELS
Every vowel sound is pronounced and they are generally short:
'a' – 'ah' as in 'park'
'e' – 'eh' as in 'bed'
'o' – 'o' as in 'hot'
'u' – 'ooh' as in 'rule'
'i' – 'eeh' as in 'police'

CONSONANTS
With regard to consonants, there are a few sounds which may be new to you:
'c' – before an 'e' it is a 'th' sound in English ('soft c'), so 'cebolla' is pronounced 'the-boyah'
'j' is pronounced like an English 'h', so 'jalapeno' becomes 'h-alapeno'
'h' is always silent
'll' – 'y' sound in English, so 'tortilla' is pronounced 'tort-y-ah'
'ñ' is pronounced like the 'ni' in 'onion'
'z' is the same as the 'soft c'

Essential vocabulary

yes/no	si/no
hello/goodbye	hola/adios
Good morning	Buenos días
Good afternoon	Buenas tardes
Good evening	Buenas noches
please	por favor
Thank you very much	Muchas gracias
You're welcome	De nada
I am sorry	Lo siento/ Disculpe
Excuse me	perdóneme

Handy phrases

I don't speak Spanish	No hablo español
Do you speak English?	¿Habla inglés?
I (don't) understand	No entiendo
Could you repeat that please?	¿Podría repetirlo por favor?
Can you speak more slowly, please?	¿Puede hablar mas despacio, por favor?

Do you understand?	¿Me entiende?
Is it possible...?	¿Sería posible....?
I want...	Quiero…
How are you?	¿Qué tal?
Fine, thank you	Muy bien, gracias
Pleased to meet you	Encantado/a (m/f)
What is your name?	¿Como se llama?
My name is ...	Me llamo …
How?	¿Cómo?
Who?	¿Quien?
Where?	¿Dónde?
When?	¿Cuando?
Why?	¿Porqué?
What is it?	¿Qué es?

Essential words

good/bad	bueno/malo
big/small	grande/pequeno
hot/cold	caliente/frío
free/busy	desocupado/ocupado
free (no charge)	gratis
toilets/wc	baño or aseos
no smoking	no fumar
here/there	aqui/allá
early/late	temprano/tarde
slow/fast	lento/ rápido
another	otra vez
before	antes
after	dopo
during	durante
near	cerca
now	ahora
up there	arriba

Getting around

Where is...?	¿Dónde está...?
Is it far/near?	¿Está lejos/cerca?
map of the city	mapa de la ciudad
tourist office	oficina turística
church	iglesia
cathedral	catedral
castle	castillo
museum	museo
town hall	ajuntemiento
garden	jardin
art gallery	galería de arte
square	plaza
street	calle
by plane/train/car	por avión/tren/coche
airport	aeropuerto
railway station	estación de tren
underground	metro
bus	autobus
a ticket to...	un billete para…
single/return	da/ida y vuelta
timetable	horario

Do I need to change?	¿Debo cambiar de plataforma?
From which platform does it leave?	¿De qué plataforma sale?
bicycle	bicicleta
on foot	a pie
What time does it open/close?	¿A qué hora abre/cierra?

DIRECTIONS

straight on	todo recto
right/left	derecha/izquierda
at the end of...	al final de...
next to	al lado de
opposite	frente a
up/down	arriba/abajo
above/below	sobre/debajo
entrance	entrada
exit	salida
I would like to go...	Quisiera ir...
bend	vuelta

In the hotel

. . . .

hotel	hotel
bed & breakfast	pensión
reservation	reserva
Do you have any rooms?	¿Tiene habitaciónes?
Do you have a room for one person/for two people?	¿Tiene una habitación para una persona/para dos personas?
I would like...	Quisiera...
a single/double room	habitación simple/doble
for one night	para una noche
for two nights	para dos noches
with a double bed	con cama doble
with twin beds	con dos camas
with a bath	con baño
with shower	con ducha
with a balcony	con balcón
a quiet room	una habitación tranquila
full board	pensión completa
Is breakfast included?	¿Está incluído el desayuno?
We are leaving tomorrow	Nos vamos mañana
At what time can you...?	¿A qué hora es possible...?
first floor	el primer piso
second floor	el segundo piso
key	llave
lift	el ascensor

Eating out

. . . .

GENERAL

I'd like to reserve a table for two (three, four, five) people	Quisiera reservar una mesa para dos (tres, cuatro, cinco) personas
The bill, please	La cuenta, por favor.
I am a vegetarian	Soy vegetariano/a
Is service included?	¿Esta incluído el servicio?
wine list	lista de vinos
What is the dish of the day?	¿Cual es el plato del dia?
What is the house specialty?	¿Cual es la especialidad de la casa?

MEALS AND MEALTIMES

meal	comida
menu	la carta
starter	primer plato
main course	plato principal
dessert	postre
breakfast	desayuno
lunch	almuerzo
dinner	cena
waiter	camarero
tip	propina
knife	cuchillo
fork	tenedor
spoon	cuchara
plate	plato
ashtray	un cenicero

MEAT AND FISH

beef	carne de vaca
lamb	cordero
pork	cochino/puerco
chicken	pollo
duck	pato
meat	carne
rare	poco hecho
medium	termino medio
well-done	bien cocido
ham	jamón
sausage	chorizo/embutido
blood sausage	morcilla
fish	pescado
shrimp	langostino/gamba
squid	pulpo
oysters	ostras

SUNDRIES

soup	sopa
bread	pan
butter	mantequilla
cheese	queso
egg	huevo
vegetables	legumbres
French fries	patatas fritas
salad	ensalada
rice	arroz
fruit	fruta
sugar	azúcar
salt	sal
pepper	pimienta
mustard	mostaza
sauce	salsa
spicy	picante
oil	aceite
vinegar	vinagre
sandwich	bocadillo
omelette	tortilla

DRINKS

water	agua
coffee	café
tea	té
milk	leche
drink (non-alcoholic)	bebida
beer	cerveza

wine	vino
still/sparkling	sin gas/con gas
red/white	tinto/blanco
sparkling wine	cava
sherry	jerez
lemonade	limonada
orange juice	zumo de naranja
bottle	botella

Shopping

How much is it?	¿cuanto cuesta?
Do you have?	¿Tiene?
Do you take credit cards?	¿Acepta tarjetas de credito?
in cash	en efectivo
I'm just looking, thank you	Sólo viendo, gracias
department store	gran almacén
supermarket	supermercado
market	mercado
antiques	antigüedades
bookshop	librería
bank	banco
chemist	farmacía
shoe shop	zapatería
post office	oficina de Correos
news-stand	kiosco de revistas
tobacconists	tabac
size	talla
small	pequeña
medium	mediana
large	grande
bigger	más grande
smaller	más pequeño
In another colour	De otro color
It's too expensive	Es demasiado caro
big/little	grande/pequeño
money	dinero
price	precio
I would like to buy	Quisiera comprar
Where can I find...?	¿Dónde puedo encontrar...?
sale goods	rebajas
secondhand objects	objetos usados/de segunda mano
bag	bolsa
belt	cinturón
book	libro
boots	bota
cap	gorra
cotton	algodón
dress	vestido
fashion	moda
gold	oro
hat	sombrero
stamp	sello
jacket (for men)	americana
jacket (for women)	chaqueta
leather	piel
linen	lino
lingerie	lencerià
raincoat	limpermeable
serviettes	servilleta
shirt	camisa

shoes	zapatos
shop	tienda
silk	seda
silver	plata
skirt	falda
socks	calzetina
square	cuadro
tablecloth	mantel
tie	corbata
toy	juguete
wool	lana

Numbers

one/first	uno/primero/a
two/second	dos/segundo/a
three/third	tres/tercero/a
four/fourth	cuatro/cuarto/a
five/fifth	cinco/quinto/a
six	seis
seven	siete
eight	ocho
nine	nueve
ten	diez
eleven	once
twelve	doce
thirteen	trece
fourteen	catorce
fifteen	quince
sixteen	dieciseis
seventeen	diecisiete
eighteen	dieciocho
nineteen	diecinueve
twenty	veinte
twenty-one	veintiuno
twenty-two/three etc.	veintidos/tres etc.
thirty	treinta
forty	cuarenta
fifty	cincuenta
sixty	sesenta
seventy	setenta
eighty	ochenta
ninety	noventa
hundred	cien
thousand	mil
two thousand	dosmil
five thousand	cincomil
million	un millon

Times and dates

yesterday	ayer
today	hoy
tomorrow	mañana
one minute	un minuto
one hour	una hora
half an hour	media hora
quarter of an hour	cuarto de hora

It's midnight	Es medianoche
It's noon	Es mediodia
It's one o'clock	Es la una
See you tomorrow	Hasta mañana
What time is it?	¿Qué hora es?
watch	reloj

Days of the week

Monday	Lunes
Tuesday	Martes
Wednesday	Miércoles
Thursday	Jueves
Friday	Viernes
Saturday	Sábado
Sunday	Domingo

Months of the year

January	Enero
February	Febrero
March	Marzo
April	Abril
May	Mayo
June	Junio
July	Julio
August	Agosto
September	Septiembre
October	Octubre
November	Noviembre
December	Diciembre

Making a phone call

phonecard	tarjeta telefónica
Do you have a phone?	¿Tiene un teléfono?
Can I leave a message?	¿Puedo dejar un mensaje?
Could you speak up, please?	¿Puede hablar más alto, por favor?
Could you speak more slowly?	¿Puede hablar mas lento?
Wait a moment, please	Espere un momento, por favor

At customs

customs officer	advanero
identity card	carta de identidad
Nothing to declare	¿Nada a declarar?
passport	pasaporte
personal objects	objetos personales

French handy words and phrases

Over the next few pages you'll find a selection of very basic French vocabulary and many apologies if the word you are looking for is missing.

Let us begin, with a very basic guide to some French grammar:
All French nouns are either masculine or feminine and gender is denoted as follows: 'the' singular is translated by le (m), la (f) or l' (in front of a word beginning with a vowel or mute 'h'; 'the' plural = les (whatever gender and in front of a vowel or mute 'h'). 'A' = un (m), une(f) (no exceptions for vowels or mute 'h').

There are two forms of the word 'you' – tu is 'you' in the singular, very informal and used with people you know, vous is 'you' in the singular but is used in formal situations and when you don't know the person, vous is also the plural form. Young people often address each other as 'tu' automatically, but when in doubt and to avoid offence, always use 'vous'.

Adjectives agree with the gender of the accompanying noun. For a singular masculine noun there is no change to the adjective, but to indicate the masculine plural, an 's' is added to the end of the adjective; an 'e' is usually added for a feminine noun and 'es' for the plural. If you are not very familiar with French don't worry too much about gender agreement when talking (unless you wish to perfect your pronunciation, as 'e' or 'es' usually makes the final consonant hard), we have used feminine versions where applicable simply to help with the understanding of written French. These are either written out in full or shown as '(e)'. Finally, if you do not know the right French word try using the English one with a French accent – it is surprising how often this works.

The verb 'to be'

I am	je suis
you are (informal/sing.)	tu es
he/she/it is	il(m)/elle(f)/il est*
we are	nous sommes
you are (formal/plural)	vous êtes
they are	ils(m)/elles(f) sont*

When you are in a hurry gender can complicate things – just say le or la, whichever comes into your head first and you will sometimes be right and usually be understood.

* The most common forms use the masculine: 'it is' = il est, 'they are'= ils sont. C'est = 'that is' or 'this is', and is not gender specific.

Essential vocabulary

yes/no	oui/non
OK	d'accord
That's fine	C'est bon
please	s'il vous plaît
thank you	merci
Good morning/Hello	Bonjour (during the day)
Good evening/night/Hello	Bonsoir (during the evening)

Hello/Goodbye (very informal)	Salut
Goodbye	Au revoir
See you soon.	bientôt
Excuse me	Excusez-moi
I am sorry	Je suis désolé(m)/désolée(f)
Pardon?	Comment?

Handy phrases

....

Do you speak English?	Parlez-vous anglais?
I don't speak French	Je ne parle pas français
I don't understand	Je ne comprends pas
Could you speak more slowly please?	Pouvez-vous parler moins vite s'il vous plaît?
Could you repeat that, please?	Pouvez-vous répéter, s'il vous plaît?
again	encore
I am English/Scottish/ Welsh/Irish/American/ Canadian/Australian/ a New Zealander	Je suis anglais(e) /écossais(e)/ gallois(e)/ irlandais(e)/ américain(e)/ canadien(ne)/ australien(ne)/ néo-zélandais(e)
My name is ...	Je m'appelle ...
What is your name?	Comment vous appelez-vous?
How are you?	Comment allez-vous?
Very well, thank you.	Très bien, merci.
Pleased to meet you.	Enchanté(e).
Mr/Mrs	Monsieur/Madame
Miss/Ms	Mademoiselle/Madame
How?	Comment?
What?	Quel (m)/Quelle (f)?
When?	Quand?
Where (is/are)?	Où (est/sont)?
Which?	Quel (m)/Quelle (f)?
Who?	Qui?
Why?	Pourquoi?

Essential words

....

good	bon/bonne
bad	mauvais/mauvaise
big	grand/grande
small	petit/petite
hot	chaud/chaude
cold	froid/froide
open	ouvert/ouverte
closed	fermé/fermée
toilets	les toilettes/les w.c.
women	dames
men	hommes
free (unoccupied)	libre
occupied	occupé/occupée
free (no charge)	gratuit/gratuite
entrance	l'entrée
exit	la sortie
prohibited	interdit/interdite
no smoking	défense de fumer

Time and space

••

PERIODS OF TIME

a minute	une minute
half an hour	une demie-heure
an hour	une heure
a week	une semaine
fortnight	une quinzaine
month	un mois
year	un an/une année
today	aujourd'hui
yesterday/tomorrow	hier/demain
morning	le matin
afternoon	l'après-midi
evening/night	e soir/la nuit
during (the night)	pendant (la nuit)
early/late	tôt/tard

TELLING THE TIME

What time is it?	Quelle heure est-il?
At what time?	A quelle heure?
(at) 1 o'clock/2 o'clock etc.	(à) une heure/deux heures etc.
half past one	une heure et demie
quarter past two	deux heures et quart
quarter to three	trois heures moins le quart
(at) midday	à midi
(at) midnight	à minuit

Getting around

••

by bicycle	à bicyclette/en vélo
by bus	en bus
by car	en voiture
by coach	en car
on foot	à pied
by plane	en avion
by taxi	en taxi
by train	en train

IN TOWN

map of the city	un plan de la ville
I am going to ...	Je vais à.....
I want to go to....	Je voudrais aller à ...
I want to get off at...	Je voudrais descendre à
platform	le quai
return ticket	un aller-retour
single ticket	un aller simple
ticket	le billet
timetable	l'horaire
airport	l'aéroport
bus/coach station	la gare routière
bus stop	l'arrêt de bus
district	le quartier/l'arrondissement
street	la rue
taxi rank	la station de taxi
tourist information office	l'office du tourisme
train station	la gare
underground	le métro

bag/handbag	le sac/le sac-à-main
case	la valise
left luggage	la consigne
luggage	les bagages

DIRECTIONS

Is it far?	Est-ce que c'est loin?
How far is it to...?	Combien de kilomètres d'ici à ...?
Is it near?	Est-ce que c'est près d'ici?
here/there	ici/là
near/far	près/loin
left/right	gauche/droite
on the left/right	à gauche/à droite
straight on	tout droit
at the end of	au bout de
up	en haut
down	en bas
above (the shop)	au-dessus (du magasin)
below (the bed)	au-dessous (le lit)
opposite (the bank)	en face (de la banque)
next to (the window)	à côté (de la fenêtre)

DRIVING

Please fill the tank (car)	Le plein, s'il vous plaît
car hire	la location de voitures
driver's licence	le permis de conduire
petrol	l'essence
rent a car	louer une voiture
unleaded	sans plomb

In the hotel

I have a reservation	J'ai une réservation
for 2 nights	pour 2 nuits
I leave	Je pars .....
I'd like a room	Je voudrais une chambre
Is breakfast included?	le petit-déjeuner est inclus?
single room	une chambre à un lit
room with double bed	une chambre à lit double
twin room	une chambre à deux lits
room with bathroom	une chambre avec salle de bains
and toilet	et toilette/W.C.
a quiet room	une chambre calme
bath	le bain
shower	la douche
with air conditioning	avec climatisation
1st/2nd floor etc	premier/deuxième étage
breakfast	le petit-déjeuner
dining room	la salle à manger
ground floor	le rez-de-chaussée (RC)
key	la clef
lift/elevator	l'ascenseur

PAYING

How much?	C'est combien, s'il vous plaît?/ Quel est le prix?
Do you accept credit cards?	Est-ce que vous acceptez les cartes de crédit?
Do you have any change?	Avez-vous de la monnaie?

(in) cash	(en) espèces
coin	le pièce de monnaie
money	l'argent
notes	les billets
price	le prix
travellers' cheques	les chèques de voyage

Eating out

∙∙∙

GENERAL

Do you have a table?	Avez-vous une table libre?
I would like to reserve a table	Je voudrais réserver une table.
I would like to eat.	Je voudrais manger.
I would like something to drink	Je voudrais boire quelque chose.
I would like to order, please	Je voudrais commander, s'il vous plait.
The bill, please.	L'addition, s'il vous plait.
I am a vegetarian.	Je suis végétarien (ne).

MEALS AND MEALTIMES

breakfast	le petit-déjeuner
cover charge	le couvert
dessert	le dessert
dinner	le dîner
dish of the day	le plat du jour
fixed price menu	la formule/le menu à prix fixe
fork	la fourchette
knife	le couteau
lunch	le déjeuner
main course	le plat principal
menu	le menu/la carte
(Is the) service included?	Est-ce que le service est compris?
soup	la soupe/le potage
spoon	la cuillère
starter	l'entrée/le hors-d'oeuvre
waiter	Monsieur
waitress	Madame, Mademoiselle
wine list	la carte des vins

COOKING STYLES

baked	cuit/cuite au four
boiled	bouilli/bouillie
fried	à la poêle
grilled	grillé/grillée
medium	à point
poached	poché/pochée
rare	saignant
steamed	à la vapeur
very rare	bleu
well done	bien cuit

MEAT, POULTRY, GAME AND OFFAL

bacon	le bacon
beef	le boeuf
chicken	le poulet
duck	le canard
frogs' legs	les cuisses de grenouilles
game	le gibier
ham	le jambon
kidneys	les rognons
lamb	l'agneau

meat	la viande
pork	le porc
rabbit	le lapin
salami style sausage (dry)	le saucisson-sec
sausage	la saucisse
snails	les escargots
steak	l'entrecôte/le steak/le bifteck
veal	le veau

FISH AND SEAFOOD

cod	le cabillaud/la morue
Dublin bay prawn/scampi	la langoustine
fish	le poisson
herring	le hareng
lobster	le homard
mullet	le rouget
mussels	les moules
oysters	les huîtres
pike	le brochet
prawns	les crevettes
salmon (smoked)	le saumon (fumé)
sea bass	le bar
seafood	les fruits de mer
skate	le raie
squid	le calmar
trout	la truite
tuna	le thon

VEGETABLES, PASTA AND RICE

cabbage	le chou
cauliflower	le chou-fleur
chips/french fries	les frites
garlic	l'ail
green beans	les haricots verts
leeks	les poireaux
onions	les oignons
pasta	les pâtes
peas	les petits pois
potatoes	les pommes-de-terre
rice	le riz
sauerkraut	la choucroute
spinach	les épinards
vegetables	les légumes

SALAD ITEMS

beetroot	la betterave
cucumber	le concombre
curly endive	la salade frisée
egg	un oeuf
green pepper/red pepper	le poivron/poivron rouge
green salad	la salade verte
lettuce	la laitue
tomato	la tomate

FRUIT

apple	la pomme
banana	la banane
blackberries	les mûres
blackcurrants	les cassis
cherries	les cerises
fresh fruit	le fruit frais
grapefruit	le pamplemousse

grapes	les raisins
lemon/lime	le citron/le citron vert
orange	l'orange
peach	la pêche
pear	la poire
plums	les prunes/les mirabelles (type of plum)
raspberries	les framboises
red/white currants	les groseilles
strawberries	les fraises

DESSERTS AND CHEESE

apple tart	la tarte aux pommes
cake	le gâteau
cheese	le fromage
cream	la crème fraîche
goat's cheese	le fromage de chèvre
ice cream	la glace

SUNDRIES

ashtray	un cendrier
bread	le pain
bread roll	le petit pain
butter	le beurre
crisps	les chips
mustard	la moutarde
napkin	la serviette
oil	l'huile
peanuts	les cacahuètes
salt/pepper	le sel/le poivre
toast	le toast
vinegar	le vinaigre

DRINKS

beer	la bière
a bottle of	une bouteille de
black coffee	un café noir
coffee	un café
with cream	un café-crème
with milk	un café au lait
a cup of	une tasse de
decaffeinated coffee	un café décaféiné/un déca
espresso coffee	un express
freshly-squeezed lemon/ orange juice	un citron pressé/une orange pressée
a glass of	un verre de
herbal tea	une tisane/infusion
with lime/verbena	au tilleul/à la verveine
with mint	à la menthe
with milk/lemon	au lait/au citron
milk	le lait
(some) mineral water	de l'eau minérale
orange juice	un jus d'orange
(some) tap water	de l'eau du robinet
(some) sugar	du sucre
tea	un thé
wine (red/white)	le vin (rouge/blanc)

Shopping (see also 'Paying' under 'In the hotel')

••

USEFUL SHOPPING VOCABULARY

I'd like to buy...	Je voudrais acheter…
Do you have…?	Avez-vous …?
How much, please?	C'est combien, s'il vous plaît?
I'm just looking, thank you	Je regarde, merci.
It's for a gift	C'est pour un cadeau.

SHOPS

antique shop	le magasin d'antiquités
baker	la boulangerie
bank	la banque
book shop	la librairie
cake shop	la pâtisserie
cheese shop	la fromagerie
chemist/drugstore	la pharmacie
clothes shop	le magasin de vêtements
delicatessen	la charcuterie
department store	le grand magasin
gift shop	le magasin de cadeaux
the market	le marché
newsagent	le magasin de journaux
post office	la poste/le PTT
shoe shop	le magasin de chaussures
the shops	les boutiques/magasins
tobacconist	le tabac
travel agent	l'agence de voyages

expensive	cher
cheap	pas cher, bon marché
sales	les soldes
size (in clothes)	la taille
size (in shoes)	la pointure
too expensive	trop cher

TELEPHONING

telephone/phone booth	le téléphone/la cabine téléphonique
phone card	la carte téléphonique
post card	la carte postale
stamps	les timbres

Months of the year

••

January	janvier
February	février
March	mars
April	avril
May	mai
June	juin
July	juillet
August	août
September	septembre
October	octobre
November	novembre
December	décembre

a year	un an/une année
a month	un mois

HACHETTE TRAVEL GUIDES

Titles available in this series:
BRITTANY (ISBN: 1 84202 007 2)
CATALONIA (ISBN: 1 84202 099 4)
CORSICA (ISBN: 1 84202 100 1)
DORDOGNE & PÉRIGORD (ISBN: 1 84202 098 6)
LANGUEDOC-ROUSSILLON (ISBN: 1 84202 008 0)
NORMANDY (ISBN: 1 84202 097 8)
POITOU-CHARENTES (ISBN: 1 84202 009 9)
PROVENCE & THE COTE D'AZUR (ISBN: 1 84202 006 4)
PYRENEES & GASCONY (ISBN: 1 84202 015 3)
SOUTH-WEST FRANCE (ISBN: 1 84202 014 5)

A GREAT WEEKEND IN . . .
Focusing on the limited amount of time available on a weekend break, these guides suggest the most entertaining and interesting ways of getting to know the city in just a few days.

A GREAT WEEKEND IN AMSTERDAM (ISBN: 1 84202 002 1)
A GREAT WEEKEND IN BARCELONA (ISBN: 1 84202 005 6)
A GREAT WEEKEND IN BERLIN (ISBN: 1 84202 061 7)
A GREAT WEEKEND IN BRUSSELS (ISBN: 1 84202 017 X)
A GREAT WEEKEND IN FLORENCE (ISBN: 1 84202 010 2)
A GREAT WEEKEND IN LISBON (ISBN: 1 84202 011 0)
A GREAT WEEKEND IN LONDON (ISBN: 1 84202 013 7)
A GREAT WEEKEND IN MADRID (ISBN: 1 84202 095 1)
A GREAT WEEKEND IN NAPLES (ISBN: 1 84202 016 1)
A GREAT WEEKEND IN NEW YORK (ISBN: 1 84202 004 8)
A GREAT WEEKEND IN PARIS (ISBN: 1 84202 001 3)
A GREAT WEEKEND IN PRAGUE (ISBN: 1 84202 000 5)
A GREAT WEEKEND IN ROME (ISBN: 1 84202 003 X)
A GREAT WEEKEND IN VENICE (ISBN: 1 84202 018 8)
A GREAT WEEKEND IN VIENNA (ISBN: 1 84202 026 9)
Coming soon:
A GREAT WEEKEND IN DUBLIN (ISBN: 1 84202 096 X)

ROUTARD
Comprehensive and reliable guides offering insider advice for the independent traveller.

CALIFORNIA, NEVADA & ARIZONA (ISBN: 1 84202 025 0)
IRELAND (ISBN: 1 84202 024 2)
PARIS (ISBN: 1 84202 027 7)
THAILAND (ISBN: 1 84202 029 3)
Coming soon:
BELGIUM (ISBN: 1 84202 022 6)
CUBA (ISBN: 1 84202 062 5)
GREEK ISLANDS & ATHENS (ISBN: 1 84202 023 4)
NORTHERN BRITTANY (ISBN: 1 84202 020 X)
PROVENCE & THE COTE D'AZUR (ISBN: 1 84202 019 6)
ROME & SOUTHERN ITALY (ISBN: 1 84202 021 8)
WEST CANADA & ONTARIO (ISBN: 1 84202 031 5)